MW01156919

# Youth in Revolt:
## The Journals of Nick Twisp

"This American cult 'Adrian Mole' is an altogether rougher, sexier, and funnier tale. . . A rollercoaster ride through the nemesis of adolescent angst." —*London Mail*

"A sussed, silly and energetic account which literally bulges with Nick Twisp's hormonal excitations. . . Faster and funnier than 14 ever felt before." —*The Punter* [UK]

"In the course of 499 pages, Nick falls in and out of favor with his divorced parents; he looks for love in all the wrong places; he invents; he schemes. He even burns down half of Berkeley. But throughout, this novel—or three novels—is extremely readable. For while Nick searches for the joys of sex, he finds a great deal more—a general *joie de vivre* and compassion that prove addictive." —*L.A. Reader*

"A hilarious six month journey through the thorny underbrush of sexual desire, frustration, and (occasionally painful) discovery. . . Payne does not offer up his characters to the altar of hackneyed change or growth. He gives us instead a wonderfully original refugee from parental cynicism and the 'gulag of the public schools' whose scorn, bad attitude, and unflagging horniness persist in a way that is engagingly real. . . There is a refreshing frankness and celebration in the writing that elevates it above the mere silliness of much of today's comic fiction." —*New Haven Advocate*

"*Youth in Revolt* . . . [is] a hefty coming-of-age novel which actually lives up to the publisher's comparisons to *A Confederacy of Dunces* and *Portnoy's Complaint*, and in many ways surpasses them... One of the funniest novels I've ever read." —*Hypno Magazine*

"Payne's ability to constantly introduce new characters and new plots while interweaving the old ones is like watching an aerialist interrupt his highwire act to take out a lawn chair, then do a headstand on it and start juggling with his feet. And then just as you're wondering how he can get out of that predicament, he sets fire to the juggling balls. It's hard to say which are more satisfying: the twists you can tell are coming or the ones that take you by surprise." —*Berkeley Express*

"It's a high honor and distinct privilege, then, to introduce C.D. Payne's totally unsentimental and extremely funny first novel, *Youth in Revolt: The Journals of Nick Twisp*. It's the antidote to Salinger's tale of the teenage saint Holden Caulfield." —*The Oregonian*

"*Youth in Revolt* is an unstintingly hilarious black comedy, almost certainly the funniest book you'll read this year... Nick is irresistible, for his first encounters with adult phenomena always seem to bring out an appropriately warped response or an almost-brilliant insight. . . Nick's voice is unique and indelible, Payne's language rich and inventive. C.D. Payne has set a high standard for himself." —*Los Angeles Times*

"A genuinely funny book, one that will have many readers laughing out loud. . . Nick is an inspired chronicler of his inner life and philosophy . . . Payne captures the trials of adolescence in these perilous times, dealing with far more than just the pangs of hormonal upheavals." —*Sonoma County Bohemian*

# Revoltingly Young

## The Journals of Nick Twisp's Younger Brother

# Revoltingly Young

## The Journals of Nick Twisp's Younger Brother

Book VI: Youth in Nevada

C.D. Payne

ISBN  0-7414-3416-4


*Published by:*

INFI∞ITY
PUBLISHING.COM

*1094 New DeHaven Street, Suite 100*
*West Conshohocken, PA 19428-2713*
*Info@buybooksontheweb.com*
*www.buybooksontheweb.com*
*Toll-free  (877) BUY BOOK*
*Local Phone (610) 941-9999*
*Fax  (610) 941-9959*

*Printed in the United States of America*

*Printed on Recycled Paper*

*Published  July 2006*

*To Joy*

A NOTE ON THE SERIES:
*Youth in Revolt* contains Books 1, 2, and 3
*Revolting Youth* is Book 4
*Young and Revolting* is Book 5
*Revoltingly Young* is Book 6
*Cut to the Twisp* contains text deleted from the post-1994 U.S. and U.K. editions of *Youth in Revolt*, plus additional short pieces.

# JUNE

SATURDAY, June 18 — My cousin Tyler Twisp is visiting Grandma Wescott and me in her dreary singlewide trailer deep in the lonely wastes of Nevada. Tyler loves everything about Winnemucca, just as I, conversely, despise every aspect of my home town. Of course, he is an immense jock who eats his own weight in grub every three days. Whereas I am a picky-eater flyweight with intellectual and cultural aspirations. Hard to believe my sinewy cousin is only 15, while I—a mere shadow in his wake—will be 16 in December. Strictly speaking, I may in fact be his uncle, since he's the son of my half-sister Joanie. But since it would be silly to have a nephew twice one's size, we prefer to regard each other as cousins.

Nevada prides itself on being the emptiest state in the nation. For example, Winnemucca is situated 165 miles east of Reno and 353 miles west of Salt Lake City. In between stretches a forbidding expanse of barren rock and scrawny sagebrush. Nice country for jackrabbits, but a challenge for any life form higher than a buzzard. If it weren't for the Internet, I'm sure my mind would have atrophied and died long ago.

Nearly 8,000 rednecks call Winnemucca home, while the population of New York City is over eight million. Therefore, according to the law of averages, my chances of residing in that great metropolis are at least *one thousand times better* than of moldering in this God-forsaken hole. Yet here I sit in a trailer that's not even within the city limits—with a thrift-shop wardrobe, nothing to do, no place to go, no girlfriend, and $4.37 to my name. Meanwhile, my cousin—a zealot for clean mountain air and challenging hikes—resides in gridlocked L.A. This strikes me as blindingly unfair.

Must stop here. Tyler wants to go over to the high school to shoot some baskets. Wish I had a gun. I'd show him how Real Men shoot baskets.

SUNDAY, June 19 — Father's Day. What a nuisance. Grandma Wescott made me call my dad—never a fun prospect. The guy is such a sourpuss. Is it my fault my mother in distant Oakland shot off most of his genitalia? Talk about your worst castration anxieties come true. Never the warmest of dads, he's become even more emotionally distant since my voice changed. He says I sound just like my half-brother Nick—a guy he really has it in for. Don't ask me why. Ever mum on my twisted family matters, Grandma says it's all "water over the dam."

Fortunately, Dad was getting ready to go to work when I called, so our desultory chat was mercifully brief. He works security for an Indian casino in California near Clear Lake. He asked me what I was doing; I said "not much." I asked him what he was doing; he said "the usual." I asked him if he got my card; he said he only goes to his post office box once a month. I asked him if he was coming to visit; he said "maybe at Christmas, but don't get your hopes up." (As if I'm pining away to see the big dork, whose support checks arrive here about as often as Halley's Comet.)

I handed over the clammy phone to Tyler, who had a lively 45-minute talk with his pop in Los Angeles, then rang off with the words "I love you, Dad." Pretty amazing, especially when you consider that he was speaking to his *step*father. Maybe that's the secret. Perhaps a kid can have a cordial and loving relationship with his dad as long as they're not actually related.

Like all Twisps, Tyler is very competitive. We are now into day two of the First Annual Wescott-Twisp Beat Your Meat Contest. Every hour on the hour we retire to the rusty metal shed at the back of the lot and flail away. First guy to fail to get it up and/or produce at least one drop loses. So far, we seem to be fairly evenly matched—except, alas, in size. I'm extremely jealous of Tyler's advantage in that department. Talk about penile overkill. I keep suggesting to Tyler that he is freakishly oversized and will never find a girlfriend to accommodate him, yet he just chuckles and remains anxiety-free as he tucks his massive tool back into his pants. Tyler has promised his mother that he will not have sex until he's 16, so he hasn't actually gone all the way with any of his numerous girlfriends. He just lets them fondle his instrument and practice their fellatio techniques. I should be so lucky. I had one girlfriend back in the sixth grade and never got past some experimental kisses. Consuela's parents objected to her seeing a non-Catholic Anglo and made her break up with me. Rather stupefying. I mean—did they imagine we were planning on getting married at age 12 and raising a pack of mixed-race Protestants?

Speaking of child brides, I've heard rumors that my half-brother Nick was married briefly when he was about my age. Hard to believe. I'd ask him if I ever saw him, but he never comes to visit and rarely answers my e-mails. He's a big-time comic juggler in Las Vegas with a too glamorous and fulfilling life (see *People* magazine) to bother with poor relations in the sticks. He does send nice Christmas/birthday presents though. Yeah, I was born on December 25, hence my dumb name: Noel Lance Wescott. Remarkably pedestrian I agree, but at least it's not Twisp.

MONDAY, June 20 — Another sports triumph for Tyler. I was obliged to forfeit this morning. I could still get it up, but the area was too raw and chafed to permit further handling. Tyler and I agree after two and a half days of incessant masturbation we are now manifesting virtually zero interest in sex. A most unusual state for us both. With my luck some cute chick will throw herself at me today and I'll be forced to decline a Golden Opportunity. Have applied some of Grandma's Avon hand cream to my inflamed member and now have the sweetest-smelling unit in town.

My friend Carlyle Bogy dropped by with his .22 rifle, and the three of us wandered up the ravine behind the trailer to take turns shooting at anything that moved. I think Tyler may have winged a lizard. Due to his constant twitching Carlyle is probably the worst shot in the state. He has extensive neurological damage from spending his toddler years in his father's clandestine methamphetamine lab. They also think he has fetal alcohol syndrome from his mother boozing it up. (I learned all this by sneaking a peek at his confidential file back when I was an office volunteer in junior high.) Carlyle lives in a foster home now as both his parents are incarcerated. He's with his fifth foster family, but he's having better luck with this latest set of hired parents (the Greenes) as they're pretty progressive and he's mostly worked through his fascination with fire. For a time there he was keeping the Winnemucca fire department on constant alert. Carlyle remains on a first-name basis with all the firemen in town.

Grandma phoned out for pizza later, but she did not invite Carlyle to stay for dinner. It bugs her that Carlyle is always going into our bathroom and helping himself to any pills he finds in the medicine cabinet. Grandma likes to take a nip now and then, but she says she doesn't dare take a drink lest she wake up with a hangover only to find there wasn't an aspirin in the place. We watched a semi-violent video and sewed on spangles. Grandma used to be a beautician, but she got increasingly broad in the beam and could no longer endure all those hours on her diabetic feet. When her sister (Aunt Deb) died, she inherited her sit-down occupation: sewing mail-order outfits for showgirls, strippers, and tap-dancers. This involves endless application of tiny spangles, rhinestones, and beads to shimmering or gauzy fabrics. I help her out sometimes in the evening while we watch TV. Rather tedious, but Grandma pays me 25 cents an hour. Pretty miserable wage, but how many kids can say they get paid to watch TV?

You wouldn't think a big jock like Tyler would be good with a needle and thread, but he approached it as another competition and once again left me in his dust. In three hours he covered the entire bodice of a midget tap-dancer's tutu with neat rows of pink sequins. Grandma was so pleased, she gave him a whole dollar.

In case you're wondering where Tyler sleeps in our cramped two-bedroom trailer, he is crashing on the lumpy sofa. My junior bed is not big enough for two, though if Uma Spurletti every drops by I'm willing to make an effort to squeeze her in. She's the cutest girl in the history of Northern Nevada and has been wearing a deep groove in my brain ever since she moved here last year. Her father is part owner of the Silver Sluice Casino downtown. I don't know if he's a mobster, but I have it on good authority that he's Italian. His daughter, I believe, regards me as an EWP (extremely weird person). It's true that I do not hang with the local teen elite, but unlike those smug cretins, I'm not entirely brain-dead either. Have to halt this train of thought. I'm in no condition to think about Uma Spurletti.

TUESDAY, June 21 — Another sunny day in the high desert. The elevation here is 4,300 feet, which as I remind Tyler is *much* higher than where he lives in L.A. He claims not to know the point of such statements, but I know he hates to be beaten at anything. Grandma was giving him a trim around the ears when my pal Stoney Holt dropped in for her usual boy's regular haircut. Her real name is Claudia, but she tends to punch people in the face who call her that. She aspires to be a lesbian, though she's even more girlfriend-less than I am. She lacks even a secret crush, since she regards all the girls in town with total disdain (and they return the favor). Stoney was always a plain, chunky girl until last year, when—during a few eventful months—her anatomy mysteriously rearranged. She now possesses a spectacular figure, which she attempts to camouflage under baggy cargo pants and oversized sweatshirts bearing rude graphics. When her baby fat retreated, it also left behind some classically chiseled cheekbones draped in pale, flawless skin. Grandma says she'd be as pretty as a model if she didn't try so hard to look like Mickey Rooney in "Boys Town."

Stoney seemed surprised to see Tyler even though I told her at least twice last week that he was coming. She also blushed when he spoke to her—an entirely novel reaction for her.

"Take a seat," said Grandma. "I'll be right with you."

Grandma treats her few hair clients like customers even though no cash exchanges hands. Stoney sprawled on the sofa and leafed through the magazines on the coffee table. Her torn sweatshirt read "Drop Dead Before I Make You."

"You got this month's *Playboy*?" she inquired.

"Wouldn't let such trash in my home," Grandma chuckled.

"Tyler and I are starting our own street gang," I said. "Would you like to join?"

Stoney planted her dusty boots on the coffee table and gave the matter some thought. "Who else is in it?"

"Just Carlyle so far."

"That guy is deranged. OK, I'm in."

"I don't want you kids getting in any trouble," cautioned Grandma.

"Noel Nothing?" sneered Stoney. "He couldn't if he tried."

"Just remember, Noel," said Grandma. "Your dad is a law enforcement officer."

As if I could forget. Has there ever been a greater inducement to crime?

7:45 p.m. We've made some progress on our gang plans. We are to be called the Upts—short for "Uptowners." We like the gritty urban edge to it, even though our town barely manages a downtown, let alone an uptown. Initially, our gang colors were yellow, and we vowed to be mortal enemies of anyone seen wearing red or blue. This decision necessitated a quick trip to the Golden Eagle Thrift Shoppe, where the pickings in yellow turned out to be slim. So we decided to go with brown, which Stoney thought was much more butch anyway. I'm not so sure. I'm now dressed head-to-toe in budget brown and look like a sanitation worker.

After completing my gangland brownout, I asked Stoney how I looked.

"You look like shit" was her cogent assessment.

Too bad the color spectrum is so limited. OK, red and blue are already taken, plus the Goths have pretty much nailed down black. That leaves green (you too can look like a hippie tree-hugger), purple (so fat ladies over 50, as Stoney points out), orange (that '70s scene), pink (just knife me, 'cause I deserve to die), or white (yes, we also paint houses). Perhaps this is the reason that like us Mussolini adopted brown for his Fascists.

As for our gang signs, we're still working on those, though we may just adopt some of Carlyle's more elaborate twitches.

The ghastly initiation rituals are set for midnight tonight. At least with all this brown the blood stains shouldn't show so much.

WEDNESDAY, June 22 — Some shocking revelations last night. My entire life has been turned upside down. We had gathered at the appointed hour in the long-abandoned hippie bus at the end of our gravel road. This is the site where too long ago I made my one and only mostly unsuccessful attempt to feel up a girl (the alluring but inhibited Consuela). Tonight we had one candle and a large bottle filched by Carlyle from his foster dad's liquor cabinet.

"OK," said Stoney, lighting the candle and adhering it with hot wax to the rusty floor, "everyone has to take three big gulps without stopping. You first, Noel Problem."

I screwed off the cap and sniffed. A mild boozy aroma. Hell, my Avon mouthwash smelled stronger than this stuff. I took three deep draughts and struggled not to expire on the spot as the fiery liquid scorched its way down through my insides.

"Nice," I choked, passing the bottle to Tyler.

He took three gigantic swallows, then wiped his mouth with the back of his hand.

"Eez good, amigo," he belched. "I like the kick of a hearty tequila."

"Glad to hear it, Tyler," twitched Carlyle, "but this stuff's vodka."

We were imbibing a distant cousin of the French fry. Perhaps a little ketchup could improve it as well.

Stoney downed her quota with a minimum of fuss and passed the bottle to Carlyle, who added yet another toxic to his poisoned system. It didn't seem to mind. Passing the bottle to me, he took out his bulky pocketknife and pried open its largest blade.

"Where should we do the cuttin'?" he inquired.

An ominous question. At that point I still felt way too sober for self-mutilation. I took another tentative sip. This stuff did not improve with experience.

"Really, we should cut where it shows like on the face," declared Stoney.

Carlyle nodded approvingly, but the proposal failed to win over the rest of the gang.

"I'm thinking of becoming a sportscaster after I retire from the pros," explained Tyler. "I need to preserve my on-camera image."

"Pussy," replied Stoney. "And what's your excuse, Noel Balls?"

"I'm thinking of going into show business like my brother Nick," I lied. "Disfiguring scars are a liability in that profession. Anyway, I know a better bonding ritual than slicing each other up."

"If Stoney's on the rag," suggested Carlyle, "we could all go down on her."

"In your dreams, dirt ball," she replied.

"What's your suggestion, cousin?" asked Tyler.

Plugging the bottle with my tongue, I took a great mock swig of vodka and passed it to Tyler. "OK, here's what we do. We confess to each other our deepest and darkest secret."

"Hey, what is this? Some kind of girls' club?" scoffed Stoney.

"I got a secret," said Carlyle, playing with his knife. "Sometimes I hear these voices in my head that tell me to do stuff. Terrible stuff."

Leave it to Carlyle to cast a pall over the gang initiation rites.

"Uh, gee, Carlyle," I said. "When you hear those voices, how about checking in with me first before you do anything? OK?"

"Sure. OK, Noel."

"Good," I said. "Is that your deepest secret?"

"Well, I know where my dad ditched the body."

Before Mr. Bogy (Carlyle's papa) went to jail his lab partner had disappeared under mysterious circumstances.

"But if I tell you," Carlyle went on, "certain relatives of mine would probably have to kill you."

"Well, I for one, don't want to know," I said. "OK, Stoney, what's your innermost secret?"

She grabbed the bottle from Tyler and gazed at him defiantly as she guzzled the raw booze. "OK, here goes, ladies. I'm a dyke."

Now it was my turn to scoff. "Some secret, Stoney. Everyone in town knows that. You'll have to do much better if you want to be in this gang."

She thought it over. "OK, but if this gets out, I'm going to pound your asses."

"It won't, Stoney," I assured her. "That's what this is all about: being gang brothers. After tonight we're going to be closer than family."

"That's not saying much," she said, taking another big swig. "OK, so here's my story. Last month I went to Reno with my mom. We went to a mall there. At Macy's we stopped at the make-up counter. Smelled all the perfume and shit. Then I let the clerk make up my face."

"Wow," I hissed. "You did?"

"Yeah, no lie. I looked at myself in the mirror. I couldn't believe what I looked like. Like some goddam movie star. Here I spent my whole life getting used to the idea of being uglier than Carlyle's butt."

"You're gorgeous, Stoney," I assured her.

"I'd hump you in a minute," seconded Carlyle.

"And die trying," she replied. "So ever since then I don't know what to think. I'm kinda confused. I'm not even totally sure I still like chicks."

"Wow!" I exclaimed again. "Really?"

"Yeah. I guess I'm messed up big time."

I noticed she wasn't looking at Tyler any more.

"That's pretty heavy, Stoney," I said. "I mean, we might be seeing you in a dress one of these days."

"I hope not," she replied. "But stranger things have happened."

"So," I said, getting down to brass tacks. "Are you attracted to brother Tyler here?"

She took another swig. "I don't know, Noel. Something weird's going on."

"Brother Tyler," I said, "are you willing to help brother Stoney?"

"Sure, I guess so. What can I do?"

I thought it over. "Tyler, I think you should and Stoney should, uh, make out."

He glanced at her doubtfully, but in a spirit of gang cooperation grunted a polite, "OK."

"Well, don't look so enthusiastic," she said.

"OK, I'm calling a five-minute time out," I announced. "You

guys go to the back of the bus and swap spit. But watch out for snakes and scorpions."

Stoney and Tyler left the circle of light for the dusty blackness of the rear of the bus. I hadn't kissed a girl in years, but I don't think I envied my cousin. Carlyle downed another swig and toyed with his knife.

"It's up in Bluebird Canyon, Noel."

"What is?"

"The goddam body."

"Don't tell me, Carlyle! Don't say another word! Jesus!"

"Sorry, Noel. You want we should make out too?"

"Don't be silly, Carlyle."

"Just checking. I never made out with anyone, Noel. Girls avoid me like the plague."

"Well, you have to use a little finesse with chicks, Carlyle. You're a bit too direct. I know girls like Uma get uncomfortable when you stare at their tits."

"I thought that's what they were for."

"Well, they are. But you have to be subtle about it."

Pretty quiet in the back. No moaning or springs squeaking. But I knew that somewhere close by inflamed lips were meeting in experimental passion. Possibly even feels were being copped. The last thing I expected to have at a gang initiation was a vicarious erection. I adjusted my pants and took another swallow of vodka. Thank God I was beginning to feel a little tipsy. How tragic it would be to discover one was immune to the effects of alcohol.

"You think maybe Stoney will do me next?" whispered Carlyle.

"I wouldn't get your hopes up. Girls generally like only one guy at a time. It's genetic, so the tribal unit will know who the father of the baby is."

"You mean they're screwing back there?"

"No, Carlyle. Just relax. Have some more vodka."

"Don't mind if I do."

Eventually, things started moving back there, and the two lovers returned to their seats by the candle.

"How was it?" leered Carlyle.

"Better than kissing you, that's for sure," replied Stoney. "OK, now it's Noel's turn. Spill your secret, dude."

I was hoping for a fuller report, but figured I'd hear Tyler's side later. I probed my soul for dark secrets.

"OK, here goes, guys. I think I'm in love with Uma Spurletti."

"Some secret!" sneered Stoney. "That's about as big a secret as the fact that that stuck-up chick wouldn't give you the sweat off her expensive nose job."

"Uma has not had a nose job," I retorted. "Her nose is naturally perfect."

"She's a rich bitch, Noel," continued Stoney. "She's so stuck up she wouldn't notice you if your dick blew out of your pants like a rocket and you dropped dead at her feet."

Another of Stoney's gross exaggerations; I do not believe I am quite that invisible.

"Uma's just reserved," I replied. "It's hard being the new girl in town."

"I hear she's not so reserved around Sloan Chandler," added Carlyle.

"That's a lie," I said. "Anyway, Sloan's away all summer at sailing camp."

Better Sloan should be away all summer in war-torn Iraq, but sailing camp would have to do. Ever since he started showing interest in Uma last semester, I've been praying his wealthy doctor father brings home some infectious microbe from the hospital. No fatal contagion so far, but I'm flexible. A tragic drowning would work just as well.

"Sloan Chandler could give any lesbian second thoughts," commented Stoney. "OK, Noel, we all know you have the hots for Uma. So out with a better secret."

"Honest, guys. That's all I can think of."

"Did you ever see your mom naked?" asked Carlyle.

"Hardly. I only saw my real mother twice. That was fully clothed and in a courtroom."

"When you beat your meat, do you ever fantasize about guys?" demanded Stoney.

"Well, when I was little, I used to feel guilty when I played with myself while watching Mr. Rogers."

"That is totally sick," she declared. "But it won't make it as your secret."

"Do you ever wet the bed?" asked Tyler, who knew perfectly well the answer to that presumptuous question.

I scowled at the traitor. "Uh, well, I used to. When I was a kid."

"How long has it been since you last wet the bed?" demanded Stoney. "And don't lie!"

Another intrusively personal question.

"Uh, well, let's see, it's been, uh . . . several months at least."

"Gross!" exclaimed Stoney. "I'd hate to see your mattress up close. Yuck!"

"It's not so bad," commented Tyler. "Mrs. Wescott keeps a plastic sheet over it."

"Tie your dick in a knot," suggested Carlyle. "That works for me."

"You can't tie your dick in a knot," exclaimed Tyler. "No one can."

"Wanta bet?" replied Carlyle. "How much you want to bet, smart guy?"

"I'll bet you five dollars," he replied.

Carlyle stood up, tugged down his shorts, pulled down some extremely grungy undershorts, and—much to his fellow gang members' astonishment—looped his very long and skinny dick into a neat knot.

"Jesus H. Christ," said Tyler.

"I'd say you just made a fast five dollars," commented Stoney.

Tyler extracted his thin teen wallet and handed over the cash.

"Want to touch it, Stoney?" leered Carlyle.

"Yuck, now I know I'm a dyke. Put that repulsive thing away and let's hear Tyler's big secret."

Carlyle untied himself, zipped up, and we turned expectantly toward Tyler.

"Well, my deepest secret concerns someone else here. I'm not sure I should spill it."

"Why not?" demanded Stoney.

"Well, if my mom finds out, she'll kill me."

"The secret must concern me," I said. "OK, Tyler, you have my permission. Let's hear it."

"You sure, Noel?"

"Spill, brother!"

"OK, Noel. Here goes. Your father isn't Lance Wescott. It's my grandfather, George Twisp. You and my mother are brother and sister."

A cataclysmic revelation I wasn't at all prepared to believe. Not for one second.

"I don't think so," I said. "They were long divorced when my mother had me. She was married to Lance Wescott."

"True, Noel. But she and her first husband got together one last time and she accidentally got pregnant with you."

My vodka-befuddled mind was reeling. It's not nice to hear you were unwanted and unplanned, though that news, at least, didn't surprise me. "How do you know all this, Tyler?"

"I was awake one night. I overheard my mother discussing it with my stepdad. It's true, Noel. You're a Twisp, not a Wescott."

"Jesus, then I really could be your uncle."

"Hell, I knew something was up," said Stoney. "You don't look like any Wescott I've ever seen. For one thing, you're not fat."

It was true. At family gatherings I was the one Wescott who didn't make the floorboards creak.

THURSDAY, June 23 — My first full day as a gang member and possible Twisp. All in all not very conducive to the placidity of one's mind. It might have been better had we just sliced each other up in that bus last night. And if I am indeed a Twisp, why have I been living for the past 15-1/2 years with Grandma Wescott? Have I no blood links at all to the Wescott family? If so, what is their interest in this errant Twisp offspring?

At least now I have a clue why my "dad" is so distant. I may not be related to the creep! Perhaps my voice reminds him more of George Twisp's than of Nick's. And who exactly is this George F. Twisp whose carelessness is alleged to have hurled me into this world? Tyler wasn't much help. He's only met his grandfather a few times and remembers him as a grouchy old guy who smelled bad. Even worse, he's nearly bald! Now I have yet another thing to worry about.

Speaking of male hormone matters, Tyler has given up trying to tie his dick in a knot. He has the required length and competitive spirit, but is much too thick (I should have his problems). I told him if he wanted a pencil dick, he should have eaten more lead paint chips when he was a kid. As I recall, that was a favorite snack of Carlyle's as a preschooler.

I'm at liberty to update my blog because my nephew has gone to the swim center with Stoney Holt. This is unprecedented in two ways. First, it is Stoney's first known date with a guy (or anyone for that matter). And second, it will mark her first public appearance in a swimsuit since she acquired her dynamic curves. By the way, Tyler reports she is quite a sexy kisser. He says we may have to resume our beat-off contest if he is to resist her spectacular charms. Damn, I wish I had some of that guy's babe magnetism. Even wannabe lesbians find him irresistible.

3:47 p.m. I just saw Uma Spurletti! She has acquired a most becoming summer glow (those Italians really know how to tan). She must not have seen me, as she crossed the street before our paths could meet. I hope my dressing entirely in brown does not cause me to blend in excessively with the desert landscape. I intended to call out a friendly greeting, but chickened out at the last moment. Although she was dressed entirely in blue, I felt no impulse to assault her (except, I fear, sexually). How odd that the mere sight of another human can be so stimulating to the nervous system.

I noticed that someone has been spray-painting "UPT" all over town. The shaky handwriting leads me to believe that it is the work of Carlyle. I suppose one should be pleased by the sudden profusion of one's cherished gang symbols, but I've always found graffiti to be rather unsettling. To me it smacks of lowlifes and lawlessness. I need to remind myself that I have joined an urban street gang, not the Cub Scouts.

There's no avoiding it: I have to get a summer job. I can't keep sponging off Grandma—especially now that we may not even be related. But what can I do that pays well and is not entirely withering to the soul? Even the halfway decent jobs like coffee jerking at Starbucks require you to be 16.

6:12 p.m. Tyler is back from his hot date. He said Stoney created quite a stir when she emerged from the bathhouse in a fluorescent orange bikini. What little it left to the imagination all the boys by the pool clearly were willing to fill in. Jaws really dropped when she spread her towel beside Tyler's and let him lovingly oil her up. He reports they had a "great time," though he did have to menace a couple of local cretins for bigoted remarks. They are to meet again tonight in the bus for more lip wrestling. If I had any balls, I'd call up Uma and invite her over to make it a foursome. Alas, in that respect I do take after my erstwhile father.

FRIDAY, June 24 — I am seething with envy and jealousy. Hanging around my handsome, virile nephew does that to a guy. He nearly went all the way last night. Stoney was more than willing—she had even brought along her own condoms. But Tyler had to decline due to that dumb promise extracted by his busybody mother. So they just made do with some extremely intimate fondling. At least you can't get a horrible disease or nine months in the maternity ward from finger fucking. But personally, I've yet to experience an orgasm in my finger. Still, I'm willing to start there and work my way down to the real thing. Tyler reports there's quite a lot of territory to explore up there, especially if you have a long finger (he does). You have to locate this bumpy zone called the G-spot. That really drives them wild. I find it improbable that I ever will be faced with such a mission, but it's good to know your targets ahead of time. Such awareness I'm sure Uma would find reassuring as she parts her shapely thighs at my approach. As if!

SATURDAY, June 25 — Stoney and I walked Tyler to the bus station for his 8:30 a.m. departure for L.A. Even at that ungodly hour, Stoney had somehow gotten it together to apply a bit of pink gloss to her smoldering lips. Not to mention what looked to my unpracticed eyes like mascara. No dress, of course, but she'd ditched the boots and brutally studded Harley belt. What a shame their budding relationship had to terminate so abruptly, but they've promised to stay in touch by e-mail. They had an impassioned clutch, then Tyler shook my hand and jumped on the bus for the long ride back to glamorous L.A. How I wish I were going with him!

After the sad departure, Stoney and I stopped by Herschon's bakery. Over iced coffee and consoling cinnamon rolls I got the full scoop.

"So, Stoney, it looks to me like you really like my nephew."

"Yeah. Tyler's OK."

"Oh? Just OK? I thought you liked him—you know, as a guy."

"I do like him, Noel. But I'm not sure how."

"I'm not following you here, Stoney."

"It's like this. I'm not sure if I like Tyler. Or if I just want to *be* like Tyler."

"Oh." I was still confused.

"I mean, do I want to sleep with the guy? Do I want him as

a boyfriend? Or do I want to be a muscular jock with a big dick?"

"Oh, right. I can see how you might be confused on that point."

"I wanted to try him on for size, but he was too chicken. I thought you guys were always ready to get laid when you got the chance."

"Well, I am, Stoney. Anytime you say."

"Now you're starting to sound like Carlyle, Noel. Don't be such a pig."

Is it me or are girls always broadcasting mixed signals?

"Sorry, Stoney. I just thought if you slept with a guy, you might have a better idea if you're really a lesbian."

"Not necessarily, Noel. Lots of dykes have slept with guys. It's a very butch thing to do—like riding motorcycles and brawling in bars."

"Oh, I see."

Being a lesbian sounds even more challenging than being an impoverished and horny teenaged youth.

SUNDAY, June 26 — Today marks five weeks since I had to change my sheets in the middle of the night. A new record for me. I hope this means I've finally turned that skanky corner. What an impediment to a satisfying love life that would be (assuming I had one). The bad news is that lately I keep waking up with my thumb in my mouth. I pray this doesn't mean I have a deep-seated need to suck stuff (like, say, cocks, for example). Most suspiciously, I wake with my other hand stuck down my shorts and wrapped around my M.F.A. (Man's Favorite Appendage). All these infantile traits lingering so long has me a bit concerned. I think what I really need is a therapeutic week in bed with Uma.

That is an even more remote fantasy now. I just received word from my blog hoster that I'm being ejected because of "obscene content." I don't see how Real Life Honestly Described can be deemed "obscene," but there you have it. And there goes my dream that while Googling her name, Uma would discover my blog and realize that she and I had a Date with Destiny. Oh well, I may not be cut out for the blogging scene anyway. The only comments I was drawing sounded like they were from middle-aged perverts masquerading as ditsy 12-year-old girls.

My bankroll is down to 19 cents. Time to watch some semi-lucrative TV with Grandma.

MONDAY, June 27 — A noisy thunderstorm in the dead of night. At that first nerve-pummeling boom I nearly bit off my thumb. I may have to buy some handcuffs on Ebay and shackle myself to the bedpost at night. Be a shame if I perished in a conflagration because I couldn't get to the key in time. I'm told these trailers can go up like aluminum-clad napalm bombs. I've turned a nasty corner here. My thumb is now even more chafed than my much-abused privates.

3:12 p.m. I may have a line on a job. I ran into Rot Dugan at the hardware store, where I was buying the cheapest garden gloves they carry. Rot's real name is Jasper, for which crime he expects his parents to burn in hell for all eternity. Long ago his bright orange hair earned him the nickname Carrot, which over time got condensed to Rot. He himself is a bit condensed, being the shortest guy in our class at a non-towering 4'6" and 81 pounds. Anyway, Rot reports his dad is looking for a "house darky" for his wedding chapel hospitality staff. The Dugans reside in an imposing plantation-style mansion that used to be a funeral home until Mr. Dugan developed a life-threatening allergy to embalming fluids. So Rot's dad cleared out the caskets and stiff clientele, and sent away for a mail-order minister's license. Now his Dixie Belle Wedding Chapel marries people in a genteel manner recalling the days of the Old South.

"Wouldn't I have to be, um, black for this position?" I inquired.

"Naw, you just have to smear on brown greasepaint and wear

a kinky wig," Rot replied. "Dad says real black people would make his customers nervous."

Sounds like blatant discrimination to me, but I doubt if many blacks in town would be lining up for a job that lets them relive their oppressed ancestors' pre-Civil War slavery days. Alas, financial desperation prevents me from taking a strong ethical stand against such overt racism. I said I would be over after supper tonight with my résumé (such as it is) in hand.

"And why, Rot, don't you do this job?" I inquired.

"Well I used to, Noel. But I got fired."

"You were fired by your own father?"

"Yeah. Too many customers were commenting that the house darky looked just like him."

TUESDAY, June 28 — I woke up at 1:08 a.m. last night. That's when the fuzzy cotton thumb of my garden glove first entered my mouth. I also woke up at 2:28, 4:51, 6:17, and 8:49. The last occasion was when Grandma tugged on my toe to tell me I had a call. It was Mr. Dugan phoning to say I was hired. I thanked him and pretended to sound pleased and enthusiastic. I suspect I mostly sounded tired, groggy, and parched. Thick cotton can really soak up the moisture from a guy's mouth.

I'm not sure about this job. Mr. Dugan impressed me as being something of a short tightwad (he's only a few inches taller than his son and a good half-foot shorter than his matronly wife). I'm to be paid a flat $5 per function plus tips. Fairly miserable, but at least most weddings are over in under 30 minutes. The truly bad news is that 90 percent of Mr. Dugan's trade consists of walk-ins. Therefore, I'm to be on call 24/7. Whenever Mr. Dugan rings my cell phone, I'm to drop everything and zip over on my bike (a brisk ten-minute ride). Worse, I'm expected to arrive made up and in costume. This means I'll have to go about my daily life in blackface and dressed like a Negro house servant circa 1840: rough breeches, fitted coat with velvet collar, homespun blouse, knotted bandana for my cravat, and battered straw hat. No wristwatch, jewelry, iPod, or running shoes permitted. Sounds dreadful, but I'm in too deep now to back out; Mrs. Dugan took my measurements last night and her husband reports she is already at work altering the costume to fit. I'm to find a pair of plain brown leather shoes (style: Junior Slave), for which they will reimburse me up to the sum of $10. Looks like another trip to the Golden Eagle Thrift Shoppe. Only one question: Why me, God?

7:12 p.m. I am now an African American named Toby (Mr. Dugan thought Noel sounded too contemporary and white). On the whole, it feels a bit strange. Mrs. Dugan let the seams out as much as possible, but I still feel like a lizard about to shed its too-small skin. And this jacket doesn't smell that good. Rot and his predecessors appear to have done a great deal of sweating in it. Grandma suggested hanging it up on the patio to air out. The wig promises to be trouble too. It's this rubbery affair like a bathing cap, covered in a quarter inch of black nappy wool. Very sweaty on hot days, such as we are expecting for the next four or five months. The greasepaint also feels rather sweaty and greasy. I hope it doesn't exacerbate my zit problem. At least my new (used) shoes feel pretty comfortable. Stoney and I found them in the hospice store, which suggested to her that the previous owner had keeled over in them. I hope not, but their minimal wear certainly implies that the prior occupant wasn't up for any arduous hikes. A bargain at only $3.99, but I intend to be reimbursed for the full $10. After all, my valuable time is worth at least that much.

No more nightly sewing for me. Grandma fears the greasepaint will rub off on the festive fabrics. I am now reduced to watching TV for free.

WEDNESDAY, June 29 — Three weddings so far today. All middle-aged couples and all apparently cold sober. Fairly meager tippers—only a gratuitous $2 thus far. This was from a couple whose van broke down on Interstate 80. While waiting for their injectors to be replaced, they decided to kill some time by getting married. I suspect they'd both had some prior experiences at the matrimonial altar. I wonder if Uma and I could ever be so casual, should Our Love progress to that stage. (Hey, *somebody's* going to marry Uma. Why shouldn't it be me?)

Toby's job is to bow and scrape, saying "yes, suh," and "yes, ma'am," as he helps the happy couple with their things. Then I shake a tambourine while Mrs. Dugan in blond spit curls and bouffant hoopskirt mans the pump organ. Or, if the clients have brought a camera, I ditch the tambourine and snap a few artsy photos. After the ceremony of union I pass out lemonade and cookies, unless they've sprung for the deluxe package, in which case mint juleps and finger sandwiches are served. In no case should Toby help himself to any of the snacks even if so instructed by the guests of honor. Nor should he EVER block the automatic video camera, for which transgression I've already received a fierce ass chewing. Sales of the commemorative videos are a big profit center, Mr. Dugan informed me.

I feel a bit self-conscious walking around town in my new 19th Century African-American persona. I noticed when I dropped into a convenience store for an emergency soda (that wig is hot), the suspicious clerk gave me the hairy eyeball the entire time. Then outside in the parking lot, an old lady walking a tiny dog stopped me to ask if the circus was in town. I shrugged, put on my best English accent, and replied, "Sorry, madam, I really couldn't say."

Passing Carlyle autographing the side of the post office, I was gratified to see that my gang brother didn't recognize me. Toby stopped to introduce himself. Carlyle was thrilled by my new identity (except for the clothes), and he quickly decided he wants to be black as well. It's true that all his favorite rap artists, movie stars, and sports heroes are black. He also thinks our gang would have much more street credibility if we altered our race.

11:45 p.m. The infantile thumb sucking has got to stop! I

have sprayed my garden gloves with bitter apple dog repellent. This vile fluid tastes worse than month-old road kill. Grandma bought a bottle a few years back to discourage our chew-happy beagle puppy, which soon broke my heart by getting eaten by a coyote. Yet another reason to move back to civilization.

Snug in my bitter gloves, I shall now go to bed thinking strictly adult thoughts that may lead inexorably to carnal self-knowledge. I am willing to take that chance.

THURSDAY, June 30 — Yuck and double yuck. My stunned taste buds are in full retreat. Such a horror, but I only had three incidents of T.S. last night. This may be the route to go if I can stand it. At breakfast this morning Grandma inquired why I've taken to wearing gloves to bed.

"Uh, I'm trying to toughen up my hands," I replied, picking through my Wheaties that now tasted like an elderly rhinoceros had pissed on them.

"I know just the thing for that, Noelly. It's called manual labor. You can start by pulling all the weeds out of my flower patch."

Damn!

5:12 p.m. What a shock. A guy in my high school got married today: Artie Prender, a soon-to-be senior (or maybe not), who ran the 440 on the track team. The bride I didn't recognize, but she was pretty cute if you like them blonde and built. Both sets of parents were there looking major annoyed. When Mr. Dugan asked if he took Tiffany as his lawfully wedded wife, Artie sighed and muttered, "Yeah, I guess so." That's when Tiffany's dad reared back and kicked him in the ass. This caused the bride to burst into tears. Inured to such drama, Mr. and Mrs. Dugan went on as if nothing had happened, but the darky stood there with mouth agape. Nobody stayed for lemonade and cookies, but Artie's dad, I'm happy to report, slipped me a $10 bill and asked me to keep my mouth shut. I suppose a baby must be on the way, though there was no sign of it to my inexperienced eye. I hope the kid receives a pleasant welcome and doesn't get shuffled off to some remote backwater like me. Of course, if the happy couple makes their home in Winnemucca, that may be hard to avoid.

Later Mr. Dugan commented that he had witnessed much worse behavior at funerals—especially if the mourners included multiple ex-wives. Mrs. Dugan agreed, noting that all in all she preferred weddings to funerals, although the money wasn't nearly as good. So true, said Mr. Dugan, who lamented that he used to clear several thousand dollars on a nice mahogany casket, but now could barely make a sawbuck on a souvenir gold-plated rose.

Personally, I'm glad that it costs less to get married than to croak, as I hope to experiment with the former one of these days. Do you suppose if I knock up his daughter, Mr. Spurletti will insist I marry Uma? Or, alternatively, will he just knock me off?

# JULY

FRIDAY, July 1 — The most depressing day of the year in the marriage biz. June is over for another entire year. People get married willingly (more or less) in June, but the rest of year their natural reluctance to commit frequently prevails. This is unlike the funeral biz where people croak reliably without regard to the calendar.

Not one to let moss grow under his Bible, Mr. Dugan put an ad in the newspaper offering a complete "Adore Ceremony" for only $29.95. Mrs. Dugan and Toby were skeptical, but, boy, were we proved wrong. All day long we were swamped by doting teen couples clutching coupons. For their 30 bucks they got a candle-lit ceremony featuring love songs on the organ, touching exchange of commitment vows, handsomely engraved certificates of adoration, and an opportunity to purchase celebratory lemonade and cookies (sorry, no free eats at those prices). A few couples exchanged rings, but the offered love tokens were all over the map. Bryan Dinger and Mindy Preel, for example, exchanged silver tongue studs.

Even though hustling the snacks added to my workload, Mr. Dugan chiseled me down to just $3 per adore service. What a cheapskate. And no tips to speak of either. I was regarded with interest by the celebrants, but no one appeared to recognize me—not that I cut that large a profile among the upperclassmen in my high school.

If I had $30 and a girlfriend, I doubt I'd blow my wad just to hear "Love Theme from Romeo and Juliet" and get a crummy certificate proving I was going steady. Still, if darling Uma found the concept charming, I expect I'd be lining up in a hurry. All this romance on the hoof today made the emotional chasm between me and Uma particularly painful. It is most stressful to be stuck on someone who is barely aware of one's existence.

8:47 p.m. Lots of firecrackers exploding along our road. I hope no one starts a wildfire that burns us all to glowing cinders. I should call up Uma and invite her to the big fireworks show Monday night. Yeah, right.

I have wiped off my greasepaint and turned off my cell phone. If someone wants to declare their mutual adoration tonight, they can sure as hell do it without me.

SATURDAY, July 2 — I had a dream last night that I was sharing a private hot tub with Uma. I was filled with anticipation because only I knew that I had switched our bathing suits to a special kind that dissolved in hot water. Anticipation quickly turned to panic, however, when the water suddenly grew cold. Frantic valve fiddling only made things worse. That's when I woke up and discovered that my five-week respite from you know what was over. So tiresome! I already go to bed in gloves. Do I have to put a clothespin on my dick as well?!

Carlyle came over after my gloomy breakfast with his foster dad's credit card number, and we were able to order him a large afro wig over the Internet. (Just try purchasing such an item in Winnemucca.) We also ordered two jumbo jars of mocha brown greasepaint (one for each of us). We've agreed that even if we can't always dress in brown, we're still upholding our gang colors if our exposed skin is brown. Carlyle also wanted to order an ex-military Soviet handgun, but I drew the line at such fraud.

The guy is scary enough just packing all those lethal-looking knives. Carlyle gave me a dozen cans of spray paint to help with the cause. Whenever he sees an open garage door, he sneaks in and helps himself to any paint stores. I pointed out that such trespass constitutes an illegal burglary.

"Aw, nobody's gonna 'rrest my ass 'cause I swiped a few cans of paint," he shrugged.

"And how many have you stolen?" I inquired.

Carlyle gave it some thought. "'Bout 600 so far, but a lot of them turned out to be empty or dried up or some useless color like pink."

7:38 p.m. Another dateless Saturday night. My 754ᵗʰ in a row (or thereabouts). The good news is that 754 Saturdays from now I'll be 29, married (to Uma?), and by then will have had several thousand vigorous bouts of intercourse under my belt. That thought sustains me.

Speaking of wanton sex, there's been another emergency wedding. Two ancient fossils got wheeled into the Dixie Belle from a local old folks home. A shift supervisor found them in bed together this morning, and the prim management insisted they get married or get out. Since they couldn't afford the latter, in they came. Though they looked about 214 to me, it turned out that he was 89 and she was 93. That's like me marrying some college sophomore! (Not a bad idea. Where do I sign up?) They got through the ceremony OK, though afterwards the bride dribbled quite a bit of her lemonade. They are honeymooning tonight back at the home, while I—young, virile, and primed for action—have only my computer for company.

I have sent an email to my brother Nick in Las Vegas demanding a complete accounting of my origins. This uncertainty is intolerable. I need to know who I am!

SUNDAY, July 3 — Another wretched night. Damn. My new policy is no beverages after 12 noon, except for cocktails with Uma. (I wish.)

This working for a living really sucks. I was supposed to go swimming with Stoney, but Toby got called in for more lousy adore ceremonies and a wedding or two. No paycheck in sight yet. I'm operating entirely on wallet fumes. Stoney is bummed because she's stuck on Tyler, but knows he's seeing his multiple L.A. girlfriends. She says guys are nothing but trouble and wishes she could go back to being a horny dyke. I said that's not very likely now that she's let the genie out of the bottle. She should just go with it, I added, and work to get in touch with her feminine side. She replied that my big fat mouth was working to get in touch with her knuckles.

7:45 p.m. New developments this afternoon. When their 3:30 reservation didn't show, Mr. Dugan sent Toby over to the Silver Sluice casino to bang on the missing couple's hotel door. While attempting an inconspicuous crossing of the lobby, who should I spy but my very own (I wish) Uma. Looking wildly attractive in a green Silver Sluice employee polo shirt, she was manning a kiosk that sold gum, candy, sunglasses and other casino necessities. I edged over to ogle the breath-mints display.

"I wouldn't try anything," she noted. "There are security cameras everywhere."

"Thanks for the warning," I replied, my heart pounding. "Are these breath mints fresh?"

"Of course. They're loaded with preservatives."

Uma rested her lovely chin on her lovely hand and studied me with interest. In this posture, I couldn't help but notice, her lovely breasts nestled sweetly on the counter.

"Any particular brand you recommend?" I asked.

"What is the nature of your problem?"

"Uh, what do you mean?"

"How bad is your breath?"

"That's a rather personal question."

Toby, I noticed, was much better at talking to Uma than I had ever been.

"I suppose, but you brought up the subject. Did that jacket shrink?"

"Yes, dreadfully. I fell into the Amazon—off a speeding river boat."

"Not wash and wear, huh?"

"Uh, no."

Toby selected a roll of mints and placed it on the counter, causing Uma to rise languidly and pass the mints under a scanner.

"That will be $1.59."

"That much, huh?" Toby removed his wallet and looking into it doubtfully. His skepticism was well founded.

"Yes, my father goes for the high markup."

"Oh dear," Toby sighed, "I seem to be a bit short at the moment."

"Not as short as Rot Dugan when he used to come in here in that outfit."

Toby colored under his layer of brown. "Oh. Rot Dugan. Right."

Uma placed the mints on the counter in front of me. "Take them. You can pay me whenever." No smile but a ghost of a glint in her lovely eyes. They were an improbable shade of pale violet-green.

"You're awfully trusting."

"Well, I know who you are."

"You do?"

"Uh-huh."

"Er, why's that?"

Lovely eyebrows were raised. "Well, we do live in the same small town."

"I know. It's a bummer. I mean, uh, being stuck out here in the boondocks."

"It's not the end of the earth, but you can see it from here."

Toby surprised himself by chuckling affably. "You can say that again. Well, I'm late for a wedding."

"Not yours, I trust."

My heart flipped over. Dare I hope she cared?

"Uh, why do you say that?"

"Well, for one thing, you have no money. And you're rather young for such a step."

"That's true, I suppose."

Uma placed the mints in my clammy hand. "Here you go."

"Thanks. Well, I'm going now."

"Have a nice day."

"You too."

I wandered off in a fog and never did track down the errant couple. When I got back to the Dixie Belle, there they were already married and guzzling their mint juleps. Mr. Dugan, I knew, would dock me the $5, but I didn't care. I'm more in love than ever. Uma knows who I am and we have already discussed marriage!

MONDAY, July 4 — Independence Day. I wish I were independent of bodily malfunctions, but alas, that is not the case. It's a mystery where all that liquid came from, since I went to bed terribly parched. I've thought of putting a rubber band around my dick, but I'm afraid it will turn black and fall off. What a blow to one's budding social life that would be.

No reply yet from my brother to my inquisitive e-mail. Those Twisps are such an uncommunicative lot.

Now I wish I'd selected a candy bar yesterday. What if Uma is under the mistaken impression I have a chronic halitosis problem? I must try to get close to her and breathe heavily, but as Toby reminds me, that is precisely the point of the entire teen dating enterprise. Can't write any more. I am being dragged off to the mountains by Grandma and old Mr. Tuelco. They love to fish. Why they feel the need to take along a hostage, I can't really say. I could be missing out on some lucrative tips today too—not that I expect Mr. Dugan to call. Grandma informed him yesterday that I was to be paid double-time for all holiday and weekend services. I think she may be tiring of Toby, who's been a bit surly lately what with his plumbing woes, thumb compulsions, and love-life distractions.

11:12 p.m. I missed out on the big fireworks show. Not to mention the parade and civic barbeque. Uma was probably there the whole time and searching desperately for me. Where was I? Stranded out by some obscure tributary of the Humboldt River in the blazing summer heat. I sprayed "UPT" on a few rocks, then hung out in the shade with my excruciatingly antiquated Gameboy. Some fish were caught and eaten. Pretty good, but nothing you couldn't find frozen and breaded at your local supermarket. Many beers were consumed, but none by me. Mr. Tuelco overdid it as usual, and Grandma had to drive his truck back. He lives down the road in an even shabbier trailer than ours. He's married, but his old lady is locked away with a bad case of Alzheimer's. He pals around sometimes with Grandma, but I don't think they're an item. The thought of them together bodily is too repulsive to contemplate. In his day Mr. Tuelco (first name Gus) was a phenomenal breeder; the whole town being lousy with his descendants, including about 27 grandkids in my school. Lots of locals grow up and move away, but for some reason the Tuelcos have never heard of this concept. They just stay put, multiply, and become fry cooks or motel maids.

I have downloaded some new music files for Stoney. Nothing too bizarre, alas, just some fairly funky industrial rock tunes from Taiwan. My best find lately was this MP3 from Ecuador that supposedly had the actual sounds of the bass player being electrocuted by his guitar. Well, somebody was certainly doing some energetic screaming. I'd been playing it constantly, but now Grandma has banned it from the trailer. She prefers country music. I say just because we're stuck out here in the sticks is no reason to wallow in the lifestyle.

Good night, Uma darling, the fireworks of my life.

TUESDAY, July 5 — No leakage and only moderate T.S. I can postpone suicide for another day. Still no e-mail reply from my famous brother. Probably too busy screwing those topless showgirls. According to Tyler, Nick used to keep some sort of pre-blog daily journal. Perhaps I have inherited a similar Twispian impulse toward compulsive navel-gazing. Too bad my life, such as it is, is so excruciatingly dull and boring.

7:12 p.m. A very strange day. Guess who waltzed into the Dixie Belle this morning? My mother! I recognized her right away even though she had aged quite a bit. She was with this very tall guy with a pink baby face and graying crew cut. So she spots me and bursts out crying. Very embarrassing as we were right in the middle of finishing up our first wedding of the day. Since the happy couple had been up all night gambling and drinking, Mrs. Dugan was serving them strong coffee instead of lemonade. Fortunately, they were still pretty plastered, so they didn't get too bothered by this hysterical interruption of their Golden Moment of Union.

The problem was that Grandma had told my mother where I was when she called, but had neglected to mention my Tobification. (Grandma has very little to say to her ex-daughter-in-law, blaming her for depriving her of any opportunity for future grandchildren.) Mother saw me and somehow must have concluded I had grown up black. I'm not sure how that's possible, but that's my relatives for you. Anyway, Mr. Dugan got very annoyed and told them they had to leave as this was a wedding chapel not a family crisis center. Well, that pissed off my mother, who reached over and yanked off Toby's wig.

"This child is *not* a Negro!" she screamed.

"Who invited her to my wedding?" asked the confused bride.

"Looks like some kind of racial thing," slurred the groom. "Are you from the KKK?"

"Scrub that off your face!" screamed my mother, ignoring his query.

"You get out of here!" bellowed my employer.

"Show some respect!" yelled his wife.

"Please, please, let's all be reasonable," said the tall man.

After we were ejected by Mr. Dugan, Mother wiped off her tears, smiled bravely, and invited me to lunch. I explained I had to go as Toby, since I could be called back to work at any time.

The tall guy (Mr. Wally Rumpkin) persuaded her to give me back my wig, and we all trooped over to the Silver Sluice for a fancy lunch in their pricey Feedbag Corral. Toby had the $21.95 T-bone steak, since I figured they owed me at least that much for nearly getting my ass canned. No sign of Uma, which is just as well 'cause my mother got pretty weepy all through lunch—especially after Toby asked her point-blank if Lance Wescott was really my dad (I don't think I would have had the nerve).

So the story straight from the horse's mouth (as it were) is that Tyler was correct. I am a 100 percent full-blooded Twisp.

"I hope that doesn't disappoint you, Noelly," she wept. "Your father was the biggest mistake I ever made in my life."

"Well, Lance Wescott was no great prize either," Toby pointed out, obliging Mr. Rumpkin to suppress a smile. I kind of like that big guy, even though he never looks you in the eye and lets my mother push him around. He used to be a truck driver until he got disabled (back trouble) from being so tall (at least seven feet).

"Are you very, very unhappy here?" Mother asked, wiping her eyes.

"It's OK."

I knew the last thing in the world I'd ever want would be to go live under the same roof with that wacky woman, even if she did reside in cosmopolitan Oakland. True, Winnemucca was a pit, but I got along OK with Grandma, she seldom butted into my life, and my dreary home town did offer that Immensity Known as Uma.

"Would you like to come to Oakland for a nice long visit?" she asked brightly. (Can mothers read minds?) "I could petition the court to permit it."

"Uh, gee thanks, Mother. But I have my job. I just joined a youth group. And school starts next month."

"I hope you don't turn out like my other children, Noel. I never hear from Nick and Joanie only stays in touch so she can give me grief."

That reminded me of something.

"Mother, is it true that Nick got married when he was my age?"

"I refuse to discuss that horrible incident and that horrible, horrible girl. I hope you're not thinking about girls, Noel. I feel there's some kind of bad seed from your father that got into Nick. He wound up getting arrested. It was a nightmare for us all."

"I always liked Nick," volunteered Mr. Rumpkin. "He's a wonderful juggler."

"Oh, pay the check, Wally. Everyone is looking at us. They're wondering why that woman with her make-up all smeared is holding that dear Negro child's hand."

I was wondering the same thing.

Parents. They *can* creep you out.

Though I wouldn't mind being adopted by Mr. Rumpkin. While shaking hands good-bye, he slipped me a wadded-up bill. Twenty dollars! What a guy.

WEDNESDAY, July 6 — Another dry night. I think the secret is to avoid dinners like spaghetti that are full of water. I hope Uma doesn't insist on cooking Italian every night after we tie the knot. Perhaps I could request my pasta dry. No, she already thinks I'm weird. I realize now I have barely more than a month to win her heart before ill-fated (I wish) Sloan Chandler returns. Toby will have to turn up his dusky charm.

Carlyle phones every half hour to ask if his afro has arrived. The guy is very anxious to repudiate his race. I keep telling him it will take at least a week to get here. I'm not sure UPS has even heard of Winnemucca.

I've been ruminating a lot about mothers. I think the act of germinating another person inside you kind of weirds them out. I used to envy kids who had mothers to tuck them into bed at night and take care of them. Not any more. I prefer grandmothers. You get the standard love and mothering, but without the biological baggage. Let's face it: how can you ever hope to have a normal relationship with a person who shat you out like a pumpkin?

5:18 p.m. A slow day in the wedding biz, so Toby sneaked away to see if Uma was manning her kiosk. She was. How I'd love to possess one of her used polo shirts for nightly snuggling (in lieu, that is, of the actual girl).

"I've got it," Toby announced, smiling brightly.

"That's too bad," said Uma. "Have you seen a doctor?"

"I mean I've got your money."

"What?"

"The $1.59 I owe you for the breath mints."

"Oh, right."

I selected an innocuous Payday candy bar and handed her my $20 bill.

"I don't need any breath mints, Uma. They were actually for Mr. Dugan."

"Uh, OK," she said, counting out my change.

"Did you see the fireworks the other night?" I asked.

"No. I missed them. How were they?"

"I missed them too."

"Oh."

The conversation was threatening to grind to a halt.

"Heard from Sloan?"

Uma, alas, brightened. "He sent me a postcard. Their boat had reached Barbados."

Where was God when I needed a hurricane?

"I hear you were dining here yesterday and holding some woman's hand."

A good sign! Uma has spies reporting on my every move.

"That was my mother. She only sees me every ten years, so she gets a bit carried away."

"My parents are divorced too."

A personal revelation!

"Is your father remarried?"

"No, thank God. He was seeing a woman in Gulfport, but he hasn't met anybody here yet."

"You lived in Mississippi?"

"For seven years. My father owned a casino boat, but he didn't like the South."

"He likes Winnemucca better?" I asked, incredulous.

"He loves it. Go figure."

A fat slob of a security guard strolled over.

"Is this person bothering you, Uma?"

"No, it's OK, Marvin."

Big dumb Marvin didn't seem to get the message.

"We don't permit loitering in this lobby, kid. You better move it."

"'Bye, Uma."

"'Bye, Noel."

Uma actually knows my name! But that pushy rent-a-cop had better watch out. He'll be sorry when the NAACP drags his sorry ass into court on a discrimination charge.

10:22 p.m. After much soul-searching I have made up my mind. The next time I see Uma I'm going to ask her out. This will be difficult, but it must be done. There are over six billion people on this planet. Even allowing for all those arranged marriages, at least one billion guys must have asked out a billion or so chicks. If Eskimos can do it, if guys garbed only in penis gourds in New Guinea can do it, if reticent English twits can do it, God dammit, so can I!

THURSDAY, July 7 — Still no e-mail reply from my loving brother Nick. Just think, if I'd asked him for the antidote to botulism poisoning, I'd be dead and buried by now.

No leakage last night again, but I forgot my garden gloves, and my red, wrinkly thumb may be ruined for life. I found a sadistic advice site on the web that recommends rubbing the nail with peppermint oil or a freshly sliced jalapeño pepper to discourage T.S. Yeah, and if that doesn't work, mothers, try amputating the offending digit with a meat cleaver.

7:25 p.m. More weddings. Sometimes it feels like everyone is getting married except me. I'd say about two-thirds of our couples are pretty affectionate, but a solid one-third interact like they were there for an IRS tax audit. I discussed this phenomenon with Grandma at dinner. She knows all about human relations from her many years of listening to the dirt from hair clients. According to her, marriage is the last step many couples take in the process of breaking up. A quick stop at the Dixie Belle is actually faster and cheaper than couples counseling. And much smarter than blowing the budget on a big church wedding right before that final split.

Silly me. I thought we were joining all those lovebirds for life.

Speaking of Cosmic Love, I'm still dateless. After working myself into a tizzy, I sent Toby in to buy another candy bar. No Uma. Her work hours seem most irregular. Fat Marvin was there giving me the evil eye. I got a closer look at that cretin's nametag. Won't you know it, he's a Tuelco—the old man's youngest son, according to Grandma. I think ol' Gus should have pulled out early that night.

10:45 p.m. I've been researching the female vagina. This is quite easy these days, thanks to the profusion of porn sites on the Internet. You can get some full-color views from a true gynecologist's perspective. Seems a pretty simple affair—at least from the outward appearance. Not nearly as much variation as you get with penises, which should be helpful for us neophytes. I think it's great there's so much information out there these days. I can just imagine how mystified my dad or grandfather must have felt when they first started poking around down there. Of course, this information exposure only heightens my desire to experience the real thing. I wonder if Uma finds the subject (carnal relations) similarly captivating?

That question I hope to answer soon.

FRIDAY, July 8 — Payday at last. No check yet, but by tonight I expect my net worth will have skyrocketed. Meanwhile, I at last received an e-mail response from my elder brother. Nick apologized for not getting back to me sooner, saying he was "away for a week in Prague for a jugglers' convention." Why is it that everyone on Earth goes to conventions but the one sub-group that really needs to mix it up: horny teenagers? Nick writes and I quote: "I have no reason to believe that Lance Wescott is not your father."

OK, either the guy is totally clueless or a compulsive liar. I'm inclined toward the latter. In my experience, we Twisps much prefer a complicated lie to the simple truth. We are by nature a devious clan.

The town's meager black population has gone up by one. Carlyle's package was delivered today. Unlike Toby, Carlyle tries to distract attention from his blue eyes and dearth of Negroid features by speaking an extreme version of ghetto English. The effect is arresting to say the least. I suggested he throttle back a notch to appear less like an offensive caricature, but he wasn't buying it. He has also modified his walk to an in-your-face ghetto strut (with twitches). More than a bit ridiculous, but I must be supportive of my fellow gang member. Now he has hit the streets in full regalia to buy a metal comb for teasing out his big '70s-style afro.

5:12 p.m. Momentous news! Toby spoke to Uma again. First he got fat Marvin out of the way by asking him if he knew some "old guy named Gus?"

"My dad's named Gus," he replied, eyeballing me suspiciously.

"That's too bad," Toby said. "I just heard he collapsed into his macaroni and cheese at the senior center."

Marvin cursed, spat, and hustled out the door.

"Is that true?" inquired Uma, adorning the gum display with her Mediterranean beauty.

"Probably somewhere on this planet," replied Toby, nervously scanning the candy bar rack. My Big Moment was approaching.

"I wish I could eat candy like you do," Uma remarked.

"Why don't you?"

"I have a grandmother who weighs 300 pounds."

"So do I. But fortunately I'm not related to mine."

Not wishing to appear too hedonistic, I put back my jumbo bar and selected a regular-size Payday.

"How did you manage that?" Uma asked, sliding my bar under the scanner.

"It's a long story."

"That will be $1.29. Do you know Mary Glasgow?"

I fished out my wallet. "Sure. I've known her since kindergarten."

True enough, but I doubt stuck-up Mary would deign to spit on me if my clothes were on fire. Uma, I knew, was tight with her.

"She's having a Christmas in July party. Are you interested?"

Toby had a mild coronary. Could it be that Uma was asking *me* out?"

"Uh, sure. Yes. Really, I'd love to. When is it?"

"Tomorrow night. Her parents are going out of town. We're supposed to dress in holiday-appropriate attire—whatever that means."

"Sounds good. What time should I pick you up?" I had to get this nailed down before she changed her mind or came to her senses.

"I don't know. Eight o'clock?"

"I'll be there."

"OK."

"OK, Uma."

"Are you intending to pay me? Or do I have to call a cop?"

"Oh, right!"

Toby paid for his item and wandered off in another golden fog.

I have an actual date with Uma!

I have joined the One Billion Club at last. This asking out

chicks was much easier than I expected.

By the way, my paycheck seemed suspiciously low. Lots of onerous deductions for frivolous taxes, plus no reimbursement for Toby's pricey used shoes. Mrs. Dugan claimed she "forgot." I let it slide, cause ol' Toby is now slaving (happily) for date money.

SATURDAY, July 9 — The most momentous day of my life. In less than 12 hours I may be holding Uma's hand (assuming I can work up the courage). Lots of overnight leakage and thumb molestation I'm attributing to nerves. My composure was not improved by Stoney arriving bright and early to grill me on these latest developments. Somehow she had heard, although I informed no one except Grandma and my employers. Just try having a secret in this town.

"Why would Uma invite *you* to Mary Glasgow's dumb party?" demanded Stoney.

"Why not? Maybe she likes me."

"You wish. No, it's got to be something else. Maybe they intend to humiliate you for trying to pass as black."

"That's Carlyle. I'm only doing Toby for the bucks."

"I fear the worst. Did you ever see the movie 'Carrie'?"

"Stoney! Uma's not like that. Besides, I'm not going to the party as Toby."

"You're not? Does your girlfriend know that? As I recall she invited Toby not Noel."

"And how, may I ask, do you know that?"

"I have my sources. Are you going as an elf?"

"Certainly not."

"It's a Christmas party, you dork."

"I know that. I thought I'd wear a red shirt and my green corduroy pants."

"You'll look like an idiot."

"Stoney, did you come over here just to undermine my confidence and make me feel bad?"

"Sure, Noel. What else are friends for?"

1:17 p.m. Carlyle's transformation to an urban minority youth has not gone down well with his foster parents. They've scheduled an emergency appointment for him on Monday with the county juvenile psychologist. Carlyle has met with this chick (Dr. Quentina Freep) many times in the past, and regards her as "kinda sexy," but "nosy as hell." At least she's black, so Carlyle expects a more sympathetic hearing than last time when he was just a "white punk" setting the county ablaze.

Carlyle loves being black, but doesn't appreciate all the scrutiny he's now receiving on the street from "honky assholes." Toby pointed out that's a fact of life in a county that's so lily white. It's too bad Carlyle didn't aspire to be Hispanic. We have lots of those, and he'd fit right in (assuming he spoke Spanish, didn't twitch, and was generally less strange).

6:17 p.m. Too nervous to eat any dinner. I expect there will be snacks at the party. I've been listening to Grandma's Christmas CDs to get in the mood and calm my nerves. Mel Torme and Tony Bennett were OK, but the Carpenters' holiday album made me feel a bit suicidal. I wonder if it's just me or does Karen Carpenter's voice provoke extreme anxiety in everyone?

7:15 p.m. Time to go. I will now leave my childhood behind and commence Life with Uma.

SUNDAY, July 10 — I slept until 1:30 in the afternoon. Not a record, but up there even for me. No leakage. After a hard workout, my kidneys were taking the night off. Very hot day. Took a shower and turned up the swamp cooler. Now roaring like a 747 that just sucked in a goose. Had to fix my own lunch as Grandma was out. No phone messages, no interesting e-mail.

Details of last night's date? Oh all right, if you insist.

Being car-less and license-less, I rode my bike to Uma's. Since I've been making a study of her life, I knew where she lived and knew it was just a few blocks from Mary Glasgow's. I ditched my bike in some shrubbery and rang the doorbell. An older Italian-looking lady opened the door. Not fat, thank God. Introduced herself as Uma's aunt Rosa. Seemed to know who I was, and did not call police to have me ejected. Made small talk in posh foyer, then Uma showed up. Dressed most provocatively in silver ice-skating costume. Leotard-like top and very short ruffled skirt. Lovely slim legs encased in matching iridescent tights. Hair pinned up and festooned with tinsel. Sparkly bejeweled Christmas tree broach fastened above left breast. Bright green eye shadow and red lipstick that coordinated nicely with my apparel. No actual ice skates, of course, just silver ballet slippers that softly caressed each lovely toe. She was like the best Christmas morning you could imagine, multiplied a million times. Somehow she even smelled like a pine forest.

"Hi, Noel," she said. "Where's that Christmas music coming from?"

"It's my iPod. I've connected it to small amplified speakers concealed in my pants pockets."

"Very ingenious."

We said good-bye to Aunt Rosa and set off for the party— linked if not by hand (I was too chicken) then by a shared sense of festive anticipation. Soon, Mel Torme gave way to Barbra Streisand. Walking in the deepening twilight with the woman of your dreams in your own cocoon of mood music is a great way to start one's Saturday night.

"Does this bra look too ridiculous?" asked Uma.

Rendered virtually speechless by her query, I inspected the area in question.

"Uh, no. You look fine, I mean great."

"I wasn't going to wear one, but my aunt insisted. She said people could see my nipples—as if every person on the planet doesn't have them."

"Uh, some people," I stammered, "some people have more than two."

"Well, don't get your hopes up in my case, Noel."

I was not entirely sure what she meant by that.

"Your aunt lives with you?"

"Yes, ever since she left the convent. She used to be a nun."

"A man? Really! She had a sex-change operation?"

"Hardly. I said 'nun.' She used to be Sister Rosa."

"Oh. Sorry."

A night of firsts: First time I had spoken to a nun. First time I had discussed intimate apparel with a girl.

"For 17 years. Can you imagine that? Then she called it quits. She wants to get married, but she hasn't had any luck finding a fellow. She needs a cultured gentleman of the old school. Catholic too, of course. Just try finding that type in Winnemucca. Know anybody?"

"Uh, I don't think so."

"Well, we've got to find her someone, Noel. I can't have an ex-nun telling me how to dress for the rest of my life."

I liked her use of "we" in that sentence. I was about 98 percent ready to grasp her dangling hand when I noticed that we had arrived at our destination. Mary Glasgow herself answered our knock and squealed out an enthusiastic "Merry Christmas!" Draping a skinny arm around her shoulder was Drew Kolstiner, my long ago grade-school next-door neighbor and best friend. His mother remarried, they sold their trailer, they moved to a fancier street, and that was that. His romantic interest in Mary Glasgow was news to me, though probably not to the rest of Winnemucca.

"Hi, Drew," I said.

"Hi, Noel. What's with the bulge in your pants?"

Everyone looked down at my crotch. Nope, nothing amiss or inflamed down there.

"Those are speakers in his pockets," volunteered Uma. "Noel's a walking Christmas concert."

"Very nice," said Mary, obviously meaning "very weird." She should talk, being dressed in fuzzy pink rabbit pajamas like Ralphie in "A Christmas Story."

I switched off my iPod, as I'd need a sound truck or a nuclear bomb to compete with the din blasting forth from the Glasgows' stereo. The CDs were being fed in by Dasan Williams, one of the few genuine African-Americans in our class. Despite the announced party theme, his cutting-edge tastes apparently did not embrace Christmas music.

We made our way into the living room, crowded with Winnemucca's teen elite. Providing the only illumination were twinkling lights strung on a bizarrely decorated artificial Christmas tree in a corner of the room.

"I hope you've brought your decorations," screamed Mary over the noise.

Uma nodded, opened her purse, extracted a limp jockstrap, and hung it on a branch next to a hood ornament off someone's Mercedes. I prayed her contribution was not a memento of some steamy encounter with Sloan Chandler.

"Where's yours, Noel?" screamed Mary.

"I didn't know we were supposed to bring any," I bellowed back.

"You have to put something on the tree!" she insisted. "Something personal!"

I removed my shirt, peeled off my sweaty t-shirt, and flung it at the tree. The crowd roared its approval. Nothing like the sight of bare flesh (even mine) to pick up the party pace.

We timed our arrival well. The doorbell rang and a harassed-looking older guy marched in with 14 large pizzas. A massive order, but his premonition came true. He left without a tip. During the ensuing gorging someone was heard to say loudly, "Oh, they're nothing but trailer trash." Then everyone made a point of politely not looking at me. Guess I know where I stand with that crowd.

Forty-five minutes later all that remained were a few picked-over crusts. The beer was gone too, and we were reduced to drinking a "punch" mixed by Drew from the contents of Mr. Glasgow's liquor cabinet. By then we had joined a group lounging out on the patio around a blazing outdoor fireplace. Nights in the high desert can be cool even in summer, so the cheery warmth was welcome—if not leather-clad Cody Wangston and his guitar. That guy is such a poseur. And applauding him politely after every song just encourages the yodeling twit. Still, I got to park right next to Uma, though I was too chicken to put my arm around her. All that booze had yet to weaken Inhibition One, although it was playing havoc with my bladder. Every ten minutes I had to stumble off toward the bushes to piss out another gallon.

"You OK, Noel?" Uma asked at one point.

"Never better," I slurred. "Need a refill?"

"No, I'm fine for now. What is it we're drinking?"

"Don't ask me. Tastes like they drained it out of a prairie dog."

"Hey, Noel," called cute Allison Linden, addressing me for the first time in her glamorous life. "Where's that big cousin of yours?"

"Went back to L.A."

"I hear he actually warmed up Stoney Holt."

"Yup, all us Wescotts are catnip to chicks."

"Shhh," hissed some girl behind us. "We're trying to hear Cody."

Hey, what is this? A goddam folk concert? Uma and I retreated to the house—now a dim scene of intensive writhing in every room. Dasan had turned down the volume and turned up the make-out music.

"How you doin', Noel," he said. "I ran into your buddy Carlyle Bogy today. What's with that dude?"

"He's sincere, Dasan. He genuinely wants to be black."

"Well, you better remind him he ain't passin' the physical. Good thing he's out here in the sticks. If he tried that act in Vegas, he'd be askin' for trouble. The brothers down there don't take that shit."

Formerly a contented resident of Nevada's largest city, Dasan had been dragged kicking and screaming to Winnemucca when his dad (a Highway Patrol cop) was transferred to this district.

"Yeah, I know."

"I hear you took over Rot Dugan's slave job."

"Uh-huh," I admitted, coloring.

"Man, they got some weird crackers in this burg. It's like the Twilight Zone out here. Am I right, Uma?"

"You are so right, Dasan," she replied, exchanging high fives with him.

I handed him a coupon.

"That's good for $10 off our deluxe adore ceremony," I explained. "Drop by anytime."

"I might do that," he replied. "You busy tomorrow, Uma?"

At long last, the booze kicked in.

"Sorry, she's taken," I said, grasping her warm hand and planting a wet one firmly on her lips.

To my utter astonishment, she kissed me back.

Uma also let me hold her hand on the walk home. I switched my iPod back on to prolong the holiday mood.

"What other kinds of music do you like, Noel?" she asked.

"Lately I've been obsessing on the Frantic Couplings."

"They're hot," she agreed. "But didn't they break up?"

"No, they just had to interrupt their tour because the lead guitarist had some psychotic episodes."

"Can't they medicate him?"

"They tried, but the music sucked. Say, where'd you get that jockstrap?"

"Why? Are you missing one?"

"No, it just doesn't seem like something the average girl carries around in her purse."

"Do I strike you as being average?"

"Hardly."

"Glad to hear it. I happened to have that item because—"

At that moment something large sailed out of the night and splattered against the back of my head, drenching me in an icy, sticky liquid. Another large balloon wobbled down out of the sky and slammed into Uma's chest.

"What the fuck!" she screamed.

We stood there dripping in stunned surprise. In the distance: the sound of fast-retreated footsteps and laughter.

"Did you see who it was?" I exclaimed.

"I saw, all right. It was your fucking friend Stoney Holt. And some black guy."

Stabbed in the back by my own gang brothers!

Uma did not let me help dry her off. She hurried up the walk to her door, muttered a fast "Good night!" and abandoned me kiss-less, forlorn, and sticky on the stoop.

I tasted a moist finger. Dr. Pepper: Carlyle's longtime beverage of choice. At least it wasn't pig's blood or cat piss.

Now is the time for the terrible reprisals to begin.

MONDAY, July 11 — I pleaded with Grandma to give Stoney nothing but rotten haircuts from now on, but she refused, citing "professional ethics." She advised me to "get over it" as "boys will be boys." She must have forgotten that she was dealing with a Twisp. As my mother demonstrated, our minimum level of retribution is castration by bullet. So I emailed Tyler that Stoney was cheating on him with Cody Wangston, northern Nevada's answer to Bob Dylan. Then I used my spray-paint stash to scrawl "sucks" over all the Upt gang graffiti I could find. That's called hurting a guy where he lives.

I've left four messages on Uma's phone with no reply so far. How can she blame me for the depravity of my former friends? That is so unfair.

4:27 p.m. Toby was on his way to the Silver Sluice with a bouquet of very expensive roses, when he was detoured by a marital summons from Mr. Dugan. The stupid bride assumed they were for her! I handed them over because she looked to be in her 87th week of pregnancy and how could you say "no" to a person that distended? At least she was landing a husband before the Big Event, although the groom (a tattooed redneck—or is that redundant?) made a point of noting that he wasn't to blame for the "peckerwood in the oven." Standing next to that perfumed blimp, I decided that any children Uma and I have will be through adoption only. Motherhood is just too gross to experience firsthand. Hell, I'd get a vasectomy right now if I could get Grandma to sign the consent form.

After the ceremony Mrs. Dugan thanked Toby for his "beautiful and generous" gesture. Wiping her eyes, she said it reaffirmed her faith in "you young people." Damn. There goes any hope of getting reimbursed by my employers for my pricey flowers. Now empty-handed, I strolled over to the Silver Sluice, where I was immediately intercepted by fat Marvin.

"Hey, that wasn't my dad! They didn't have no medical emergency up' the Senior Center!"

"Does your father drive an old red pickup with the spare tire mounted on the side?"

"Yeah, it's a Chevy. A '53."

"Well, a truck like that just careered off the I-95 overpass!"

"Shit!" bellowed Marvin, hurrying toward the door. "I'm third in line to inherit that truck!"

Uma eyed me coolly as Toby approached her kiosk.

"You're such a liar, Noel Wescott."

Well at least she was speaking to me.

"And *you* don't return people's phone calls," Toby pointed out.

"I don't recall ever giving you my phone number. And it's not in the book either."

"No, but luckily it's programmed into Mary Glasgow's speed-dialer."

"So, you're a sneak too. I might have expected as much."

"I'm very sorry about what happened, Uma. I have terminated my friendship with those responsible. I even bought you a very nice mixed bouquet of roses."

"Which is where exactly?"

"Which is brightening the wedding day of an expectant

mother. There was a slight misunderstanding just now at the Dixie Belle."

"I don't think I appreciate not receiving your very nice flowers. The gesture seems rather hollow."

"Not according to Mrs. Dugan. She thought it was extremely touching. Would you like to speak to her on my cell phone?"

"Not particularly. You will have to buy something if you intend to monopolize my time here."

Toby selected two Payday candy bars; Uma ran them under her scanner. I paid, then offered one to her. She leaned back and unwrapped it warily. Did she imagine I had sneaked in earlier and sabotaged the sweets?

"What is it you want, Noel Wescott?" she asked, munching her peanutty bar.

"Uhmm, I don't know," I said.

I did know, of course, but somehow I didn't feel this was the right time to bring up marriage.

"I, I'd like to be your friend," I continued, nibbling nervously on my bar.

Uma sighed.

"You know, Noel, women like chocolate. Indeed, for most of us it's an essential. Yet this is *not* a chocolate bar. The first thing you have ever given me, besides my non-existent flowers, is an inappropriate candy bar. Doesn't that tell you something?"

My mind reeled. I didn't quite see her point.

"Do you know what Sloan Chandler brought me before he left for that stupid sailing camp?"

"What?"

"A two-pound box of chocolates."

Damn that thoughtful mariner!

"And do you know what I did with his lovely chocolates?"

"No. What?"

"I brought them here and put them out in the employee lounge. Did that idiot imagine I was going to eat two pounds of fattening candy?"

"The cad should be shot," I noted.

"Well, guys are living on their own planet. That's all there is to it."

"So, uh, Uma, would you like to go out again?"

"Not particularly, Noel. But thanks for asking."

Uma turned away to hustle sunglasses to three priests. Crushed, Toby wandered off into the blazing heat of the raw Nevada day.

Suicide or murder? Which do you suppose is the more appropriate course?

TUESDAY, July 12 — I'm a mess. Vast leakage last night and rampant thumb oralfication. Meanwhile, Stoney Holt persists in dropping by, even though I have informed her that her loathsome person is anathema to me. Were she not so physically intimidating, I believe we might have come to blows this morning.

"So she dumped you for good, huh?" she commented, helping herself unbidden to the last breakfast roll on the premises. "Well, you should thank me."

I resisted a very strong impulse to grab a steak knife from the drawer.

"You're insane."

"She's a B.G., Noel. This 'incident' as you call it proves it. Got any herbal tea?"

"Some friend! You're wrecking my life."

"No tea, huh? Face it, Noel, only a first-class bitch goddess would react the way she did to a little hazing. Believe me, I know the type. She's nothing but trouble."

"I'm going to call the police and have you arrested for trespassing."

"What you need to do, Noel, is get a life. And while you're at it, get a little emotional backbone. Don't put all your eggs in one basket. Am I pissed at you for all the lies you told Tyler about me? Hell, yes. But am I going off the deep end? No way.

I know the sun doesn't rise and set on your cousin."

"He's my goddam nephew. I hope every person you ever go out with dumps you in the cruelest way possible."

"That's a very nasty thing to wish on anyone, Noel."

"I mean it. I consider you a human plague. If you were a bug, I'd step on you."

"And if you were a man, I would punch you out. But fortunately for you, you're just a little bed-wetting creep. Thanks for the pastry."

"Thanks for dropping dead as soon as possible. And don't slam the door on your way out."

She flipped me both fingers and slammed the door. Shaking all over, I sat down and tried to think of one happy thought. Tertiary leprosy, I thought. I can be grateful I don't have tertiary leprosy.

9:45 p.m. A busy day. Five weddings and two adore ceremonies. My tips have gone way up since Toby's been so emotionally on edge (and, embarrassingly, a bit weepy). Clients must assume the darky is sniffling at their happiness. I appreciate the extra income and have noted it in the column headed "Reasons Not To Commit Suicide." So far, my list is not very compelling.

WEDNESDAY, July 13 — Carlyle and I have decided to expel Stoney from the Upts gang. We have notified her of this decision via official e-mail. We also informed her that she is no longer permitted to wear brown. Knowing Carlyle, he could not have been the brains behind the balloon assault. Therefore, I've decided to overlook his participation in that outrage. I've also persuaded him that the vandal currently sabotaging Upts graffiti could only be gang turncoat Stoney Holt. For these treacherous acts, Carlyle has vowed to exact a terrible revenge.

Carlyle continues to be the blackest of Winnemucca's faux Negroes. Apparently Dr. Quentina Freep regards his impulse toward race reversal as the least alarming of his numerous mental disturbances. She even commiserates with his desire to be black. After all, what has being white ever done for him? She advised his foster parents to play it cool and wait for "this phase" to pass. In the meantime, she has lent them a cookbook of soul food recipes. I hope it's a good one. Carlyle has invited Toby over for dinner tomorrow night.

THURSDAY, July 14 — New depths of despair. This morning I received a copy of a libelous e-mail that "Heart of Stone" had sent to Uma. It read:

> Yo Uma!
> You may be interested to know that a friend of yours (a certain N.W.) has a serious problem with chronic bed-wetting and thumb sucking. The big baby told me he has the hots for you.
> —A friend.

Damn. I can't believe she did that. She must really hate my guts. Sure, we had a disagreement, some hot words were exchanged, but I never thought she'd stoop that low. I mean, we were friends for a long time. I was the victim of a fair amount of social ostracism just from hanging out with her. Now, I don't know what to think. Things are really spinning out of control around here. At least now I have Uma's e-mail address, not that it does me much good. I wonder who Stoney got it from?

Well, I can never face Uma again—that's for sure. Don't know what my alternatives are. Can't really think straight at the moment.

11:35 p.m. Well, I made it through the day. Still among the living and non-incarcerated. Toby saw Stoney downtown on his way to a wedding. She was dressed entirely in brown. Now I know what the expression "saw red" means. My entire field of vision turned blood red when I spotted her. Swept by very violent impulses such as have landed many hapless dudes on Death Row. Good thing Toby's tight clothes limit his pocket capacity. Even access to a sharp pencil could be dangerous when that chick is encountered. As it was, we looked the other way and ignored each other.

Didn't feel very social, but went to Carlyle's house for dinner. Another rude shock. The Mrs. Greene who is his latest foster mom is the very same Mrs. Greene who was my third-grade teacher. Somehow I never made the connection. Of all my teachers back then she's the one I would have picked to be my mom. Now Carlyle's living out my childhood fantasy. She looked exactly the same and seemed to recognize me despite my Tobification. She said "Hi, Noel!" and gave me a very motherly hug. She even exuded that nice chalky vanilla smell like The Ideal Mother. Mr. Greene was there too and seemed equally nice. He used to be a software engineer, but now repairs slot machines at all the casinos in town. Hard to believe he goes to bed every night with Mrs. Greene and probably fools around with her too.

Dinner was quite good if a little tense. Mr. Greene barbecued ribs out back on their patio. A handy guy, he's constructed an elaborate outdoor grill out of adobe block. Must weigh at least 100 tons. A real exercise in applied bodybuilding. The ribs came out a little charred, but we all dug in with enthusiasm. The cornbread was good too, though if I never face collard greens again it will be too soon. Carlyle got in trouble when he asked his surrogate mom to pass the "motherfuckin' potato salad."

"Carlyle, we have asked you not to use that word," Mr. Greene sternly reminded him.

"I gots to say it, Poppie! Man, you just can't be black otherwise."

"Now, Carlyle," began Mrs. Greene in a tone I recognized from long ago, "do you know what a motherfucker is?"

Toby dropped his rib bone. Never in my entire life did I expect to hear that word from those lips.

"Say what?" Carlyle replied.

"A motherfucker," she continued pedagogically, "is a person who has sexual congress with a woman who has given birth.

Now what does that have to do with my potato salad?"

Carlyle looked at me for assistance. No way Toby was handling that hot potato. I stared down at my plate and rearranged my greens.

"Your mother asked you a question," Mr. Greene reminded him.

"Fuck if I know," Carlyle grunted.

Our hosts exchanged grim glances and sighed.

"Noel," said Mrs. Greene, "don't you agree that ethnic colloquialisms are all right in their place, but are not appropriate at the dinner table with one's parents and guests?"

Carlyle looked at me and twitched. It was a twitch I recognized as an Upts gang sign. Damn, I was now stuck between a gang brother and my fantasy mother.

"I remember all of my multiplication tables, Mrs. Greene," I replied, enthusiastically changing the subject. "You were such a great teacher. Six times seven, that's 46!"

"I believe it's 42, Noel," she replied. "As I recall, math was never your strong suit. And what do you like to study in school now?"

Truthfully, all I could think of was sex education, but I replied, "English and writing."

"Toby's writin' his own motherfuckin' blog," Carlyle added.

More sighs from the adults. What I can't understand is why Mrs. Greene, after herding 35 screaming third-graders all day, would want to come home and take on a foster kid like Carlyle. They certainly don't look that hard up for bucks. Hell, their TV's at least 48 inches across. Is being a foster parent that lucrative?

FRIDAY, July 15 — I'm going to L.A. to visit Tyler! I leave this afternoon. Grandma made all the arrangements and even bought my bus ticket. She said I needed a change of scenery. Boy, do I ever. Too bad they don't sell tickets to Mars. She called Mr. Dugan and said their slave would be gone for an entire week.

He groused, but what can he do? I'm in totally tight with his wife, and Toby's getting really good at hustling those profitable extra-cost items. Bottom line: they know they've got a good thing going. So they're sticking Rot back into my oversized slave clothes while Toby's away (I'm dropping them off when I pick up my paycheck). I hope he doesn't stink them up again. Looks to me like all of that kid's growth genes are going into b.o.

7:25 p.m. On the bus to L.A. I'm writing this on a laptop I got a few months ago at a garage sale for $5. The guy was asking $15, but I made him an offer he couldn't refuse. Believe it or not, this baby packs a Pentium 75 and Windows 95. There are vines creeping over gravestones in cemeteries faster than this sucker. Forget WiFi or cruising the Web. All I can do are word processing and a few primitive games like hangman and chess. The battery was deceased, so I sawed open the plastic and re-placed the cells with standard rechargeables. Works like a charm. At least the screen is color. I hear they once made laptops with monochrome screens, if you can imagine that.

Nevada may generally suck, but the scenery can be semi awe-inspiring in spots. We are now cruising down Route 395 on the eastern side of the Sierras. To the west out my grungy window a whole line of peaks is turning golden in the fading light. I think nature puts on these grand displays to help us humans forget our troubles. I look out the window and almost get choked up by the soaring majesty. Better than looking in the other di-rection where a snoring old fart is drooling down both sides of his unshaven chin. Somehow I knew when he got on in Carson City that he was going to plop down next to me. Smells like a liquor store too.

I'm trying not to think about Uma. I wonder how many people she's discussed my sphincter control issues with? Probably be all over town by the time I get back. Should I change my return ticket for one going to Oakland? Lots of people live with moth-ers even wackier than mine. Why should I be so particular?

SATURDAY, July 16 — Tyler and his stepdad were nice enough to come pick me up even though it was nearly midnight when the bus got in. They live way out in the Valley, but fortunately the freeways weren't too clogged at that hour. Call me a rube from the sticks, but rolling down the pass when you first hit that sea of lights on the outskirts of L.A. is a mind-blowing sight. So many millions of people sprawled out across what was once empty sagebrush. And any time of the day or night a good fraction of them are out roaring around on the freeways.

Bill (Tyler's stepdad) picked me up in his awesome 1968 Pontiac GTO. He also has a Harley and a few other bikes as well. He's an electrician by trade and very mechanically oriented. His full name is William Teslar Tibble, but everyone calls him Bill. Grandma has a theory that everyone looks at least a little bit like some movie or television actor. She claims I look like Brandon De Wilde, whoever that is. Applying her theory, I'd say Bill resembles a shorter, stockier, and grubbier version of Kevin Costner.

Even though Bill formally adopted Tyler, my nephew still goes by the name Twisp. He says he kept it to honor his mother for all those years she took care of him as a struggling single mom. Tyler Twisp or Tyler Tibble—I'd say you're stuck in Name Hell either way. Technically, I may be a Twisp, but it would take a very large bribe to get me to change my name.

My sister Joanie was still up and gave me a big hug when we arrived. She was looking older, but not yet in the repulsive category. She used to be a glamorous airline hostess, then worked as a travel agent. When online reservations made that job redundant, she went into the antique business. She and Bill are out scouring yard sales now. They do that every Saturday morning. She has a booth at a collective store in West Hollywood where she unloads her junk. Plus, she sells stuff at the Rose Bowl Flea Market, where actual movie stars sometimes paw over her items. I wouldn't mind a few pawing over me right now.

The Tibble-Twisps reside in a modest stucco ranch crammed

with zany 1950s furnishings. Rather like living in a Technicolor cartoon: lots of bold colors, wild patterns, and flamboyant shapes. Dominating the living room is an immense glass cabinet packed with glittering silver and gold trophies. That impressive display must provide a constant ego boost to my athletic nephew. So many awards and medals and ribbons reminding him that he is an achiever of superlatives, a vanquisher of lesser beings. And how many trophies have I won? So far none. Competitive nose picking is not yet an Olympic event.

Since Joanie's house is not set up for visitors, I slept in their camping trailer parked next to the garage. It's the kind where the back end folds down like a ramp so you can load in your bikes or other toys. Bill has two quads that they take out to the desert and zoom around on. Tyler says it's tons of fun. Too bad you can't do it this time of year (too hot). I noticed that some- one put a plastic shower curtain under my sheet on the trailer bed. My reputation precedes me. Fortunately, I passed a dry night—my first in a while. And my bitter apple garden gloves kept T.S. to a minimum.

Can't write any more. Tyler has too much fun on the agenda. One of them is named Awanee.

SUNDAY, July 17 — Another bone dry night. I'm begin- ning to think it's not the bladder, it's the state. Let us not forget I am a native Californian. Nevada is an alien environment for me.

So far Joanie and I are the only ones up. She just fixed me a massive breakfast. While I ate, we had a chat on family topics.

"My mother just paid me a surprise visit," I informed her.

"Oh, really? She's my mother too, but you can have her. How was she?"

"OK when she wasn't crying or grabbing my hand. She told me my real dad was George Twisp."

"Oh. She spilled the beans, huh?" Joanie sipped her coffee. "Well, I'm glad that secret's out. Yep, we're all Twisps. Lucky us."

"So why am I living with Grandma Wescott?"

"Well, it seemed like the best solution at the time. And that's what the judge decreed. How bad is it?"

"Uh, not that bad. We get along OK. I just can't figure out why Grandma's going to all the bother."

"Well, she always seemed like a nice lady. I don't know what happened to her son. Is he much of a pain?"

"I hardly ever see him."

"Well, you're lucky. What a bastard. Perhaps your grandma figured she screwed up so bad on the first one, she wants to make amends with you."

"I think her husband wasn't the greatest. She doesn't talk much about him."

"So maybe that's where Lance got his personality. Stands to reason."

I nibbled my bacon and cleared my throat.

"So. Any chance I can meet him?"

"Who, Noelly?"

"George F. Twisp. My dad. I hear he lives in L.A."

Joanie slumped back in her chrome dinette chair and stared out the window.

"There's a concept, Noel," she said at last. "I'll have to think about that one."

"We could invite him to dinner," I suggested. "And maybe Nick too. It could be a family reunion."

"I'm not sure that's a good idea with Twisps," she replied. "Besides, I already called Nick when I heard you were coming. He wasn't there. His girlfriend Ada said he went to Prague."

"But he was just there."

"Well, he went back. He must have liked it. Ada didn't seem too tickled either."

My glamorous brother. I wonder what he's up to?

No sign of Tyler yet. That big guy can really sleep. Must be hard keeping all those muscles charged up. Gives me time to note yesterday's highlight, which was our evening excursion to the Barber College to hear the Pickled Punks. We went with Tyler's B-list girlfriend Ericka Stabb and her bud (my date) Awanee Doma. Although Ericka only rates a B, Tyler often goes out with her to clubs because she has a driver's license and a rad Mazda. She's also adept at getting her friends into places with age restrictions. That girl can flirt. Awanee and I are both pretty shy, so it was a bit uncomfortable being thrown together. Still, we managed to relate a bit. Her father's Mexican and her mother's Vietnamese. Pretty attractive in an exotic way. Very thin and petite, although nature hadn't skimped on her chest enhancements—not that I got anywhere near them. She in no way reminded me of Uma, which was good.

The Barber College used to be exactly that in the basement of a once fancy, now derelict building in Hollywood. They cleared out the barber chairs, but kept all the ornate pink marble and mirrors. All those hard surfaces make for a very loud environment when the Pickled Punks got cranked up. Tyler knew it was my kind of band—about 14 levels beyond maniacally frenzied. The place was jammed and hotter than blazes, so everyone got very sweaty and crazed. My eardrums are still pulsating. Needless to say, we have nothing like them (or the club) in Winnemucca.

In case you're not up on your carnie lingo, "pickled punks" are those weird and scary fetuses they used to have floating in jars in carnival sideshows. In keeping with their name, the Pickled Punks featured a large backlit jar in front of their drummer. I worked my way up close, but found it contained nothing more than one tired-looking pig fetus. Not even a two-headed one. That was the sole disappointment I experienced from that band. Their music was so awesome, I bought one of their self-produced CDs. As I forked over my money I made a mental note to burn a copy for Stoney, then remembered I hate her guts. It's hard losing your friends.

Afterwards we parked at Tyler's high school in a private spot he knows behind the athletic building. Tyler and Ericka went at it (within limits) in the front seat, while Awanee and I chatted in the back seat. Sorry, but I'm just not capable of throwing myself at total strangers—even if they have very kissable lips and tiny, bare knees that call out for caressing.

9:12 p.m. Got blasted by the sun today, so I may zone out early. Tyler and I went with the B Team to the beach. The Pacific Ocean is another convenient amenity that's lacking in Winnemucca. We parked in Santa Monica by the pier and walked all the way to Venice and back. Tyler walked a few blocks on his hands. Quite the showoff in more ways than one. I'm not sure he realizes that in this posture those strolling beside him have a straight shot down his baggy swim trunks at the prize sausage and two furry kiwis nestled within. I noticed Awanee was studying them with interest. Tyler reports that she, like everyone else in our party save Ms. Stabb, is a restive virgin. We camped on the sand and got pretty silly, so I feel like I'm breaking the ice with her a bit. Very sweet and cute as a button, but not many sparks—at least on my side. Too bad I can't be like Tyler. He enjoys his girlfriends as one would a juicy steak or a fine cigar: with genuine pleasure, but little emotional involvement. Much more sensible than my approach, which is to fall like a brick and then try to cope with the catastrophe.

Tyler's cell phone is constantly ringing with girls, girlfriends, and more girls checking in. To this credit, Tyler is very straightforward. He told them all he was hanging at the beach with Ericka. He even got a call from Stoney, who told him he shouldn't believe a word I said about her. Well, the joke was on her because I hadn't mentioned her once. I'm doing my best to put all things Winnemuccan out of mind.

To my horror I just calculated I've spent $48 in two days. I've got to throttle back on the extravagances. No way I can maintain a Bill Gates vacation lifestyle on Toby's slave income.

MONDAY, July 18 — Urine-free again. I'm beginning to think the bed-wetting was all a myth. Good news: It's now 3:26 p.m. and I've yet to spend a nickel. After breakfast Tyler and I walked over to his buddy Zack's house to lift weights with him and Duncan (another teammate). That is, I walked and Tyler rode his skateboard. He also surfs, but his true passion in that line of neck-breaking activities is snowboarding. That's another reason he envies me for living in blizzard-prone Winnemucca. I've told him he can come shovel out our driveway any time. On the way over he alerted me that he had told Zack and Duncan that I was a noted high-desert wrestler.

"And why exactly did you say that, Tyler?"

"Well, these guys have very narrow bandwidths, Noel. They can't really relate to non-jocks. And I could hardly say you were a linebacker."

"But I know nothing about wrestling."

Though I'm willing to experiment with Awanee, should she prove sports-minded.

"Just say you're in the flyweight division and are very competitive statewide."

"Won't they notice my lack of muscles?"

"Just keep your shirt on."

I did, not that Zack and Duncan paid me much mind. They were more interested in ribbing Tyler for riding a skateboard. It seems your diehard jocks don't go in for that form of transportation. Perhaps they find the wheels too silly and small. There was nothing small about Tyler's buddies. Zack could pass for normal in dim light, but Duncan had a neck on him that would make a telephone pole envious. They all grunted away on giant weights in Zack's garage, while the Nevada wrestler sat it out due to an alleged hamstring pull. Actually, I'm not sure where my hamstring is or if I even have one. I toyed with a barbell and tried to add appropriately macho remarks to a conversation that dealt chiefly with arcane football strategy, contouring the Latissimus dorsi, and pussy.

Now Tyler is at football practice and I'm catching up on my blog. He has football practice every afternoon this week, for which he was most apologetic. I don't really mind. In truth, keeping up with my nephew can be pretty exhausting.

11:12 p.m. If I can get to bed without being charged, I will have experienced the perfect budget vacation day. Total expenditures: $0.00. I did go out for snacks with Joanie this afternoon, but she paid. I helped her arrange her newly acquired items in her sales space in the antique collective. This store is located in a considerably more mauve neighborhood than you will find in Winnemucca. There were guys walking around holding hands, which would rate as suicidal behavior in most of Nevada.

I was amazed at the outrageousness of Joanie's prices, but she says her inventory turns over steadily. It's kind of spooky hanging out in a building stuffed to the rafters with the detritus of countless dead people. Me, I prefer items that are new, modern, and come from the factory wrapped in three layers of sanitary plastic. Joanie says that's because I've grown up in an old trailer surrounded by gloom and decay. People always react against what they've known as kids. Glad to hear it. That means as an adult I will be living amid swanky surroundings in a big city with throngs of nubile chicks at my beck and call.

TUESDAY, July 19 — A rather boring day until Tyler came home from football practice. There's not much to do out here in the burbs with no car and the adults all off scrounging a living. I watched TV, checked my e-mail (terminally sparse) on Tyler's computer, and snooped around. Not a photo of George F. Twisp on the premises. That guy is perhaps not greatly beloved. I did find an entry for him in Joanie's address book. No phone number, but I made a note of his address. I also checked out the garage, where I discovered Bill's elaborate shop (which explains why all the cars are parked outside). Joanie says one day she counted 38 gasoline-powered machines on their property—not counting Bill's speedboat that he keeps in a storage lot. Tyler says from what he can tell his parents still have a functioning sex life because Bill is so good at figuring out how things work.

Knowing him he probably has the shop manual for the female reproductive system.

After dinner Tyler asked me if I wanted to go meet a chick.

"Sure," I replied. "Is she from the A-list or the B-list?"

"I don't know. I haven't met her yet. She sounds pretty cool on the telephone."

"So how did you hook up?"

"She found me through Myspace.com. She zeroed in on me 'cause of my name."

"Tyler or Twisp?"

"Twisp. This girl claims her aunt was once married to a guy named Nick Twisp."

"Hmm. I think this is a chick we need to meet."

Tyler recruited thick-necked Duncan to do the driving. He pilots (insanely) one of those small Japanese pickups. Of course, the skinny wrestler had to sit in the middle. I felt like a third testicle in a very tight scrotum. We snaked through many winding canyons in Bel Air before locating Miss Veeva Saunders' street. I had never seen such a ritzy neighborhood.

"How much do you suppose these houses go for?" I asked.

"Millions and millions," replied Tyler. "Unless it's a fixer."

The Saunders' manse was not a fixer. It rambled across a ridge-top with a mind-boggling 360-degree view that extended all the way to the luminous aqua waters of the Pacific. A very handsome middle-aged man answered our knock.

"Noel?" he asked.

"Uh, yeah," I said, surprised that he knew my name.

"And you must be Tyler," he said, smiling at my nephew.

"Uh, right," he replied. "We've come to see Veeva."

The man shook everyone's hand and welcomed us in. "Upstairs, fellows. Third door on the right."

We trooped up a curving staircase that must have given the carpenters fits to build.

"That's weird, Noel," whispered Tyler. "I never mentioned your name to Veeva."

"Yeah, well he seemed to know who we are," I whispered back.

We found the door, met the chick, and made the fumbled introductions. Veeva was a nervous, edgy blonde on the thin side. Very intense blue eyes. Extraordinarily neat and orderly teeth like the braces had just come off. Not yet beautiful, but you could tell she was working up to it. Her boudoir was like no kid's room I'd ever seen. More like an elegant apartment where Gloria Vanderbilt or Jackie O might hang out.

Veeva draped her bony frame on a divan and motioned for us to take a seat. I sat on a curvy armchair upholstered in silver-and-cream striped silk. Very thin legs like maybe it was the sideline of some pencil factory. Not comfortable but oddly stimulating to the spine.

"Your room's, uh, very nice," said Tyler.

"Oh, thank you," she replied. "I collaborated with Mother's decorator. We're still looking for a few final accessories to pull it all together. No theme, exactly, but the inspiration was Manhattan in the forties. I really wanted some Ruhlmann pieces, but even the reproductions are fabulously beyond our reach. Of course, working with a decorator was fun, but you have to reign them in. Their tastes can be so hideous if unsupervised."

"Say, how old are you?" demanded Duncan.

"Fourteen. Not that it matters. What are you—the bodyguard?"

"Duncan's my driver," explained Tyler.

There was something about this chick that brought out the pretentiousness in a guy.

"Was that your father who let us in?" I asked.

"Yes. Paul Saunders, the impresario. You've probably heard of him. Isn't he marvelous? My friends say I'm such a daddy's girl. It's true, of course. I dread how daunting it will be to find a husband who could measure up to him in any way. Connie is so fortunate."

"Who's Connie?" I asked.

"My mother," she replied, nodding toward a photo in a silver frame on an anorexic sideboard. "She's rather insane."

"Your mother's Asian?" asked Tyler, surprised.

"She's Polish on both sides. Fortunately for their children, Daddy is as WASP as they come. My mother is an enthusiast for cosmetic surgery. Years ago she was going through a Chinese phase. She says when I'm 16 she'll let them attend to my horrible nose."

"It looks fine to me," I said.

Veeva rested her azure gaze upon me. "I think it's marvelous that Nick Twisp has a baby brother. I can imagine he looked just like you at your age: weedy and rather endearingly useless."

I made a note of that comment for later deciphering.

"You've met my brother?" I asked.

"Several times, but years ago. He once juggled half my Barbie collection. You can imagine the impression that made on a young girl. Mother still phones him occasionally, but is very tightlipped about their chats. That is so like her. She can be such a selfish bitch. She gave me that photo of herself for my birthday. Of course, I have to leave it out for a requisite time, then into a drawer it's going. The frame I rather like. I may use it for my boyfriend's photo."

"Who's your boyfriend?" demanded Duncan.

"I don't have one currently. My standards are impossibly high. To be frank, though, you're not in the running."

Duncan scratched his crew cut and pondered this put-down.

"Is your mother home now?" asked Tyler.

"No. Can't you tell? The house is so free of her oppressive presence. She's at a Philharmonic board meeting. She's on lots of boards. I find it very boring."

"Do you have any brothers and sisters?" I asked.

"Two wretched brothers—both younger—whom I have contrived to have exiled to summer camp. We are nearly alone here—just as I prefer it. Family life can be so enervating."

"What kind of dumb name is Veeva," demanded Duncan,

still trying to stretch his inelastic mind around this peculiar chick.

"Is he always so blunt?" asked Veeva.

"He's a linebacker," explained Tyler.

"OK, if you say so. Well, according to Mother, I was conceived while viewing an Elvis Presley movie—'Viva Las Vegas.' Hence my name."

"It's a good thing they weren't watching 'Harum Scarum'," noted Tyler.

"Yes, or 'Clambake,' 'Spinout,' or 'Tickle Me'," replied Veeva, obviously familiar with such Presleyan speculations. "Would you like something to drink? We could go out by the pool. There might be a sunset worth our time."

We all trooped down to the pool, which was hung off in space on metal stilts. A large window inset in the side gave anyone underwater a sweeping if murky view of the lights of Beverly Hills. A Latina housekeeper set out a large tray of beverages and sandwiches, then discreetly withdrew. What a lifestyle. Even the sun had been commandeered to dress up the darkening sky with aesthetically correct purples and pinks.

Duncan gulped his drink and made a face.

"It's grapefruit and wheat grass juice," said Veeva. "One of my many compulsions. The sandwiches are shredded carrot and tofu cream cheese. Animals should be cherished not eaten. Sorry, but that's how I feel."

We made the best of it and munched away politely.

"Was it at a drive-in movie?" queried Duncan.

"Was what?" asked Veeva.

"Where they was screwing when they had you," he elaborated.

Veeva shuddered. "I hardly think so. Tyler dear, your driver is so . . . one point oh."

"Tell us about your aunt," Tyler prompted.

"Ah, my aunt Sheeni. Real name Sheridan. My father's baby sister. Very beautiful and brilliant, of course. She hates America. Never comes here. They live in Lyon. Married to a very sexy young Frenchman. Two adorable kids. So French, but then they are exactly that. I'm campaigning to have my brothers sent to a harsh old-world boarding school where only French is spoken. No luck so far. It could do them both a world of good."

"You visited your aunt?" I asked.

"Once. Two years ago. I screamed to go back to France this summer, but Mother must punish me for my refusal to submit to her tyranny."

"Did your aunt say anything about my brother?" I asked.

"No, unfortunately. Well, I didn't know anything about her earlier marriage then. I've asked her since about it on the phone, but she clams up. No one wants to talk about it."

"Same with my mother," said Tyler. "She's Nick's sister and she refuses to discuss it."

"My mother won't say boo either," I noted. "Though she seems to harbor a very strong dislike for your aunt."

"We've got to get to the bottom of this," Veeva declared. "I sense a dark and terribly romantic secret. Are you with me, boys?"

Two of the three males nodded in the affirmative. Duncan was still in shock from the refreshments.

WEDNESDAY, July 20 — Another dry night. I am so ready for bed sharing. Speaking of which, I shuffled into the house this morning and there was Tyler breakfasting with Wylie, a decidedly A-list girlfriend. The movie star she most resembles is Reese Witherspoon, I kid you not. It turns out they have a standing date for breakfast on Wednesdays. That's the only time she could pin him down. Hard to believe. If she were my girl-friend, I'd be clearing my calendar months in advance. Wylie fancies herself a cook. She made us both cinnamon toast. I was looking forward to the accompanying dishes, but her menu stopped there. Wylie's future husband may be dining out fre-quently—not that he'll care. While we nibbled our toast, Wylie chastised me for not calling Awanee for two entire days. I pointed out that in fact I've never telephoned that girl.

"And may I ask why not?" she demanded. "Awanee likes you a lot."

"Well, I'm leaving in a few days. I live about 700 miles away in another state. God knows when I'll ever be back. And nobody's yet invented a way to have sex over the phone."

"What are you saying?" demanded Wylie, perhaps not the most perceptive of chicks.

I spelled it out for her. "This relationship is doomed!"

"You guys are so unromantic," she sighed. "Kiss me, Tyler."

He did. What a breakfast that guy had. I don't know about him, but after she left I had to return to the trailer for some pressure relief work.

7:43 p.m. I spent the day with Veeva in West Hollywood. Sister Joan dropped me off at this immense building on Melrose the locals call the Blue Whale. Its real name is the Pacific Design Center, and it's Veeva's constant haunt. A couple of hundred showrooms featuring edgy furnishings you won't find at your local Wal-Mart. Looked like the kind of place kids would get tossed out of, but everyone seemed happy to see Veeva. A real ordeal for the feet. We trooped all over, scouting for accessories, smirking at the gaucheries, and revisiting all those tempting pieces she had to forego for space or budget reasons. It's a shocking crime that Veeva had only $75,000 to spend on her room makeover. I pointed out that sum would buy five trailers on my road and probably the occupants as well.

"But I don't want five trailers," she replied. "I just want a room that won't embarrass me when I invite my friends over. You have no idea what a joke my budget was. When I first started on my project, some of the snootier showrooms suggested I try looking at IKEA."

"How mortifying for you."

She ignored the sarcasm. "Well, the shoe was on the other foot when I informed them who my mother was. They changed their tune in a hurry."

I made a mental note to mention Connie Saunders the next time I needed to impress a decorator.

After grinding our feet down to the bone, we had a late lunch in the Blue Whale's trendy restaurant. Veeva said she would pay as long as I didn't order anything "that walked or swam." She forgot to exclude "slithered," but there was no snake or lizard on the menu. We both had Caesar salads with grilled asparagus. Tasty if not exactly filling. I was so ready for a burger too.

While munching our salads, Veeva casually inquired if Tyler had a girlfriend.

"No, Tyler does not have a girlfriend," I replied. "He has about 37 girlfriends. For example, he breakfasted this morning with Wylie, who looks like a fresh-faced Reese Witherspoon."

"You lie."

"I don't lie."

"His parents let her sleep over?"

"No, she drops by at 9 a.m. every Wednesday. Tyler has promised his mom he won't have sex until he's 16. Now me, I have taken no such vow of chastity."

"And how many girlfriends do you have?"

"Well, locally I'm only breaking one heart at the moment. But I just blew into town late Friday."

"And how about in—what's the name of your little town?"

"Winnemucca. It's an Indian name meaning 'bored out of my skull.' Well, I have this chick there I was putting the moves on."

"But she dumped you?"

"I'd rather not discuss it. So how many guys have you slept with?"

"None so far, but I have impossibly—"

"Right," I interjected, "you have *impossibly* high standards."

"That's why I find it so appealing that Tyler's a Twisp."

"I'm more of a Twisp than he is. Nick is my actual brother. Did you see that article about him in *People* magazine last year?"

"Of course. I took the liberty of forwarding it to Aunt Sheeni."

"What did she say about it?"

"Nothing. That woman is a sphinx about her past."

"We could get married too," I suggested, doing something suggestive with an asparagus spear. Who says only Tyler and Toby can flirt with girls?

"That's an idea. Do you love me, Noel darling?"

"I could work my way up to it if I tried."

"Well if I can't land Tyler, I'll keep you in mind."

"Why be one in a crowd with Tyler when you can have all of me?"

"Oh, perhaps I like the challenge."

To make up for my protein and romantic deprivations, I ordered two desserts. Veeva didn't seem to mind. Amazingly, she refused to sample either the fudge cake or the nectarine-apricot tart. Such willpower is beyond me. And that girl could stand to put on a few pounds too. Somehow the conversation got around to my long-lost father.

"But you're going to see him aren't you?" she asked, excited.

"I don't know. My sister doesn't seem to be making much progress on a reunion."

"Then we'll go see him ourselves, Noel. We'll go there tomorrow! I'm sure he can tell us about Nick and Sheeni."

We worked out the details, then Veeva paid the check—by credit card. She's had her own American Express card since she was ten.

"It's rather convenient," she admitted. "But I know it's just another way for Mother to monitor my activities. She's such a control freak. If she doesn't get off my back, I may have to marry you, Noel. Just to get out of the house and drive her insane."

"Sounds good to me."

Whatever her motivation, I'm sure the honeymoon would prove amply diverting. I wonder what kind of honeymoon Nick Twisp had?

We swapped cell phone numbers and parted with a farewell

kiss—a light one on the lips. Everyone does that in L.A., even the guys.

I took city transit back to the Valley. Many tedious waits and tricky transfers, but I made it back eventually. I was glad I did. Joanie made burgers for dinner.

9:12 p.m. Veeva just called. She reports her father suggested I phone my grandmother as she may have some interesting news.

"How the hell does your father know I have a grandmother?" I asked.

"Search me, Noel, but he was rather insistent. What's Tyler doing now?"

"He's out in his stepdad's GTO receiving a blowjob from a redhead named Fleur."

"He is not."

"OK, don't believe me. I better call my granny. See you tomorrow. I love you."

"You do not."

Somehow flirting with Veeva just came naturally to me. As opposed to talking to A-list Fleur, who left me terminally tongue-tied. It's true she's sitting out in the GTO with my nephew, though what exactly they're up to, I can't say. I haven't figured out whom she looks like yet. Maybe a young Elizabeth Taylor with freckles.

9:38 p.m. OK, I'd been feeling a bit guilty for not checking in with Grandma, but as I remind myself, she's not really my grandmother. I just phoned but no one answered. Sort of worrying, then I remembered that Wednesdays are Bingo Night at the senior center.

11:34 p.m. Finally got through to Grandma. After a tedious discussion of our mutual activities and her bingo travails, she spilled some disturbing news. Yesterday a girl dropped by looking for me.

"I told you, Grandma, I'm not having anything to do with Stoney."

"It wasn't Stoney, Noel. Heck though, why don't you two

kiss and make up? No, this was some other girl."

"Well, who?"

"I don't know. She told me her name. I forgot to write it down. Something like Irma Spumoni."

"Uma!?"

"Yeah, that was it. Very nice girl. Maybe she was that Italian girl you took to the party."

"You didn't let her in did you?"

"Of course I did. It was a hot day. I made her some iced tea. We had a nice chat."

Uma has seen the inside of my trailer! She knows I live in squalor!

"You didn't let her into my bedroom did you?"

"No, Noelly. Why would she want to go in there? Do you have something of hers?"

"No, Grandma. Did she ask you if I have any, uh, bad habits?"

"No, Noelly. She was a very nice girl. Are you two in some kind of trouble? Noelly, you know there are condoms in the medicine cabinet, and these days you really have to think about safe sex."

No way I was going to discuss that topic with my grandmother.

"Relax, Grandma. Jesus, I never touched her. She doesn't even like me."

"I don't know, Noelly. I think you should give her a chance. Rome wasn't built in a day."

Thank God Uma was foiled in her snooping. She never got into my bedroom to check my mattress. How can I ever return to that town? How?

THURSDAY, July 21 — Like a branch of Niagara Falls on the trailer bed last night. Just the mention of W————a sabotages my plumbing. Very embarrassing to have to sneak into Joanie's laundry room this morning to wash my bedding. And my thumb looks like it passed the night plugging some dike in Holland.

Tyler so wanted to go with me today, but he had football practice. Why do those big guys have to practice so much just to run around and slam into each other? The appeal of that game eludes me, although I do appreciate the skimpy outfits on the cheerleaders. I took the bus to North Hollywood, then rode the Metro train to downtown. Yes, you can get around sprawling L.A. without a car, though nobody in their right mind does it unless they have to. As agreed, I hooked up with Veeva in front of the swanky Biltmore Hotel. She arrived by taxi from her Bel Air pad only 20 minutes late. I hate to think what that ride cost. She gave me a perky smile and a perkier kiss. I could get used to kissing that chick if I had the opportunity. She was dressed very stylishly in a pale gray ensemble that probably cost more than my entire lifetime clothing budget. It must be nice having rich parents (or any parents for that matter).

I was having second thoughts about the whole enterprise, but Veeva took my hand and led me down some grim side streets to the building matching George Twisp's address. It was a dingy old red-brick residence hotel with some down-and-out types lingering out front. I was aggressively panhandled of all my change, then allowed to proceed into the building. The bearded and turbaned Indian man behind an armored grill in the dim lobby said Mr. Twisp was out, but mostly likely could be found in Pershing Square.

"What does he look like?" I asked.

"Just look for an elderly bald fellow with pigeons," the man replied.

We retraced our steps and entered the park (across the street from the Biltmore) that we had crossed earlier. Veeva said Pershing Square had once been lush and beautiful, but in the 1950s they tore it up to build an underground parking garage and carted all the palm trees off to Disneyland for the Jungle Cruise ride. Now it was a bleak urban space with lots of concrete, a Legos-on-steroids fountain, and a monstrous purple bell tower that looked like something from another planet. Not the sort of place I'd choose to meet the man who engendered my being, but those were the cards life had dealt me. After a few minutes we spotted an shabby old guy sitting on a bench with three pigeons perched on his white-flecked shoulders. He wasn't feeding them; they were just hanging out in the sun and cooing softly. I was all for walking right on by, but Veeva tugged me to a halt in front of him. I swallowed and cleared my throat.

"Excuse me, sir," I said. "Are you by any change George F. Twisp?"

He and the pigeons looked up at me suspiciously.

"Who the hell wants to know?"

"Uh, I'm a friend of, uh, Nick . . . Nick Twisp."

"Then tell that son of a bitch his goddam check is late."

"Excuse me?"

The man took a swig from a bottle in a brown paper bag.

"My check. I'm supposed to get it by the 15th. It's late. If I don't pay my rent by the first, I'm out on the fucking street!"

The man smelled of booze, but was not obviously drunk. Of course, it was still early in the day. Teeth the color of old piano keys, with a few prominent ones missing. Was it possible my father did not own a toothbrush?

"Actually, uh, Nick is in Prague," I explained. "That may be why your check is delayed."

"In Prague? What'd that dirtball do—defect?"

"Uh, I don't think they have Communists over there any more. He went to a convention of jugglers."

"Do you mind if we sit down?" asked Veeva.

"It's a free country. Don't sit too close. You'll bug my friends."

"You enjoy pigeons?" Veeva asked.

The man stared at her defiantly. "What kind of question is that?"

An uncomfortable impasse; I tried to keep the conversation rolling.

"Have you trained those birds?" I asked.

"Nope. They trained me. They trained me to sit here and let them shit on me. Took a while, but pigeons are pretty patient. Do you have twenty bucks?"

I pulled out my wallet and handed my father $20. He slipped the bill furtively into a pocket and took another swig.

"Would you mind answering a few questions about your son Nick?" I asked.

"I thought you were buddies with him."

"Well, uh, I am, but he doesn't talk very much about his past."

"Why should he? The kid was a total fuck-up from the get-go."

"How so?" asked Veeva.

"Hell, he burned down half of Berkeley. Then he shot some fat lawyer. Then he kidnapped some girl that he knocked up and took her to France. The French cops nailed his ass though. Serves him right. Went to the slammer. I washed my hands of him."

"Yet now he's supporting you," Veeva pointed out.

"The ungrateful bastard sends me a pittance when he feels like it. Man, I paid child support on that kid for years. He owes me."

"Don't you collect Social Security?" I asked.

"Shit no. Not old enough."

"How old are you?" I asked.

"I don't know. Sixty, I guess."

Veeva and I exchanged glances of wonderment. The guy looked at least 75. So much for those Twisp anti-aging genes. Fortunately, I have always expected to die young.

"I could have been a man of property," he went on. "I was hooked up solid with a wealthy woman. Rita had the bucks big time. And she was nuts about me too."

"What happened?" asked Veeva.

"Sabotaged by her damn dogs. A couple of nasty little Chihuahuas."

"They didn't like you?" I asked.

He took another swallow.

"Nope. And I always treated them like royalty too. A couple of runty mutts and here I sit in bird shit heaven."

"Did Nick get married to that girl?" asked Veeva.

"He claimed he did. Fuck, the little squirt was only 14 at the time."

"Do you ever think about, uh, Nick's brother?" I asked.

"His what?"

"His brother," said Veeva. "Your other son. The one who lives in Nevada."

"He's not my son. I'm not getting on the hook for another one of her goddam bastards. I paid all the fucking child support I'm paying."

"He may not be interested in your money," I replied.

"I prefer pigeons," he said, tickling one of his companions under its beak. "They're all the family I need."

We asked him a few more questions about Nick, but he couldn't add much in the way of details. Veeva and I stood up.

"I'll e-mail Nick and remind him about your check," I said.

"You do that. And thanks for the loan. What's your name, kid?"

"Uh, Michael."

"Nice talkin' to you, Mike."

"Take care, Mr. Twisp," said Veeva.

"Yeah, you too. And kick a Chihuahua for me."

I didn't feel much like eating, but Veeva took me to lunch in nearby Little Tokyo. We had miso soup and California rolls. I'm not sure Veeva ever gets any protein. We agreed my father was a sorry case, but that he had divulged some interesting information, if it could be believed.

"I really think Nick and Sheeni *were* married," Veeva declared.

"How can a 14-year-old on the run get married?"

"I don't know, Noel. I'll have to do some research on that. Do you think she was really pregnant?"

"I don't know. A smart girl like her doesn't seem like the type."

"If she was, she must have had an abortion. They're easy to obtain in France. Of course, it is an enlightened and civilized nation."

"I wonder who that lawyer was that Nick supposedly shot?"

"That part I doubt, Noel. If he shot some lawyer, he'd still be in jail. My grandfather's a lawyer and those guys stick together."

"Yeah, that's true."

"You know, Noel, my grandmother is named Rita and raises Chihuahuas. She's rich too, of course. And single."

"It's a big world, Veeva. Even if what he said was true, I very much doubt my father was banging your grandmother. Though it's a cross-family tradition we could start sometime."

"Cool your jets, Noel. I'm like total jailbait."

"Yeah, well I bet you wouldn't say that to Tyler."

She changed the subject.

"So how come you didn't tell him your real name?"

"Ah, what's the point? I met the guy. I satisfied my curiosity. OK, that's that. I don't think I'll be seeing him again."

"No, he's kind of a bastard. I'm glad you and Tyler don't look anything like him."

"Yeah, me too."

To contrast paternal heritages, we then discussed Veeva's dad. He puts on concerts and owns his own record company. Too bad he only handles jazz musicians.

"Well, it's great that he's so successful," I said. "Seems like a tough business."

"It is. Daddy's done very well, but of course, he's never made much money at it."

"Then how come you're living in the Taj Mahal?"

"My mother's loaded. That's her one saving grace."

"Your father should sign the Pickled Punks."

"What's that, Noel?"

"A completely awesome band I heard in Hollywood. They're fabulous."

"Well, I'll mention your suggestion to him. Say, what was your grandmother's news last night?"

"Oh, nothing much," I lied. "I think your father was a little out to lunch on that one."

Veeva walked me back to the Metro station for our sad parting. Who knows when my next trip to L.A. will be? Nor was it likely she'd be stopping by Winnemucca any time soon. We both agreed it sucks that I live on the back side of the moon. She gave me a hug and her warmest kiss so far. If anyone could make me forget Uma, it was that crazy chick. We seemed to connect on all bases—or at least I did. So we said good-bye, and I headed back to the Valley.

10:37 p.m. I just spent the last 45 minutes running my probing hand over a female form. This is very pleasant work if you can get it. Wylie and Awanee came over, and we took a cruise to nowhere with Tyler in the GTO. This is a compromise my nephew has hammered out with his parents. He's allowed to entertain chicks in the car, but not in the trailer with its superior privacy and areas to stretch out. As a further inhibition against wanton acts, Tyler knows that any stains left on the GTO seats will be regarded as grounds for homicide by his stepdad. Steaming up the windows in the driveway, however, is permitted.

Awanee and I in the back seat broke through our reserve big time. She has quite a delectable body from what I can tell (and I could tell quite a lot). Very proficient kisser too. Toward the end she slipped a small but busy hand down my pants with explosive results. Much more satisfying than my own feeble efforts along that line. I was prepared to return the favor, but she kept her thighs tightly clamped. Anyway, I appreciated the experience and her willing spirit. At last I may have exorcized the ghost of Consuela, my doomed grammar school love. Not to mention a certain Nevada gum and mints purveyor.

FRIDAY, July 22 — On the bus east. Why is it that vacations always come to an end? It seems like I just got to L.A.

Beautiful weather today too to make the parting even more poignant. Distant mountains now loomed where impervious smog once lingered. Clogged though it is, L.A. can still pass for a paradise in the sun when it tries. Bill had to go to work, but Joanie took me and Tyler out for a farewell breakfast. She apologized for not being able to get in touch with my dad. I assured her it was no big deal and not to bother in the future. Of course, I had told Tyler about our encounter in the park, but his lips are sealed. Awanee called while I was scarfing my pancakes, and I assured her I would keep in touch by e-mail. She seemed quite bummed by my leaving, but what's a guy to do?

My sister gave me a souvenir t-shirt from Mariposa, California—a place neither of us had ever been, but she liked the butterfly design. She said I'm like a butterfly about to emerge from its cocoon and take wing. Could be, or it could just be a shirt she scored at a recent garage sale and it proved too small for Tyler. In any case, I thanked her for the gift.

Just passed the Nevada state line. You can always tell you're in Nevada by the lunar landscape and absurd summer heat. The driver just reported over the intercom that the outside temperature is 112 degrees. I don't know how people out here coped in the days before air conditioning. Of course, no one ever moved here who wasn't a bit batty in the first place.

SATURDAY, July 23 — Back home in my trailer hovel. It doesn't look any better after a week's absence. I'm trying not to imagine Uma sitting at our rickety table and contemplating my gnarly home environment.

Veeva called bright and early (11:30 a.m.). She's convinced the only solution is for me to go live with my sister in L.A. This is doubtful for many reasons. Their house is quite small (only two bedrooms), so where would I fit in? Plus, I'm not sure I'd want to live perpetually in the shadow of my accomplished and handsome nephew. Tyler's stepdad is pretty laid-back, but even if my sister agreed to take me in, she exhibits signs of being temperamental and high-strung. After all, she is a full-blooded

Twisp. I told Veeva I'd give it some thought. She had other news as well. Surprisingly, her father has agreed to go hear the Pickled Punks. And she's now convinced that my father and her grandmother were once lovers.

"My skepticism is boundless," I sneered.

"Wait, Noel, hear me out. I asked my father about it—in a very discreet way—and do you know what he said?"

"You're insane?"

"No. He said go ask your mother."

"Proving what?"

"Proving he knew it was true, but didn't want to be the person who confirmed it."

"Well, I suppose you could interpret it that way. Are you going to ask your mother?"

"No, that would be completely pointless."

"How about your grandmother?"

"That's a thought. She doesn't like me much though."

"Why not?"

"She says I remind her too much of her daughter. None of the females in my family gets along except for me and Aunt Sheeni. Noel, there are all these connections between our families!"

"I know. That's why we have to run away and get married. Then we could live together in your tastefully decorated room."

"Not likely. Boys are so hard on nice things. I do like you, Noel. I find I'm really upset that you've gone away. And what's this I hear about you and some slut named Awanee?"

L.A. is a very big place, but news still gets around fast.

5:38 p.m. Too hot to do anything but lie in my room and listen to the Pickled Punks over and over again at maximum volume—not that my cheap speakers in any way reproduce the actual concert experience. For some reason this seems to be bothering Grandma. She suggested I call up "Irma" and "invite her out to go bowling." Not being the world's greatest masochist, I have declined.

11:12 p.m. Carlyle and I just passed a boring few hours loitering downtown. In my absence he Africanized his name to Jamal, but I keep slipping up and addressing him by his old "honky slave name." Each time I do so he punches me in the arm as a form of aversion therapy. He reports a few nights ago he used the leather awl on his pocket knife to puncture all four tires on the Holt family's Buick. I'm glad he did this while I was away so Stoney can't blame me. No sign of our former gang brother, thank God. Just the mention of her name is for some reason extremely anxiety-provoking. And that's precisely what I don't need any more of.

SUNDAY, July 24 — I'm up to three dry nights in a row, a positive sign of improving mental health. I wish.

Awanee has e-mailed me 17 photos of herself in a variety of attractive poses (all fully clothed, alas). She demands at least that many of me. This will be tough as no occupant of this trailer has ever shown the slightest interest in photography (or owns a camera). She also suggests I get a video cam for my computer so she can watch me in my room anytime she needs my company. As if I wish to broadcast to the world my incessant self-abuse. I don't know what the typical daily average is for youths my age, but I fear I may be dangerously raising the curve.

8:47 p.m. Rot Dugan just dropped by with Toby's slave costume—once again reeking of bad b.o. If that kid ever tires of the nickname Rot, he can always change it to Stinky. Rot reports his father will have a "nice surprise" for me tomorrow. What that might be he refused to say. Why must work be such a source of constant dread?

I decided to make a list of all the reasons I am not a popular person in this town. 1. I'm poor. 2. I live in a trailer. 3. I'm not tall, dark, and athletic. 4. I dress poorly and my grooming habits are not the best. 5. I have weird friends. 6. I don't suck up to teachers to get good grades. 7. I am willing to work as a Negro slave for money. 8. I could care less if my high school beats Elko (arch rivals) in any sport. 9. I lack a friendly, outgoing personality. 10. I'm self-centered yet deficient in self-confidence.

To my credit: 1. I'm not outrageously ugly—my looks having been compared favorably to Brandon De Wilde, a deceased actor. 2. Some people find me intelligent. 3. I have well-developed and rather sophisticated musical tastes. 4. I shower regularly and rarely smell that bad. 5. I am loyal to my friends, unless stabbed in the back. 6. I am a decent person who tries to treat people well. 7. I am sensitive to the feelings of others. 8. I believe I have a lot of love to give to a special person. 9. I am not an abuser of cigarettes, snuff, or drugs. 10. I have a famous and glamorous brother.

Speaking of Nick, I e-mailed him a reminder to send that check to our father. As long as he has the checkbook out, I wish he'd take a hint and send a monthly stipend to me. At least I wouldn't blow all his largesse on booze and pigeon feed.

MONDAY, July 25 — The heat wave continues. Too bad we can't save up all this merciless heat and spread it around next January. Winter in Winnemucca in a drafty old trailer: the best argument yet for the imperative of suicide.

It was with a heavy heart that I made myself up as Toby and returned to work. The first thing Mr. Dugan said to me was that he was "very tired" of my grandmother's "unreasonable demands," and if I didn't "shape up" I would be "out the door." Guess he wasn't interested in hearing about what I did on my summer vacation. Even worse, my employer's had another marketing inspiration (the ominous "nice surprise"). At his direction a sign company has fashioned an advertising sandwich board, which Toby is to wear while marching up and down Main Street every hour on the hour. This contraption consists of two large signs (joined at the top by vinyl straps) that drape over the victim and hang down fore and aft. Fastened to the bottom of each sign are small bells which "tinkle merrily" (Mrs. Dugan's phrase) while one walks. The front sign reads: "Wedding Bells Are Ringing at Dixie Belle Wedding Chapel!" This is the "teaser" message. The rear "hard sell" sign reads: "Get Married Now! No App't Needed! Also Loving Adore Ceremonies! Affordable for all!"

Since Toby is paid by the service and not by the hour, we had to negotiate a rate for this added work. Considering the heat and the humiliation factor, Toby felt $500 per forced march was a reasonable rate. Mr. Dugan countered with a very paltry $1. After strenuous negotiations, we settled on $2 per stroll.

The good news: The signs, made of a thin corrugated plastic, were not excessively heavy. The bad news: The signs bounced annoyingly against one's person with every step. They inhibited the free-flow of air, leading to rapid overheating of the wearer. The rattling bells set off a terrific din, causing people to rush out of buildings to see what the ruckus was. The approaching apparition tended to draw rude comments from passersby and to antagonize vicious dogs.

As agreed upon, Toby walked four blocks up, crossed the street, walked eight blocks down, crossed the street, then walked four blocks back. This route, I was mortified to see, took me directly past the Silver Sluice casino. On my fourth circuit of the day Uma came out and blocked my path.

"Hi, Noel," she said.

"Hi, Uma. Your toes are glistening."

It was true. Gold and silver glitter alternated on each perfect toenail on display in her fashionable sandals.

"Nice of you to notice. Mary Glasgow and I got a little bored yesterday. Noel, I haven't seen you much lately."

"Well, you told me you weren't interested in going out with me."

"I may have said something to that effect, meaning on that particular day I wasn't interested in going out with anyone. But I didn't expect you to disappear off the planet."

I wasn't sure I was hearing what I thought I was hearing.

"Uh, I went to L.A."

"So your grandmother informed me. How was it?"

"Super. We went to the beach. Went to a cool club and heard a great band. I met some nice gir—I mean, people."

"Sounds great. I'd like to hear all about it."

"You would? Didn't you get that awful e-mail about me?"

"The rantings of a jealous female, Noel. I think Stoney Holt must be in love with you."

"What?"

"Why else would she be so jealous? Want to come over after dinner? If it's still this hot, we could cool off in my pool."

She was either inviting me over or I was having hallucinations from impending sunstroke.

"Sure, OK," I stammered.

"Great. You look a little ridiculous, Noel. And there's blood on your sock."

"Yes, I know. Old Mrs. Frey's schnauzer got to me."

"You should get it attended to. Dog bites can be nasty."

Possibly, but at that moment I was feeling no pain.

11:36 p.m. It's amazing how fast one's life can turn around. Sure, it's all just chemistry in the brain, but, man, it can be pleasant when you get those enzymes lined up right. To keep things under control in my swim trunks, which I slipped on under my cutoffs, I had a couple of vigorous bouts of self-abuse before I went over to Uma's. Girls may have to take similar precautions, though somehow I doubt it. Uma answered the door in a fairly modest, but nevertheless coronary-inducing blue-and-white striped bikini. She introduced me to her father, who shook my hand and said he admired my initiative. I feared he was referring to my designs on his daughter, but it turns out he was complimenting Toby for his advertising efforts in today's heat. To my surprise, Mr. Spurletti did not look at all Italian, having light brown hair and blue eyes. He was of an adequate but non-intimidating height and did not appear to be packing heat. From some angles he looked a bit like Burt Lancaster. I found him eminently suitable as a prospective father-in-law.

Uma's graciously landscaped backyard pool was not as large

as Veeva's, but it was a heavenly venue for splashing around with the girl of your dreams. The water was an ideal temperature for prolonged soaking, though the chlorine stung a bit on my ravaged ankle. We swam around for a while, then drifted to a corner of the deep end where we held onto the tile edge, treaded water, and talked. Occasionally, a lip was nuzzled. I told her the highlights of my trip, minus the more romantic bits, such as fondling Awanee's intimate parts and proposing marriage to Veeva. She expressed sympathy when I told her about meeting my father and seemed intrigued by our quest to find out more about my brother and his tumultuous teen years. She said she had caught his act in Vegas last fall, which she found "amazing and hilarious." She said she enjoyed meeting my grandmother, so I told her the whole sorry tale of how I came to live in a trailer in Winnemucca.

"Your mother shot off your stepfather's penis!" she exclaimed.

"Well, most of it I guess. I haven't really seen it. And the testicles too, of course. It was a large-caliber weapon—the gun I mean."

"I'm sure she was entirely justified."

More enthusiasm for summary castration than I would have preferred, but I let it pass. Since the conversation had entered a spicy zone, I decided to go with the flow.

"So finish your story about the jockstrap," I said, pulling her to me with my free arm. I liked the way certain anatomical protrusions brushed against my chest.

"My aunt Rosa is watching from her window, you know," she cautioned.

"Yeah, I thought I spotted someone up there. Is she likely to scream or call the cops?"

"More likely a priest. We can't do anything too overt out here. And your erection will have to subside before we get out of the pool."

So much for my earlier prophylactic measures.

"Sorry about that," I said.

"Why apologize? I'm taking it as a compliment. The jock-strap was a souvenir from a slumber party in Gulfport when I was 10. In the middle of the night we raided the bedroom of my friend Tali's brother."

"That must have shook him up."

"He was away at college. We each took turns trying it on. But we got a little hysterical and woke up Tali's mother. I had it on under my pajamas and wound up wearing it home. After that, those girls all called me Jock."

"Shall I call you Jock?"

"No. Those times are past."

My flattering boner never did subside, so eventually I had to exit the pool with my back to the house. I slipped on my t-shirt and cutoffs, gave Uma a good-night kiss and squeeze, and sneaked out by the side gate.

Life in dear old Winnemucca is looking up. I pinch myself, but it's still true. I have heard the expression "your erection" from Uma's sweet lips.

TUESDAY, July 26 — Toby came out this morning to ride his bike to work and discovered that someone had slashed both tires. I don't see why I have to suffer at the hands of Stoney in retaliation for vandalism committed by Carlyle. I notice she didn't mess with the tires of Grandma's Honda Civic. One does not sabotage the car of the person who cuts your hair. Good thing for her my brain is so awash right now in blissed-out dopamine. Otherwise, I'd have to devise some swift and ter-rible revenge. Sorry, Uma, I don't think Stoney likes me or is feeling jealous; I just think she's a mean bitch.

It must have been a slow news day in Winnemucca. A re-porter for the local paper came out and snapped some photos of Toby wearing his sandwich board. She also asked me a few ques-tions about my life and job. Mr. Dugan was thrilled to hear of this potential free advertising. He says the next time a Reno TV news crew is in town for a bad freeway pile-up (their usual reason for visiting Winnemucca), he'll try to get them to squeeze in a feature spot on Toby. Over my very dead body I thought to myself, scratching my sore ankle. Thanks to Mrs. Dugan, Toby now has a small can of spray dog repellant clipped to his belt. Very inappropriate to the antebellum look, but my employers don't want to get their asses sued.

Uma helped Toby pick out a birthday card for my brother, who will soon be 30. We got some nasty looks in the drugstore as Winnemuccans appear not to approve of mixed-race couples. Such scorn only made Toby even more affectionate toward the pretty white girl. I hope he doesn't wind up getting lynched. While checking out the cards, Uma casually asked if I knew some girl named Awanee. Tyler must have blabbed to Stoney, who then e-mailed Uma. It's enough to make a guy paranoid. I was stammering out a vigorous denial, but Uma assured me the matter was of no consequence. No, she didn't sound pissed either. She says she's interested in psychology (her intended future major in college) and from all of her reading has developed a keen empathy for the sexual needs of teenage boys. That may explain why she didn't run screaming from the pool last night when my you-know-what brushed against her. Perhaps her "empathy" will extend to submitting soon to my indomitable lusts. I must work up the nerve to inquire if she is a virgin.

10:12 p.m. Buying new tires and tubes for my bike wiped out most of my last paycheck. This is a feud I cannot afford. I have called off Jamal (formerly Carlyle) and e-mailed Stoney, apologizing for any misunderstandings between us and reinstating her membership in the Upts gang. I hope this gets that vindictive chick off my back. I suspect an endorphin imbalance in her brain. I need to find her a girlfriend and/or boyfriend as soon as possible to channel all that surplus energy into something positive like getting laid. That girl needs it bad. (Don't we all!)

WEDNESDAY, July 27 — Veeva called this morning to report that she had talked to her granny in Arizona. More confirmation of my father's near miss at great wealth. First, Veeva's grandmother demanded to know if Connie (Veeva's mom) had blabbed about the George Twisp affair, then she indignantly denied all. Very depressing. I'm sure if my dad had married Veeva's granny, at least a few of those bucks would have trickled down to me. No way my mother's lawyers would have let him squirm out of his lawful child-support obligations. DNA tests would have been performed and my father's fat wallet nailed to the courthouse door. I could be dressing better now and listening to the Pickled Punks in full Dolby® surround-sound stereo.

Somehow Veeva suspected there'd been a change in my love life.

"You seem a little distant, Noel," she complained.

"I'm 700 miles away, Veeva. I might as well be living on Mars."

"Why don't you tell me you love me any more?"

"Because I know you only have eyes for Tyler."

"Are any of Tyler's girlfriends, you know, really pretty?"

"Only the A-list girls. They're all knockouts. The rest are just better than average."

"I think you're saying that just to torment me."

"Of course, they're not rich like you are, but I don't think that matters much to Tyler."

"Does it matter to you?"

It did, but I denied it.

"Are you seeing anyone there in Wapakoneta?"

"It's Winnemucca. I have some female friends."

"Anyone special?"

"Not really."

"I can tell you're lying, Noel. There is someone. It's that girl you were telling me about before. Have you slept with her?"

"Not yet."

"I'm very happy for you, Noel."

"You don't sound very happy, Veeva."

"Our lives are destined to intertwine in many ways, Noel.

It's true with Nick and Sheeni, and it's true with us. It's a fate I know we cannot escape."

"What makes you so sure?"

"I just know it, Noel. Like I know Tyler will break my heart. Talk to you soon."

"'Bye, Veeva. I love you."

"I love you too."

5:15 p.m. Momentous news. Sweaty, sign-draped Toby encountered Uma outside the casino, and she's agreed to drop by tonight. This may be Bingo Night for more than just my grandmother. I've been vacuuming and straightening up like a madman. Fifteen years of clutter is a lot to cope with. Call me a cockeyed optimist, but I also installed fresh sheets on my little bed.

11:27 p.m. Grandma was feeling somewhat tired, but I reminded her how much she loved bingo and waved a relieved good-bye as she drove off in her huffing old Honda. Uma was supposed to arrive at 7:30. By 7:45 I was a nervous wreck, but shortly thereafter she rolled up on a very deluxe mountain bike. She dismounted and we kissed under the patio awning. I invited her in for a Coke.

"Where's your grandmother?" she asked, removing her bike helmet and shaking out her lovely hair.

"She's away at Bingo Night."

"Oh, I see."

I handed her a frosty glass and smiled seductively. We clicked glasses and sipped our drinks. Uma sat on the sofa and looked around.

"This place is neat as a pin," she commented, I hope approvingly.

"We try, Uma. Of course, on your first visit I'd been away for a few days. Grandma isn't much of a housekeeper left on her own. Still, I realize it's a precipitous decline from your exalted home environment."

"I don't know. I like it. I like the nice varnished wood on the walls. What is it—birch?"

"Hell if I know."

We put down our drinks and indulged in a long and passionate kiss. Very inflaming to the senses. After a prolonged interval, we paused.

"Uma, darling, would you like to retire to my bedroom?"

"I don't know, Noel. I think we should discuss the situation."

I was in no condition for human speech, but managed to inquire what she had in mind.

"Well, we could discuss our respective virginities."

"Oh, right."

"Now, I've always heard that for a girl's first time she should do it with an older guy. You know, someone who's had some experience and knows what he's doing."

"Well, there's something to be said for that, I suppose," I grudgingly conceded.

"I mean two virgins going at it is the worst possible scenario, Noel. We could fail miserably and both be traumatized for life."

"Well, I'm willing to risk it, Uma."

"The other thing is what having sex does to a relationship."

"It elevates it to a much higher plane, darling."

"Not from what I've seen. It just causes lots of jealousy, hard feelings, and possessiveness."

Crushing disappointment, though Uma helped me cope by placing my hand on her breast. Infinitely more pleasurable than touching Awanee's. Don't ask me why.

"Do you like old movies, Noel?"

"Sure I guess so."

I liked the way her nipple stiffened when I caressed it through her shirt.

"Movies have become the myths of our culture. You see these great old movies, but everyone up there on the screen is dead now. The actors are like talking and moving two-dimensional ghosts. Kind of a celluloid window into another time. Did you ever see the film 'Hud'?"

"Uh, I don't think so."

"Melvin Douglas is in it. He plays this old broken-down rancher. Very decrepit. But slip in another DVD, and now you can see him in 'Ninotchka,' when he was young and handsome and debonair, and charming his way into Greta Garbo's heart."

"I didn't see that one either."

I slipped my hand under her shirt. Much nicer that way. Why do breasts feel so divinely entrancing?

"I saw 'Hud' last year—with my aunt Rosa. We liked it a lot. Of course, she went for Paul Newman, but do you know who I liked in that movie?"

"The old guy, uh, Melvin Douglas?"

"No. I liked the young kid: Brandon De Wilde."

"Oh." It was all beginning to make sense to me now.

"You know, Noel, you could be Brandon De Wilde's younger brother. The resemblance is striking."

"Yeah, I've heard that before. Is that why you like me?"

"Who's to say, Noel? I like your warm hand on my breast. I like that hard part of you pressing into my thigh. I like your laugh. I like your version of Toby. Much more imaginative than Rot's. I like your sneakiness in trying to get me alone out here. I like your kisses."

I liked hers too. We lay entwined on the sofa and kissed for two straight hours by the clock. It was by far the greatest two hours of my entire life.

THURSDAY, July 28 — A dry night and no thumb-sucking either. If my lips hadn't received their quota of oral gratification last night, there'd be no hope for them. I've been thinking it over. Sure, it could be hazardous for two virgins to have sex. But how healthy in the long run is all that frustrating celibacy? Damn, I should never have been so reserved in L.A. Had I been practicing like mad with Awanee, I'd be totally up to speed now for Uma.

Stoney called early, and I met her for breakfast at the pan-
cake place on Main Street. We apologized mutually for the ug-
liness of the past weeks. It was good to get that behind us, though
I still feel some resentment toward her. She was appalled to hear
of my romantic progress with Uma. I don't know why Stoney is
so dead set against her. I assured Stoney it was very healing to
the psyche to lay hands on the warm body of a loved one.

"I know that," she replied. "Don't forget, I got pretty far
along with Tyler."

"Sure, that's all well and good, Stoney, but you've got to
hook up with someone local. People need this sort of thing more
than once a year."

"I hate this town and everyone in it."

"You don't hate Sloan Chandler."

"No, I suppose not. He's coming back from sailing camp next
Thursday."

Damn, only a week in which to convince Uma to marry me.
A daunting task.

"Stoney, you've got to forget all this looking-butch business.
Face it: you're not a dyke."

"How can you be so sure?"

"Because there are plenty of attractive girls in town, and
you've never once had the hots for any of them."

"That's true."

"So you've got to start dolling yourself up and making a play
for Sloan. You're the prettiest girl in town with a fabulous body,
so just get used to it."

"You sound like my mother, Noel."

"Well, once in a while even mothers know what they're talking about."

"Not my mom. She's a total fake and phony."

Long-suffering Mrs. Holt always seemed perfectly nice to
me, but I wasn't going to open that can of worms.

"OK, forget your mother. Just do this for yourself."

"But if I do that, my mother will have won. The bitch will be
so smug."

"Cut the cord, Stoney. Jesus, don't ruin your life just to get back at your mother. Shit, just ignore her. That's what I do with my mother."

"Yeah, well it's easier for you. Your mother's in another fucking state. All my mom has to do is look at me, and I want to murder her."

"What about your father?"

"You mean my stepdad? Every time I come out of my room, that creep undresses me with his eyes."

No wonder Stoney was a mess. Her home life sounded even unhealthier than mine. I tried to reassure her.

"All guys do that, Stoney. The incest taboo is very weak in males. You shouldn't take it personally. What you've got to do is divorce your parents. Even though you have to live with them for a few more years, now is the time to separate emotionally from them. Be your own person."

"Yeah, that's right. What the fuck do I care what those assholes think?"

"Right. And maybe consider cleaning up your language. Guys don't find chicks who swear all that attractive."

"Not feminine, huh?"

"Not very."

"Shit, I guess I should have played more with Barbie when I was a kid and less with my battery-powered Harley."

So it *was* Mrs. Holt's fault. There's a good lesson for parents: inappropriate toy choices can come back to haunt you later.

4:12 p.m. Mr. Dugan added a new leg to Toby's circuit today (at no increase in pay). I now have to take a detour through the main floor and gift shop of the Buckaroo Hall of Fame, one of our local cowboy-theme tourist attractions. He's made some kind of arrangement with the management there. On one of my walks this afternoon Toby had to fire a warning spritz of dog repellent at Biggie Smalls, a cute but hostile Boston Terrier mix. Its owner came roaring out and screamed at me. She ranted that she would *never ever* employ the services of the Dixie Belle Wedding

Chapel. Toby held his tongue and did not point out that as she was ugly, old, and grotesquely overweight that was not likely to happen anyway. I did pull down a sock to flash my still-draining dog bite.

Later Toby detoured through the Silver Sluice and had a nice chat with Uma. She invited me over for dinner tonight. Fat Marvin Tuelco burned like fire when Toby kissed her, but he is under strict orders not to mess with the boss's daughter or her friends. Yes, complaints had been made.

10:45 p.m. Trying to make a good impression, I was right on time at Uma's house. It was just the three of us for dinner: me, my future wife, and her aunt Rosa. Uma's dad was busy at work training some new dealers. He's chartered a fleet of buses to snag more seniors and is anticipating a boost in traffic. The casino business is very competitive these days since all the Indian tribes started muscling in on the action. Aunt Rosa made chicken cacciatore, one of her specialties. Very delicious. I can only hope Uma proves as culinarily gifted down the road. The conversation, though, got a little scary in spots.

"Noel, are you Catholic?" asked Aunt Rosa, getting down to basics.

My Consuela experience had prepared me for such a question.

"Yes, I am," I lied.

"That's odd," she commented, "I don't recall seeing you in the congregation at St. Paul's."

"Uh, we usually go to the Church of Christ. It's closer."

Eyebrows were raised around the table, some in warning.

"The Church of Christ! How extraordinary! That's certainly taking ecumenicalism to a new level."

"Well, my grandmother can't walk very far—though she prefers St. Paul's, of course."

Aunt Rosa appeared somewhat mollified.

"And when, Noel, was your last confession?"

Uma smiled into her plate; it appeared she was enjoying my

grilling.

"Uh, my last confession? Yes, uh, that was last week. Very, uh, absolving."

"You sound most devout, Noel. Did you have Father Gillis or Father Sheldrake?"

"Uh, I don't know. It was kind of dark and they were behind a screen."

"Well, of course. But you can always tell which is which from their voices. I generally prefer Father Gillis. He takes one's transgressions much more seriously. Sin is no frivolous matter to him."

"Yes, well, fortunately I don't have that many sins. Speaking personally, that is."

"We are all sinners, Noel. I believe I witnessed some in our back-yard pool. Very recently, in fact."

I colored and shoveled in the chicken. Uma was right. We needed to get that uptight religious chick married off. If she weren't around, Uma and I could be going at it in style and comfort.

After dinner we loaded the dishwasher and cleaned up, while Aunt Rosa retired to the family room to watch TV. Uma sneaked us a glass of wine and I sneaked many scorching kisses. Then we went out and sat by the pool in adjoining lounge chairs and watched the sun go down. I screwed up my courage, grasped my darling's hand, and told her I loved her.

"I don't know if we're mature enough for love, Noel. I certainly share your sense of intense infatuation. I enjoyed being alone with you last night."

"Me too."

"I never realized that our bodies react so strongly to kissing. It really is a powerful antecedent to intercourse. I got quite wet after a time."

I appreciated that Uma now felt comfortable enough with me to discuss the state of her vagina.

"Yes, Uma, I seem to respond to kissing in that way also."

"You do indeed, Noel. Though from what I can see, you can

get turned on just from talking."

I looked down. She had a point there.

FRIDAY, July 29 — Toby has achieved his 15 minutes of fame. The *Humboldt Star* came out today, and there he was with sandwich board on the front page of the inside section. Here is the news article in its entirety:

> Wedding's Longest March?
>
> WINNEMUCCA - Local teen Noel L. Wescott, 15, can now be seen treading the boards of downtown in his role as super salesman for a local wedding chapel. He also assists at weddings and commitment ceremonies, where he plays the role of "Toby," a 19th Century rustic servant.
>
> Wescott reports he enjoys the work and is happy to do his part to bring both residents and visitors closer together. The hard-working youth calculates by the end of summer he will have carried his signs over 2,500 miles. That's a lot of shoe leather devoted to love.

Are those people incapable of basic math? I just made up that mileage estimate off the top of my head. I can't believe they actually printed it. The photo wasn't that flattering as young Toby was sweating like a pig.

Nevertheless, Grandma was thrilled and rushed out to buy a dozen copies. I scanned the article into my computer and e-mailed the file to Awanee. She'll have to be content with that photo until I can scrape up some more. Perhaps I can dig up some shots of Brandon De Wilde on the Web and pass those off as candid views of her absent beau. I also sent the story to my brother, though he has yet to reply to my last e-mail. Even if he is still in Europe, he must have taken along some sort of laptop. I feel I just don't rate with that guy. He could be a vital father figure for me if he wasn't so fucking aloof.

Mr. Dugan commented that in future interviews I should insist they mention the full name, address, and operating hours of his business. He also was pissed that in cropping the photo the editors seemed more interested in showing Toby than his sign. I hope I don't wind up some small-town businessman grubbing for dollars like my boss. God knows what I'll be when I grow up. At present I have no discernible occupational aspirations, although I think being a roadie for a rock band might suit me. As long as I don't have to lug anything heavy.

On one of his rounds this afternoon Toby ran into Mrs. Greene, my fantasy mom. She congratulated me on my news article, then spilled her guts. It seems Jamal has signed up with an online dating service and has been corresponding with some 23-year-old black woman in Reno. Well, that explains why I hadn't heard lately from my pal.

"If that woman shows up in town, I'm going to have her arrested!" Mrs. Greene declared. "Carlyle is only 15!"

True enough, but what parents don't understand is a 23-year-old woman is exactly what a 15-year-old boy needs. For example, I could use one right now to help me get ready for Uma. I mean high school sex-education classes are helpful, but there's no substitute for practical experience. I wonder if Jamal's babe has a friend?

9:37 p.m. Jamal just went home empty-handed. He came over to borrow bus fare to Reno, but I had to decline. I pleaded poverty, but actually I didn't want to piss off Mrs. Greene. I hope he doesn't do anything desperate. He seems quite gone on Rashilla, even though they've never met and only spoken a few times by phone.

"This Rashilla," I inquired, "does she think you're black?"

"Sure. I sent her my picher."

"And you want to have sex with her?"

"Yeah, and so does she. The bitch say she wants to untie my dick."

"You told her about that feature, did you?"

"Right on, baby."

"If you like her, why are you calling her a bitch?"

"That's just the lingo, dude. Get with the program."

"And what happens when you take off your clothes and she finds out the rest of you is white?"

"No problem, man. It's going to be like really dark. Dig it?"

"And if you spend the night, will it be really dark the next morning?"

"Damn!"

Jamal gave the matter some thought.

"Well, by then the bitch will be like totally digging me. She won't mind."

"Jamal, it's not legal for a chick that old to have sex with a kid our age."

"Why the fuck not? We couldn't be havin' no sex if the guy wasn't turned on."

"A valid point, but I don't write the laws. You could both be arrested."

"Tell it to the judge, man. Don't be tellin' it to me!"

11:15 p.m. Had a long phone chat with Uma. She has such a sexy voice I felt like I was getting an erection in my ear. Is that possible? I told her about Jamal, and she thinks we should sign up her aunt Rosa for online dating. A great idea. It's the perfect way to troll for cultivated and single Catholic men who dig ex-nuns who can cook.

"Has your aunt Rosa ever had a date?" I asked.

"Not to my knowledge."

"Wow. That's a lot of years of going without."

"I know. It's no wonder she's always vacuuming. A dust ball doesn't stand a chance in this house."

"I noticed it was pretty spotless. I miss you, darling."

"I'm only a mile a way."

"Shall I come over and sneak up to your room?"

"I don't think so. You'll have even more to talk about in confession."

"What?"

"My aunt's going to check you out with the priests, you know. I couldn't believe you said what you did. I've been thinking it over. We'll have to get you to confession soon."

"Are you out of your mind? I'm not a Catholic!"

"Don't worry, Noel. I can coach you."

"I'll be struck dead by lightning, Uma. The Pope will send his agents after me with instructions to shoot to kill!"

"Well, the alternative is having Aunt Rosa totally pissed at you. The one thing worse for her than being non-Catholic is being a lying non-Catholic. She'll make it hard for me to see you."

Damn. Now I have to go spill my guts to some nosy priest. All for the off chance of getting laid. And what assurance do I have that my pious confessor hasn't been buggering some altar boy?

11:53 p.m. I downloaded some songs from a band that Uma recommended, the Winking Pixies. Pretty cool group. If they ever link up with my current favorite band, they'd be the Winking Pickled Pixie Punks. On that note, I think I'll hit the sack.

SATURDAY, July 30 — On the bus to Las Vegas. Yeah, I'm going to visit my brother. It wasn't his idea or mine. Veeva phoned early this morning and said it was time to "beard the lion in its den." She knows Nick is back because her mother talked to him last night. He's also scheduled to perform this weekend. I'm meeting Veeva and Tyler in Vegas, and we're going to get my brother to spill about his past or die trying. The whole idea sounds kind of half-baked and impulsive, but there's no resisting Veeva once she's made up her mind. I had to call up and cancel my date with Uma. We were going to watch "Hud" on DVD at her house and hope that the adults hit the sack early. This "physical intimacy" business is amazingly addictive. To hell with my brother and his tempestuous youth. All I really want to do is hole up with Uma somewhere private and merge our living flesh.

If the spying chick sitting next to me doesn't stop trying to read what I'm typing on this screen, I'm going to bean her over the head with my laptop.

There, that did it.

She looked at me like I was a maniac, got up, and moved to another seat.

I can't say I blame her for snooping. The scenery out the window is beyond boring.

8:12 p.m. Veeva met me at the sweltering bus station. Not surprisingly, she had jetted to Vegas first-class. A quick one-hour flight, while I'd been rattling around on that damn bus all day long. After greeting me with an extremely warm kiss, she said Tyler had decided at the last minute that football practice was more important than an illuminating weekend in Vegas with us. I suppose you don't win all those trophies without some seriously misplaced priorities.

We took a cab to Nick's house. Fortunately, Veeva had Mapquest directions to his address from downtown since our Pakistani cabdriver was clueless. He says Las Vegas is growing so fast there's no way he can keep up with all the new streets and developments. My brother's house is this big two-story stucco affair on top of a desert rise that had been shaved off flat. Nice views in all directions if you like the sight of endless tile-roofed houses swallowing up the desert. No way I'd want to be one of the guys who had to swing a hammer for a living in that sizzling heat.

Nick wasn't there, but his girlfriend Ada Olson let us in. She was quite surprised to hear we had decided to pay him a birthday visit. The house was full of boxes like someone was moving, which turned out to be the case.

"So why are you moving, Ada?" I asked. She was an extremely cute blond I would rate at least a 9.5 on a scale of 10.

"Oh, the usual reason."

"What's that?"

"Don't be dense, Noel," hissed Veeva.

"I don't get it," I insisted.

Veeva sighed. "OK, Noel, somebody here has found a new squeeze."

"You're ditching my brother, huh?" I asked.

"Quite the contrary," she replied.

"Then why are *you* the one moving?" asked Veeva. "If I may be so nosy."

"Oh, I don't know," she replied. "This was Nick's house before I arrived. I'm trying to avoid things getting too ugly. How long have you had dentures?"

Veeva laughed. "Everyone asks me that. They're real."

"Really?" said Ada. "Mind if I look at them? I'm an oral surgeon."

"Be my guest," said Veeva, opening wide.

"Extraordinary," said Ada. "You have absolutely the most perfect teeth I've ever seen."

"I know," replied Veeva. "My dentist is so proud. He says my teeth should be on the list of Southern California attractions like Knotts Berry Farm and Disneyland."

I can't believe my brother's dumping this chick. Beautiful looks, great body, nice personality, good job, and free dental care to boot. The guy must be seriously deranged.

Have to stop here. Ada is taking us out for a late dinner.

11:36 p.m. No sign of my brother yet. Ada says he has two evening shows and doesn't usually get home until well after midnight. Fortunately, his house has five bedrooms, so everyone's making themselves at home. Exiled Ada's camping out in the guest suite over the attached three-car garage. Her new place won't be ready until Monday. My room is upstairs in the back, overlooking the pool and spa. Ol' Nick is doing way better than even I imagined. Yup, I've got to put the bite on that guy. And soon.

Ada took us out to a fancy seafood and steak place around the corner from the Liberace Museum. Since Veeva wasn't paying, I got to eat actual meat. She had the mushroom risotto and tried not to cringe as Ada and I masticated our fellow creatures. Hard to believe that arid Nevada has given rise to a city this huge and sprawling. Ada says it's easier to understand Las Vegas if you just think of it as the most distant suburb of Los Angeles.

In her discrete way, Veeva pumped Ada for information about my brother, but she didn't have much to report. She says Nick is very private about his personal life and past. She was amazed to hear he might have been married once, as she had long since concluded the guy was allergic to that word. Nor had she ever heard of his keeping a daily journal—although she says he is quite literate and well-read for a guy who never went to college. (I'm not sure we Twisps are that educable by conventional means.)

"So what was he doing in Prague?" asked Veeva.

"Looking up some old flame," Ada replied, letting most of a nice filet go to waste.

"You think it's serious?" Veeva asked.

"Who's to say? She's returning the visit next week though."

Too bad I couldn't stay to meet this chick. She must be one incredible knockout. Perhaps even in Uma's class.

Veeva tried to steer the conversation in a happier direction. "Did you meet Nick in the dentist's chair?"

"No, but I wouldn't mind getting him back there for a root canal or two. We met in a skydiving class."

"You jumped out of an airplane together?" I asked.

"Well, sort of, Noel. He liked to tell people that when we met we fell for each other big time."

My brother made a joke. I'm amazed. The few times I've talked to him he always seemed so deadly serious.

SUNDAY, July 31 — By 8:00 a.m. it was already over 90 degrees outside. My brother must blow a big bundle every month on air conditioning. Veeva and I got up early and scrounged for breakfast in Nick's spotless kitchen. I scrambled some eggs while Veeva marveled that I knew which end of the skillet to hold.

She's one of those pampered kids who grow up thinking that cooking is an art known only to Latina housekeepers. Since eggs don't walk or swim, she condescended to eat her half of my sloppy creation: a cheese and ortega chili omelet.

"Notice anything unusual about your brother's house?" she asked, sipping her herbal tea.

"He has five bedrooms for one lonely guy?"

"Well, there's that too. But did you notice his decor is totally generic? This place feels like a furnished model home that he simply moved into. My room, for example, has all the personality of a guest suite at the Holiday Inn. And a person could wither and die in that sterile living room."

"Well, guys aren't generally big on home decor."

"I don't know, Noel. This feels like the place of a person who doesn't express his personality. Who keeps everything suppressed. A guy who has lots of secrets. This is the home of a man who is treading water while waiting for his life to begin."

Where do girls come up with stuff like that? To me it seemed like a perfectly fine house; I'd live in it in a minute. I'd hate to think what Veeva would conclude about me if she ever got the chance to snoop through my squalid trailer.

No sign of Ada, but eventually my brother wandered down looking bleary-eyed, unshaven, and annoyed.

"Happy birthday!" Veeva and I called out.

"Yeah, yeah. You know, Noel, you guys should have talked to me first. This isn't really the best time for a visit."

"We wanted to surprise you," I replied.

"A person only turns 30 once," added Veeva, bubbling with forced goodwill. My brother, though, wasn't buying it.

"Does your mother know you're here?"

"More or less, Uncle Nick. Aren't you going to give me a hug?"

He did so reluctantly and then shook my clammy hand.

"Ada called me at work last night about you two. You know she's moving out."

"We know, Uncle Nick. And we both think you're being a real beast."

Nick smiled and studied her. "I hardly recognized you, Veeva. You're growing up. You remind me of someone I once knew."

"And that would be," she replied, "my aunt Sheeni perhaps?"

"Has your mother been talking about me?"

"I wish. She's a total clam on all things Twispian. You know I visited Sheeni in France a couple of years ago."

"Well, we'll have to talk about that sometime. How about we all go out for breakfast? Then we can see about getting you both back home."

We went out for a second breakfast, and Veeva turned up the charm. She got Nick to agree to let us stay at least through his birthday. She called her mother from the restaurant booth, and both she and Nick talked to her. Mrs. Saunders was pissed, but not hysterical. Veeva had cut out without permission, but thoughtfully had left a note. And now that Connie was reassured her daughter hadn't been sold into white slavery, she was looking forward to spending a few days alone with her handsome husband.

Veeva persuaded Nick we could be his "emotional support team" while he went through this "difficult period." She even got him to spill some about the mystery chick from Prague. It's a gal named Reina Vesely whom he met years ago while touring with a circus in France. She has a trained parrot act and a former husband (a clown), who recently ran off with a Polish slack rope walker. Very long distance for conducting a romance, plus the chick has two rugrats. I vote he stays home and marries the dentist.

When Veeva went to the restroom, Nick asked me if there was anything going on between us. I assured him I already had a girlfriend in Winnemucca.

"Glad to hear it," he replied. "You know Veeva's still pretty young. Her mother was always a handful, and the Saunders side can be even more difficult."

Now was the time to strike while the iron was hot.

"So you were married to her aunt Sheeni at the age of 14?"

My brother blushed and looked down at his plate.

"We were never married, Noel. Not legally at any rate. We, we were together for a time—a short time. It was a painful, uh, interval. I try not to think about it."

"But it sounds like it was pretty exciting. You ran away to France together?"

"We did that. We lived in a garret in Paris."

"And you were only 14?"

"Well, I turned 15 at some point. It was a rough year."

"That's my age now. And you shot some lawyer?"

"Who have you been talking to, Noel?"

"Our dad. I saw him in L.A. He wants you to send him his check."

"I did. It's sent automatically by my bank. It must have been delayed briefly in the mail."

"And the dead lawyer?"

"He didn't die. I just winged him."

"Why did you shoot him?"

"It was an accident. The gun went off in my hand. I hope you never fool around with firearms, Noel."

"I'm not planning on it, Nick. So how come you don't marry Ada? She's very nice."

"She is indeed. I don't know. My relations with women have always been, uh, complicated. I hope you have an easier time of it."

"I'd like to get married to Uma. Right now."

"Well, you've got a lot of growing up to do before you get married. Believe me, Noel, I speak from experience."

He clammed up when Veeva returned. I find it interesting he didn't blink when I mentioned "our dad." So Nick was in on the secret all along. I knew he was lying about that. I wonder how much of what he told me today was the truth? It's always hard to tell with us Twisps.

When we got back, Ada was in the kitchen separating her pans from Nick's pan. She and Nick hardly spoke, but only glanced at each other with these incredibly pain-laden looks. I don't see why people have to torture each other like that. I say just hook up with someone you like and stay hooked up. Maybe have a kid or two to cement the adhesion.

Veeva volunteered to help Ada with her packing and whispered to me to "find the diary." Yeah, like I'm supposed to discover on a shelf somewhere this leather-bound set of volumes inscribed in gold-leaf on the spine: "My Rebellious Teen Years by Nicholas F. Twisp." Guys who keep diaries tend not to leave them around for prying houseguests to snoop through. I gave it a shot though, and spotted some bookshelves in this office-type room where my brother was juggling a half-dozen balls.

"Juggling is like playing a horn," he remarked, not stopping. "You have to practice daily or you lose your chops."

"Are those billiard balls?"

"Yeah. They're a nice size for my hands and the weight works my muscles. Want to try?"

"No thanks. Mind if I look at your books?"

"Go ahead, but be careful. Some of them are rare and valuable old books on juggling."

People write books about juggling? Sounds incredibly boring. I noticed a framed photograph on the wall behind his desk. Nick was shaking the hand of some well-preserved blond while juggling four martini glasses with his left hand.

"Who's the lady?" I asked.

"That's Nancy Sinatra. She caught my act one night."

Probably half the celebrities in the world have seen my brother's act, but the one he showcases on his wall is Nancy Sinatra. Go figure.

"You like Nancy Sinatra for some reason?"

"Sure. She's very nice. And that's as close as I'll ever get to shaking her old man's hand."

Sometimes my brother seems more like 50 than 15 years older

than me. No diaries were spotted, though I did find a photo album from his childhood in Oakland. Lots of faded color shots of the happy young couple and their two romping youngsters. Hard to believe that handsome young advertising executive with the pipe and all the hair is now providing roosts for pigeons on Skid Row. My once-pretty mother looked fairly normal 25 years ago too, though Nick assured me she was a trial even back then.

4:13 p.m. I just talked to Uma for over an hour on my brother's phone. I figure with all the calls he's making to Reina in distant Prague my splurge won't even make a blip on his massive bill. Uma was loitering behind the counter at work and wanted to know every detail of what I'd been doing down south. Being incredibly smart as well as beautiful, she pointed out that like me Nick might have been noting his daily activities on a computer.

"I suppose they had computers 15 years ago," I conceded. "But my brother doesn't strike me as an early adopter. He has an entire shelf of Frank Sinatra albums, all on vinyl if you can believe it. He has an incredible stereo, but the amp uses tubes. You have to wait for the thing to warm up before you hear any sound."

"My father has one too, Noel. Many audiophiles prefer the supposedly warmer sound of tube equipment. I think they just like to fuss with expensive gear. Does Nick have a computer?"

"Oh, sure. It puts mine to shame. I notice he has a nice laptop too. You think I should check them out, darling?"

"Well, that wouldn't be very ethical, Noel."

"Right. I'll get right on it."

11:46 p.m. Nick took us out for a fancy dinner at the casino where he works, then we watched his first show of the evening from a choice reserved table. All the beverages we wanted too, as long as they were alcohol-free. I don't know why they imagine Las Vegas is a town anyone would wish to experience dead sober. Nick had a second show to perform later, so he had Derek, his personal assistant, drive us back. I didn't know jugglers required personal assistants, but that's my brother's glamorous lifestyle for you.

It was impressive seeing his name in huge letters on the marquee of the Normandie casino. That's one of the newer ones on the Strip. It's a re-creation of the 1930s French luxury liner done in three-quarter scale. The original ship must have been a monster, since the downsized replica is still nearly 800 feet long and towers above that part of the Strip. Every contour is outlined in colored lights—over two million in all. The ship is "berthed" in its own patch of artificial ocean, and every hour on the hour it "steams away" with a great blasting of whistles, raising of gangplanks, waving of crowds, and shooting off of paper streamers. It's all an illusion, of course, because what actually moves is the pier, not the ship (which is in fact a non-floating building planted solidly on a regular foundation). Rather well done though, with waves streaming by the hull and a matching tugboat puffing away. Nick says they keep the imported sea gulls hanging around by surreptitiously supplying them with leftovers from the ship's many restaurants. There are six laborers on staff whose sole job it is to scrape up the bird crap and shoo away pigeons.

The Normandie's interior is done up very swankily in Art Deco style, though Veeva pointed out if you look closely, the "rare woods" were mostly just tarted-up sheetrock. We ate dinner in the immense Main Salon, which according to a blurb on the menu had been one of the largest and grandest rooms ever afloat. In the Las Vegas version, all of the replica Lalique chandeliers sway back and forth in unison, so you do sort of feel like you're at sea. The simulation of motion is so effective, Nick says some diners have been known to turn green and toss their cookies. Not to worry, the waiters carry concealed barf bags.

Midway through our meal the chandeliers began to sway wildly, and the captain came on the P.A. system to apologize for the "rough seas." For the next ten minutes all the waiters staggered about like they could barely keep their footing. Rather silly, but fun.

Our table was right next to this vast three-story-high bas-relief sculpture of "Normandy peasant life." I guess in the old days some of those Normandy peasant gals were running around as topless as Las Vegas showgirls. The sculptor Alfred Janniot did his original in carved red marble highlighted with gold gilding, but even Veeva had to concede the Vegas plaster replica was rather well done. Everything was first rate (including my steak), but we could have skipped the waiter's annoying French accent, which was as fake as Carlyle's afro.

If we Twisps weren't so competitive, I'd have to say my brother was the greatest juggler I've ever seen. None of the usual clichés for him, like swinging away on flaming torches or chainsaws with their motors running. He tosses four crystal glasses in the air, then four eggs, and sets each glass down with an unbroken egg now resting inside it—one of which he cracks open to prove it was real. Or he juggles six lit candles, then steps forward so they fall behind him. Yet when he then moves aside, the candles have all disappeared. Or he launches a set of golf clubs high above him, then grabs each club as it descends and smacks a series of balls lined up on tees. Good thing the balls are plastic since he hits them straight at the audience. All the while he keeps up an amusing banter with his assistant, a scantily clad babe named Henrietta, whom we met backstage after the show. I thought her well-spangled assets were real, but Veeva assured me that like everything else in Vegas they were crowd-pleasing simulations. Still, she's another attractive local dame that Nick could marry instead of running after some chick 8,000 miles away—and both of them on the rebound to boot.

# AUGUST

MONDAY, August 1 — Middle of the night sometime. No sleep on the menu with Veeva on the prowl. She said we had to tackle Nick's computer before he got back from work. It booted fine with no password required. Lots and lots of files, but Veeva suggested we search for any containing the name Sheeni in the text. Easy and quick with Nick's stallion of a processor. It found only one file though, an e-mail message earlier this year from Trent Preston.

"Trent Preston the actor?" asked Veeva.

"Probably. My brother hobnobs with all the greats."

Here is the text of the message:

Hi, Nick.

Back in Paris after a few days in Barcelona, one of our favorite cities. I saw Sheeni for lunch yesterday. They were here on wine business. She sends her regards. She was looking extraordinarily beautiful. Not to be sexist, but I think these may be her peak years. She's well, but her spirits seemed a little down. I think she may be feeling discouraged that her career has not progressed as well as she would have liked. Of course, she dotes on her children, though she would never admit it. Frankly, I'm surprised that she turned out to be such a devoted mother. She is taking them all over the city on her usual missions of cultural enrichment. I've accepted a challenging role in a Franco-German-Norwegian production, so must get back to the darn script. Many pages to learn, since I like to go into rehearsals well prepared. We leave for Oslo on Friday. Sorry, no possibility of getting back to the States until perhaps the fall. Violet has an idea for a new routine for you. She will be calling you one of these days. She sends her love.

Talk to you soon.

Trent

"Damn, that's not very enlightening," said Veeva. "Well, perhaps Nick didn't use my aunt's name in his diaries. He might have used a pet name."

"Like what?"

"I don't know. Like Snookums or Twinkle Toes."

"I could call Uma that. She polishes her toenails and sprinkles them with glitter. It's amazing."

"Enough about that small town hick, Noel. Jesus!"

"Uma is not a hick. She's lived most of her life in Mississippi."

"One of our great cosmopolitan centers. OK, search for Saunders instead."

That effort turned up two e-mails from Connie Saunders, both complaining in the bitterest terms about her difficult daughter. Veeva read them with interest, then snarled, "Yeah, well you ain't seen nothing yet, lady. OK, what other words would you find in the diary of a teenage boy? Search for wanking."

"You're the boss," I sighed.

All the standard terms for self-abuse turned up nothing. Nick's elusive diary was not on that computer. It might have been on his laptop, but that machine, we discovered, required a password to access.

"Fuck and double fuck," said Veeva. "Well, we'll just have to give this house a thorough search. Leave no stone unturned!"

We finished in Nick's bedroom just as we heard his BMW pull into the driveway. No diary, but we now knew a great deal about my brother's personal tastes in underwear, ties, cufflinks, cologne, condoms, bedside reading material (mostly *Amusement Business* and *Billboard* magazines), sex lubes, shampoo, men's cosmetics, and shaving apparatus (why does one guy need six electric razors?). And why does he have one white anklet sock matted in a silver frame above his dresser? Oh, and he also takes Rogaine to battle the dreaded Twispian curse of scalp-baring baldness. I'd never heard of the stuff, but Veeva says they sell it by the trainload in L.A.

She kissed me in the hallway, said we'd do the rest of the house tomorrow, and scampered off toward her bedroom. It's 2:08, blog readers. Time for this dude to turn in. Oh, one last note: today is my brother's 30th birthday. The guy's youth is now behind him.

1:15 p.m. Another scorching day. Veeva says Las Vegas is the waiting room to Hell in more ways than one. She roused me from bed at the ungodly hour of 8:30. Didn't even knock. Just barged in and surprised me with my usual morning boner. I was embarrassed, but she says having younger brothers has destroyed any fascination she might have had for the ups and downs of male anatomy. She dragged me out of bed to finish searching the house before Nick woke up. Only the FBI could have given the place a more thorough going-over. No luck at all. I was beginning to think the Journals of Nick Twisp were all a myth.

Nick finally hauled his birthday carcass out of bed, and Veeva volunteered to take us all out to breakfast. No sign of Ada. We went to a local place, which turned out not to take American Express, so my brother ended up paying again. I felt bad because we hadn't even bothered to scrounge up a present for him. I felt worse when he asked us if we were looking for anything in particular in his house or just snooping around. Damn, and I thought we'd been pretty careful to return everything just as we found it.

Veeva smiled and turned on the charm. "We're looking for your diary, Uncle Nick. We want to know all about your eventful past with my aunt Sheeni."

"Did she send you to find it? Is that what she's worried about?"

The guy seemed more than a little paranoid, even if he was turning 30, losing his hair, and breaking up with his girlfriend.

"No way, Uncle Nick. My aunt's never said boo about your diary. We're just curious."

"Well, if she asks, you can tell her I've copied my journal files onto two CDs. One is in my safe deposit drawer in my bank; the other is in the safe of my attorney. Those are the only two copies and there they will stay until my death."

Jesus, his diary must be even spicier and more incriminating than we had supposed. I wonder how hard it is to break into a lawyer's safe?

"You're being awfully secretive about your past, Uncle Nick," Veeva scolded.

"Well, Sheeni also kept a journal during our time together," he replied, still not smiling. "If you're so interested, why don't you bug her to read her account?"

"Thanks for the information," smiled Veeva. "We'll do just that!"

On the way back, Veeva made us stop in a shopping center to buy a cake and candles for our host. She says supermarket bakery cakes are inedible, but we bought one anyway. I wanted chocolate, she preferred carrot, so we went with the latter. I paid this time, as not even I could make my brother buy his own birthday cake. We also got him one of those shiny metallic birthday balloons on a stick. Very festive. I sure hope my 30th birthday is cheerier than his was turning out to be.

5:36 p.m. Kind of a boring afternoon, until Ada arrived with the moving van. Veeva said it wasn't a surprise that all the passable furnishings got carted off by her. Personally, I think it was a little cruel of Ada to move out on her ex-boyfriend's birthday—even if he was two-timing her with some Czech bimbo. Nick holed up in his office and worked on his computer while the movers were here. After they left, Veeva and I went swimming in Nick's pool, but it really was too hot to stay outside even in the shade. Winnemucca may suck, but it rarely gets this absurdly hot.

Nick just phoned out for pizza. We're going to have an early dinner, blow out the candles, then my brother is meeting some friends to "get very drunk." Nope, we're not invited, though he said we were free to watch anything on TV from his DVD collection. Perhaps we can find something R-rated starring that sexy beast Brandon De Wilde.

11:47 p.m. A momentous night. We never did get around to watching a movie. Instead Veeva wanted to talk about my brother. We spun a couple of his Frank Sinatra platters (to use the terminology of the era), and I scarfed down two more pieces of birthday cake. Interestingly, although we bought the cake that Veeva preferred, she didn't actually deign to eat any. Veeva nibbled a celery stick and commented that Nick being such a Frank Sinatra fan proved that he was a romantic at heart.

"Sounds pretty square to me," I replied. "Are you sure this record is playing at the correct speed?"

"Relax, Noel, it's a slow tempo ballad. You know in his day Frank was considered very cool and hip—a real trendsetter."

"When was that? 1812?"

"Just shut up and listen. OK, I've worked out a possible scenario. Nick and Sheeni fall in love, they have sex but the condom breaks or slips off or something. No birth control method is absolutely reliable. So they decide to run away to France, which Sheeni loved even back then. Of course, they have no money, but they hear about this rich lawyer in Ukiah. Nick robs him, but the gun goes off and the lawyer gets perforated. Now they really have to beat it, so they catch the next plane to France."

"I guess that makes sense, Veeva. So what happens next? Why did they break up?"

"Well, you notice how hostile Nick is when he talks about Sheeni? Your brother is still very bitter. They must have had a fight and maybe she ditched him. It could be that Nick didn't want her to get the abortion."

"I don't know, my brother doesn't seem very big on kids."

"That's true, and my aunt loves my little cousins to bits. Perhaps it was Nick who was championing the abortion."

"Yeah, according to my mother, he wasn't too thrilled to hear she was going to have me. He wanted her to get rid of me too."

Yup, if Nick had any clout, I'd have been a bit of ectoplasm in the vacuum at Planned Parenthood. A close call for me.

"That's only natural, Noel. Siblings are very competitive. I might be a much nicer person today if my brothers hadn't come along."

"I think you're pretty nice."

"Then kiss me, dummy. Why do you suppose we're listening to this music?"

So we kissed a long time while Frank crooned away about love and loneliness and longing and despair. Somewhat inconvenient for making out, though, because you have to get up every 20 minutes to flip the record over. And by then some of us were impaired by throbbing erections. Still, I suppose it was an improvement over the days when you had to stop every three minutes to wind the Victrola and change the needle.

On the third album Veeva dropped her bombshell.

"I think now is the time," she announced. "We should do it."

My heart stopped beating for a nearly a minute.

"You think we should?" I said at last. "I hear it's not so good when two virgins go at it."

"Don't be ridiculous, Noel. It's *always* good for the guy. It's usually unpleasant for the girl, but fortunately for you I'm a realist and have zero expectations. Now go upstairs and grab a couple of your brother's condoms."

"Should I get the lube too?"

"I hardly think that will be necessary. But get a couple of bath towels. We don't want to mess up his ugly sofa."

"We could do it in a bed."

"Nah, I like the ambiance we've got going here. Just hurry before I chicken out."

And so we did it right there on the sofa while Frank sang about being miserable at three o'clock in the morning. Veeva took off all of her clothes. Quite amazing. The first time I had seen a chick stark naked. Very nice breasts and lots of smooth white skin. Blondish pubic hair pruned fashionably short for easy access. Pretty soon I had the condom on and she was guiding me to the spot. A bit of resistance, but suddenly I was sliding all the way inside. Without thinking about it I knew to start gliding in and out. Veeva moaned and said not to stop. Well, even encased in latex, my wang was having a hell of a grand time, but I wasn't prepared for how great the rest of it felt too—her breasts against my chest, her arms around me, her lips softly kissing mine. No way I could stop that runaway freight train. I gushed several gallons into the condom, withdrew, and suggested we take a brief breather.

"That was a lot easier than I expected, Noel. I think it's good that you're not that large."

Not exactly music to a guy's ears, but I managed to get hard again soon. I slipped on the other condom and returned to that magical fairyland of silky warmth and delicious friction. This time we went at it for quite a while—the rubber helped. I don't really see how guys could last for more than two seconds going in there bareback. We got a coordinated rhythm going that didn't stop when the record ended. The last part we did while the needle went round and round in the groove. I came again in another wrenching explosion, then Veeva showed me how to stroke her clitoris lightly with the tip of my finger until this activity yielded some prolonged seismic shocks. After that we put our clothes back on and indulged in leisurely kisses while Frank sang away.

Veeva said we would remember this night for the rest of our lives.

"I'm glad my first time wasn't horrible and I did it with a Twisp—just like my aunt Sheeni. And in Nick's house too. That's special."

"And even with his own condoms," I pointed out. "I hope they're not the same ill-fated brand he was using with Sheeni."

"Don't get me paranoid, Noel. I am *not* getting pregnant."

"Glad to hear it."

I wanted to sleep with Veeva in her room, but she said it would be too tempting, and we didn't dare borrow any more condoms from Nick's stash. Our having sex was a development she didn't want getting back to her mother, as she would kill her for sure. So we kissed in the hallway, whispered "I love you," and retreated to our separate bedrooms.

No sign of my brother yet. Quite the night. He turned 30 and I lost my virginity. Wow, I still can't believe it. I feel different though. Maybe more mature or something.

TUESDAY, August 2 — Hurtling north through the Nevada desert. That sounds more interesting than saying I'm on the bus back to Winnemucca. Veeva found temptation hard to resist, and sneaked into my room early this morning. Her robe she left on the rug beside my bed. We necked and fondled to a frenzied pitch, then took turns trying out oral sex. I went first. Rather aromatic, but nice. Her item is easier to feel with your tongue than your finger. Quite a tiny thing to be so packed with nerves. I like that for this task you can get very close to your work; the pussy at that distance is quite a marvelous thing to behold. Veeva seemed to be enjoying my efforts and soon was flopping about like one of ol' Mr. Tuelco's rainbow trout, fresh from the mountain stream. Then she did me. Amazing to feel someone's warm mouth engulfing you, and their tongue swirling around your tip and down just a bit into your opening. Veeva seemed a little grossed out when I came, but as they lecture us in school: a person's actions have consequences. She swallowed most of it, which may have violated her principles. Those little guys never walked, but I imagine they were swimming like mad.

No sign of my brother's Beemer, but he came wandering out of his bedroom around 10:00 looking much the worse for wear. He was delivered here sometime last night by cab. I made him some breakfast and he gradually revived. He didn't seem so depressed now that his birthday was over and Ada had moved out. Pretty soon we were yucking it up over family history, such as the time he tried changing my diaper as a baby and I wiggled loose.

"The loudest crack I ever heard," Nick declared, "was that poor kid's head hitting the floor."

"Well, that explains a lot," said Veeva. "I was wondering about Noel."

"At least I have an excuse," I retorted. "Your impairments are purely genetic."

We also got my brother to divulge that he and Sheeni had tied the knot in a place called Yazoo City, Mississippi. Nick lied about his age and used a fake I.D., which is why (he claims) the marriage didn't count. Hell, for all he knows, he might still be legally married to Veeva's aunt, her French spouse notwithstanding. I like that Nick got married in Mississippi, former home of my own dear love. Perhaps we can get hitched there too. I must research Mississippi marriage laws; they seem promisingly lax.

Eventually, Nick phoned his assistant Derek, who arrived to take us to the airport and bus station before going on to locate his boss's car. I gave my brother an actual hug, and he slipped me a $100 bill. I guess, all in all, it's a good thing having a brother. Interestingly, Nick never says "good-bye." That's considered bad luck in his profession. Instead he said, "See you down the road, kid."

In Derek's car Veeva and I didn't say much, since little personal assistants can have big ears. She did whisper she had some news which she would tell me about later. God, I hope she hasn't figured out already that's she's pregnant.

Damn! I can't remember what the hell we did with those used condoms!

4:15 p.m. Still on the road. The foam died long ago in these seats, something most of the lard butts on this bus may not have noticed, but my skinny ass is whimpering in agony. To distract myself I've been thinking about Uma. I realize now it's possible to have wild sex with one chick while remaining loyal in your heart to another. In fact, I feel I love Uma even more now that I've had a foretaste of our future lovemaking. Somehow I have to convey to her the good news that I am now experienced sexually (what she seeks in a first-time partner) without giving her the impression that I cheated on her. This will take some finagling. I don't feel she should mind my practicing with someone else in order to bring improved skills to bear on her.

All this sounded perfectly logical until I asked myself whether I'd mind if Uma practiced similarly on say Sloan Chandler. I found this wouldn't bother me as long as I got to strangle Sloan later with my bare hands. There's a logical explanation for this dichotomy: Guys can have sex impersonally, but it's always more significant for chicks because they are accepting another person inside them. Therefore that deed can never be shrugged off by the wronged boyfriend (me, for example). Chicks, though, may not perceive the crystalline clarity of this reasoning. For example, I notice Ada wasn't hanging around long after Nick cheated on her. She also expressed a desire to work in his mouth with sharp instruments—and probably without anesthetic.

The other troubling aspect of my present situation is I really like Veeva and would very much like to get it on with her again. I do love that girl—just not the same way that I love Uma. It appears that three generations of our families have been going at it. Clearly, we have a well-demonstrated sexual affinity. Let's face it: you can't fight destiny when it's that strong.

Of course, I can't delude myself either. If things had worked out as Veeva had planned, it would have been Tyler she was putting the moves on in Nick's house and not me. I wonder if he could have upheld his chastity vow with Veeva clamoring to do it? Fortunately, the Fates intervened, and thanks to the manly sport of football I now have a sex life.

9:27 p.m. It's always hard to come back to this trailer after one has been some place nice. I think this is why most trailer residents never go anywhere except (as is frequently the case) to jail. Grandma was happy to see me, though she reported that my employer was shocked and appalled to hear I'd left town again. Hey, aren't people allowed to have personal lives?

I called my darling and found her camping for the night at Mary Glasgow's. Already new toenail adornments have been experimented with. Why is it that chicks can have sleep-overs, but if guys try it, everyone assumes they're testing for the re-make of *Brokeback Mountain*? We chatted for a bit, and she agreed to swing by tomorrow for Bingo Night.

I got some interesting e-mails. First, I received an angry one from Awanee informing me that she was breaking up with me. She felt that I was distant and indifferent, and she thought Toby was blatantly racist. Probably correct on all three counts. I re-plied that I would always cherish our times together—brief as they were, and that she could keep the ring. The addendum I tacked on to mess with her head.

I also got this e-mail from Veeva, which I'm pasting here in its entirety:

> Hi, Noel Sweetie!!
>
> I've been calling you ALL day!! Why don't you AN-SWER?! Did you FORGET to turn on your cell phone?!! [Veeva likes to shout in her e-mails. She's also appar-ently unfamiliar with the geography of central Nevada. The few towns along Route 95 have about 12 people each; nobody's investing big bucks to install cellular tow-ers out there.] I had an AMAZING time with you. You are such a NEAT person. Btw, I know how you guys like to BRAG about your CONQUESTS. If possible, though, could you not BLAB to Tyler about us? I would

REALLY appreciate it!!! [Actually, guys don't brag about these things; they merely swap information just as chicks do. But I suppose I can consider her request.]

Another slight NITPICK: You left the used items and torn WRAPPERS right by Nick's sofa. Not very BRIGHT!! Fortunately, I found them and DISPOSED of them in time. I also made a GREAT DISCOVERY!!! While putting away the records, I found a LETTER from SHEENI to NICK in one of the album covers. It was in a Frank Sinatra album titled "My One and Only Love." Get it???? My ONE and ONLY Love!!! Nick still LOVES Sheeni!!! That is why his LIFE is on HOLD!!! [Or the letter might just have slipped in there by mistake. If he loves only Sheeni, why is he now throwing himself at Reina?] In the letter Sheeni apologizes for DITCHING Nick!!! It appears she left him WITHOUT A WORD!!! Also, she mentions falling in love with a CLOWN named Alfredo Nunez and hiding out with his brother's family in southern France. I found out something INTERESTING about that clown!!! [Could it be the same clown that Reina was married to? That would be getting too incestuous.] We MUST discuss this!!! Please CALL me A.S.A.P.!!!!
LOVE you!!!
Veeva

Is that girl intense or what? No wonder she's such a firecracker in the sack. I gave her a call, and of course her LINE was BUSY!!! Uh-oh, now she's got me doing it.

11:14 p.m. Finally got through to Veeva. She explained she had been discussing her weekend with her girlfriend Maddy. More likely bragging about her conquest, but I let that one pass.

"So what's this about some clown?" I asked.

"I found a picture of him on the Web, Noel. Guess what?"

"What?"

"Alfredo Nunez is a dwarf!"

"Oh, really? You mean Sheeni ditched my brother for a dwarf?"

Another blow to the tattered Twispian ego.

"Apparently so, Noel. Now, here's where it gets interesting. While I was staying with my aunt in Lyon, François warned me not to go down in their cellar because he had some valuable wines stored there."

"Who's François?"

"Aunt Sheeni's husband, of course. The guy is totally devastating. Well, I had no interest in their damn cellar until he told me to keep out of it."

"So naturally you had to explore it."

"Naturally, I did, though I wasn't interested in his dusty old wine bottles. But I found this storage room with a bunch of old piled-up boxes and trunks."

"Which you snooped through."

"Did I ever. It was most interesting. Well, I uncovered an ancient French-language typewriter. In a battered old case. And do you know what I discovered in a pocket of that case?"

"Alfredo Nunez the dwarf?"

"No, idiot. I found a photo. A most curious photo."

"OK, so tell me."

"It was the photograph of a dwarf in a green suit holding a little baby."

"Do you think it was Alfredo?"

"Well, it's been a couple of years, but I'm almost positive it's the same guy. He's very dark, but the baby was light-skinned and blond. It looked like a little girl."

"So what are you saying?"

"Sheeni didn't have an abortion, Noel."

"Really? You think not?"

"I'm almost sure of it. You have a niece and I have a cousin—somewhere—that we didn't even know about."

"Wow, that's amazing. That means my brother might have a daughter around our age."

"That's right, Noel. And I don't think he's even aware of her existence. This explains a lot."

"Like what?"

"Like why my aunt is so secretive about her past. I'll bet François doesn't know about her first child either."

"You think not?"

"I doubt it. French men are very charming, but they can be pretty traditional in their attitudes."

"But surely someone in your family must know if Sheeni had the kid."

"Well, perhaps my father, but I doubt it. No one even heard from her until after she was married. She like totally disappeared."

"Weren't your grandparents concerned?"

"My father's parents are a case, Noel. You'd have to meet them to believe them. We hardly ever visit them. They're like these total Bible thumpers up in Ukiah. My dad also disappeared for years when he was young. Sheeni mentions that in her letter, but I knew that already."

"You've got to see if your father knows anything about the kid, Veeva."

"I'll try, Noel, but it won't be easy. Daddy hates talking about his family—not that I blame him."

My brother a father at age 15? The same age as me. Very shocking indeed.

WEDNESDAY, August 3 — No sign of bed-wetting or thumb-sucking for days. And no zits either. More proof of the healing properties of the human touch (in all its tantalizing forms). Has anyone noticed that when a guy gets an erection it rises to the optimal angle for sliding into the receptive vagina? I mean was that well thought out or what? Too bad, though, they didn't give us guys a little more control over our orgasm timing. I hear some lizards can do it for 12 hours, which may explain why no lizard has ever won the Nobel Prize in anything.

It was with a heavy heart that I applied Toby's greasepaint this morning. Why does work have to be such an imposition on one's time and lifestyle? Mr. Dugan was in fine form when I finally showed up. You'd think I was single-handedly trying to bankrupt the guy. He ranted on about how all the jobs were going to China because nobody in this country wanted to work any more. That's funny, I thought the jobs were going over there because China was a police state with no unions, no benefits to pay, no environmental laws, and millions of workers willing to be exploited for 25 cents a hour. It's like every patriotic Republican's dream business climate. I didn't tell him that. I just swallowed meekly and muttered something about visiting my sick brother down south. Then I was off with my signboard in the blazing sun. On my second round Uma called and said to meet her at St. Paul's church at 3:30. Damn, what a guy has to do these days for love.

6:12 p.m. Here is a blow-by-blow account of Toby's first encounter with a holy father in a Catholic confessional:

Toby: Hi, Father, this is Noel, uh Noel Wescott. Bless me for I have, uh, sinned. It's been, uh, six months or so since my last confession.

Priest: Aren't you the boy whose picture was in the paper?

Toby: Uh, right. That's me.

Priest: I don't recall your being a member of this parish.

Toby: Uh, yeah well, we usually sit in a rear pew. Like way in the back.

Priest: You know your employer is not really a minister. He has no theological training. He used to be a mortician. The man is a charlatan.

Toby: Oh. Uh, I just carry his signs. Do you want to hear my sins? I've got them all lined up.

Priest: And what is this 'adore ceremony' you people offer?

Toby: Well, it's kind of a marketing deal. You get your candle-lit mood lighting and your organ music and your certificate. The snacks and keepsakes are extra though.

Priest: I'll tell you what it is, young man. It is a bogus sanction for sin—for fornication by the youth of this community. Yours is a vile enterprise that should be stopped.

Toby: Uh, well my guess is a lot of the kids were getting it on even before they got the certificate. Our service is just kind of a going-steady ritual. Mostly the girls like it. But, really I just carry the signs.

Priest: I see. You're just obeying orders.

Toby: Right. Now about my sins . . .

Priest: Where did you receive your catechism and communion?

Toby: Uh, well, I was home sick for a few years. I did it all by mail.

Priest: Very curious indeed. And what are the sacraments of the church?

Toby: The sacraments? Uhmm, I don't think I recall those. Not right off-hand.

Priest: You know, Mr. Wescott, this is a church of God. It is no place to be playing games.

Toby: Uh, maybe I should just go now.

Priest: If you have a sincere interest in the church, I suggest you call the office and make an appointment. Are you involved with a Catholic girl?

Toby: Who me? No, not at all.

Priest: I certainly hope not. You sound like a most unsuitable young man.

Toby: Uh, right. Well, take it easy.

Priest: You get the hell out of here!

Damn, that was brutal. I didn't spill the whole conversation to Uma, but she says we're now in much worse shape than before. She took it as a very bad sign that I wasn't assigned any Hail Marys or Our Fathers to say. For some reason I drew Father Gillis, who normally is in Elko harassing infirm oldsters on Wednesday afternoons. She had anticipated my encountering laid-back Father Sheldrake, a native Nevadan well-steeped in our frontier culture. That priest can be relied upon to keep things in perspective.

The only good news is that Uma and Mary Glasgow have filled out a profile for Aunt Rosa at Match.com. They noted she was a great cook and loved housework, so they are already attracting responses from marriage-minded males. Our only hope is to get her distracted by hunky and pious suitors as soon as possible.

11:22 p.m. An unsettling evening. Uma came over for Bingo Night and took off her shoes for show and tell. Her toenails were now a deep midnight blue covered in a profusion of tiny glow-in-the-dark stars, comets, planets, and moons. Very dramatic with the lights off, which I accomplished without delay. Extreme snuggling then ensued. Eventually, our garments were quite awry as they say in the police reports. I probed for Umanian G-spots, while she familiarized herself with my bare inflamed member.

"What happens when I stroke up and down like this?" she inquired.

"Your popularity goes way up. And how does this feel, darling?"

"Quite stimulating indeed. Oh, my!"

"I know something even better."

I did her with my tongue (as practiced with Veeva), and she went off like the noon fire whistle. Tasted very similar, though her button seemed more pronounced. She wasn't ready for full reciprocation, but did the job manually with very satisfactory results.

"So this sticky stuff is what makes babies. It certainly shoots out with great velocity."

"Yeah, sorry it got in your hair."

"Better there than some places. You're all stiff again, Noel. Shall I do it some more?"

"Sure. If you like."

She did.

"There's less volume this time and it's somewhat runnier," she observed. "All the trouble you went to make it, and it just winds up in a hankie."

"Not to worry, Uma. I've got a bottomless supply."

We did up our zippers, snaps, and buttons, and lay together on our ratty couch. I nuzzled her ear and told her all I had learned in the last few days about my brother and his possible offspring.

"What I can't understand, Noel, is why an intelligent girl like Sheeni agreed to marry him—even if she was pregnant."

"Why shouldn't see marry him? If she loved him?"

"Well, clearly she didn't care that much for him. And she was much too young."

"She was 15—that's not so young. Lots of people get married when they're 15."

"Like who, for instance?"

"Well, like various country and western singers. And millions of people in places like India and China."

"That's because women are oppressed in those cultures."

"I'd like to marry you, Uma."

"That's sweet, Noel. But aren't you confusing lust with love?"

"I don't think so. The sex part is nice, but it's you who I love. My brother fell in love with Sheeni when he was 14 and according to Veeva he's still stuck on her all these years later. She says his whole life has been on hold because of her. It's not just lust with us Twisps."

"Then, Noel honey, I'm going to do you a favor—a big favor."

"What's that, darling?"

"I'm not going to see you again."

"What!!!"

Nope. No further explanations. Uma got up off the couch, put on her socks, shoes, and bike helmet, and pedaled off into the darkness.

I can only assume this is some kind of joke. Not very funny though.

THURSDAY, August 4 — A miserable night. I called Uma around midnight in a panic, but her aunt Rosa answered. She said Uma did not wish to speak to me. She also said she'd had a disturbing conversation about me with Father Gillis, and that I was not to call their home ever again.

Damn! What did I do? What did I say?

Grandma dropped a bundle on her diabetes supplies and was having trouble making this month's rent. So I donated Nick's crisp $100 bill to the cause. She said she'd accept it as a loan, but I told her she didn't have to pay me back. A guy doesn't need any spending money to lie around a trailer in a state of acute emotional paralysis.

Stoney dropped by while I was staring suicidally at my cereal bowl. I hardly recognized her. She had a flattering new hairdo, was nicely made up with lipstick and all the trimmings, was wearing a neat new blouse and skirt, and had installed attractive gold earrings completely devoid of skulls, snakes, or Harley insignias.

"Something wrong with those cornflakes?" she asked. "They're getting awfully soggy."

"I'm not hungry."

"Hit another speed bump with your bitch goddess?"

"If you're referring to Uma, she appears to have dumped me."

"Shit! I knew that was coming."

"Why, Stoney?"

"You forget, dude. Sloan Chandler returns today."

"Oh, right."

"Face it, Noel. You were just a mid-summer fill-in for that bitch."

"You think so, Stoney?"

"It's obvious. But what that slut doesn't realize is she's got some competition now. How do I look?"

"Amazingly feminine, Stoney. I hardly recognized you. How does it feel to wear a skirt?"

"Nice ventilation in hot weather, but I feel a little vulnerable. I mean if you're not careful when you sit down anyone can get a clear shot at your beaver. Guess what color panties I got on today?"

"Virginal white?"

"Pink! Can you believe that? My mom's in seventh heaven, the bitch. Heard about Jamal?"

"Who?"

"Jamal Bogy, our fellow gang member. He's black like you. Likes to autograph every tree and wall in town."

"What's he done now?"

"He disappeared. Gone. Kaput."

"When?"

"Saturday. His foster parents are major pissed. They drove to Reno and found that black woman he'd been talking to. She claims she hadn't seen him."

"Did they tell her that Jamal was white?"

"They mentioned that detail. And also that he was only 15. She promised to call them if he turned up. You heard from him?"

"Not a word. 'Course I was in Vegas."

"How was that?"

"Nice. Can you keep a secret?"

"Sure."

"I got laid."

"You lie!"

"No, honest. It's true. I crossed the great divide."

"You did! Who with?"

"Veeva. But you can't tell anyone! Especially Tyler."

"You got some ass, dude! So how come you're sitting here all miserable?"

"I don't know. It was nice, but I'm still stuck on Uma."

"That'll pass. I thought that Veeva chick was 14."

"Well, she's a very mature 14."

"You popped her cherry?"

"Uh-huh."

"How'd she take it?"

"Great. She liked it."

"She just say that, or did she really mean it?"

"No, Stoney, she had a good time. She wasn't faking it. So you might like it too—if you get it on with Sloan."

"Well, that's good news. You didn't get any off Uma, huh?"

"No, but we'd made quite a bit of progress. She was very loving—right up until she walked out the door."

"Chicks are weird, dude. Take it from me. I am one, and I'm always amazing myself with the shit I pull. I think it's the hormones. Turn your head."

"Why?"

"I got to scratch my pussy. It's really hard in a goddam skirt."

I turned my head and she scratched away. Yes, there's more to being feminine than just changing your wardrobe.

6:18 p.m. Somehow I got up the energy to Tobify myself and slunk off to work. I tried to see Uma on one of my rounds, but fat Marvin intercepted me and said I was officially banned from the casino property. He then hustled Toby bodily out the door, bending one of my signs in the process. Of course, he is going to pay dearly for that assault. Toby is back to sniffling through weddings, being even more acutely aware now that my own has been indefinitely postponed. One bride today reminded me of an older and less pretty Uma. She was marrying a total slob of a guy in a flashy polyester suit and bad hairpiece. I couldn't imagine how she would want to crawl into bed with that creep, let alone sleep with him for the rest of her unnatural life. Stoney's so right. Chicks are weird.

Veeva phoned while Toby was shuffling along Main Street. She didn't seem wildly sympathetic when I told her about Uma, but then I suppose she regards her as the competition. She reported that she had approached her father about possible mystery cousins.

"What did he say, Veeva?"

"He said any questions I had about Aunt Sheeni should be addressed to Aunt Sheeni."

"Are you taking that as an affirmative?"

"I don't know, Noel. Possibly. Daddy can put on such a poker face when he tries. I think it's from all those years of living with my mother. She can be so intrusive."

"Are you going to ask your aunt?"

"I've already sent her a very delicately phrased e-mail. We'll see how she responds. You know that Reina person?"

"My brother's old flame? Yeah."

"Well, I mentioned her to my father, and he was most interested to hear she was coming to visit Nick. I think he may have known her ages ago."

"It's a small world, I guess."

"God, Noel, you sound so depressed!"

"Mere depression would be a great improvement."

"Shall I come there to cheer you up?"

"Will you?!"

"I wish. My horrible mother has confiscated my American Express card for one entire week. How's a person supposed to function? Daddy's a bit pissed at you too."

"Why? You didn't tell him about us, did you?"

"Of course not, silly. Parents can be so unreasonable about their children's sex lives. No doubt because their own is so unsatisfactory. My father's rather intuitive though. He may suspect something is going on. And your Pickled Punks shot him down."

"What?"

"Yeah, he went and talked to them about a recording deal, but they said he was too small-potatoes for them."

"Really?"

"Typical L.A. attitude. Even the obscure garage bands have delusions of grandeur."

"The Pickled Punks are no garage band."

"Yeah, well, they're not exactly the Rolling Stones either!"

On his last round of the afternoon Toby had to duck into an alley when Sloan Chandler himself passed by. I don't think he saw me. Sloan was looking very tanned and tremendously fit, like he'd been tugging on heavy anchor chains all summer. My guess is he grew an inch or two as well, and his light brown hair was now tinged with golden highlights, possibly from the tropical sun (or so he would have us believe). In other words, he had not been shanghaied by pirates, maimed by a shark, ravaged by dysentery, cut to pieces on a coral reef, or brutally assaulted in some dockside saloon. What's worse, the twit was strolling in the direction of the Silver Sluice with a large bouquet of mixed roses in his manly hand. It was all I could do to restrain Toby from emptying a can of dog repellent in his steely blue eyes.

10:36 p.m. No call yet from Uma saying it was all a big misunderstanding. Grandma made me eat some dinner, then I got on my bike and cruised around Uma's neighborhood. No sign of her, but I did see her vile aunt leaving in a car driven by some bald guy. They were both dressed to the nines. Could Uma have lined up a date for her already? I hope the guy turns out to be a notorious Protestant rapist wanted in 29 states, though he looked more like a salesman driving his bland company car.

I hope Nick didn't feel this bad when Sheeni cut out on him. God, perhaps I should take up juggling to get through these interminable black hours.

FRIDAY, August 5 — Still in blackest despair, but at least my bladder is behaving itself. No obvious signs of overnight thumb sucking either. I'm not making any wild claims though, since I've been wrong so many times before. I got an e-mail from Awanee indignantly denying that I had ever given her a ring. I replied that I had slipped my grandmother's heirloom platinum ring into the pocket of her shorts as a surprise, and that I hoped she'd find it soon since it was appraised last year for over $18,000 as the three antique pear-shaped diamonds were of a quality virtually unobtainable these days. I added if she didn't find it, we'd both be in big trouble when my grandmother discovers it missing from her jewelry box. I'm not sure exactly why I wrote that, except Awanee seems rather gullible and perhaps I feel the need to spread some of my misery around. Besides, that chick had her nerve trying to dump me.

Toby shuffled past the Silver Sluice casino six times today, and at no time did Uma come rushing out to apologize for summarily ditching me. Yet each time as I approached the building a small flame of hopeful expectation flickered in my heart. So much for the eternal optimism of youth.

8:12 p.m. To cheer me up Grandma made my favorite meal for dinner: broiled pork chops. She left them under the propane flame until they were black and cinder-like all the way through—just the way I like them. I also like my toast severely burnt, which the timid cooks in restaurants rarely seem to understand—though I frequently send it back. Now my heart also is broiled to a crisp, which seems somehow appropriate.

At least there was something diverting on TV tonight. Some nutcase in Sacramento swiped a hearse that was idling in the driveway of a funeral home, and has now been chased halfway down the state on live TV. The Highway Patrol hasn't tried to stop it, because they don't want to risk having it crash and the governor's deceased mother (the stiff in the back) getting accidentally cremated on the I-5 freeway. The news guys reporting the chase say it's the biggest highway story since a confused O.J. Simpson tooled around L.A. in his white Bronco while holding a gun to his head. They've been speculating that the driver may be headed to Mexico since the hearse has two gas tanks and is capable of at least 700 miles. I hope the guy makes it and, while he's at it, swings by here to pick me up.

9:37 p.m. Driven to desperate measures, I called Mary Glasgow to see if she had any news about Uma. She didn't want to talk long because she said she was watching something interesting on TV and I was "a horrible filthy beast."

"Why do you say that?" I asked. "What did I do?"

"You know what you did, Noel Wescott. And Uma is perfectly miserable. I hope you're satisfied!"

She then hung up on me. Very confusing, but it was interesting to hear that Uma was suffering too. All this time I'd been imagining her engaged in unspeakable acts with Sloan Chandler.

11:28 p.m. The guy made it all the way to Anaheim before ditching the hearse in the parking lot of Disneyland. They're searching for him now with police dogs and helicopters equipped with infrared cameras. Half the cops in L.A. are on the scene, but so are a couple thousand park-goers wanting to get home. It's a real madhouse. Naturally, all the bystanders they've been interviewing are saying they hope the guy gets away. More proof that civilization is just a thin veneer over our wild and crazed human species.

It's a jungle out there, says Grandma.

She may be right. I hope so at any rate.

SATURDAY, August 6 — Stoney Holt dropped by early this morning with some amazing news. She burst right into my bedroom and had a good laugh at my morning boner pronging up under my thin blanket. Pure penis envy if you ask me.

She reported that the cops took some fresh prints off the hearse interior and have tentatively identified the escaped hijacker as a teen runaway from rural Nevada named Carlyle Bogy. The only point they're a bit confused over is that the hijacker was black, while young Carlyle is alleged to be white.

"Oh my God!" I exclaimed. "That's incredible! How did Carlyle get to Sacramento?"

"Who knows?" she replied, sitting on my bed, then jumping back up.

"Relax, Stoney. I didn't wet it."

"You swear?"

"I swear."

She gingerly sat back down.

"Here's another interesting fact, Noel. While barreling down the freeway at 90 miles an hour, Jamal took the time to spray UPT all over the dashboard and headliner."

"He didn't!"

"Yup. He even managed to mark up part of the casket. They're lucky he didn't rape the stiff while he was at it."

"Oh, damn! I didn't even know that idiot could drive."

"Yeah, well according to the radio, Jamal stole his first car at the age of seven when they were living in Idaho. It's still a record for that state."

"Come to think of it, Stoney, I remember back in grade school his bragging about something like that, but I always assumed he was making it up."

"Yeah, me too. Guess he showed us."

WEDNESDAY, August 10 — (Written in the abandoned hippie bus at the end of my road.) Sorry, blog readers, if you're wondering what happened to the previous three days, I've been in the custody of the Winnemucca Police and Humboldt County Sheriff's Department. I was locked up in juvenile hall along with some of my rather scary peers. Today I was released into Grandma's custody, but I have a court hearing scheduled next week.

The cops arrived on Saturday with a search warrant and found my stash of spray paint with Jamal's fingerprints all over the cans. They also seized Toby's mocha greasepaint and nappy wig. Plus, my cell phone, my computer, and all its peripherals. Fortunately, they missed my $5 laptop which I had left in plain sight on the back seat of Grandma's Honda. No e-mail now, though, since my laptop lacks a modem. Anyway, the cops now regard me as a fellow gang conspirator. They raided Stoney's house too, but she had wisely ditched her paint cans in the Humboldt River. Too bad she hadn't thought to alert me to do the same. The truth is, I'd forgotten all about them, since as I've stated here previously I'm not a big fan of graffiti. As if the cops believed that statement!

Grandma called my brother, who's agreed to help out with my legal expenses. Unfortunately, he had to hear about this mess on the day that Reina arrived from Prague. He's probably ready to disown me now.

The good news is I don't have to dress up like Toby any more. After all the inflammatory (and wildly inaccurate) stories in the newspaper and on TV, Mr. Dugan phoned Grandma to inform her that I was canned. Apparently deciding it's unwise to trust anyone except family, he's given the job back to Rot— assuming they can find him another wig. Good riddance, I say, though I could use the money and it's unlikely anyone else in town will hire a notorious gang member.

No, they haven't caught Jamal yet, though the cops are convinced that I know exactly where he is. These people seem to have maddeningly one-track minds. Of course, they're under big pressure from the authorities in California, who are pissed off that their governor got embarrassed on TV by some puny 15-year-old kid. The idiot TV news people keep referring to Jamal as the "Uptight Hearse Hijacker." Don't they realize that UPT stands for the Uptowners gang? Jamal is many things, but uptight is not one of them.

Now I wish I'd been a bit more circumspect in my blog. Fortunately, I'd protected my computer with a security program I downloaded off the Web that's supposed to be hacker-proof. No way the cops are going to make me cough up that password. I'm familiar with the Bill of Rights and a citizen's protections against self-incrimination. Not that the sheriff's officers impressed me as being particularly computer savvy. Their booking software, I noticed, seemed so poorly executed as to be laughable. I suggested I might be able to improve it, but they told me to "just worry about my future if I don't help them find Carlyle Bogy." Very, very one-track minds. I'm thankful, at least, that my blog was only on my hard drive and no longer splashed publicly across the Internet. Still, I'm not taking any more chances. My laptop I intend to conceal here in the bus until everything blows over or I'm incarcerated.

I wet the bed nightly in juvenile hall, sparking great derision from my fellow inmates. The food was terrible, the communal shower room was a nightmare, and the only activities to pass the time were watching TV (tuned to the dumbest, most violent programs) and playing basketball. Not my favorite sport, and the inmates there play that game like it's rugby with a bigger ball. I'm praying the judge gives me probation as not even gambling-rich Nevada can afford my hit on their prison laundry budget.

No word from dearest Uma, who I last saw and held in my arms one week ago tonight. My darling probably considers herself well rid of me now.

It's all very confusing. I am now a criminal with an arrest record, although I'm not at all sure what exactly I did wrong.

THURSDAY, August 11 — Grandma's diabetes sugar levels have been very high the past few days. She hasn't said so, but I suppose it's from all the stress induced by you know what. It didn't help that her son has been calling and screaming that she should "throw that bum out on his ass." He must not have liked my Father's Day card. It has occurred to me that since Uma doesn't want me and I might be going to jail soon, I have no compelling reason to go on living. It's too bad that all the means of suicide I can think of are so scary. I'm such a coward when it comes to cutting myself, jumping off an Interstate overpass, or even suffocating myself in my own bed under a plastic bag. I'm amazed that people can work up the nerve to do such things. They must be in even worse shape than I am—if that's somehow possible.

6:47 p.m. More bad news. Sheriff's Detective Lloyd Moroni dropped by this afternoon to put the screws to me some more. Thankfully Grandma was up at the clinic getting her blood checked. He has a daughter in my class named Ruth Ann, who I once had a crush on for about five minutes. I think I was just feeling sorry for her because everyone called her Rough And Moronic. Her dad sat on the sofa, removed some papers from his briefcase, and got down to business.

"OK, Noel, you know some girl named Veeva Saunders?"

"Uh, I don't think so."

"Well, that's interesting because she's left four messages for you on your cell phone."

"Oh, right. Veeva lives in L.A. She doesn't know Carlyle."

"So you say. Of course, that's the area where Carlyle was last seen."

"She has nothing to do with him. Carlyle is not the type of person she would be caught dead associating with."

"OK, Noel, you know some girl named Uma Spurletti?"

"Yes, she's, uh, she's a girl in my class." A ray of hope. "Has she been leaving messages for me too?"

"I'll ask the questions, Noel. We sent your computer to Carson City. They peeled your hard drive like an onion. You made some incriminating statements about those two girls, did you not?"

A very unsettling feeling rippled across the base of my scrotum.

"It was all a fantasy! None of it was true!"

"So you say, Noel. But I don't think their parents would enjoy reading it, do you?"

"Uh, no. I guess not."

"Right. They wouldn't. So why don't you tell me where Carlyle is?"

"Believe me, I would tell you if I knew."

"I've dealt with you gang types before, Noel. I know you think it's a macho thing sticking up for your homies, but how would you like to go back to Vegas to answer a charge of statutory rape?"

I totally lost it then. Wailing, shrieking, the works. I think even Detective Moroni was taken aback. He got me some Kleenex from the bathroom and told me to pull myself together.

"If you read my blog," I sobbed, "then you know I had nothing to do with Carlyle stealing that hearse."

"I thought you said it was all a fantasy? You can't have it both ways, Noel."

"All I can tell you is Carlyle really wants to be black. If he's anywhere in L.A., it would be in some black neighborhood. He would probably be going by the name of Jamal."

"Yeah, well we got that much from his foster parents. You need to tell me something I don't know, Noel."

I wracked my brain and finally thought of something.

"The body of his father's murdered partner! Carlyle told me they ditched it up in Bluebird Canyon."

"What? I'm not interested in the whereabouts of some deceased lowlife, Noel. You think about it, kid. You produce some useful information on Carlyle, or I talk to Mr. Saunders and Mr. Spurletti. They might not be as nice to you as I'm being."

If there's a color worse than the bleakest black, that is where my life has now sunk to.

FRIDAY, August 12 — Some disturbing phone calls last night. The first was from my sister Joanie in L.A. The cops had just hauled away Tyler for questioning, and she was going off the deep end. She said if her son got in trouble with the law, he wouldn't be able to play high-school sports, wouldn't get an athletic scholarship to USC (his intended college), wouldn't go on to have a highly lucrative career in the pros, and would wind up a Skid Row failure like our father. All because of my pernicious influence. I told her Tyler wasn't in very deep, and she should just relax and not worry. Then she called me some very unsisterly names and hung up. So much for that precious fraternal butterfly about to take wing.

While I was still shaking from that call, Veeva phoned demanding to know why I hadn't returned any of her calls. I explained my many reasons and inquired why she hadn't thought to call on our land line sooner as we were in the book.

"Not being stupid, I thought of that, Noel, but I couldn't remember your damn last name. I just think of you as a Twisp. Finally, I called Tyler and got your phone number from his mom. She's rather hysterical you know."

"I know. The cops got Tyler for being in our gang."

"Two rather cute and young L.A.P.D. officers were just here asking me about your idiot pal. I don't know why they imagine

I'd be clued in on your Glocca Morra criminal associates."

"That's Winnemucca, Veeva."

"Whatever. I didn't even know you guys were in a gang with that hearse hijacker. It came as a complete shock to me."

"Well, it's not much of a gang."

"No, you're just splashed across the front page of every newspaper in the state. Fortunately, everything's in a big uproar here. My mother hardly noticed the cops."

"What's going on?"

"My parents had a monster fight. Daddy said he had to go to Vegas on business, but my mother accused him of wanting to see Nick's Czech girlfriend."

"What did he say?"

"I'm not sure. Daddy tends to mumble during fights, and it's hard to hear him over Mother's screaming."

"Did he go?"

"Oh, he went. Last night. My mother's been totally insane ever since. She was so distracted, I got her to give me my credit card back early."

"Damn, Veeva, your father and my brother might be stuck on the same woman."

"I know. It's all very unsettling. I'm feeling almost as jealous as Mother."

"You're such a daddy's girl, Veeva."

"Well, that's no secret. That's why it's such a positive step that I did it with you. Speaking of sleeping with Twisps, I heard back from Aunt Sheeni."

"About her kid? What did she say?"

"She said and I quote: 'You must have been watching too much American TV.' How's that for a copout?"

"Yeah, Veeva, if it wasn't true, you'd think she'd be denying it more vigorously than that."

"Exactly my feeling, Noel. Now tell me all about jail!"

We discussed my prison experiences, declared our mutual regard, and promised to keep in touch. I didn't tell her about the cops finding my blog and threatening to expose our affair. There's no point in everyone in the Saunders' household coming unglued. And I want to keep Veeva on my side as long as possible. A guy needs at least one friend in his life.

5:12 p.m. Despite the scorching weather, I had to get away. Grandma packed me a bag lunch and I took a long bike ride out of town. One good thing about Winnemucca, you don't have to travel far to find Total Solitude.

If you take the time to look closely, I suppose the landscape is not as desolate as it seems. I ate my lunch beside a dried-up stream. The best way to end it, I decided, would be to hike far out of town with a small collapsible shovel, find a tall sand bank, and tunnel into it until it caves in on top of you. It would all be over in a few minutes, and chances are nobody would ever find you. You'd just disappear. In a few thousand years the sand bank might wash away, and some future Future Civilization would discover your bones and speculate about your demise. Probably they'd never suspect you were escaping a rape charge and a love affair that went bad. If I copied my blog onto a CD and stuck it in my pocket, do you suppose they'd be able to read it in 5009? Most likely it would be way too obsolete by then.

SATURDAY, August 13 — The phone rang in the middle of the night. It was Jamal Bogy himself. All in all, the fugitive seemed pretty cheerful.

"Jesus, Jamal, why'd you steal that hearse?"

"Shit, Noel, you ever tried hitchhikin' as a black dude? Man, you could grow old and die waitin' for a ride."

"What were you doing in Sacramento?"

"Well, bro', first I hitched to Reno 'cause you weren't givin' me no bus money."

"You saw Rashilla?"

"Yeah, man. It didn't work out with that bitch. I didn't tell her I was white, but she didn't tell me she was fat. So I figured I'd come that far, hell, I might as well go to Disneyland."

"Yeah, well, you chose an odd way to get there."

"You watch me on TV, dude? Man, that was a blast haulin' down the road with all those 'copters chasin' my ass. That Cadillac had some balls! I mean it could go! I gots to get me one of those cars!"

"So how'd you escape the cops?"

"Piece of cake, dude. I rolled under some parked car, wiped off my paint, and stuck my afro in my backpack. Then I hooked up with this family, said I got separated from my parents, and they gave me a lift to Pasadena."

"So you're in Pasadena?"

"I was. Man, that's a white-bread town. Got my black ass out of there in a hurry."

From my experience only his underwear was dark, but I didn't contest the point.

"So where are you now?"

"I hooked up with these dudes. They invited me to share their crib."

"Which is where?"

"Damn, Noel, I gots to go. Just checkin' in, bro'. Got to crash now. We're making a big run tomorrow to pick up some reefer."

"A run to where?"

"Hasta la vista, dude!"

Even though it was 3:12 by the clock, I immediately phoned Detective Moroni and told him that Carlyle Bogy might be trying to cross the border into Mexico tomorrow in the company of marijuana smugglers. He thanked me, but said I should never again call him at that hour unless Jesus Christ on a pogo stick had just cruised into the Silver Sluice looking for some action. Damn, how was I supposed to know my information could wait 'til morning? I thought it was a Vital Breakthrough.

11:14 a.m. I've hauled the battery from Grandma's Honda out to the hippie bus to recharge my laptop. I hope she doesn't mind.

A Federal Express truck arrived after breakfast and delivered an overnight package from Veeva. She's lent me her spare cell phone until the cops return mine. Those assholes better not be running up a bunch of charges on my number. I tested out the new phone by checking in with Stoney. Her parents were pissed to hear she'd joined a gang, and she's now totally grounded except for going out on dates with guys.

"Not that Sloan's likely to phone after this scandal," she sighed. "Are you grounded too?"

"No way. Grandma knows I'm innocent."

"You're so lucky not to have real parents, Noel. I'm thinking seriously of murdering mine."

"Don't do anything rash, Stoney. Maybe you should give Sloan a call."

"And say what? Invite him over to view my gang tattoos?"

Sure, it's hard for guys to work up the nerve to ask chicks out. But it's probably harder for girls to wait around hoping the guy they like wakes up to their existence.

4:14 p.m. My emasculated stepfather Lance Wescott just roared into the driveway. Things have gotten very ugly indeed.

SUNDAY, August 14 — I'm on the road. I'm putting the dust of Winnemucca behind me. I would like to have seen Uma one last time before I left, but that wasn't in the cards. I left a note for Grandma and cut out early this morning. I have my backpack, my laptop, and $87.43 in cash. Not much assets to show for 15-1/2 years on this planet. Way too little to be splurging on bus tickets, so I walked down Main Street and loitered by the front gate of an RV park. When a rig with California plates was exiting, I tugged open the rear door of the trailer and hopped in. Fortunately, the guy was headed west. It was one of those giant rolling homes on wheels where the front third extends up over the bed of the truck towing it. I think they're called fifth-wheel trailers. Seemed oddly cramped inside, but then I figured out that was because all the slide-out sections had been sucked inside for moving. I sat in a recliner and watched my home town retreating in the early morning light through the huge rear window. I poured myself a glass of water and later used the toilet in the fancy bathroom. Got a little nervous when the guy stopped for gas in Stockton. I thought they might come in for lunch, but they headed into the truck-stop restaurant instead (after nearly giving me a heart attack when they stopped to lock the trailer door). It was an old guy and his perky younger wife. I found some barbecued chicken in the refrigerator and some corn chips in a cupboard. The only thing cold they had to drink was beer, so I stuck with water. Finished it off with some great homemade chocolate cake. Beats standing by the highway in the heat with your thumb out.

We headed down Route 99 in the afternoon and got all the way to Bakersfield before they pulled off the freeway. I didn't know where they were headed, so when they stopped at a light, I bailed out and walked back to the freeway interchange. I had a budget dinner in a truck-stop diner, then walked around the lot asking the truckers idling there if anyone was going to L.A. A younger guy who looked fairly unmenacing agreed to give me a lift. He'd been driving a long time (and fudging his logbook), so he needed someone to talk with to help him stay awake. We crawled up the Grapevine at about eight miles per hour, and I told him all about the events of the last few days. He said he left home at 16 and lied about his age to get in the army. He didn't recommend that course of action, but said at least the army gave him experience driving big trucks. He was an on-call driver now, which he liked because it left him plenty of time to go surfing. He talked about surfing non-stop for the next three hours, which Tyler probably would have found fascinating. He dropped me off in West L.A., and I took a city bus into Santa Monica.

It's now after 11 p.m. and I'm bedded down for the night in some bushes next to the Civic Auditorium a few blocks from the ocean. Rather scary and not that comfortable, but it seems fairly deserted around here. Still pretty warm, so I don't think I'll freeze to death. It's worrisome being on my own, but at least

I don't have to listen to Lance Wescott's fat mouth any more. I'm thinking of changing my name. Perhaps I should just bite the bullet and go with Twisp.

Noel Twisp.

I could live with that.

TUESDAY, August 16 — Sorry to have skipped a day, but yesterday was hectic in the extreme. Anyway, Veeva doesn't understand why I bother to write a blog, since it isn't actually posted on the Web. I told her that noting what I do and feel every day makes my life seem slightly more worth living. She seemed to accept that and said maybe in 20 years her children will be desperate to read it. Hard to imagine Veeva as a mom. The good news is she's had her period, so those condoms in Vegas were doing their job. The bad news is I am no longer recording our intimate activities (should they occur) in case this laptop falls into the wrong hands.

I was planning on sleeping in doorways along Venice Beach and panhandling tourists for spare change, but darling Veeva has come to my rescue (at least temporarily). She has secreted me in her granny's old house in Bel Air about a half-mile from her own posh pad. Mrs. Rita Krusinowski (her grandmother) now lives near Phoenix, but has retained her old home for when the Arizona summer heat proves too oppressive. It was 116 degrees there yesterday, but Rita would rather swelter in the desert (says Veeva) than face her daughter and her grandchildren in L.A. She allegedly prefers the company of her Chihuahua dogs and a one-armed chef/chauffeur/handyman/companion named Dogo.

The house isn't entirely deserted though. I'm sharing these once palatial premises with Señora Garonne, the elderly mother of the Saunders' housekeeper Benecia. Although she does not quite have all of her marbles, she is employed as a caretaker by Mrs. Krusinowski. I'm not sure what care she takes, since the place is looking a bit decrepit—and that's saying something from a guy used to life in a squalid trailer. Señora Garonne is under the impression that I am Veeva's brother James (still salted away at camp). Every time we pass in a hallway she exclaims at how Nipsie has grown. I cornered Veeva on this point, and she admitted that her brother (the elder of the two) is only 11. Years ago he acquired the nickname "Nipsie," but Veeva felt the topic was too tiresome to go into further.

Bel Air is nice (the view from up here is to die for), but it's a bit far off the beaten track for a kid with no car. I found a dusty old ten-speed in the garage though, and I'm using it for transportation. Veeva thinks it might have belonged to Dogo. I wanted to move into his old quarters above the garage, but that door is locked and no one seems to have the key. So I took the farthest bedroom from Señora Garonne, and Veeva and I may or may not have gotten reacquainted there several times so far with the door securely closed.

Of course, Veeva had to let Benecia in on my presence, since she frequently looks in on her mom and brings her groceries, but she's agreed to stay mum. Señora Garonne is a much better cook than my grandmother, though she gets confused sometimes and does things like thicken the chicken soup with powdered sugar. Her English used to be pretty good, but Veeva says that her adopted language is now dribbling out with her marbles. We get along OK with a combination of English and my schoolyard Spanish. I'm learning to answer to the name Nipsie. I'm also trying to be helpful so her daughter will view my presence here favorably. I don't know if Benecia suspects Veeva's interest in me is more than casual. I hope not. According to Benecia, my brother Nick once hid out up here when the cops were after him. I guess it's a Twisp family tradition.

Speaking of cops, there's been no news of Carlyle being captured at the border. Detective Moroni probably thinks I made that story up, and is now even more committed to nailing my bloodied scalp to his wall.

Life would be OK if I didn't have to worry about that and obsess about Uma the rest of the time. Why am I so stuck on that chick? The guy who said 'better to have loved and lost than never to have loved at all' was completely full of shit.

WEDNESDAY, August 17 — Grandma's 77th birthday. Sorry to have missed it. I didn't dare send her a card or call her either. I hope she's OK, and if Lance is still there, he takes her out some place nice for dinner. She should have an easier time of it now without me there to run up her expenses.

Two weeks since Uma split from my life. I try not to wonder how she's getting on with Sloan Chandler. I must put Winnemucca behind me. That part of my life is over.

Veeva reports her father is due back from Vegas tonight. No word yet how anyone is making out with Reina. I guess I'm rooting for my brother. Connie Saunders is totally pissed at Veeva for blabbing about Reina's arrival in the U.S., as if she was supposed to know of her father's interest in that babe. Connie even accused her daughter of trying to break up her marriage. The irony is that according to what Veeva has been able to piece together over the years, it was her mom who intrigued to throw her own father at Paul Saunders's then girlfriend so Connie could make a play for him. She succeeded, the Krusinowskis got divorced, then her father croaked from a heart attack, leaving a big chunk of his fortune to Paul's old girlfriend. (Something Connie is still burned up about.) Well, Veeva recently called this woman (named Lacey) and found out it was all true.

Where things really get kinky is that before Lacey hooked up with Paul, she was living with my own father. It was Nick who brought them together! Veeva thinks her mother's scheming was lower than low, although she's willing to concede that if Connie hadn't made the play, Veeva wouldn't be around today to sneer at it. I'm thankful my own genesis hadn't hinged on such a convoluted set of circumstances. My parents just got loaded and went at it for old time's sake.

I'm beginning to see that mothers and daughters can be extremely competitive. For example, Veeva feels that her mother resents her because she has developed very nice breasts, while her mother's own impressive rack is entirely fake. Why this creates friction in a family I don't really comprehend. Shouldn't mothers be proud of their daughters' attributes? Not that my alleged fathers have ever demonstrated any pride in my accomplishments, meager as they may be.

7:14 p.m. Veeva just called me with the news of the day. I was kind of hoping to see her, but I suppose she has her own exciting life to lead. She finally got through to Tyler, who's been switching off his cell phone because his coach says all those calls from girls were interfering with his concentration on football. He's the quarterback of his team and has to stay alert. Tyler reports the cops released him pretty fast when they realized an all-city athlete wouldn't lie about the whereabouts of a despicable gangbanger like Carlyle. As if a guy is trustworthy just because he has muscles, wears a jockstrap, and knows which end of a football to hold.

Tyler further reported that Awanee is in a panic and has turned her entire house upside down trying to find a valuable ring that I supposedly gave her. So I had to explain that story to Veeva without making it sound like I ever had a romantic interest in the girl. Not easy and I don't think Veeva found my prevarications particularly credible.

The big news is the uproar that has been created by the disappearance of Noel Twisp (formerly Wescott). Apparently, I've been missed. In fact, my mother is threatening to sic her lawyer on Grandma for gross child neglect. My disappearance has been reported to the cops, and all friends and relatives have been alerted to be on the lookout for me. Damn, I may be seeing my photo on milk cartons soon. Jesus, thousands of kids leave home every day. How come they're making such a fuss about me? Are they that desperate to see my puny ass behind bars?

Veeva stayed clammed about me until we can be sure that Tyler is to be trusted. Of course, my continued disappearance also gives her an excuse to check in frequently with that guy. Should we be going at it, I wonder if she's daydreaming about

Tyler while I'm imagining it is Uma who may or may not be reclining in my arms.

THURSDAY, August 18 — Today is the day of my scheduled hearing in juvenile court. I guess that makes me an official fugitive from justice—like Dr. Richard Kimball and Carlyle Bogy. You'd think media interest in that uptight hijacker would be fading by now, but no such luck. Today's *Los Angeles Times* had a big in-depth feature story about white youths who want to be black. Turns out Jamal and Toby have a lot of company out there in the 'burbs of L.A. Now my on-the-lam gang brother is a big cultural hero to those dudes. One of the kids featured in the article was shown wearing a t-shirt that read "Bogy on Carlyle!" under the graphic of a hearse sprayed with a big UPT symbol. Looked very professionally done. And why aren't we being paid royalties for such use?

Veeva took me out to lunch in Beverly Hills. She's been complaining bitterly about my wardrobe, but what's a guy to do? How many teen runaways have the funds to dress like fashion models? She says she wants to introduce me to her friends, but I can sense she doesn't want them to think she's going out with some geeky rube from the sticks. As it was, the stuffy restaurant had to lend me a jacket and tie to go with my ragged cutoffs and scuffed running shoes.

Over gourmet but vegetarian lunches we discussed the latest developments in Vegas. My brother is blowing the joint. According to Veeva's dad, Reina thinks Las Vegas is an amusing place to spend a weekend, but not sustainable of daily human existence. No way is she planting her refined Continental sensibilities in that desert inferno. So Nick is following her back to Europe. He's terminating his engagement at the Normandie casino and will attempt to lease his house.

"You mean he's moving to Prague!" I exclaimed.

"No, the plan right now is for all four of them to live together in Paris. If everything works out, Nick might adopt her children—assuming he learns Czech, they learn English, or everyone settles on French."

"Wow, my brother's moving to the same country as your aunt Sheeni. I wonder if he'll look her up?"

"Yeah, I'd love to be an eyewitness to that reunion."

"Your dad flamed out, huh?"

"Sounds like it. I've never seen him looking so miserable. He hasn't said so, but I think Reina may be the only woman he ever loved."

"Why didn't they hook up back then?"

"Well, when they first met, she was 17 and he was 25. That's a pretty big age difference. Plus, my mother was waging total war to get him to marry her. Now he's 40 and Reina's 32—a very appropriate age mix for marriage."

I suppose, though I've yet to see a seven-year-old that appealed to me.

"So, Veeva, is your mother still pissed?"

"She may be, but she's being completely loving toward him now. It's all rather sickening. Parents seem completely oblivious that they are acting out these soap operas in front of their children. Do they imagine we are completely blind?"

"You'd rather your father just stuck it out with your mom?"

"Not at all, Noel. My father deserves to be happy. I realize now that it is my task to make sure that happens—if not with Reina, than with someone equally suitable."

"Your mother will kill you!"

"We're destined to clash, Noel. It's inevitable. In some way I think we've both always known that."

After lunch Veeva did a little light shopping while I marveled at the prices. In one swanky shop I couldn't even buy a handkerchief with my entire net worth (which is dropping alarmingly; I *must* get a job). Then we taxied back to my place, where we engaged in some mutually rewarding activities in my room. Good thing I cleaned out all those small packaged items in Grandma's medicine cabinet before departing.

Later Veeva showed me this interesting area in a remote section of the grounds. It's an overgrown ravine that looks like something out of a Tarzan movie. It had once been her grandfather's pride and joy: a tropically landscaped black-bottom pool. After he died, the water was drained, but too many kids were sneaking in to skateboard in its concrete void. So Mrs. Krusinowski had the pool filled in with dirt. You can still make out its location from the boulders that outlined part of its rim. Even spookier was the former cabana, which had been built into the hillside like a cave. It had been professionally decorated in wild leopard-skin prints, but now it was a dank and dripping crypt like something out of a horror movie. Movable cave walls once could motor back at the touch of a button to reveal sweeping city views, but now all the machinery had long since rusted stuck. Veeva says if she inherits the house someday, she plans to restore everything to its original condition. Seems rather expensively ambitious. Why not just enjoy the ruins and give the money to me instead?

Veeva nixed my plan to rustle up some grass-mowing jobs in the neighborhood using the dusty power mower I spotted in the garage. She says everyone hires real gardeners. It seems you have to be fully professional to get work in this town. You can't just push a mower over someone's yard. You have to know about fertilizers, herbicides, natural pest control, exotic plant care, irrigation systems, Fung Shui principles—the works. If you so much as scalped a hummock, you could wind up getting sued for thousands. People take their landscaping very seriously in a city where image is everything. Meanwhile, my bankroll is down to $53 and change. Panhandling for spare change looms ahead.

For dinner Señora Garonne made delicious enchiladas from yesterday's roast pork. It's now Nipsie's daily job to warm the tortillas over the gas flame. She says she thinks it's very sweet that Nipsie spends so much time with his sister.

Yes, I agreed, we're quite a loving family.

FRIDAY, August 19 — Less than two weeks until school starts. If I had a secure place to stay and a steady income, I'd think about enrolling in high school here. It would be nice to make some friends and not feel so isolated up on this hill. I wonder if I'd fit in better in a Los Angeles high school, or would wind up orbiting on the social fringe like I did in Winnemucca. Veeva, of course, goes to a fancy private school, where she is one of the supreme mandarins of her class. All bow before her beauty, smarts, style, and wealth—or so she would have me believe.

Unsettling breakfast reading today on the front page of the *Times*: A boxed letter to the editor from a noted fugitive. It read (with the spelling corrected):

> Hey, you jerks!
> Get with the program! UPT means Uptowners not Uptight! We're the m————g Uptowners Gang!
> I like your city (except for the cops), so I'll be hanging here a while. All you cute sisters out there should look me up. I'm the hottest dude around.
> UPT forever!
> Carlyle "Jamal" Bogy.

A caption noted that the letter had been authenticated by the police from details it contained that the newspaper chose not to print.

I find it amazing that Jamal is still at large. The guy is not that slippery. After every suspicious fire back in Winnemucca, he was always in handcuffs within ten minutes.

Feeling nostalgic for my home town, I phoned Stoney Holt after breakfast for an update. She hadn't heard from Jamal, but I gave her my new cell phone number and asked her to call me immediately with his location if he checks in. Stoney reported that my grandmother is most upset that I ran away.

"Well, her son was screaming at me to get out," I replied. "Not to mention threatening my life."

"Yeah, so I heard. She says Lance is an even bigger blowhard than his dad. She wants you to call her."

"Well, I'll think about it, Stoney. But what if the cops are tapping her phone line?"

"Jesus, Noel, you're sounding kinda paranoid. Where are you anyway?"

I told her I was holed up in a cabin by a lake outside Buffalo, Wyoming. I'm not sure that chick's entirely to be trusted. Detective Moroni might be putting the screws to her as well. She advised me to rustle up a warm coat as winter arrives early in Wyoming. Stoney hasn't had a date yet with Sloan Chandler, but she's been running into him frequently at the swim center.

"I thought you were grounded, Stoney?"

"I am, but my idiot parents realized I wasn't likely to be asked out unless I went to a place where there were actual guys. I hope you don't mind, but I told Sloan that you nailed Uma."

"What!?"

"Well, you told me that you practically did."

"But why did you blab about it to Sloan?"

"I wanted him to know your bitch goddess was a slut, so he'd dump her and go out with me."

"But Uma will think it was me who told you about us."

"Which, of course, it was, Noel. Anyway, why do you care what that bitch thinks? She dumped you, remember?"

"So what did Sloan say?"

"He said Uma would never be interested in a dorky creep like you. So I told him to ask around who took Uma to Mary Glasgow's party. He said he would. God, Sloan looks so sexy when he skips shaving for a few days. I wish I could grow stubble like that."

I reminded her that she was neither a guy nor a dyke and asked her to keep me posted if she saw Sloan and Uma together anywhere.

So Sloan thinks I'm a creep, huh? Another enemy to add to my list for terrible retribution.

6:17 p.m. Veeva came over this afternoon in a fever of excitement. No, she wasn't jonesing for my bod. She had just heard from Tyler. He reported that he had been doing more research on the Web on Alfredo Nunez, the clown. Tyler found out that Sheeni's dwarfish ex-boyfriend is engaged this summer with a circus touring the western provinces of Canada.

"It's the Hercules Circus," noted Veeva. "It's owned by Greeks and they have one ring under canvas, whatever that means."

"You guys should go up there and check him out," I suggested.

"Well, one of us must, Noel. Tyler, of course, is consumed with football mania. And I have to get ready for the start of school."

She looked at me expectantly.

"Well, I can't go crossing the Canadian border, Veeva. I'm a fucking fugitive. I'd get nailed by the cops for sure."

"You don't have to cross any borders, Noel. According to their website, the tour dips down into Washington state next week. They open in Spokane on Wednesday."

"I can't go to Spokane, Veeva. I don't have any money."

Veeva agreed that was a problem. Like most Americans, she has access to loads of credit, but can lay hands on precious little ready cash. She's promised to see what she can do though. I don't see why I'm the sucker who has to go trooping all over the country to track down my brother's missing kid. Somehow, though, Veeva was making it all seem fairly logical in my bedroom this afternoon.

9:42 p.m. I see from *L.A. Weekly* that the Pickled Punks are appearing again tonight in Hollywood. I'd love to go, but it's a long bike ride from here, plus I can't afford the cover charge. Car-free poverty really sucks—especially when you're surrounded by the faded trappings of great wealth. Despite the Krusinowski millions, there is only one working television in this dump—which Señora Garonne keeps resolutely tuned to bizarre Spanish-language soap operas and game shows. No, Nipsie is not even to think of touching the remote. So to pass the time, I've been swiping books from old man Krusinowski's dusty library. I'm now reading *The Viking Book of Poetry of the English Speaking World*. Rather pretentious title for a bunch of dry old poems by long-dead white guys (and a few poetical chicks). I did like these lines by Robert Browning:

> I send my heart up to thee, all my heart
>   In this my singing.
> For the stars help me, and the sea bears part;
>   The very night is clinging
> Closer to Venice' streets to leave one space
>   Above me, whence thy face
> May light my joyous heart to thee its dwelling-place.

So I send my heart up to thee, Uma, that you may glance up at some starry Nevada sky and perhaps think of me.

SATURDAY, August 20 — Disaster! While I was picking my way through a steaming bowl of tripe soup (Señora Garonne is into exotic breakfast eats), a gigantic motorhome rumbled up the driveway.

"Señora Krusinowski *esta aquí*!" exclaimed the flustered housekeeper.

While she hurried out the front door to greet her arriving employer, I was gathering up my stuff as best I could and running out the back door. I've placed an emergency call to Veeva and am holed up temporarily in the jungle by the dead pool. Veeva says it's unlikely anyone will come down here, but if they do, I should hide in the cabana cave. Easy for her to say. There's enough musty mold spores in that crypt to kill an entire ward of asthmatics.

1:26 p.m. Now I wish I'd downed a bit more of that repulsive tripe. I'm beyond famished.

I've been spying on the house from some well-placed bushes. A one-armed bald guy covered with tattoos (Dogo?) leveled the motorhome and slid out its many ancillary rooms. Looks like they're not just stopping by to pick up fresh socks. The most lavish land yacht I've ever seen, it's styled like a boat, with fancy gilt letters on its stern spelling out *Spring Forth - Phoenix, Ariz.* After plugging a cable into an outlet by the garage and adjusting a satellite dish on the *Spring Forth's* roof, the man sprung four yapping Chihuahuas from the interior and took them for a walk. Somehow with just one hand he was able to keep all four leashes from tangling.

Meanwhile, Veeva had arrived by taxi and disappeared inside the house. God knows what she told her grandmother about young "Nipsie's" presence there and his abrupt departure. Then, about a half-hour ago, she exited with the fabled matriarch herself, a gaunt old lady with blondish hair (a wig?). Just think, if my father had played his cards right, I might be addressing her as "Granny" myself, instead of lurking in her shrubbery like some undernourished Peeping Tom. I might even have gotten to ride somewhere in their fancy RV.

They piled into this little boat-shaped car that was towed in behind the motorhome and drove off (to police headquarters? to the FBI?) with Dogo behind the wheel. Mrs. Krusinowski didn't appear obviously pissed, so I'm hoping they just went some place for lunch. The name on the back of the nautical car was "*Plock II*," whatever that means. Perhaps the sign painter misspelled "pluck."

1:48 p.m. Veeva just called from the ladies' room of a restaurant in Westwood. I'm to clear out the rest of my stuff and meet her in the parking lot of a convenience store on Beverly Glen Boulevard. That's a long way to lug all my stuff, but at least I can look forward to a hotdog and slurpie when I get there.

5:38 p.m. I had to cool my heels in the parking lot for nearly an hour before Veeva showed up. And they pipe out this irritating classical music to discourage that sort of loitering. While cabbing to our next destination, Veeva explained how she had dealt with the crisis.

"I told my grandmother you were Pedro, Benecia's nephew, who was there to look after Benecia's mother. So Señora Garonne wouldn't think she was being watched over, we let her believe that Pedro was my brother Nipsie."

"And why did Pedro run out the back door?"

"Skittish Pedro feared he might be turned over to the INS."

"OK, and why was Veeva spending so much time in Pedro's room with the door closed?"

"In the first place, Noel, I don't think Señora Garonne is likely to mention that fact. If she does, I'll just tell Grandmother that I was helping him with his English."

"You're a genius, Veeva. A goddam fucking genius!"

"No, I'm just really smart and rather manipulative. I did my best to get Grandmother to say how long she planned to stay, but she's always cagey about such details. We'll just have to play it by ear."

"Why is her car named *Plock II*?"

"Well, her big land yacht used to be called the *Plock*. That's a city in Poland where her husband's family was from. Grandmother's Polish too, but her side mostly came from Krakow. So after her husband ditched her for a younger babe and then croaked, she decided the old name had to go."

"Why *Spring Forth*?"

"Easy. With her cheating ex-husband now planted in Forest Lawn, the lively widow was ready to do just that. Plus, it's kind of an in-joke, since Grandfather made all his money manufacturing truck springs. She kept the old name on the little boat car to remind her deceased husband exactly who was now leading whom down the highway of life."

"You chicks don't take any prisoners do you?"

"Not typically, Noel. Now here's some things you should know about my friend Maddy: Number one, she may try to seduce you. Number two, she has the biggest mouth in town, so I'll find out in a hurry if you betray me."

"OK, OK. So why are Maddy's parents letting some kid they

don't even know stay in their guestroom for a few days?"

"Well, we've had to tell one small white lie."

"OK, lay it on me."

"Both your parents were killed this morning in a car wreck on the 405 Freeway."

"What!?"

"So remember to look sad and grief-stricken. And keep your hands off Maddy."

Maddy Dockweiler lives with her parents and older brother in a Tudor mansion in Beverly Hills that's almost as swanky as Veeva's. Her dad is a big accounting cheese at Paramount. He helps make sure that none of their movies ever shows an actual profit. Her mother is a well-known therapist to the stars. Maddy has her mother's olive complexion, long black hair, and personality gearshift stuck permanently at "In Your Face."

The painful introductions were made in their grand Old English foyer. It had all the period accouterments except two knights dueling with swords. Everyone was doing their best to be gracious and consoling toward newly orphaned Jake Darko, who was certainly nervous if not emotionally devastated. Mrs. Dockweiler gave me a fierce hug and said she was available for grief counseling 24/7. I thanked her and said I'd probably do OK on my own for now. Somehow I made it to the lower-level guestroom with my stuff, but Maddy pushed her way in before I could shut the door.

"God, from Veeva's description I thought you'd be much cuter."

"Uh, no . . . I guess, I'm not. What's my name again?"

"Jake Darko. Don't you love it?"

"Uh, it's OK."

"All my friends have huge crushes on the actor Jake Gyllenhaal. He's an alumnus of our school. You'll recall he made quite an impression starring in the film *Donnie Darko*."

"Uh, I don't think I saw that movie."

"Oh, you really should, Jake. Well, I'll let you get unpacked.

Dinner's at 7:00. Try not to let my mother get her claws into you."

"What should I do?"

"Just don't encourage her."

Maddy then let out a piercing scream that about blew me out of my shoes.

"Don't you love the echo in this room?" she inquired, dancing out the door.

I walked over and checked the knob. Just as I feared. No lock.

11:08 p.m. On a pain scale of one to ten, I'd rate dinner a 9.6. Mrs. Dockweiler did her professional best to draw me out, but I took refuge in monosyllabic mumbling. Fortunately, the eats were great, though I fear I surprised my hosts with my hearty appetite. Yeah, kids can be so callous these days. I had to keep making up stuff when the Dockweilers asked me about siblings, what my parents did, where I lived, who was arranging the funeral, why no relatives were available to take me in, etc. God, it will be a miracle if I can keep my story straight. Mr. Dockweiler probably wouldn't notice, but his wife is trained to root out everyone's darkest and deepest secrets. Fortunately, Maddy and Marty (her 16-year-old brother) tried as best they could to distract her. I don't see how those two kids can stand it. I'm sure if she were my mother, I would have run away from home even sooner.

Marty let me check my e-mail on his state-of-the-art computer. He also has all the latest game consoles. No e-mail from Uma, but I had messages from Nick, Tyler, and Awanee urging me to check in right away. My brother added that his lawyers can deal with the cops, and I should call him collect before he leaves for Paris. Too bad that guy's credibility is so low. If his lawyers are so smart, how come he had to spend half his teen years locked up? Of course, I haven't winged anyone with a gun—not yet at any rate. I didn't dare send any replies, fearing the cops might trace them back to Marty's computer.

Maddy's brother seems as retiring as his sister is aggressive. They don't look much alike except for the exact same heavily lidded brown eyes borrowed intact from their dad. No way Mr. Dockweiler could ever weasel out of a lawsuit contesting their paternity.

The good thing about hanging out in Marty's room is his sister can't get at you there. They have a house rule that each bedroom is a personal sanctuary—no other family members allowed unless expressly invited. I'm praying that also applies to the guestroom. Marty showed me some of his video games and asked if it was true that I was a founding member of the notorious Uptowners gang.

"Yeah. In fact, I'm the one who came up with the name."

"That is so cool. Do you really know Carlyle Bogy?"

"I've known him since kindergarten. Want to know an interesting fact about that guy?"

"Sure, Jake."

"Carlyle can tie his dick in a knot."

"How do you know that? Are you lovers?"

"Uh, no, but I've seen him do it."

"That's amazing. Is it true you're also getting it on with Veeva Saunders?"

Veeva is one to talk about people wagging their tongues.

"Yeah, I suppose so."

"Do you like her as much as Carlyle?"

Marty was not as laid back as I'd first assumed. Nor did he listen very well.

"I like her fine. Why?"

"Just asking. Has anyone told you, Jake, that you look like Brandon De Wilde?"

"People have mentioned it. I'm surprised you even know about that actor. He was way before our time."

"I have DVDs of many of his films and most of his TV appearances."

"Wow, you must really like the guy."

"My grandfather worked on the crew of his TV show 'Jamie' back in the 1950s. Brandon was still a kid actor then. It only ran one season. He died in a car wreck—just like your imaginary parents."

"Yeah, I heard that. He was only 30."

The same age as my brother Nick. Just goes to show you never know what's coming around the next corner.

"Brandon was on his way to appear in a stage production of 'Butterflies Are Free.' Isn't that ironic, Jake?"

"Is it, Marty?"

"Sure, Jake. Butterflies are free, but people die in car crashes. You know, there's a butterfly on your T-shirt."

I looked down.

"Yeah, my sister gave me this shirt. It's not really my style."

"I think it's fucking amazing, Jake. Just absolutely fucking awesome!"

So far, kids in L.A. seem way more intense than your average teen redneck back in Winnemucca.

I have wedged the back of a desk chair against the doorknob like they do in the movies. At the very least, it should slow down any intruders. My mattress is surprisingly lumpy for the Dockweilers being so loaded. It is also besmirched with some suspicious stains. Probably a hand-me-down from their kids' toilet training days. I pray to God I don't add to the designs as the housekeeper would probably scream rape if I showed up uninvited in her laundry room with my sheets. I was doing OK in that department at the Krusinowski manse, but then I was feeling a bit more relaxed there. This being a houseguest is rather stressful to the nerves.

Probably I should do a little loud sobbing now for the benefit of my hosts. I think I'll skip it though and just hit the sack. Perhaps I'll be able to work up a few orphan's tears at breakfast. That should keep them satisfied for a while.

SUNDAY, August 21 — The Dockweilers and houseguest drove to Venice this morning for breakfast at an outdoor café near one of the canals. I don't see why people move to Europe when you can get virtually the same ambience right here. And here the waitresses wear cute form-hugging tops and speak your own language.

Grieving, I've decided, is a lot like moping, which I've had tons of experience at. So I moped all through breakfast, while downing a large omelet plus two breakfast pastries. I spotted a fellow diner who reminded me of Uma, so I let out a genuine sniffle as well. Good thing too, because Mrs. Dockweiler watched me like a hawk the entire time. I think she's decided she has a professional responsibility to get me through this crisis. God help any of her family members if somebody close to them actually dies. I'm sure she'd make everyone feel at least ten times worse.

Midway through the meal I excused myself to take a call from Veeva. She reported that the minute Connie Saunders heard her mother was in town she made plans to escape with her hubby to romantic Santa Barbara for a few days—just the two of them.

"I think she's hoping to reinvigorate her marriage," commented Veeva. "Fat chance of that."

I begged Veeva to let me come stay with her while her parents were away, but she said it was too risky.

"Maddy Dockweiler is a total pain!" I complained. "She keeps putting me down."

"Oh, she always does that with her friends' boyfriends. I could be going out with Tyler and she'd still find a way to get a dig in at him. It's just her coping mechanism, Noel."

"That implies you feel Tyler is some kind of ultimate, Veeva—the boyfriend beyond reproach."

"Don't be silly, Noel. I was just using him as an example."

"No, Veeva, there was a clear superiority over me implied in that statement. That was a putdown worthy of Maddy herself."

"Well, Noel, you're always letting me know how I don't measure up to your precious Uma. And frankly I'm sick of it."

"Veeva darling, I think you're great. I love the time we spend together."

"I like you too, Noel. You're very special to me."

"Then you'll let me come stay with you?"

"Forget it! You don't know my mother. She'd sniff the air and know I'd had a man in the place. The woman is some kind of she-wolf."

Now moping for real, I returned to the table and said the call was from my Aunt Min in Dallas consulting on the choice of colors for the funeral.

"Aren't the colors usually black?" inquired Mr. Dockweiler.

"Not in my family," I replied, "When my Uncle Phil died, he went out in shades of teal and gold. And Grandma Edna specified lavender and baby blue. Laid out for viewing, she made quite a memorable display."

Later we all got a break from Maddy's mouth when she went to the beach with her surfing club. According to her brother, she joined that group to meet boys, but so far has achieved intimate contact only with manta rays and jellyfish. Marty prefers tennis and insisted that we bang some balls back and forth on the Dockweiler's private court. Believe it or not, when they bought the house it came with a lavish swimming pool, but they ripped it out to put in a tennis court. Is that insane, or what? To me that's like tearing apart your Rolls Royce to make a go-kart from the wheels.

Marty gave me a lesson in the proper way to serve a tennis ball (as if I cared), while his mother spied on us from the house. Remembering to mope, I paused occasionally to wipe away an imaginary tear. Then we went up to his room to sample more of his video games, and I played him my Pickled Punks CD on his righteous stereo. Impressed he was not. He plays trumpet in his school's jazz band, and prefers the music of Miles Davis—even though that guy has been dead for years.

The time went by pretty fast and the eats were good too, even though it was the housekeeper's day off. In keeping with a family tradition, Mr. Dockweiler made dinner (he does that every Sunday night). Tonight he made his mother's old recipe for peppered ham casserole. I had three helpings, though I had to pick out all the artichoke hearts. Yuck. They might have been big back in his mother's day, but I told him I didn't think anyone was eating them any more. He said he would "take that under advisement," whatever that means. Maddy only insulted me three times during the meal; she must have been feeling mellow from her day in Malibu.

Then we watched a DVD on their giant plasma TV of a Paramount movie that won't be released to theaters for months. It was a comedy that I think someone of the mental capacity of Carlyle Bogy might enjoy. Maddy told her dad it was a "royal stinker," but he said not to worry because they had already recovered the costs of production and hadn't even finished selling all the "secondary rights."

All in all, a fairly pleasant day, and it didn't cost me a cent. I think this houseguest racket may be better than I first assumed. The secret, I think, is to get invited some place nice like Beverly Hills instead of, say, a trailer park in the sticks, where they might expect you to help with the dishes and chip in for the eats.

MONDAY, August 22 — The chair against the door worked fine, except the intruder came in through the French doors. Terrified, I switched on a lamp and there was Marty Dockweiler in his flannel bathrobe. He was carrying a half-full bottle of red wine and two glasses.

"Care for a drink, Jake?" he asked.

I looked at the clock on the night stand.

"Marty, it's 2:47 in the goddam morning."

"I'm taking that as an affirmative, Jake." He filled both glasses and handed one to me.

"Actually, Jake, it's only 1:47. That clock was never adjusted to Daylight Savings Time. We don't get that many guests down here because of the mold problem. How do you like the wine?"

I took a tentative sip. My first taste of wine. Not bad—only a notch or two degraded from the original grape juice.

"It's OK, Marty. Did you swipe this from your parents' stash?"

"You're such a throwback, Jake. I find that charming. Mind if I sit down?"

Since the chair was busy blocking the door, I moved my feet aside and he sat on the bed. He nodded toward the door.

"Was that chair there to keep me out?"

"I was thinking more of your scary sister."

"Glad to hear it. Maddy seems to be exhibiting an unusual hostility toward you. She's very competitive with Veeva, you know."

"Then why did she agree to hide me out?"

"Because she and Veeva are best friends. They'd do anything for each other. Do you sleep in the nude?"

"No, I sleep in my shorts. How 'bout you?"

"In the buff. Always. More wine?"

"OK."

Marty splashed more wine in my glass, and I took a big swig. Unlike vodka, this stuff improved with use. Something fluttered by the lampshade, startling me.

"It's only a moth, Jake. It must have come in with me. A moth has joined the butterfly."

Marty impressed me as a kid who was fixated on butterflies. I asked him if he collected them.

"You're my first, Jake. My first and best."

The guy wasn't making much sense, so I figured he must have started earlier on the wine with a full bottle. His speech was a bit slurred too.

"I like your dad, Marty. Your mother's OK too."

"That's a joke, Jake. You don't have to bullshit me. And I'm not going to bullshit you. OK?"

"OK, Marty. It's a deal."

"The thing is, Jake. It's like this. I've got it all figured out. You've got two choices here. More wine?"

"OK."

Marty emptied the bottle into our glasses.

"What are my two choices, Marty?" I hoped they wouldn't be too difficult because my head was beginning to spin.

"Number one, Jake, I can go upstairs and tell my parents who you really are."

"Not a very nice choice, Marty."

"No, not very nice, Jake. Or, number two you can invite me into that bed."

That choice didn't sound very nice either. I told him I was a bed-wetter from way back. He said he'd risk it, switched off the lamp, and shoved in beside me. I sensed immediately that he had left his flannel robe behind. Kind of an awkward situation for my muddled brain to cope with. A realization began to dawn.

"Marty, are you gay?" I asked, pulling away from his embrace.

"There's no such thing, Jake. Everyone is bisexual, only some of us choose to admit it to ourselves."

Damn, was that a yes or no? I couldn't really tell, although his clammy hand down my shorts was pointing toward the affirmative. I told him I was straight and had two girlfriends. He reminded me that I only had two choices. So, to make a long story short, the houseguest received a more or less compulsory blowjob and then a tearful apology. Marty said he loved me deeply despite my being an uncultured clod, and I said he should go away and leave me alone. Eventually, he did.

Only the second blowjob of my life and I had to receive it from a guy. Even worse, it was not unenjoyable. In fact, I came rather more explosively than I did with Veeva. I'm hoping that can be attributed to a general relaxation induced by the wine and not a hitherto unsuspected sexual inclination. That is another problem I just don't need.

The adults had both gone to work by the time I wandered into the kitchen looking for breakfast. Too bad too, because my dull headache from the wine would have enhanced any simulations of grief. Maddy said I looked like a homeless person and deigned to point out the cupboard containing the cold cereal. No sign of Marty, not that I was looking for him. I ate two bowls of organic granola, then tried calling Veeva. No answer so I left a message.

Now I have finished updating my blog and await the next houseguest activity. What does the proper houseguest do to avert excruciating boredom when he's not fending off amorous assaults? Dare I sneak upstairs and snoop?

4:12 p.m. No call back yet from Veeva. Where is that chick? I had lunch out on the terrace with Marty. Excellent tamales made by the Dockweiler's morose housekeeper. I decided I can't hate a guy just because he loves me and thinks I'm an uncultured clod. Plus, he had gone out this morning and bought some antique games for my laptop. Very sedate ones, of course, so as not to tax my anemic processor. We kept the conversation on computers and did not broach the unmentionables. I'd probably like the guy if he wasn't hung up on Brandon and butterflies and me.

When we were finishing up dessert, Marty's mom came home, kissed her son, and invited the houseguest up to her office. Ominous feelings of dread washed over me as I trooped up those carpeted stairs behind her. I knew which room was her office, since I had given it a thorough inspection a few hours before. Her file cabinets had revealed some interesting facts that some prominent celebrities would probably pay Big Money not to have revealed. She dumped her purse on a shelf, closed the door, and waved to me to take a seat on the sofa. We both sat, got comfortable, and smiled at each other across her cluttered desk.

"How are you, Jake dear?" she asked.

"Not too bad. God, I still can't believe my parents are dead."

"I have some good news for you, Jake. I had my administrative assistant check with the Highway Patrol. There were no fatalities on the 405 Freeway last week."

"Oh. . . Really? . . . Well, uh, that's a relief."

"I'm rather disappointed that you guys felt the need to lie to me, Jake."

"Oh, you know, huh? Did Maddy tell you?"

"She didn't have to, Jake. I see with a mother's eyes."

"Oh. Are you going to call the cops?"

"Of course not, Jake. You've done nothing wrong in my eyes. I'm very happy for you, in fact."

I didn't quite see how she could be so thrilled that I was a fugitive from justice. Was it possible she was one of those left-wing Hollywood liberals?

"Then you'll let me hide out here?" I asked.

"You don't need to hide, Jake. We're completely understanding. Marty is old enough to make his own choices. We're happy that he's chosen such a nice person as you."

"What!?"

"Forgive me, Jake. I don't want you to think that I'm prying into your affairs. But I know that you two fellows spent last night together. And that's perfectly OK with us."

"It is?"

"Of course. So you didn't have to invent that crazy story about your parents dying just to spend the weekend here with my son."

No doubt about it now, she was one of those Hollywood liberals.

"Oh, OK," I replied.

"And please forgive another motherly trespass," she added, reaching for her purse. "Here's a small gift—for both of you."

She handed me a white paper bag. I peeked inside. Two dozen condoms—lubricated with the deluxe nipple ends. An expensive brand too.

"Uh, gee thanks, Mrs. Dockweiler. I can use these."

"I hope you do, Jake. Enjoy them in good health!"

A bit embarrassing, but I appreciated the gesture. My stash had been getting rather depleted.

TUESDAY, August 23 — On the bus to Spokane. Got on last night at 11:30. Been riding all night and we're still in California. How is that possible? Well, this bus does things like stop for 50 interminable minutes in Modesto in the middle of the night. Then it's on to Lodi, Stockton, Sacramento, Marysville, and on and on and on. We just passed Mount Shasta, a tall mountain that looms up all by itself over the dry brown plains of Northern California. Still a few patches of snow on its summit. Personally, I'd rather be flying over that mountain in a fast and comfortable jet, but Veeva insisted there was no way she could get such a charge past her mother's eagle eye.

My trip is being funded through a generous grant from Rita Krusinowski, who handed $700 in cash to Veeva yesterday for "school supplies." Must be some expensive pencils in L.A. Veeva wanted to split it with me, but I made her hand over the whole bundle. It's not that big of a wad for traveling across three states in search of a dwarf. Veeva got the windfall after spending the day buttering up her granny at a dog show in Costa Mesa. That's why she wasn't answering her phone: she didn't want to "interrupt the magic." The show was restricted to little dogs, so the yap factor—she informed me later—was not to be believed. What we kids have to do for a little spending money.

We had quite a torrid good-bye kiss at the bus station. I didn't tell Veeva about my episode with Marty, but I expect she'll hear about it from Maddy. I hope it's not blabbed over the entire L.A. basin. I got a kiss as well from Marty when the houseguest was leaving, but only on the cheek. I suppose I should feel flattered that someone found me attractive, since so comparatively few have felt that impulse. I wonder if he's right that we're all bi at heart? Well, he certainly wasn't proving his thesis, since he registered a stone cold zero on my attraction meter. The gusher in bed I'm attributing solely to applied friction in the dark.

2:37 p.m. Only able to doze on this bus, so now feeling like a zombie. We just took on a new driver in Bend, Oregon—a place that's probably the butt of countless rude jokes. Very pretty country though, with daubs of gold among the green from trees getting an early start on fall. Had a long chat with a girl going as far away as her money would take her from a scary-sounding ex-boyfriend. She was wearing sunglasses over her black eye and chomping on nicotine gum to quell her raging urges on this non-smoking bus. I'm glad now that Grandma raised hell so I never got hooked on cigarettes. Two packs a day killed her husband pretty quick—not that the world is missing that bastard.

Seems to me this business shouldn't take long. I'll go to the circus, find the clown, and nail him on the missing kid. If all goes well, I should be back in L.A. by the weekend. Perhaps by then Veeva's granny will have hit the road, and Nipsie can move back into his old room. If not, I may have to go back to fending off lovesick Marty.

10:30 p.m. Homeless shelter, downtown Spokane. The only accommodations I could dredge up. Went to a half-dozen motels along the main drag, but nobody would rent a room to a kid on his own. They all wanted a credit card in case I went berserk and busted up the room. This shelter is pretty down and out, but at least they provide lockers to secure your valuables overnight. I hope I don't pick up any bugs or diseases. The smelly cots don't look super comfortable, but I'm so exhausted I don't expect I'll have any trouble sleeping through the snuffling and snoring.

Spokane is another place like Winnemucca that you wonder how it came into existence in the middle of nowhere. Much bigger than my home town though. A wild-looking river roars through the center of town on its way to somewhere. Kind of scary being alone in a strange city, but at least I have some money in my pocket and I can say I'm seeing a bit of the country.

WEDNESDAY, August 24 — Gathered up my stuff and had breakfast at a café downtown. When I went to pay, I discovered my wallet had been cleaned out. It appears somebody tampered with my locker. The only money I had was the $50 bill Veeva told me to fold up and hide in my shoe. Less than $45 to my name now that I've paid the check. I can't believe how much that sucks. People are such rotten filthy bastards. The asshole did leave me my laptop, since it's probably too worthless to steal.

Walked about a mile to the fairgrounds, where I saw the circus setting up. The big tent was already up and men were moving stuff into it. There was a line of people waiting by an office trailer, so I joined it. I filled out an application, and a middle-aged lady with enormous glasses gave me a test. She handed me a $20 bill and had me make change from a money drawer for a purchase of $6.73. I knew the secret is to forget about subtraction and just do it with addition. You start with the figure of $6.73 and add coins and bills until you come to $20. A simple test, but most of the applicants looked like they'd never even seen a sum as large as $20. I was one of three temps hired to fill out the crew of refreshments vendors. Fortunately for me, the circus sometimes takes on locals in the bigger towns for such jobs. Pay is minimum wage, plus anything you can hustle from tips.

On the application I gave my name as Jake Darko and my age as 17. I kind of like the name Jake. It's less frou-frou than Noel, and Darko also has a certain dark appeal. They asked for a Social Security number, so I wrote down one that Veeva had gotten from Benecia, her resourceful housekeeper. According to Veeva, it's an internal control number used for debugging, so the computers won't challenge it. Don't ask me how Benecia got hold of it. Perhaps some of her relatives use it too. Now I'm hoping I can find some corner in the fairgrounds to stash my stuff and hole up tonight after the evening show.

7:48 p.m. All in all, a rotten day. A sparse crowd for the first matinee, so there was lots of competition among the vendors to hawk our overpriced snacks. The lucky guys got to hustle floss (cotton candy), but I was loaded down with back-breaking cans of soda. Very exhausting work trooping up and down the risers while trying not to bash people in the head with your load. Lots of cash to handle because about nine customers in ten pay with a $20 bill. One idiot tried to pay a $2 tab with a $100 bill, but I indignantly refused. I mean *nobody* had the correct change.

I did get to watch the show a bit. Several clowns were tumbling about in the center ring, but I figured that the short one with the mustache was Alfredo. I cornered him as he was going into this smaller tent for dinner (we local hires are on our own for eats). The guy totally blew me off. He said he didn't know anyone named Sheeni Saunders and didn't know anything about some kid. Then as we were getting ready for the evening show, the vendor crew-chief told me I was fired. He said I was too light for the job, lacked hustle, and that "complaints were received." He gave me 20 bucks for my labor and told me to beat it.

I just called Veeva and she got totally pissed. She blamed me for losing her $700 and said I should have used more finesse with Alfredo. No, she didn't have any more cash to send me, so I'm stuck up here in Washington state with less than $60 in my pocket. I'm not sure if it was Alfredo who complained, or the customer with the hundred bucks, or the guy whose daughter's hand I stepped on. I thought that kid was never going to stop howling. Veeva said if it had been Alfredo who had me canned, that meant he knows stuff and doesn't want me around. Very true, but what can I do about it now?

I should never have agreed to go on this crazy chase in the first place. Guys should never say yes to anything when they're lying in bed with a naked chick. Yeah, and I don't give a damn what any cop who may read this thinks about that incriminating statement. So maybe the aforementioned chick was 43, and it was she who was molesting me.

FRIDAY, August 26 — Sorry I skipped a day. Too much going on. I decided since I came this far I couldn't just give up. I passed another miserable shift under shrubbery on Wednesday. Summer nights in Spokane, I discovered, are much colder than in Santa Monica. The ground seemed noticeably harder too. Next time I run away from home I'll remember to bring a sleeping bag and air mattress.

It occurred to me that one of the ways rich people get ahead is by exploiting their family connections. There I was homeless and freezing under a bush when I had a brother who'd been in *People* magazine.

I didn't recall the Hercules Circus having any jugglers, but I had seen a guy who had an interesting act balancing a small pug dog on his nose. That could be interpreted as a form of juggling. After defrosting in a nearby donut shop, I returned to the fair-grounds and tracked down the man, who was walking three pug dogs (all wearing cute bow ties on their collars) by an encamp-ment of large trailers. I asked him if he knew Nick Twisp.

"The juggler?" he asked warily as his dogs sniffed my shoes. "I've met him a few times. Why?"

"He's my brother and I need a job."

"How do I know you're his brother?"

"Well, ask me a question about him."

"What kind of car does he have?"

"He drives a BMW. A gray one with a dent in the rear quar-ter panel from where a guy kicked it in a road-rage incident."

"If you say so. And where does he perform?"

"Formerly at the Normandie casino in Vegas, but he's mov-ing to Paris."

"Really? I hadn't heard that. OK, I suppose you could be his brother. Do you have an act?"

"No, sorry."

"Any skills?"

"Not really. But I work cheap."

I had to wait around all day, but eventually I got in to see the head boss, a balding older Greek fellow (and husband of the lady with the big glasses) named Balasi Patsatzis. He asked me more questions about my brother, and some personal ones too, like was I really 17 and did my family know where I was? I answered those more or less untruthfully, and he finally agreed to try me out for a week or two to determine "the cut of my mustard." My job is mostly janitorial: I clean the office and bunkhouse trailers, plus all the restrooms (called donikers for some reason). I also pick up litter on the lot and operate the bounce house on the midway before and after performances. This is a vinyl structure in the shape of a circus wagon, kept inflated by an electric blower, where kids go in with their shoes off and bounce their little brains out. I'm working 11 hours a day, seven days a week for $95 a week, plus room and board. All I have to do is stick it out for seven weeks, and I'll be back financially where I was when I started. I hope my brother had a better time of it when he ran away to that circus in France.

Will try to write more tomorrow if I have the strength.

SATURDAY, August 27 — We jumped to Coeur d'Alene, Idaho this morning. Not that far; only took an hour. A scenic town on a big blue lake. Lots of townies turned out to watch the big tent go up. They even bused in school kids for the spectacle. A tractor tugs up the two tall center masts, then electric motors on the masts lift up the tent. Next, the crew installs the quarter poles and side poles, hammers in the stakes, unfolds the bleachers, connects up the lights and sound system, and rigs up the equipment for the aerial acts. If it's a hot day like today, they connect up a truck with this huge swamp cooler to blow chilled air into the big top. Meanwhile, the marquee and dining tents are going up, and I'm struggling to unroll the heavy bounce house and get it inflated. In a bit under three hours, the show is ready to open and I'm ready to collapse.

Some circuses use elephants to put up their tents, but Mr. Patsatzis is not big on animal acts. He says they're too much trouble, and he would rather pour a little gas into a tractor than a lot of hay into an elephant. The only exotic animals traveling with the show (excluding Marcel the clown's little monkey and Mr. Barker's pug dogs) are four ostriches ridden by a family of acrobatic Hungarians named Herczegh (pronounced like a vigorous sneeze).

The big tent has seating for about 1,300. When at least 1,000 of them are occupied, Mr. Patsatzis looks slightly less fraught with worry. When the crowd is sparse, he slaps his forehead and moans "Tonight we eat the ostriches!" So far, though, they've stayed off the menu (except for their eggs which on a good morning can feed the entire company). Running a circus is hard on the nerves and on the wallet. Even when the house is full, not all of the seats are paid for. The sponsoring organization or club in each town distributes plenty of Annie Oakleys (free tickets) to kids. Then the kids drag along their parents, who have to fork over for admission, souvenir booklets, balloons, refreshments, etc. Thankfully, the sponsors are contractually obligated to provide port-a-potties, so I don't have to swab up after thousands of slobs.

Since we moved today, only two performances are scheduled. Tomorrow we have three. Circus people are real masochists for work. Probably not the neatest folks on the planet either. All of the trailer restrooms were way overdue for scrubbing. I don't know what they would have done if I hadn't come along. Probably board them up as health menaces. Those roustabouts may be able to pound in huge metal stakes and muscle around great rolls of tent fabric, but they can't hit the side of a barn when they take a piss.

I certainly hope I don't have to spend my life swinging brooms, pushing vacuums, and swabbing toilets. I see now why Nick taught himself to juggle. There's lots to be said for having a marketable skill out here in the real world.

SUNDAY, August 28 — I've been catching a few more snatches of the show. This Señor Alfredo Nunez seems to be something of a big shot in the circus world. He's the only one of the four clowns who gets introduced by name. If there's a Señora Nunez somewhere, she's not in evidence. He lives alone in one of the fancier trailers and drives a big Dodge diesel pickup equipped with a booster seat and pedal extensions. Those trucks,

I know, don't come cheap. He's been totally ignoring me on the lot and in the dining tent.

By the way, the eats are pretty good and they don't skimp on the servings. They can't really, because everyone works up massive appetites slaving so hard. Mostly the kids sit together for meals. There are quite a few, including some pretty girls around my age. Some are performers and some are just brats who travel with their parents. So far they haven't had much to say to the new janitor. I think Randy has been bad-mouthing me to them. He's a nasty little runt with yellow smoker's teeth who claims to be 18, but I have my doubts. If Marty thinks I'm an uncultured clod, he should meet this guy—truly your redneck's redneck. Randy works in the commissary as the helper assistant—a job I would rate as even crummier than mine. When I showed up, they made him move out of a bunkhouse trailer and sleep in the pantry of the commissary trailer. It wasn't my idea, but he still hates my guts.

Depending on their length, the bunkhouse trailers have 10 or 12 tiny roomettes and one communal bathroom in the rear. The earlier you get up, the better your chance of getting in the shower and scoring some hot water. If you bogart the shower too long, a muscular and likely tattooed arm will reach in and yank you out by your hair. Each cell has half a bunk bed, a small closet, storage cupboard, two drawers, one window, a crank-up roof vent, and its own entry door to the outside. If you have an upper bunk like I do, that means the guy on the other side of the thin divider wall has a lower bunk. Fortunately, my neighbor doesn't snore, but I can hear when he snorts, farts, or beats his meat. The actual floor space available for roaming measures 23 inches by 59 inches (less than 10 square feet), so it's not for claustrophobes. Since there's no air conditioning, the rooms can get pretty hot when you're trying to sneak a nap after lunch (not that Mr. Patsatzis or his minions encourage such indulgences). His philosophy is "If you've got time to lean, you've got time to clean." I prefer "You've got nothing to lose by swiping a snooze."

10:48 p.m. Señor Nunez likes to linger in the cook tent after dinner and serenade the stragglers with his accordion. Not my kind of music, but he's pretty good. Tonight he decided to come sit near the janitor while squeezing his box.

"I hear you're the brother of Nick Twisp, the juggler," he commented, shifting his cigarette to a corner of his mouth.

"That's right."

"Then how come your name is Darko?"

"I prefer it to Twisp."

"I knew your brother in Paris years ago."

"Then you had to know Sheeni Saunders."

"I knew her slightly."

"That's not what she said in a letter to my brother."

"What did she say?"

"That you helped her stay with your brother. That she once loved you."

"She said that?"

"Yup."

He smiled, but his fingers shifted into an even sadder tune. Upbeat musically he was not. "She never had her baby, Jake Darko. She got rid of it."

"I don't think so."

"What makes you say that?"

"She has a photo of you. You're holding a newborn."

"There are lots of babies in this world, Jake."

"Yeah, well this one was blond."

"That doesn't prove anything."

"It proves something if Sheeni kept that picture all these years. And kept it hidden."

"You don't know anything, Jake Darko. But you remind me of your brother. He was my friend."

"Yeah? Some friend you turned out to be."

I just checked in with Veeva. She's severely depressed because her brothers are back from summer camp. She feels that they are a plague upon her psyche. (I don't particularly mind my brother and sister, but then I never had to live with them.) She's also depressed because she went to Tyler's first football game of the season Friday night, and was appalled by the number of girls cheering lustily just for him (his team won, naturally).

"Did he pay any attention to you?" I asked.

"Precious little, Jake. I don't think my tits are big enough to suit him."

"Your tits are fine, Veeva. I'd like to have a session with them right now."

"Don't be obscene, Jake. I swore Tyler to secrecy, and told him you were on the case up in Washington."

"I hope we can trust him to keep his trap shut. And I'm in Idaho now."

"How is it?"

"Oh, not bad. Lot of trees and hills. Phone reception is OK so far."

"Made it with any girls yet?"

"Not yet, but I've got my eye on a few."

"I'll bet you have. I miss you, Noel."

"I miss you too."

It was true. My whole body ached for her. I think it's easier to do without sex when you're a virgin, and the sexual appeal of chicks is all theoretical. Now that I know what I'm missing, the pangs are way more acute. But one thing to be said for working like a slave, it does help take a guy's mind off Uma.

MONDAY, August 29 — Stoney Holt called me as I was eating my bacon and eggs. This I do warily after I found a still smoldering cigarette butt between my pancakes yesterday. I had assumed the lump was a pat of dairy-fresh butter. Mr. Povey, the stout black man who commands the big six-burner stove, claimed ignorance of how it happened, but I know it was sabotage by Randy. I had seen him loitering near the griddle when I was passing along with my tray. The butt was his brand too.

Stoney has made progress toward becoming a woman. She

reported she went on a date Friday evening with Sloan Chandler. They went horseback riding and afterwards he kissed her in the barn as restless stallions looked on enviously.

"How was it?" I asked.

"Very nice, Noel, though the sexy stubble is not so great up close. It feels kind of creepy, like you're kissing a dog's butt. Sloan told me I was the 34th girl he's kissed since the fourth grade. The guy's been keeping track on his little pocket computer."

"Yeah, well some guys are into statistics, Stoney. Don't let it get to you. Did you see him again on Saturday?"

"I wish. He went to a big pool party at your ex-bitch goddess's house."

"What!"

"Yeah, he says he likes me, but since we're not going steady, he sees no reason why he can't go out with other chicks too. I'm thinking of giving him a reason, like maybe breaking both of his arms."

"Just be feminine and seductive, Stoney. You'll be going steady with the guy soon if you play your cards right."

"I hope you're right, Noel. Otherwise, I may have to tangle seriously with that Uma bitch."

Uma hosted a pool party for Sloan and pals on Saturday night. So much for her feeling "miserable" about our breakup. She seems to have recovered quickly from that trauma. Damn, I wish I could say the same.

Stoney also reported that Detective Moroni checks in regularly to see if she's heard from Jamal (she hadn't) or me. She assured me that she hasn't told him zip about me. I hope she's telling the truth. She claims the Winnemucca cops may have big hard-ons to find Carlyle, but actually they're secretly pleased that he put our little town on the law enforcement map. She says hunting for Carlyle is a nice diversion from their usual fare of rousting card cheats at the Silver Sluice and busting meth dealers.

4:18 p.m. I got into serious trouble today with Endre Kanavos, the boss's nephew and the Greek in charge of the midway crew. (All our crew bosses are Grecians, as the second President Bush called that ethnicity.) Some local lowlife sneaked behind the bounce house when I wasn't looking and slashed it with a knife. Apparently, soft air-filled structures are irresistible targets to vandals—like giant balloons they feel compelled to burst. All the kids started screaming when it collapsed on them, but I think they were more disappointed that the fun was over than scared. I got my ass chewed while Endre applied a patch to the gash. According to him, my job is to take tickets, manage the kids in line, prevent any roughhousing inside, toss out kids when their time is up, and guard the entire perimeter. Also alert patrons that tempting treats are available at the snack trailer, help lost children find their parents, pick up stray litter, and generally Stay Alert. Most important: I must do all that with a big friendly smile!

Yeah, right. I thought it was the Greeks who invented logical thought. What fantasy world is he living in?

10:27 p.m. Circus people like to hang out after the last show and shoot the breeze, but tonight I headed straight back to my tiny roomette. I think I overdosed on people this past week. Too many new faces to deal with. Big change for a kid who grew up in a lonely trailer on an isolated road in the middle of nowhere. Not much quiet and solitude in a circus, where everyone is piled up on top of each other. People say circuses are "just one big family," as if that were a good thing. You could say the same thing about high school, where the rigid hierarchy calls the shots, everyone competes for attention and status, and the weak or unconventional get forced to the fringes. At least in high school you can go home at 3:30. Here you have everyone in your face every waking hour of the day—not to mention a guy sleeping three feet under your butt at night.

TUESDAY, August 30 — School started in Winnemucca yesterday. How odd not to look forward to seeing Uma in class

189 | Revolting Young

every day. The rest of the experience I may not miss so much. There are kids in this circus who have never been to school a day in their lives. An example of this are Nerea and Miren Lurrieta, who dress in flashy leotards and hop around on a neon-lit trampoline. Seems like an odd thing to do daily with one's parents (and little brother Iker), but they accept turning somer-saults in midair and landing on their dad's brawny shoulders as perfectly normal. They're petite twins about my age and seem quite intelligent despite being entirely home-schooled. Miren, especially, always has her head in a book. They're from Bilbao, a city in northern Spain on the Bay of Biscay—though they re-gard themselves more as Basque than Spanish. They speak En-glish with slight but very endearing accents and are virtually identical. Fortunately for identification purposes, Nerea now dyes her light brown hair a vivid tangerine. Both are somewhat intimidating as they're quite attractive, amazingly fit from a life-time of exercise, and, I think, rather conceited. Walking around between shows in their silver and gold satin capes, they look like costumed heroines from some adventure video game. Much too haughty to notice the new janitor, although lately I've seen signs of a thaw.

So far the friendliest of the performing kids are a couple of Korean brothers, Sam and Jin Pak. Sam's 14 and Jin's 16 (they both seem younger though). They do a very nervous-making aerial act with their father and two uncles on a network of over-sized bungee cords. Lots of plunging from high platforms and bouncing back up to grab tiny handholds or each other. Quite exciting, to be sure, though I think I'll stick to cleaning toilets. They like to practice juggling in their spare time, so are always eager to discuss my famous brother. Both are secretly stuck on the Lurrieta twins, which is not surprising considering how those girls fill out a leotard. I notice Randy pants after them too in his crude and offensive way. What a loser, yet somehow these rednecks always seem to achieve reproductive success.

5:42 p.m. Big crowds today for a Tuesday. Mrs. Patsatzis

says they have a very competent advance man, who arrives a few days ahead of the circus in each town to stir up interest and promote ticket sales. The guy doing that job is her very own daughter Syna. I'm not likely to meet her, since she's always on the road ahead of us. Mrs. Patsatzis claims her daughter is a great beauty, but has trouble meeting men because she's never in one place for more than three or four days. She used to have a thing going with Mr. Barker (the pug balancer), but he got tired of never seeing her and recently married Mrs. Patsatzis's niece Dorcas (another knockout), who does a cloudswing act. This has created some bad blood between Syna and Dorcas, who are cousins and once were as close as sisters. It also pissed off some relatives back in Greece because Dorcas married a non-Greek. God forbid, says Mrs. Patsatzis, that they should ever find out what Dorcas's husband does for a living. Interestingly, Mr. Barker changed his name from Parker (as more fitting for his act), but his wife hates being called Mrs. Barker.

Mrs. Patsatzis also divulged that Señor Nunez has been agitating to have the new janitor canned. Fortunately for me, her husband doesn't believe in firing employees unless they prove incompetent or do something wrong. She thinks that clown is getting "too big for his britches," which would not be difficult since they started out so abbreviated in the first place.

Yeah, Mrs. Patsatzis is a chatty person. She spends long hours every day in the office trailer counting money and doing the books, so she loves to talk when she finds a willing listener. She says if I stick around and work hard, she may marry me off in a few years to one of her younger nieces (right now there are 11 to choose from). If any of them look like Dorcas, I may take her up on the offer.

11:27 p.m. I had an interesting talk after dinner with the tall clown Marcel. It turns out he knew my brother years ago when Nick was traveling with that circus in France. In fact, Marcel claims that he was the one who taught my brother how to juggle. It sounds like Nick had an even worse job than mine. He had to clean all the animal cages and sleep in a truck with two smelly camels. And to duck the French cops, he was shoveling all that shit while trying to pass himself off as a little old lady. Marcel didn't know anything about Sheeni Saunders and her alleged baby, but he warned me that Alfredo Nunez hates my brother and therefore likely has it in for me as well. He says I should watch out for that dwarf, as those little guys can sometimes be ruthless. I thanked him for the advice, and then he asked me what Nick was doing now. When I told him that my brother was off to Paris to live with Reina Vesely, he turned white as a sheet. Then he muttered something I didn't quite catch and abruptly left the table. Very weird. This Reina must be quite a babe to have all these guys so stirred up. And Marcel is really old too—I'd say at least 50.

Most of the occupants of the bunkhouse trailer have little TVs in their rooms, but I've been making do with my pilfered poetry book. These lines from "The Vagabond" by Robert Louis Stevenson seem to apply to us circus folk:

> Give the face of earth around,
>   And the road before me.
> Wealth I ask not, hope nor love,
>   Nor a friend to know me;
> All I ask the heaven above,
>   And the road below me.

I hear we jump to a new town tomorrow. It's a little odd being in Idaho, a state I almost never thought about, even though it's right next door to Nevada. I came up with the first line of a poem about prostitution here: "There once was a ho from Idaho."

This poetry business is not as easy as it looks. Will work on line two tomorrow. Very tired, so I will now say "See you all down the road."

WEDNESDAY, August 31 — We're in Moscow. No, not the one in Russia. We drove an hour and a half down the highway over endless rolling hills and are still in Idaho. A sign by the city limits welcomed us to the "Dry Pea and Lentil Capital of the Nation." Some college is also located here, although no cute coeds turned out to watch the tents go up. Might be a nice town, but all we ever see are the same fast-food joints and big-box chain stores out by the fairgrounds. Not much variation in the outskirts of cities these days. There's a semi-tall hill looming in the distance which a little boy with pink cotton candy in his hair informed me was called Moscow Mountain.

My brother is in Paris and I'm in Moscow. Yes, we Twisps do get around, except my brother doesn't have to travel with toilet brush in hand. I hope this cleaning toilets all day doesn't permanently prejudice me against humankind. So far I'd estimate I've swabbed up a ton and a half of stray pubic hair and other nasty surprises. Too bad people can't just expel waste products out their noses while they breathe. Or produce tidy little packages— hermetically sealed in natural plastic—that emerge ready for sanitary disposal. I believe this area is ripe for some creative genetic engineering. Just think of all the forests that could be saved by eliminating the need for toilet paper. Nor do I feel it is healthy for an impressionable male youth to handle bulky bags of used tampons. Don't blame me if this job warps me for life.

6:05 p.m. I was cleaning up litter in the vicinity of the trampoline, when Miren Lurrieta asked me if I wanted to try it out. I said sure, tore off my shoes, and hopped aboard. She showed me how to jump up and down in the center and warned me not to get too close to the edge. Now simple bouncing is fun, but it turns out that doing anything fancier like landing on your knees or back is much more challenging. My body has had 15-1/2 years to get used to gravity telling it that if I tried something like that it would hurt like hell. So it's very hard to overcome your instinctual resistance to such maneuvers. Despite Miren's coaxing, I found I just couldn't do it. She smiled and said not to worry because such fear was natural, and I could overcome it with practice. I did enjoy sitting on the metal trampoline edge and watching her demonstrate her mastery. I couldn't help marveling how her state-of-the-art jogging bra let her leap about with virtually zero bounce. I wouldn't mind examining its construction someday if I got the chance.

Miren told me that she and her sister already have taken and passed their GEDs (high school equivalency exam). They're thinking of leaving the circus and going away to college in a year. She concedes doing so would be a difficult step, since traveling with circuses is the only life they've ever known. She wants to study literature, but her sister thinks they should get business degrees so they can run their own circus someday. Miren was most impressed when I brought my poetry book into the cookhouse tent yesterday. I told her I was writing a poem, but insisted it was much too personal to show to anyone.

Miren seems the shyer of the two sisters. She has a very cute way of sneaking peeks at you while she talks: little flickers of intelligent interest that dart out at you from her lovely blue eyes. Most enchanting. Amazingly, she also applies glitter to her toenails just like Uma. It appears I have a serious weakness for such foot adornments. Of course, Miren decorates her toes in her professional capacity as a circus performer. As they say in this business: "Flash is cash." Uma, on the other hand (or foot), merely does so to ensnare susceptible youths for the purpose of breaking their hearts.

10:52 p.m. I got two surprises at dinner tonight. First, as I was passing along in line, loathsome Randy leaned forward over the steam table and whispered that if I didn't stop "messing with Miren" he was going to slip rat poison into my eats. I felt like carving him up with my butter knife (he has a prominent Adam's apple that cries out for stabbing). But I told him to cool it and "leave me the hell alone."

Then, as I was finishing my excellent dessert, Alfredo Nunez plopped his be-accordioned self down near me for another chat.

"Any requests?" he inquired. I asked if he knew "Razor Blades in My Socks" by the Pickled Punks. He didn't, so he played another doleful dirge from his vast repertoire of mournful melodies. When that weeper was over, he took out his cigarettes and offered me one. I shook my head, he shrugged, lit up, then asked me if I had been sent here by my brother. I said no, that I rarely saw Nick and was entirely on my own. He pondered that while puffing away, then squeezed out another depressive's lament.

"You know, Jake," he said at last, "I was more the father of that baby than Nick was."

"Oh, really? How did you manage that?"

"Because if it wasn't for me, that baby would never have been born. I'm the one who talked Sheeni into having it."

"Then you admit Sheeni had the kid?"

"Did I ever deny it?"

"I seem to recall you did."

"I gave Sheeni a sanctuary—a place to hide out from Nick and her parents. I could have got in trouble for that. Wound up in jail even. No?"

"If you say so. So where's the kid now?"

"It's a sad story, Jake. I wanted to spare you the details."

"I can take it."

"My brother's family was taking care of Sarah on their farm near Albi. That was the *nina's* name: Sarah Nunez. *Muy bonita.* But there was a bad flu going around the next winter. Little Sarah died."

Señor Nunez produced an authentic tear to accompany that statement.

"She died, huh? That's convenient. Have you got a death certificate to prove it?"

"What?"

"A death certificate. I'm sure they must issue them in France when someone dies. Show me the death certificate, and I'll believe you."

"Why should I show you anything?"

"If my brother's child died, he has a right to know about it."

"Why, Jake Darko? Hasn't he believed all these years that the child was dead?"

I conceded that point, but insisted that the particulars of the death were relevant and must be produced.

"You are a hard person, Jake," he sighed, flicking away his cigarette butt. "There is no place in a circus for a person like you."

"I do my job."

"There is more to life than doing a job, Jake. That is what you Americans do not understand."

# SEPTEMBER

THURSDAY, September 1 — I have now been with this circus for one week. Already I have cleaned a lifetime of toilets and pushed a vacuum the equivalent of half-way around the globe. The litter I have picked up would fill Yankee stadium way up to the cheap seats or bury Randy to a depth of 3,712 feet (sounds like a good idea).

Jin Pak let me check my e-mail this morning on his computer in the Paks' big fifth-wheel trailer. He lives there with his mother and father, two uncles, and brother. The four bachelors sleep in bunks in a tiny room in the rear. His uncles are engaged to gals back in Korea, but both fiancées are mired in long waiting lists for visas. So everyone has to content themselves with lives of convivial celibacy and aerial bungee soaring

Jin has a nice laptop which he connects to the Internet via Bluetooth and his cell phone. Slow for Web cruising, but it does the job for e-mail. I had another message from Nick. Nothing like running away to get my brother's attention at last. He wants me to call him collect at his hotel in Paris. I noted the number in case I should need it sometime. Another e-mail from Awanee informed me that her father had consulted a lawyer, who advised them that they were not liable for any lost rings. She also said that her friend Wylie (Tyler's Reese Witherspoon look-alike girlfriend) was having her Voodoo class put a curse on me. The things you can study these days in Los Angeles high schools.

Tyler also checked in. He may be the only football jock in L.A. whose e-mail messages are always perfectly composed and properly spelled. I hope they don't hold that against him in his application to USC. He reported that Stoney Holt has been trying to make him jealous by e-mailing him daily updates on her romantic activities with "some stud named Sloan Chandler." Tyler didn't seem too concerned, but he did ask me if Sloan was as formidable as Stoney claimed.

I took a chance and replied to Tyler's e-mail. I told him Sloan was nothing special and asked him if he could find out anything on the Internet about Sarah Nunez, a one-year-old child who may have died 14 years ago of influenza in Albi, France.

Still no e-mail messages from Uma, always a fresh source of acute pain.

Speaking of which, Sam and Jin are convinced that Randy and I are destined to duke it out one of these days. To help me prepare for battle, they've been showing me some TaeKwonDo (Korean martial arts) stances and attack moves. I now know the rudiments of the cat and horse stance, thrashing kick, guarding and rising blocks, hammer fist, palmhand strike, and spearfinger thrust.

I don't know, I've never been very good at physical combat. My usual tactic is to frighten away my opponent with a violently hemorrhaging projectile nosebleed (my nose not his). I'm not particularly anxious to tangle with Randy, since he carries a big blade in a sheath on his belt. All redneck youths seem to have those. I think they're presented to them in the hospital when they're born—along with the greasy comb, a coupon for a free tattoo, and that first starter pack of cigarettes.

They're expecting big crowds today, so must end here. I'm wondering why Veeva hasn't called lately. Have I been forgotten already? Is Idaho that far off the map?

FRIDAY, September 2 — The start of the big Labor Day weekend and the end of the summer salad days for circuses. After Monday, I'm told, it will be much harder to dredge up profitable audiences. Townies see frost on a pumpkin and retreat to their houses for six months. They only come out to shovel snow and shop at Wal-Mart.

At last I seem to have achieved a social breakthrough at the kids' table in the cookhouse tent. People seem willing to acknowledge my existence—even those forbiddingly reserved ostrich-jockeys Kardos and Vrsula Herczegh. Kardos is very tall, very thin, and very pale. His sister is equally pale and tall, but only thin in spots. Her narrow waist is the smallest I've seen on anyone over the age of eight. A real hourglass figure like your grandpa used to drool over. And a face that's almost too lovely for sustained viewing—like you don't rate high enough even to lay your eyes on her. Now imagine all that beauty in sparkly purple tights astride a galloping ostrich. It makes for a real eye-opener at 6:30 in the morning.

Kardos is no slouch in the looks department either. My guess is Nerea Lurrieta is semi-infatuated with him, but any flirting with that guy is a challenge since the whole family speaks the barest rudiments of English. Mostly they chatter away in Hungarian, a very foreign-sounding tongue. This is the Herczeghs' first circus tour in North America. If I spoke Hungarian I would ask them if ostrich-riding was a traditional pastime back in their homeland. Since I don't, I'm content to sit next to Miren and discuss the books she's been reading.

This summer Miren has worked her way through Jane Austen, the Bronte sisters, and now she is happily lapping up Anthony Trollope. She says she doesn't understand why there aren't monuments to Trollope in every city in the English-speaking world. I couldn't answer that question since I had never heard of the guy. I do my best, though, to make intelligent-sounding comments. I was never much of a fiction reader, preferring to spend my idle hours cruising the Web or watching videos. When

I felt like reading, I'd usually crack open a juicy computer magazine. This doesn't surprise Miren, who—typical of Europeans—regards America as a nation of lazy thinkers, tubby sports nuts, and narrow-minded religious wackos.

One good thing about circus life, I can sit next to Miren for breakfast, lunch, and dinner. No way I could do that in the real world unless we were married or something. Every time I take the seat beside her, Randy scowls at me from across the steam table. I notice this morning he fished out the limpest, most fat-laden strips of bacon to dump on my plate. He also burned my toast, not realizing that's exactly how I prefer it. All this sabotage is for naught, since Miren assured me that she regards him as a Total Creep and has steadfastly snubbed his crude overtures. His sister was even more blunt, having warned Randy to maintain a minimum five-meter distance from her at all times or she'll call a cop. Yet he remains undeterred, being both supremely confident of his appeal to chicks and profoundly ignorant of the metric system.

8:48 a.m. I sneaked a break from my toilet duties and phoned Veeva in L.A. Her manner at first was distinctly chilly. Maddy had not only blabbed, she had wildly exaggerated my entanglements with her horny brother.

"She said you guys couldn't keep your hands off each other," Veeva noted. "Her mother thinks you're practically engaged."

"All lies," I protested. "We just played a few video games in his room."

"Then Marty didn't spend the night with you in their guestroom?"

"Well, he tried, but I kicked him out. Jesus, Veeva, do I strike you as being gay?"

"One never knows these days, Noel, though your tastes do seem rather unrefined for someone of that persuasion. Of course, living all those years in Minnetonka could explain that."

"It's Winnemucca!"

"Whatever. It's really not anything to keep bragging about, Noel."

I sighed and brought her up-to-date on my latest conversation with Señor Nunez. She agreed that he had spilled some potentially valuable information that we should follow up on. And, like me, she thought the untimely flu death sounded a bit too convenient. She said she would check in with Tyler to see if he had discovered anything more about young Sarah Nunez. Meanwhile, she suggests I break into the dwarf's trailer and poke around. I pointed out that a crime like that would be difficult to manage since everything on the lot is kept locked up tight because all these larcenous townies will steal you blind. She told me to use my "Twisp street smarts" to find a way in.

Easy for her to say. She's not the one facing arrest for breaking and entering—or worse if the dwarf catches me in the act.

Veeva then filled me in on the latest Reina Vesely news. The reason that chick sent Veeva's dad packing back to California was not that she didn't love him. She said if she let him abandon his wife and children, then she and Paul would be no better than her ex-husband who had deserted his own family.

"Sounds reasonable to me," I commented.

"Not at all, Noel. Don't you see? If they love each other, they should be together. I mean, it would be hard on us, but we'd survive."

"You wouldn't mind if your father moved to France and you never saw him again?"

"Of course, I'd mind. Daddy is the vital buffer between me and my mother. Half the time he's the only thing keeping us from murdering each other. But I love my father, Noel. I want to see him happy."

Wow, it's possible to love a parent. I suppose I love Grandma, but then we're not actually related.

"How happy is he likely to be, Veeva? Even if Reina overcame her scruples and married him, your mother would probably guilt-trip him to death."

"I know. My mother is so manipulative it's scary. I sometimes think everything would be so much simpler if my father were an attractive and wealthy widower with three adorable children."

"Don't do it, Veeva. You'd never get away with it."

"I know, Noel. My mother's probably already placed a letter with her attorney fingering me as the prime suspect in the event of her untimely death."

"So what are you going to do, Veeva?"

"I don't know, Noel. But I have to do something before Reina marries your damn brother."

"Is that likely to happen?"

"My father fears it may. It may be Reina's way of sacrificing her true love and closing off that avenue for good."

"Well, you're just hearing your father's side of things. Reina may in fact love my brother."

"Don't be silly, Noel. There's no way your brother could be loved as deeply as my father. Daddy is a wonderful and extraordinary man. Your brother's a fucking juggler."

I knew better than to argue that point with the world's most rabid daddy's girl. I gave her a big wet phone kiss and rang off.

Wow, my brother may be getting married again. I hope I'm invited to the wedding this time.

5:18 p.m. One of Mr. Barker's dogs got loose today, and everyone had to drop what they were doing and go hunt for him. Mr. Barker was pretty frantic. Apparently, purebred pug dogs are a desired item, and people are not above stealing them. I scored some major brownie points (and a $10 reward) by locating the lost beast. He was licking a greasy pan that Randy had ditched in some bushes rather than going to the trouble of scrubbing it. How I enjoyed watching that turd get his ass chewed by stern Mr. Povey for that misdemeanor.

Mr. Barker invited me into his nice trailer for a celebratory glass of sherry. Now there's a drink that's quite a major comedown from the original grape juice. Virtually undrinkable, but I tried to be polite and gulped down most of it. My host gave me a tour, showing me the actual bed where he cuddles nightly with the voluptuous Dorcas Barker. I'd balance more than a pug on my nose to swap places with that lucky dude, who—unaccountably—doesn't seem all that thrilled with his lot in life. Apparently, having a dog act in a circus is a source of considerable career frustration.

Sure, people applaud when you balance a small fawn pug on your nose—but it turns out they're applauding the dog not the performer. They don't give much credit to the guy who 1. spent years training the dog to stand perfectly rigid, and 2. has mastered the very difficult art of balancing a 14-pound canine on a remarkably small perch—namely the end of his nose.

"Hell, my wife gets a much bigger hand for swinging around on a velvet sling with half her tits hanging out," he complained, swigging down another glass of sherry.

True enough, but they're remarkably applaudable tits.

"Then why do you do it, Mr. Barker?"

"I don't know, Jake. I guess I've always liked dogs—especially pugs. They're not the brightest breed on the block, but they're incredibly loyal and eager to please."

His loyal dogs lay at his feet and beamed up at him. Today they were modeling yellow polka-dot bow ties clipped to matching rhinestone-studded collars.

"Does your wife like them too?" I asked.

"I thought she did, Jake, but lately she's been agitating to have them thrown out of our bedroom. Can you imagine that?"

"They sleep with you in bed?" I asked, shocked.

"Of course, Jake. Dogs are pack animals. And the pack always sleeps together in a big pile. It's very pleasant and cozy on a cold night."

I wanted to ask him how the dogs fit in when he was having sex with Dorcas, but I feared he'd get offended and demand his $10 back. So I thanked him for the sherry and added that I thought he had the best act in our show. I think that compliment meant something to him coming from the brother of the illustrious Nick Twisp.

SATURDAY, September 3 — Payday at last. I got my $95 in cash, just the way I like it. No deductions for Uncle Sam or Social Security. Why should a kid have to fork over part of his meager wage to underwrite the retirement of a bunch of free-loading Baby Boomers?

That was today's good news.

The bad news is that two of the younger roustabouts left to go back to college. Which freed up Randy to move back into the bunkhouse trailer, specifically the roomette adjoining mine. His repulsive unwashed person is now installed on the bunk directly below me. Yuck. I can feel waves of Randroid creepiness ooz-ing through the thin divider walls. Not to mention the tinny blasts of his cheap radio tuned to the trashiest possible rural lowlife station. The idiot also smokes in bed and very likely will incinerate both of us one of these nights.

We jumped this morning to Grangeville, a small prairie town at the foot of the Bitterroot Mountains. I'm supposed to ride in the cab of the generator truck, but I find I can grab another hour's sleep by staying put in my roomette while we roll along. Although Grangeville is the seat of Idaho County (which is larger than the entire state of New Jersey), only 3,300 reclusive folks call it home. The population of the county is barely 15,000, but Mr. Patsatzis is optimistic that a large fraction of them will turn out for the circus. After all, what else is there to do around here? Not that they have much time to think it over. After three shows today, we jump again tomorrow. Mr. Patsatzis says small towns can be lucrative—especially on big holiday weekends—but it doesn't pay to hang around.

Time to man the bounce house, a task I'm now coming to rate even below toilet swabbing. All that boinging up and down must addle those little kids' brains. They become so loud and unruly I just want to murder them. And their obnoxiously in-dulgent parents are so damn protective. Hey, why shouldn't I give their little bastard's arm a slight tug or twist when he dis-obeys my instructions? What I really need is a cattle prod to handle the kids, a whip to use on their parents, and a machine gun to take out those sneaky fabric slashers. Too bad life can't be more like a video game—extremely violent with many satisfyingly sadistic opportunities to score.

5:47 p.m. Looks like my acrobat lessons are over. I was taking a ten-minute break between shows with Miren on the trampoline when her father told me to lay off. He wasn't very nice about it either. He said it was a "professional circus prop," not a toy for anyone in the company to use. Miren protested, but he said their insurance doesn't cover use by "outsiders." Guess I know where I stand with that dude.

As I was walking back to the bounce house, Señor Nunez stopped me to say he has something to show me. No, he wouldn't say what it was, but he invited me to have a drink with him in his trailer after the evening performance. Should be interesting, since Miren says his decor is not to be believed.

SUNDAY, September 4 — I'm screwed. I mean like totally screwed. Things are still a little fuzzy. I remember going to Señor Nunez's messy trailer, furnished in ornate kid-sized Mexican furniture. Kind of surreal with this mind-boggling clutter of clown memorabilia packed in everywhere. I remember he was drinking rum in pineapple juice and fixed one for me. Rather tasty and tropical. Then things start to get hazy. I remember feeling woozy like I was going to throw up and then I must have passed out. Later (much later?) I woke up damp and shivering. I was lying in a ditch in the middle of a forest. How I got there I couldn't tell you. A half moon overhead gave off enough light for me to see I'd been dumped beside what looked like an old logging road.

Crawling to my feet, I was trying to curse that damn dwarf, but my mouth wouldn't work. It was stuffed with little squares of paper. I spit out this sticky wad and was trying to figure out if it was a message or Sarah Nunez's death certificate or something when things began to get really weird. It felt like the trees were starting to close in on me. I sat on a rock to get my bearings and tried not to panic, but I kept getting more and more anxious. I started hearing these strange noises like animals creeping up on me and weird voices of people I couldn't see. I could feel muscles in my body I'd never noticed before clinching up and shutting down. Then it felt like my mind was somehow becoming detached from my body and that was really scary. Complete and total panic set it.

I shut my eyes and saw eight glowing red eyes staring back at me. That wasn't working, so I opened my eyes and saw my hands and forearms were now covered with tattoos. Only these tattoos were moving like some kind of animated nightmare cartoon. Then I really lost it and threw myself back into the ditch. It felt like the ground was moving under me like I'd landed on a pile of 500 squirming rats. I started to scream, only it sounded like the massed voices of an entire city, a whole universe of people. Then I watched terrified as two furry arms unwound from my stomach. Fearing they were going to strangle me, I thought my pounding heart would burst, but the arms embraced me gently around the shoulders, which felt oddly comforting, although I didn't like the prickliness of the hairs. Somehow I could sense the touch of every individual hair. I also could sense a different color for each follicle, including a whole galaxy of luminous colors that were entirely new to my eyes. I stared up at the moonlit trees, which seemed to take the shape of infinitely branching geometric designs. I watched fascinated as the stars in the violet-black sky rearranged themselves to form new constellations and pulsed out profound messages directly into my brain.

Don't ask me how long I lay in that ditch. It seemed like hours and hours. I saw vision after vision like I'd plugged into some miraculous alien world. Sometimes I shivered from cold and sometimes I felt a warm tropical breeze like I was lying on a beach in Hawaii. Then the night sky began to lighten and I could feel the furry arms gradually release their grip. I became aware of a shooting pain in my hip from where I'd been lying for hours on a sharp rock. I crawled to my feet again and started walking back and forth to get warm. I had a sweatshirt on over my t-shirt, but was very, very cold and my teeth were chattering.

I tried to get a sense of where I was: steep hills covered in dense forest. I figured I probably wasn't that far in off some highway, but I didn't know which way to walk. I listened for the sound of passing cars, but heard nothing except morning bird chatter. I still felt woozy and a little sick to my stomach. I wasn't sleepy at all, even though I'd been awake most of the night. I found the wad of paper I spit out and examined it. Little paper squares covered in brightly colored designs. Didn't mean anything to me, but I stuck the soggy mess in my pocket. I felt around in my other pockets. No wallet and no cell phone. That dwarf had cleaned me out. I was starting to feel hungry too.

I remembered from somewhere that if you're lost in the woods, it's best to walk downhill. So I set off down the logging road. Every time I came to a branch in the road, I took the lane that appeared to be going downhill. But I must have missed the turnoff to the highway. I walked for hours and wasn't getting anywhere. Sometimes the roads I followed petered out and I had to backtrack. The sun was well past overhead when I came to a big mountain stream tumbling down through giant boulders. I took a long drink of the icy water and decided to follow the stream as best I could. I struggled around rocks and over ravines for at least another hour when I rounded a point and spotted an old guy in boots up to his waist standing in the stream and flicking a fishing rod back and forth.

The men weren't too happy to see me. It was a guy in his 30s named Gary and his laconic father-in-law. They had driven there in a four-wheel-drive pickup with a camper mounted on the back. At first they wanted me to wait until Monday afternoon for a lift back to Grangeville, but I managed to talk Gary into interrupting his trout-fishing holiday to give me a ride back to the highway. He also grudgingly fixed me a peanut butter sandwich. The trip back to the main road was 13.7 miles by Gary's odometer. It appeared I'd been walking entirely the wrong direction the whole time. Gary said if I hadn't found them there was not much between me and distant Montana except thousands of square miles of national forest. He dropped me on the asphalt and pointed the direction I should hitch to get back to Grangeville. Not many cars came by, so it was dusk by the time I made it back to the fairgrounds.

Of course, the Hercules Circus had long since departed. I walked around and found most of my stuff dumped in a drainage ditch. I shoved the muddy clothes into my backpack, rescued my battered poetry book from a puddle, and retrieved my $5 laptop from where it had lodged behind a rock. The thing still works as demonstrated by this sad blog entry, which I'm typing at the rear table of the only café still open this time of night in Grangeville. I just ate an entire extra-large, family-sized pepperoni pizza and still feel like I could wedge in another slice or two. Thank God for the $50 bill in my shoe. Never did find my cell phone, so communication is a problem. No, I don't know where the circus was headed next, and nope I never bothered to write down their phone number. No, I don't have a place to spend the night.

As I noted before, I'm screwed. Big time.

MONDAY, September 5 — Labor Day in Grangeville, Idaho. Not the most festive of holidays in this burg. Most of the stores and businesses are closed down tight, including the café where I was hoping to eat breakfast. So I had to content myself with a plastic-wrapped pastry from a gas station. I asked the clerk why I couldn't find a working pay phone in town. She seemed to think it was because everyone had cell phones these days. So sorry, but company policy prevented her from letting me use their phone. She suggested if it was an emergency that I walk over to the sheriff's office and ask to use their phone. Of course, that was the one building in town Dr. Richard Kimball and I weren't going anywhere near.

It had rained overnight, but I had stayed dry. If you walk down a residential street in small towns in rural Idaho, you'll discover that lots of houses have trailers or motorhomes parked next to them. And in such locales people are not as inclined to lock their doors. The second trailer I tried was unsecured. Smelled a bit musty inside, but I made myself at home. Didn't dare switch on a light, but I found a sleeping bag rolled up in a cupboard so I didn't freeze. Slept like a dead dwarf, but woke up early enough to sneak out without being seen. The RV toilet flushing mechanism didn't seem to be working, so I left behind an unpleasant memento in the bowl.

3:13 p.m. I'm in a laundromat in a little shopping center. My clothes are finishing up in a dryer. I knotted my soggy poetry book inside a t-shirt and tossed it in as well. A nice Mexican lady with four little kids just lent me her cell phone and I made a collect call to Veeva in L.A. Actually, she was in Newport Beach where she had been dragged by her parents to watch young Nipsie (the real one) compete in a video game tournament. Therefore, she could not access a computer to look up the Hercules Circus tour schedule. She did clear up a few mysteries. She said the knockout drops they used on me were likely chloral hydrate or gamma-hydroxybutyrate (GHB), which are popular "date rape" drugs. She knows all about such menaces because her paranoid mother is always handing her articles to read and warning her never to leave her beverage unattended at parties. The little paper squares are called blotters, and each of them contains a potent hit of LSD. The normal practice, Veeva informed me, was to put one or two of them under your tongue. Packing in a great wad of them definitely was not recommended.

"Sounds like someone wanted to send you on a very bad trip," she commented.

"Yeah, well, they did."

"Have you had any flashbacks yet?"

"No," I replied, alarmed. "Is that common?"

"Mostly for chronic users, Noel, but since you did a whole

lifetime's worth in one night, you may have some. Don't they know anything about acid in Owatonna?"

"That's Winnemucca, Veeva. No, we're totally into meth there."

"I hear that stuff turns your teeth to cheese. God, Noel, what are you going to do?"

"I'm considering therapeutic suicide."

"I guess you'll have to stay put. I'll overnight you another cell phone and the circus schedule in care of general delivery there. It should be at the post office by Wednesday."

"Oh, fuck!" I groaned. "Can you add some cash too?"

"I'll try, Noel. God, the situations you get yourself into!"

I didn't point out that I wouldn't be stranded in Podunkville, USA with an acid-fried brain if it weren't for her.

TUESDAY, September 6 — More rain. Cold too. Does Idaho go straight from summer to winter? I'm holed up in the little public library. They have a computer with an Internet connection, so I was able to find the circus schedule. I also e-mailed Mr. Patsatzis that I had been inadvertently detained in Grangeville and to please hold my job open for me. Also did some emergency research on LSD flashbacks. They can happen any time—even years later! I did find out that many famous people have taken LSD and still get written up regularly in *People* magazine. All of which makes me hopeful that I have not permanently toasted my brain.

I got kicked out of my trailer last night. The homeowner's little ratty dog sniffed me out and barked his damn head off like I was Charles Manson on a crime spree. All the other ones I tried were locked. So I sat up in the laundromat until it closed at midnight, then crashed behind a dumpster in an alley. I don't know how the homeless survive in cold climates. Perhaps they don't and nobody cares. First thing this morning after the stores opened I blew $8.99 from my dwindling stash for the warmest thrift-shop coat I could find. I think it may be intended for chicks, since the buttons are arrayed down the wrong side. Plus, in direct daylight the burnt rust color veers suspiciously toward pink.

Feeling and looking extremely grungy. Haven't showered or brushed my teeth since Saturday. Move over, Dad. I expect pigeons will be roosting on me soon.

WEDNESDAY, September 7 — Veeva's package contained her brother Nipsie's spare cell phone, one measly crummy $20 bill, the now redundant circus schedule, and this note:

> Darling Noel,
> I looked up Grangeville in Daddy's atlas. It's in the MIDDLE of NOWHERE! Hope you are COPING and holding together physically and MENTALLY. You sounded in a VERY bad STATE on the phone. Alas, Tyler has been able to find out NOTHING about Sarah Nunez. That dwarf may be LYING. You must deploy all your WILES against him. I realize you have mostly failed MISERABLY so far, but I DO have confidence in you. Remember, Noel, you are a TWISP—the most CUNNING and RESOURCEFUL of men. Sorry, this is all the cash I could muster. School is commencing and one is simply OVERWHELMED by financial necessities. Btw, Maddy reports her brother is MISSING you terribly. He keeps babbling about his LOST BUTTERFLY. Thought you'd like to know.
> Also loving you,
> Veeva
>
> P.S. While I was at it, I looked up Winnemucca on the map. Your home town is ABSURDLY remote. You are WELL out of there!

Thanks a pantsful, kid, as I once heard my brother say to Ada when they were discussing which corkscrew he would be permitted to retain.

12:07 p.m. Had the cheapest budget lunch I could find,

211 | REVOLTINGLY YOUNG

washed my face in a gas station restroom, and am about to blow this burg.

Montana here I come!

FRIDAY, September 9 — Sorry I skipped a day. One of these days, blog readers, I may just decide to skip the rest of my life. No, there is no such thing as justice in this world. I knew that already, but I got slapped with a fresh reminder yesterday. Señor Nunez denied any knowledge of my alleged kidnapping, and I think Mr. Patsatzis believed him. It was not just my word against the dwarf's. His story was corroborated by Randy, who testified that when I returned from Señor Nunez's trailer last Saturday night, I asked him if he wanted to drop some acid with me. The lying asshole also stated that I was always abusing various substances and asking him where I could score drugs.

Mr. Patsatzis was ready to send me on my way, but his wife said she thought I deserved another chance if I promised to renounce drugs and stay straight.

So now everyone in the show thinks I'm a deadbeat drughead, and Randy is walking around pleased as punch.

6:28 p.m. We're in Missoula. All these small western towns are starting to look alike to me. Business is way down because of the lousy weather. You wouldn't believe the mud everyone tracked into my nice clean donikers while I was away. Very demoralizing. If I'm going to be subjected to LSD flashbacks, I wish they'd happen while I'm hunched sponge in hand over a stinking toilet. An out-of-body experience would be most welcome then.

I had to sit with Jin and Sam Pak at dinner tonight because the Lurrieta sisters have been warned by their parents not to associate with me. Jin was hot to arrange a duel of honor with Randy, but I told him I was still too wasted from my ordeal in Idaho. Señor Nunez, who serenaded everyone after dinner as if nothing had happened, is back to pretending I don't exist. As I was leaving the cookhouse tent, that strange tall clown Marcel sidled up to me to chat. He reminded me that he had warned me about the dwarf, and added that he had seen Alfredo and Randy around midnight last Saturday muscling my unconscious person into the back of the big Dodge pickup. When I demanded to know why he hadn't tried to stop them, he replied that he never gets involved in such affairs. And no, he wouldn't go with me to the boss to back up my story. His parting words were, "Frankly, Jake, I thought we'd seen the last of you. I was amazed when you turned up here again alive." Not that he seemed care one way or the other if I'd lived or died.

11:49 p.m. If I had a gun, I could fire it straight down into my mattress and kill Randy. What an intriguing idea, except I'm not sure eliminating that moron would merit the destruction of a perfectly good mattress. As I was pondering these matters, someone tapped lightly on my roomette door. I feared it was Señor Nunez back to finish the job, but it turned out to be darling Miren. Since my quarters were not secure from eavesdropping slimeballs, we sneaked off in the rain to the cab of the swamp-cooler truck. It smelled of diesel fuel and old seat covers, but I found that if you snuggled close to Miren, you hardly noticed such things. I gave her the full scoop on what happened to me, and she gave me a great deal of sincere and welcome sympathy. By then we were rather fully embraced, so I tried an experimental kiss. Extreme fireworks such as I had known only briefly with Uma. I don't know if all that acid expanded my mind, but I had never before experienced such a feeling of complete union with another person. It was like a direct connection through our lips from one beating heart to another.

Miren had to get back, but she promised to try to see me again when she could.

What a revelation. Is it possible there's another girl in this universe for me besides Uma?

SATURDAY, September 10 — We jumped this morning to Butte, an old mining town perched on the edge of a giant hole in the ground. I'm told this is an abandoned open-pit copper mine, now filled with acidic water so toxic it will boil the flesh right off your bones. A real environmental disaster, but helpful for attracting tourists, who come to gawk at its scary immensity. Mr. Patsatzis is hoping some of them will come to look at us. Butte is also the birthplace of Evel Knievel, a bus- and canyon-jumping daredevil who inspired generations of dirt bikers and snowboarders to sail off into the sky in bone-crunching disregard of gravity.

The gray clouds have all blown away and things are starting to dry out. A soggy circus is a very forlorn thing, which may be why they call our type of smaller circus a "mud show."

While waiting for the first bounce house customers to show up, I used my latest hand-me-down cell phone to check in with my old pal Stoney Holt, who informed me that she has now experienced heterosexual lovemaking three times with studly Sloan Chandler.

"So how is it?" I asked.

"Aw, it's OK. Hurt sorta bad the first time. I mean that's a pretty big thing to be shoving in a guy."

"You didn't enjoy it?"

"Not really. I'm not seeing what all the fuss is about, Noel."

"Well, perhaps Sloan is just a clumsy lover."

"I don't know. He seems to be doing the usual stuff. I like it when he goes down on me, but then I could get some cute chick to do that. And I wouldn't have to pretend to be some feminine princess all the time."

"Well maybe you are a dyke, Stoney."

"I don't know, I think sometimes I am, but then I see him with that bitch Uma and I want him really bad."

"Is he making it with her too?" I asked, attempting to sound marginally disinterested.

"He claims not, but I know all you guys are lying assholes in that department."

"I think you should keep doing it, Stoney. Some chicks just take longer to get warmed up to sex."

"That's easy for you to say, Noel. You're not the guy with the pussy getting banged."

"I know, Stoney, but lots of chicks just can't get enough of it once they get, you know, stretched out."

By then there was a parent in my face wondering what the hell I was talking about. I took her tickets, admitted her two rugrats, and told Stoney I had to go. She reminded me to call my grandmother and said she'd call my new cell phone number if she heard from Carlyle.

I can't let Stoney break up with Sloan. She's my only hope of keeping him away from Uma. I know he's just the sort of experienced male that misguided Uma would be inclined to yield her virginity to. If only there were some way I could make Stoney's complaints known to Uma. Not to mention contrast them with the numerous good times enjoyed by Veeva with yours truly. Clearly, the facts prove that I am the preferred sexual partner for restless virgins.

11:14 p.m. Pretty good crowds today. Mrs. Patsatzis said her daughter the advance man did some heavy flirting with a bigwig in the Butte schools, who agreed to distribute an Annie Oakley (free ticket) to every grammar school kid in town. The bounce house alone did over $400 in business, which pays for a whole month of my valuable services.

After the last show Kardos Herczegh stopped me to ask in his very halting English if I would sell him some weed. He was disappointed when I replied that I wasn't in that line of work, but invited me to share a joint with him. This we did in the cab of the ostrich truck. Quite powerful, mind-expanding stuff. In reviewing my experiences with various intoxicants, I'd have to say it's more likely that I'll wind up addicted to drugs than alcohol. Kardos smokes several joints a day, which is how he copes with missing his girlfriend back in Sopron and having to ride ostriches for a living. He speaks only about 200 baby English words, but is fluent in German, which overlaps much more with English than Hungarian. So whenever he'd get stuck for a word,

215 | REVOLTINGLY YOUNG

he'd say it in German and I'd try to figure it out. (I, needless to say, know no German.) A tough way to communicate, but his potent grass helped grease the language skids.

Kardos would rather be going to a university in Germany to become a sanitation engineer. He says you can get a very good job in Hungary with a German technical degree. Hard to believe a good-looking guy like him wants to devote his life to cleaning up the stuff people flush down toilets, but there you have it. His parents, though, are insisting that he stick with the family trade even though he finds it boring and unchallenging. Plus, he doesn't care much for ostriches except grilled with garlic and onions. Plus, he's horny in the extreme because all the attractive chicks in this circus are either married or too young. He had his eye on Dorcas, but then she ran off with the "damn dog man."

He said he knew Nerea was interested, but didn't dare go near her. Basque parents, he explained, are even less enlightened than Hungarian ones. If he so much as touched Nerea, who is only 15, and her father found out about it, he would likely be: 1. Brutally killed, 2. Arrested and prosecuted for rape, 3. Forced to marry her at gunpoint, or 4. A combination of the above. He wasn't taking any chances and advised me to steer clear of Miren as well.

Damn, how can I do that now that I've tasted her sweet lips? I've had the appetizer and am more than ready to sample the main course.

SUNDAY, September 11 — I found a large fried cockroach in my scrambled ostrich egg this morning. Head chef Mr. Povey insisted the bug hadn't come from his "spotless kitchen," but we all know its source. These provocations can only end in violent bloodshed. I must recall my UPT heritage and prepare for a fight to the finish. Too bad I have virtually no muscles and weigh a scant 131 pounds.

Things weren't entirely grim this morning. A note was passed to me from Miren inviting me to "attend church" with her. She left with her Bible in hand as she does nearly every Sunday morning, and I met up with her a few blocks away. We strolled into town and explored its sleepy streets. Parts were almost like a ghost town. Whole city blocks of old brick and wooden buildings were boarded up and abandoned. None of the churches we passed appealed to Miren, so we found a café open downtown and had a coffee. I held her warm hand under the table and we discussed her father's temperament. Yes, he was excessively protective toward his daughters and no, he did not regard me with favor. Yes, he had a German Luger concealed in their trailer, and yes, as a veteran of the Spanish Army he knew how to use it. Yes, his restrictions bothered her, but they really bugged her sister, who has been scanning their audiences for cute boys for as long as Miren could remember. Having tried and failed all summer to get Kardos alone, Nerea was thinking seriously of giving up on Hungarian men. Miren feared she might next focus her amorous attentions on me. I told her not to worry, and we exchanged an invigorating coffee-flavored kiss. She looked amazingly desirable dressed for worship in her hand-crocheted head scarf of white lace. Almost like some of the brides that Toby used to escort along the bridal path.

That's a thought. Except that I'm a fugitive and have no money, I can think of no compelling reason why we shouldn't run away and get married.

It's true. When I'm with Miren, I can barely remember what that chick Uma looked like.

10:18 p.m. I've been observing Señor Nunez. That dwarf always locks his trailer door when he exits and slips his key ring into his pants pocket. All the clowns change into their costumes in a small "clown alley" tent in the back yard behind the big top. According to Miren, each of them has a trunk in which they stow their street clothes while performing. Señor Nunez secures his trunk with a combination padlock. Presumably, he also locks his key ring inside, since his various costumes have only big floppy pockets for props.

I've borrowed a flashlight from the cleaning supplies cabinet. I will now go into maximum stealth mode to see what I can see.

11:31 p.m. I'm back. Pretty quiet out there on the lot. Only person about was Mr. Barker walking his pugs before that final assault on bed and Dorcas. I sneaked into the little tent and located the trunk with the combination padlock. Fortunately, it's a fairly common brand. I tried my high-school locker combination, but not surprisingly that didn't work. Still, I think I've worked out a plan. It will probably get me arrested or killed, but, hey, it's a plan.

MONDAY, September 12 — Vrsula Herczegh (Kardos's beautiful sister) and I went through the line together this morning, then switched trays. When she fished a cigarette butt out of her oatmeal, she complained loudly and indignantly to Mr. Patsatzis. The complaints of a performer (even in unintelligible Hungarian) count way more with that Greek than some lowly janitor's. They didn't have to call in Sherlock Holmes to figure out whose butt it was. Only one dirtball on our team smokes Kools, and that was the Randroid behind the counter. He got his skinny ass chewed by the big boss himself, and I enjoyed a pristine and hearty breakfast in the company of Hungary's prettiest 16-year-old. Too bad she's not fluent in German like her brother. We could only converse at toddler level employing the simplest of English words. We didn't get very far socially, which is just as well as Miren was directing some nasty looks at us from down the table. Once we're married, I expect she will be keeping me on a very short leash.

After breakfast I walked into town and bought the various items I need for tonight's major felony. I'm doing it tonight, because if I allow myself any more time to think about it, I'm sure I'll chicken out. And that's just not in the Twispian Creed.

11:49 p.m. I feel a little lightheaded. I expect it's from extreme nerves or too much smoking. Anyway, during tonight's bust out (when the clowns entertain the arriving townies), I sneaked into their tent with my new bolt-cutters concealed under my coat. Its carbon-steel jaws snapped through Señor Nunez's $6.99 padlock like it was so much cheese. I know how much his lock cost, because after I fished out his key ring from his pants, I slapped on an identical padlock that I had purchased yesterday. That should keep the clown busy for a while.

Two minutes later I was sneaking unobserved (I hope) into his trailer. I closed all his blinds and switched on my borrowed flashlight. Pretty creepy. That guy may be the world's shortest lousy housekeeper. Really, if you're going to live full-time in a trailer, you have to make an effort to be a little neat or things quickly descend into chaos.

I started in the front living room. I found a small plastic shampoo bottle in the cupboard where he stored his booze. I screwed off the cap and sniffed. Not shampoo, but some clear, odorless liquid. Date rape anyone? I slipped the bottle into my jacket pocket. Under a pillow on the messy built-in sofa I found a scary-looking blue steel handgun. Perhaps he had planned to use it on me if the knockout drops hadn't worked. The weapon I also pocketed, reasoning that Alfredo was one guy I didn't want packing heat. Besides, I figured the gun might help even the odds if I ever found myself going up against Randy's knife. In another cupboard I found a stack of *Little People* magazines—some sort of lifestyle journal for dwarves. Kind of interesting, but I had no time for light reading.

The kitchen was too disgusting for more than a cursory going over. Despite the hearty meals served in the cookhouse, it appeared that Señor Nunez liked to snack. The bathroom yielded nothing but an involuntary shudder. On to the rear bedroom. Not surprisingly, slovenly Alfredo did not make his bed or hang up his clothes. I found a big stash of personal papers in cardboard boxes under his bed. Lots of scrapbooks filled with press clippings about the noted Mexican clown. The guy had received laudatory reviews all over the world, yet here he was entertaining retired copper miners in Butte, Montana. Seemed like some-

219 | R<small>EVOLTINGLY</small> Y<small>OUNG</small>

thing of a comedown, but I suppose at his age he was regarded as over the hill. Yet I can testify he still convulsed audiences at every show.

Big piles of dusty sheet music, but under them I found a bound packet of old letters; most of them in Spanish and nothing that looked like it came from Aunt Sheeni. Certainly nothing mentioning Sarah Nunez or her death, and I checked through all the papers carefully. In another box I found an envelope of old photos, and as I was going through them I heard a key turn in the front door.

Damn!

I switched off my light, pocketed the photos, slid the box back under the bed, and peered forward around the bedroom door. I watched alarmed as Randy switched on the overhead light and scratched his balls. Apparently the Randroid had his own key to Alfredo's trailer. Cozy for the redneck, but unanticipated by me.

Randy helped himself to a beer from the frig, turned on the TV, and slipped in a DVD. He flopped down on the sofa and fast-forwarded with the remote. The screen was pointed away from me, but the low-grade synthesized music and sounds of rhythmic grunting suggested he was not viewing a highbrow film. Sure enough, he proceeded to pull down his trousers and grab hold of his disgusting privates. A beer can in one hand and his dick in the other—what more could a redneck want?

Double damn!

I hoped he'd get it over quickly, but Randy wasn't that kind of guy. He just pawed himself enough to keep things aroused and tingling while what sounded like 14 people and a donkey went at it on the screen.

Fuck!

I looked at the illuminated clock on Alfredo's nightstand. Time was moving on, even if Randy wasn't. And how come all those cigarettes hadn't stunted that guy's growth? Very bushy too, suggesting a genetic link between extreme obnoxiousness and an overabundance of pubic hair.

I contemplated the bedroom windows. The rear one might have been big enough to climb through, but there was way too much clutter on the vanity desk to get at it. My only escape was out the front door.

Fortunately, the trailer I'd chosen to break into was the home of a clown with packrat tendencies. It took me about five minutes of silent searching to find everything I needed.

When I was ready, I composed myself, took a deep breath, uttered a piercing scream and ran toward the oafish masturbator with a large (albeit plastic) hatchet raised over my head in a most threatening manner. He turned white with fright and dove toward the floor, while I hurtled out the door and dashed madly toward the ostrich truck. There I quickly ditched my hatchet, blond fright wig, satanic skull mask, and colorful Mexican serape. I then ambled casually into the back entrance of the big top and blended in with the departing townies. Randy rushed in about a minute later for a hurried conference with you know who.

A half hour later Mr. Patsatzis knocked on my roomette door. Lurking behind him was an indignant dwarf. I denied any knowledge of the incident and invited them in to look around. Somehow they all squeezed into my tiny home, and a thorough search was conducted. I was found to be in possession of none of Señor Nunez's personal property. Mr. Patsatzis apologized for the intrusion, and suggested to his star clown that he withdraw his accusations. This he declined to do and made what I assumed were threatening statements in rapid Spanish. They left, but the threats are continuing.

These are being uttered by my sexually unfulfilled neighbor across the partition.

I've responded by suggesting repeatedly that he blow it out his ass.

It's amazing how the ownership of a handgun can change one's attitude toward these ruffians.

TUESDAY, September 13 — A beautiful morning under a big blue Montana sky. The air is so clear and crisp you just want to suck in as much of it as you can. My plan worked very nicely, thank you. Kardos met me by the cookhouse tent and handed over the small items I had given him yesterday for safekeeping (he is concealing several other items for me as well). These I distributed to fellow conspirators when they arrived for breakfast. After everyone went through the line, we sat down at our usual table. Soon a loud commotion was raised as victim after victim scooped a nasty cigarette butt from their oatmeal. It was the final straw for Mr. Patsatzis. Randy—vainly protesting his innocence—was dragged out from behind the counter, stripped of his hairnet and soiled apron, and discharged on the spot. He has been paid off in full and kicked off the lot.

Yes, it was well worth all the trouble I went to tracking down a convenience store in Butte that would sell a pack of Kools to a 15-year-old. And then having to smoke all those ghastly menthol-laden cigarettes down to Randroid-length butts (he doesn't let any of his valuable tobacco go to waste). Toward the end of the pack the nicotine was starting to feel pretty good, like one more drag and I'd be addicted for life. Still, even a nasty death from lung cancer might have been worth it to see the back of that repulsive cretin. Things are looking up!

10:47 a.m. A major setback. Mr. Patsatzis has relieved me temporarily of all bounce house duties and "promoted" me to acting assistant kitchen helper. Yes, I'm to do all my regular cleaning tasks, plus Randy's old job. At no increase in pay!

I didn't dare protest much, since the boss man reminded me that I was still on employee probation. He did say I probably wouldn't have to do both jobs for long. Just until the next kid shows up who wants to run away to a glamorous life in the circus.

1:26 p.m. The lunch rush is over. I have 14 seconds to rest up before dinner preparations begin. This morning I sneaked out of the commissary trailer to phone Veeva. She whispered she was in French class and couldn't talk. I told her to get her ass out into the hallway as it was urgent. A minute later she called me back.

"OK, Noel, what's so damn important?"

I brought her up to speed on my adventures in Señor Nunez's trailer, and told her that I found a photo under his bed that was rather puzzling.

"What photo?" she asked.

"Well, it's a wallet-size photo of a little blond girl holding a stuffed animal. On the back someone wrote in pencil 'Veeva S. at 19 months'."

"That's bizarre. What kind of stuffed animal is it?"

"Uh, it looks like a monkey or something."

"That would be Gilbert my gorilla. He was my favorite toy when I was a kid. I think I know that photo. Do I have a pink ribbon in my hair?"

"Yeah, you look kind of retarded."

"Jesus, Noel, that's creepy. Why would that dwarf have my picture under his bed?"

"Well, I've been giving it some thought, Veeva. I've come up with one possible explanation: Sheeni had her baby and her own brother adopted it."

Silence on my phone. I gave it a shake.

"Veeva, are you there?"

"I'm here, Noel. I think . . . that's . . . preposterous."

"I don't know, Veeva. It explains a lot. Who's your one relative you most resemble?"

"My aunt Sheeni?"

"That's right. And who is the only female relative with whom you have any rapport?"

"My aunt Sheeni?"

"So you yourself have said. And the reason you get along so badly with your mother is because—."

"—she's actually my wicked stepmother?"

"You guessed it. That could be why she didn't let you go

back to France this summer. She doesn't want you to get too close to your real mother."

"That sounds like her, but I don't know, Noel. The time line's all wrong. Sheeni's baby would be at least six months older than me."

"Well, parents have been known to fudge birth dates. You know, so it doesn't look like the kid arrived too soon after the wedding. You could be older, Veeva. You seem pretty mature for 14."

An understatement, if ever there was one.

"Jesus, Noel, that would make Nick Twisp my father. But he's never acted very fatherly toward me."

"The guy's in the dark, Veeva. You can tell that from the letter Aunt Sheeni wrote to him."

"God, Noel, this is too much. Too much to deal with. Now I wish I hadn't sent that letter."

"What letter?"

"I wrote a long letter to Reina Vesely last week outlining all the reasons she should dump Nick and marry my father. I could be wrecking my actual father's happiness!"

"Well, perhaps it won't change her mind."

"Jesus, Noel, I've been screwing my own uncle. That's incest!"

"Is it, Veeva? I thought uncles could marry their nieces."

"Well, perhaps in places like West Virginia or Mississippi. In those states they're probably just relieved you're marrying someone besides your own brother. Christ, Noel! Tyler is my first cousin!"

"Yeah, I guess you'll have to lay off that guy too."

"I can't talk any more, Noel. I have to go to the restroom and have a nervous breakdown."

She hung up before I could point out that the reason she liked her father so much was because he wasn't actually her dad. And that was the linchpin in my whole case.

Tyler is my nephew, Veeva is my niece, and I've fooled around sexually with both of them. Jesus, maybe I am just a piece of poor white trailer trash.

8:47 p.m. I may be peeling potatoes in my sleep tonight. Mr. Povey learned his trade in the Navy, and doesn't believe in convenience foods. Everything in his kitchen is made from scratch. Did you ever peel potatoes for 87 ravenous circus employees? Thank God the commissary trailer isn't set up for large-scale dishwashing; everything is served on paper plates. Still, there are countless pans, trays, cutlery items, coffee urns, etc. to be scrubbed and scoured. Not to mention all the counters, steam tables, sinks, stove, and grill.

No wonder Randy had such a bad attitude. He had the worst job on the planet.

At least now I can pick out the choicest chops and biggest slices of pie to deposit lovingly on the plates of Miren and her scowling parents. (They appear to hate my guts.) My darling has promised to meet me again later tonight in the swamp-cooler truck. How I look forward to her sweet lips!

WEDNESDAY, September 14 — We jumped this morning to Bozeman, another cowboy western town surrounded by rugged mountains. Darn, and I never made it to the World Museum of Mining back in Butte.

Some reproachful glances across the counter this morning from sweet Miren. I dropped off in my bunk last night and slept right through our rendezvous. It was all Randy's fault because he wasn't on the other side of the wall making his usual racket. I slipped a note under her toast apologizing abjectly for standing her up, but she still seems pretty frosty. Why can't we skip all this sneaking around and just get married? Tired as I was last night, I'm sure I would have revived if my own nubile young bride had crawled fully unclothed into our cozy bed.

11:08 a.m. While swabbing out the ladies' doniker, I was confronted by Nerea, my potential sister-in-law. She demanded to know if I was merely toying with her sister. I assured her that I liked Miren immensely, but am excessively fatigued at times from non-stop toil. Nerea parked her taut buns on a sink and suggested I work up an act so I can skip all this boring drudgery.

"Can't you juggle, Jake?" she demanded.

"Not even one ball," I replied.

Running down the list of possibilities, we discovered that I possessed not one skill that anyone in their right mind would pay good money to see.

"My father might like you better if you had an act," she pointed out. "He doesn't like us hanging around the laborers."

"Well, Kardos has an act and he's scared to death of your father."

"He told you that?"

"Yup."

"Kardos—does he like me?"

"Well, he has a girlfriend back in Hungary. But he'd be interested in you if you were older."

"I am plenty old enough for that boy."

"That may be, but your father may not agree and he has a gun."

"How about you tell Kardos that I will sabotage Papa's gun?"

"That won't work, Nerea. Kardos doesn't want any trouble."

"Yes, but I want him. Very much."

"And I want your sister very much."

"I tell you a secret, Jake. If you get my sister pregnant, my papa will make you marry her."

"He won't kill me first?"

"He'll want to, but *mi madre* will put her foot down. She'll make him accept you, even if you're not Basque. But if you ever desert my sister and her babies, then he will kill you for sure."

I didn't like the conviction with which she said that.

"But I don't have any money, Nerea."

"If you marry my sister, Papa will train you on the trampoline. You could do it—you have an acrobat's build. No muscles to speak of, but they will come. Then you will have an act and a career. There will always be circuses in this world, Jake."

I told her I'd think it over.

Jesus, do I really want to get married, be a father, and hop around on a trampoline for the rest of my life?

That's kind of a big decision for a 15-year-old to make.

Another question: If I married Miren, could I keep my hands off my sexy sister-in-law and her flaming tangerine hair?

9:38 p.m. Veeva thinks I'm insane to think about marrying anyone at my age.

"Didn't you learn anything from your brother's example?" she inquired cellularly from her gracious $75,000 room.

"Your dad's doing OK, Veeva," I replied from my cramped trailer roomette. "He has a lucrative juggling gig and several scorching girlfriends. He's also living in Paris, which beats Bozeman, Montana by a mile."

"Several miles I should think, Noel. But I'm not so sure Uncle Nick is my dad. I put the question to Daddy this morning and he said the whole idea was absurd. He said he could show me my birth certificate and the receipts from the hospital where I was born."

"Well, then perhaps you are his kid after all."

"I'd like to think so, Noel, but I can't be sure. Daddy sounded a little glib on that topic, like he'd been rehearsed. It would be just like my mother to cover all her tracks. Of course, she'd have a birth certificate and hospital receipts. I wouldn't put it past to her to have faked a video of my delivery."

"Do they have one of those?"

"Just of my younger brother. It's completely gross and X-rated. No, I do not want to watch that woman's shaved privates getting dilated. She made me watch it last year so I'd always use birth control. It worked too. Promise me you won't seduce that circus girl without using protection."

"Well, I'll think about it."

"Noel, you've got to ask that clown what he knows about that photo of me."

"How can I do that, Veeva? In the first place, he's not speaking to me and wants to murder me. And second, if I ask about the photo, he'd have proof that I was the one who robbed his trailer and he'd have me fired. Plus, you know anything he'd tell me would probably be a lie anyway. The guy is not to be trusted."

"Damn, Noel, I need this matter resolved. I need to know who the hell I am!"

I assured her I sympathized completely with her predicament. After all, I went through a similar period of anguished paternal uncertainty earlier this summer—right before getting that final dreaded confirmation that I was a Twisp. Yes, I know how that chick feels.

THURSDAY, September 15 — Lots of cute college girls on the lot today wearing very little to speak of (the hot weather has returned). Our appearance in Bozeman is being sponsored by one of the sororities at the university here. It's their main fund-raising event of the year. I'm not sure what they do with the money they raise. Probably buy beer and snacks for all those fraternity brothers dropping by.

I stayed awake long enough last night to meet Miren in the cab of the swamp-cooler truck. But we didn't have much time together—or privacy. We looked up from an impassioned clinch, and there was Señor Nunez perched on the running board and staring in the window at us. What a shock. The disgusting pervert had followed me!

I leaped from the truck and confronted him. I told him to go away and leave us alone.

"I want my pistol back," he exclaimed. "It belonged to my father. And his father before him."

Sounds like he came from generations of well-armed Mexicans. I told him I didn't know anything about his damn pistol.

"It is very old, Jake. If you try to fire it, it will likely blow your hand off."

"I'm not saying I have your stupid gun, but if you tell me the truth about Sheeni's baby, you might get it back."

"That I cannot do, Jake."

"Why the fuck not?"

"Because I made a sacred promise to Sheeni. I promised I would say nothing to no one about her child. And Alfredo Nunez is a man of honor who keeps his word."

"Some honor," I scoffed. "You drugged and kidnapped me. You stole my money. You tried to kill me!"

"I just wanted to frighten you into going away, Jake. I didn't know anything about the LSD. That was Randy's doing."

"You think I believe that?"

"Believe what you like, Jake. But I will give you a warning. You must not go near Miren or Nerea. Not ever. I know their father. He does not approve of you. If you persist, he will do much worse to you than I ever did."

"Just mind your own business," I replied. "And don't go following me around!"

"You are an incredibly stupid kid," he hissed, turning and walking away.

I returned to the truck, but the cab was now empty. Darling Miren had bailed on me.

This morning I slipped a note under her toast asking her to meet me in town in one hour. She read my message and flashed me a cautious smile, which I'm taking as an assent.

Señor Nunez's continued recalcitrance has obliged me to adopt Randy's heinous tactics. Today he received on his plate bacon of a greasy limpness that would gag a famished dog.

3:08 p.m. The fates are conspiring to keep Miren and me apart. I was three blocks from the lot this morning when Randy stepped out from behind a tree, said "Whoa there, Jake," and swung his fist at me. I ducked and immediately adopted the basic TaeKwonDo defensive stance. I focused my mind to a razor point and thought of my body as an impregnable fortress. That's when Randy socked me hard in the stomach and I lost my breakfast. As I was bent over retching, he swung up into my nose—

triggering a great fountain of blood. Then he slammed his fists down on the back of my neck, sending me crashing to the hard pavement. I crumpled into a ball and received kick after fierce kick from his pointy redneck boots. The ones to the kidneys were especially punishing, although the blows to the balls were also major distractions. Eventually, he stopped, thrust something that felt like a still-lit cigarette butt into my bloody mouth, said "See you around, Jake," and walked away.

Miren found me and somehow got me back to the circus. Mr. Patsatzis wanted to take me to a hospital, but I didn't want to deal with doctors and cops possibly asking for my identity. I said I was OK and just needed to rest up a bit. Miren washed my cut lip and finally got it to stop bleeding. I've been sacked out in my roomette, which is rather enervating as the heat is most oppressive today. Plus, it's been hard crawling in and out of my high bunk to go to the doniker, where I've been pissing out blood. Kind of scary. I'm hoping it stops soon. Miren has been nice about checking in on me even though her father doesn't like it one bit. I suppose he thinks I got what was coming to me.

Can't type any more. Hurts too much.

FRIDAY, September 16 — Didn't sleep much last night. Too sore. My body has really stiffened up on me. I can barely walk. Piss, though has gone from a bright cherry red to a soft blushing pink, so that trend seems promising. Look like hell in the doniker mirror. Left black eye nearly swollen shut. One of my front incisors is loose. If it falls out, I'll be left with that true trailer-trash smile.

Jin Pak has been bringing me my meals on a tray. He's not too thrilled by my martial arts performance. He says I should have chased less after Miren and concentrated more on my TaeKwonDo lessons. Of course, we all know that he likes her too. I told him he should make a play for Nerea, since she wasn't getting anywhere with Kardos. He merely shrugged and told me to eat my soup. Hot liquids though really torture my blistered mouth. Jin said Spivey, Jacques, and some of the other roustabouts have been out looking for Randy, but they think he's probably skipped town. I'm not taking any chances though. I have retrieved all of my purloined Señor Nunez items from Kardos and have secreted them close at hand in my cupboard. This time I'll be ready for that hooligan if he returns.

Jin did have some good news to report. With me laid up and Mr. Povey screaming for help, Mr. Patsatzis had to get serious about finding a replacement for Randy. He's hired a local college freshman who just flunked out even though school had only been in session for two weeks. Sounds like the guy has the right mental equipment for the job.

Later, I heard him moving his stuff into the roomette next door. He has a merry whistle. Probably relieved to be done with the college thing and getting on with life. Hope he doesn't get too discouraged by the reality of what Life is about to hand him.

I took a nap, and then Kardos dropped by and we smoked some medical marijuana. Made me feel a lot better. I might have the energy to try to make it to the cookhouse tent for dinner.

7:28 p.m. Miren brought me a dinner tray, so I stuck it out in the roomette with her. Nothing like looking like a corpse to win sympathy points from loved ones. Probably at her father's insistence, she brought along her brother Iker as chaperon. No place to sit, except next to me on the bunk, so she leaned against a wall and Iker squatted on the floor. He's eight and seemed quite impressed that I'd been in a fight. He asked me what it felt like when Randy popped the lit cigarette into my mouth.

"Not very pleasant," I replied, showing him the ugly blister on my tongue. "But the blood put it out pretty quick."

"Your face looks horrible," he remarked. "Like some movie monster."

"Iker!" protested his sister. "You shouldn't say such things to people."

"It's true," he replied. "I bet not even you'd want to kiss Jake now."

She took that dare and gently kissed the monster on his swollen lips.

There was a flash of light, a puff of smoke, and I was transformed into a handsome young prince.

I wish.

SATURDAY, September 17 — My cell phone rang in the middle of the night. That Nipsie has the most juvenile taste in ring tones. Good thing I don't receive many incoming calls when I'm out in public. Anyway, it was Veeva phoning from the stratosphere somewhere over Kansas. She's taking a red-eye flight to Paris, France. As usual, her parents are clueless. They think she's in Oxnard for a weekend speech tournament. She figures that will give her a few days' head start before they start tracking down her credit card charges.

"I need to know who I am, Noel. I intend to get this matter resolved one way or the other."

"Sounds like a good idea to me, Veeva. As you requested, I put the question again to Señor Nunez. He claims he's made a sacred promise to your aunt Sheeni to keep his lips zipped."

"Noel, why is your speech so garbled? Have you been drinking?"

I explained that I had been pummeled mercilessly by the dwarf's lowlife accomplice.

"Dammit, Noel, these guys play rough. I hope you landed some good blows yourself."

"Not really, but I think I gave him a hell of a dry-cleaning bill. There was blood all over the place—unfortunately all of it mine."

"That's terrible, Noel. Are you all right?"

"Well, I'm getting better."

We had to end the conversation there because the new Randy started pounding on the wall.

Besides being airless little boxes, these roomettes offer absolutely no soundproofing. Of course, I hadn't raised a peep earlier in the evening when my new neighbor was saying good-bye to his girlfriend. They went at it for quite a while, and I was kept fully informed at all times where exactly he was putting it.

We jumped this morning to Billings, the Los Angeles of Montana. This town is so large, it boasts an actual skyline featuring several high-rise buildings. We're parked pretty far from the city center, so I doubt I'll be sampling many of its cosmopolitan delights. A short drive from Billings is the spot where General Armstrong Custer lost his scalp to the Indians. Interestingly, General Custer was from the same small town in Ohio as Clark Gable, although Errol Flynn played him in the movie.

I felt well enough to limp to the cookhouse tent for breakfast, where I was served by the new Randy—a pleasant-looking guy named Joe. Didn't catch his last name, but Mr. Povey was addressing him as "Joe College." I apologized for the late-night phone call, and he said "no problem." He may have been sincere too, since the bacon he forked over was nicely lean and crisp. I took a seat beside Vrsula Herczegh, who was most solicitous. It's nice to have someone blindingly beautiful to converse with when you're feeling lousy and praying each painful bite doesn't knock out your loose tooth.

Took a shower after breakfast and had a candid look at my naked body (rarely a thrill even for me). My entire gonadal region is tinged a repellent purplish-blue. It could be the biggest bruise in human history. Snapped a photo of it for posterity with my cell phone camera. Hope everything is still working down there. I'll have to check it out one of these days. Piss is still pink, but growing fainter. We Twisps are built to take abuse.

6:37 p.m. I cleaned all eight donikers on my circuit today. Mr. Patsatzis declared "if you can walk you can work." My theory is "if you can barely hobble, you can huddle in your hovel," but the boss man wasn't buying it. Pretty fatiguing, even if I was rather cursory and slapdash in performing my duties.

Had a chat outside the commissary trailer with Joe College (real name Joe Allis). He's feeling a bit stunned by the workload, but what really bugs him is having to wear a hairnet. He has quite a crop of wavy black hair that he hates to imprison artificially in such a girlish manner. He feels it is ruining his looks.

(The guy may be a bit vain.) He asked Mr. Povey if he could wear a manly baseball cap instead, but that proposal got nixed. Mr. Povey claims health department regulations require standard hairnets, or alternatively, he's welcome to shave his head. But "bald and proud" is not a lifestyle choice our kitchen helper is willing to consider.

Joe asked me if I wanted to switch jobs, but—not being insane—I declined. He also asked me if Vrsula was my girlfriend. I said I was secretly engaged to Miren, and he was welcome to her sister or Vrsula. I feel it's wise to work out these territorial issues first thing to avoid possible conflicts later. I've fished enough gross contaminants out of my grub.

11:46 p.m. Kardos has exhausted his reefer supply (he'd been buying from Randy), so he brought over a therapeutic bottle of red wine and a stash of paper cups. Not bad and, I suppose, easier on one's lungs. He has worked out a solution to all of our problems. He proposes that I marry his sister, take over his spot on Orsolya (their star ostrich), and then he will be free to go to Germany to study sanitary engineering.

I told him the offer was tempting, but what was the point of marrying his lovely sister if I was just going to break my neck on some rampaging ostrich? He admitted that male ostriches can be obstreperous, but said his family only travels with tame and sweet-tempered females. He claimed in a week he could teach me everything I'd need to know to perform his riding stunts. I thanked him for the offer, but said I'd rather marry Miren and learn to be an acrobat on the trampoline. At least it doesn't gallop around at 30 miles an hour. He said fair enough, but how about I sleep with his sister first before I decide?

An intriguing proposal. I asked him if he had discussed the idea with Vrsula. He said no, but he could tell she liked me. All I had to do was give her some encouragement. I asked him how I could do that without pissing off Miren. He said it wouldn't be a problem as European girls were used to their boyfriends sleeping around.

The whole thing sounded semi-plausible to my wine-steeped brain, but now I'm not so sure. Besides, I just saw Vrsula loitering on the ring curb with Joe College. Now there's a guy who doesn't let any cobwebs grow on his unit. Perhaps that's why he flunked out.

SUNDAY, September 18 — Another middle-of-the-night phone call from Veeva. I climbed down out of my bunk and took my phone outside so as not to disturb my neighbor. Veeva caught a train south from Paris and is now staying in a youth hostel in Albi. She says the French countryside is amazingly beautiful this time of year. I told her Montana was not bad either. She's located the office where the district birth records are kept and will be going there when they open tomorrow. In the meantime, she's been sucking Euros out of bank ATMs in anticipation of her parents guillotining her credit card. She says Albi looks like a much nicer place to be from than "boring L.A." If it proves to be her birthplace, she intends to look into obtaining dual U.S.-French citizenship in case she decides someday to reside in France. I hope she doesn't, since that'd be pretty far to travel for my yearly incest quota. She was up for chatting some more, but I told her I was freezing my balls off and rang off.

9:12 a.m. It's all coming together. Notes have been smuggled back and forth, and I've persuaded Kardos to lend me his credit card. Sunday morning in Billings: time for a true religious experience.

2:17 p.m. Miren and I arrived at the sexually suggestive Bighorn Inn just after 10 a.m. She was wearing her lace head scarf and carrying her Bible. The motel is located near the campus of Montana State; so the desk clerk may have been used to young people appearing at all hours of the day and night without much luggage. I told him we needed a room for "Bible studies."

"Single or double?" he asked.

"What?"

"Do you need a single bed or double beds?"

"Uh, single," I blushed.

He assigned us a non-smoking room on the second floor, and I paid him $68.40 in very hard-earned cash. He didn't even require a credit card, although he did ask me if I'd been in some kind of accident.

I told him I was a lion tamer with the circus and had been mauled recently by one of my "big cats." I don't think he believed me.

Both Miren and I were pretty nervous when we got to the room. We kicked off our shoes and crawled into bed fully clothed. I told her I loved her very much, and she said I was the nicest boy she'd ever met. We kissed and gradually peeled off each other's layers. Just as I suspected, Miren has quite delectable breasts: rather large and nicely firm with compact rosy nipples. While I was getting acquainted with them, she pulled off my underwear, but I told her not to look at my body.

"Why not, Jake?"

"The bruises are too revolting."

Of course, then she had to see for herself. She tugged back the covers, looked at my crotch, and was visibly appalled. Not exactly the Romeo and Juliet moment one anticipates on such occasions.

"We should have insisted you go to the hospital, Jake. Those injuries look serious."

"It's not as bad as it looks, Miren. See, things are still working."

"Will it hurt if I touch it?"

"I'd say it will hurt more if you don't."

Things eventually reached quite a frenzied state, and Miren inquired about birth control. I told her I'd brought along some condoms, but asked if she really wanted me to use one.

"What do you mean, Jake?"

"Well, I thought we could make a nice baby and get married."

"What!?"

I told her about my conversation with her sister and Nerea's plan to bring me into the Lurrieta family. Miren laughed and said no she does not want to have my child and get married. She said I should just ignore her sister, who thinks she can run Miren's life because she (Nerea) is the elder by 14 minutes. Miren intends to go to college and study literature. She says any babies coming along in the next few years in the Lurrieta family will be due to her boy-crazy sister not her.

I suppose I felt mostly relieved by that news. We got the condom on and went at it. Unlike with Veeva, it slipped right in without any hindrance. All of Miren's body is incredibly toned, so she was able to do things with her pelvic muscles that are probably illegal in most states. Even though it hurt sometimes to move, I had an orgasm that detonated all the way up to the tips of my ears. Miren seemed to be having a good time too, especially on the second go-around when I lasted longer.

Afterwards, we lay there together for as long as we dared. She told me about her childhood in Spain and I told her about growing up in rural Nevada. The one thing we have in common is that we both spent most of our lives living in trailers or caravans. Of course, Miren traveled around in hers, while mine was going nowhere fast. Miren snuggled against me and said she loved the way we fit together. I kissed her and tried not to think how transitory our connection may be. I suppose we could think about going to the same college—assuming I had the money and grades to get into one. It's a real pain trying to do anything major in life when you're only 15. It's hard to follow your dreams when you're swabbing toilets for peanuts and on the lam from the cops.

When we turned in the key at the motel office, Miren picked up a complimentary newspaper from a stack on the counter. A boxed story on the bottom of page one caught my eye: "Hearse Hijacker Nabbed in L.A."

Yeah, they nailed Carlyle at last. They arrested him in City Hall while he was attempting to obtain a marriage license under a false name. The clerk got suspicious when he pulled out a giant roll of money and peeled off a $100 bill. When the cops grabbed him, he was found to be in possession of $7,300 in cash and wearing several thousand dollars worth of chunky gold jewelry. He'd also had a fancy diamond and platinum grillwork installed in his front teeth and now has quite the dazzling smile. The bride-to-be was a 17-year-old whose name was withheld because she's a minor.

Carlyle just proved my point. He followed his dream and look where it got him.

8:45 p.m. I finally got through to Stoney. She said all of Winnemucca is in an uproar over the arrest of the town's favorite son. She heard on the grapevine that Mrs. Carlyle Bogy-to-be is expecting a little surprise. I'm sure it will be with Carlyle as the father. No, she hasn't heard if Carlyle's intended is black, but that's what everyone assumes. She said Carlyle is facing a battery of charges and may not get out of jail until his kid is in the fourth grade. We agreed that could be a blessing in disguise for both the mom and the kid.

I told her about my interlude in Billings with Miren. Stoney said she has no faith in my taste in women and could only hope Miren wasn't another bitch goddess like Uma. I assured her that was not the case, and that we were very compatible.

Speaking of which, Stoney has figured out the cause of her sexual problems. Sloan had been putting too much of himself into the act and kept banging into her cervix (whatever that is). Things have improved in that department since he's been exercising some restraint.

"Uh, how big is that guy?" I asked.

"I'd say he's just over the line into the freak category, Noel. Just my luck I have to get stuck on the biggest stud around."

"He's bigger than Tyler?" I asked, incredulous.

"Oh, way bigger. No comparison really."

Damn, I hope Uma knows what she's letting herself in for. Stoney said she's been dressing nice and putting on her make-up every day. Since she started associating with Sloan and his crowd, her popularity quotient has gone way up at Winnemucca High. Girls who used to look past her like she was invisible or a stain on the wall now say hi to her in the hallways. Some have been encouraging her to try out for cheerleader.

"God, Stoney," I exclaimed, "your life has been totally transformed!"

"Yeah, Noel, I guess it has. But one thing hasn't changed."

"What's that?"

"I still want to murder my mother and buy a Harley with the insurance money."

MONDAY, September 19. I've been thinking things over. I have now slept with 2-1/2 chicks. (I'm only counting Uma as half since we didn't go all the way.) People might think I'm wantonly promiscuous, but I truly and deeply care for all those girls. I'm willing to marry them in this order: Miren, Uma, Veeva, and Vrsula. I put the last one on the list in case the other three fall through. Veeva might rank higher than Uma if it weren't for the incest issue. I'm really pissed at Uma; I've been checking my e-mail regularly on Jin's computer and she hasn't once bothered to write. I mean *what* is going on with that chick?

I suppose I'm thinking more about her now since Miren quashed our marriage plans. I think I was getting used to the idea of going into marriage, fatherhood, and trampolining full time.

Now I'm back to being a lonely high-school dropout fugitive with no discernible future.

At breakfast this morning Vrsula kept saying something unintelligible about Humphrey Bogart. I finally figured out that she was suggesting I might wind up with a scar on my lip like him. As long as girls don't object to kissing me, that would be OK by me. I'm more worried about my loose tooth, which at last is showing signs of taking root again. Still, I won't be opening any beer bottles with my teeth for a while.

I don't think Joe College likes me dining with Vrsula. The bacon this morning was rather sub-par and he also burned my toast. He has taken to tying a dishtowel over his hairnet, so he looks like a Bedouin. Now Mr. Povey is addressing him as Joseph of Arabia.

1:22 p.m. I just received a dressing down in the ladies' doniker from Nerea for blowing the marriage deal with her sister. It turns out I wasn't supposed to discuss the matter with Miren. According to Nerea, I should have just sabotaged the condom and impregnated her through stealth.

I was a bit surprised that Nerea was so up-to-date on my sex life. It appears those girls aren't into keeping secrets from each other. She said her sister likes me a lot and hopes to meet me again "for church" next Sunday. Sounds like a great idea if I can afford it, but those motel rooms take a giant bite out of my paltry income. Perhaps I can negotiate a discount, since we're only there for a few hours—although the wear and tear on the mattress can be substantial.

Next time, says Nerea, I should "be a man" and make sure "the sperm reaches the egg." I protested that Miren would hate me if I did that, but Nerea said a woman's hormones change once she's pregnant and Miren would love me even more. She says the female body does that automatically so the woman won't despise the man for putting her through nine months of "horrible pain and sheer hell." Sounds reasonable to me.

6:27 p.m. Amazing news. Veeva just checked in from Albi, France. To her utter astonishment, she found not one but two birth listings for "S. Saunders, non-citizen." Registered on the 8th of December fifteen years ago were the births of Emma B. Saunders and Marie A. Saunders. No father was listed for either of them.

"Do you realize what this means, Noel?" she asked breathlessly.

"Uhmm, you're a Sagittarius?"

"Exactly! I'm a Sagittarius with a missing twin sister somewhere. And here's the confirmation: My false birthday was June 16, which made me a Gemini—the sign of twins!"

"I'm not following the connection, Veeva."

"Don't you see, Noel? It would be just like my mother to give me a fake birthday with that reference to twins. Her sadism can be so subtle."

"Wow, that's amazing. So where's your missing sister?"

"That's what I've been trying to find out. I spent all day searching for that dwarf's brother. But there don't appears to be any Nunezes living in this district. I don't know, he may have moved away or been deported or something. It's very discouraging. I did find out that no Nunez—named Sarah or otherwise—has died in this province in the past 15 years."

"Then Alfredo is lying as usual."

"Yes, and now you must get him to tell the truth."

Easy for her to say. I don't think she has a clue how formidable that dwarf really is.

"So what are you going to do now, Veeva?"

"Head to Lyon, of course. It's time for a heart-to-heart talk with Sheeni."

"Sounds good, Veeva. You can threaten to expose her to her husband if she doesn't come clean."

"I couldn't do that to my own mother, Noel. And what was that disgusting photo you sent to my cell phone?"

"Those are my bruised privates, Veeva. I thought you'd like to see the price I'm paying for this quest of yours."

"It's your quest too, Noel. Aren't you interested in locating your missing niece?"

I suppose, though I think "Uncle Noel" has more than enough nieces and nephews already.

11:57 p.m. No more visitors after dark. That's my new rule and I intend to stick to it. I answered a loud rap on my door this evening, and there was Miren's florid-faced papa pointing his very scary Luger at me. He forced his way inside and announced he had come "to exterminate some *asqueroso* vermin." His breath smelled strongly of garlic, cigars, and booze. I backed up as far as I could and asked for the particulars of his complaint against me.

"You know what you did, you degenerate *pajiera*. You sneaked into the women's doniker today and molested my Nerea."

"Excuse me! I was *cleaning* the women's doniker today, and she dropped by to chat. It was all totally innocent."

"You had the door closed!"

"The door has one of those spring thingies on it, Mr. Lurrieta. It closes automatically."

"And you've had your *pringao* hands on my Miren. That I cannot forgive!"

I had put more than my hands on her, but this I did not point out.

He stuck the steel barrel of his gun into my bruised abdomen. At that range, I knew, I could hardly count on him to miss.

"Will you grant me one last request, Mr. Lurrieta?"

"What's that, *malnacido*?"

"Will you share a glass of wine with me?"

"*Si, claro*. I appreciate a *chupaverga* who goes bravely to his maker."

I got him to withdraw his firearm an inch or two, turned around in the confined space, opened my cupboard door, and spotted Señor Nunez's pistol. I knew it was loaded because I had checked it out previously. If the gun actually worked, I might be able to get off the first shot, but did I want to have a gun battle with a drunken Spaniard in a room no bigger than a coffin? I decided to go with Plan B. I very shakily poured some of Kardos's wine into two paper cups and covertly added a splash from the shampoo bottle into one of them. I turned around and was virtually certain I handed the proper cup to the guy with the gun.

We clinked cups, said "Salud!" and Mr. Lurrieta downed his with a mighty gulp. I took a tentative sip and managed an ingratiating smile.

"Drink up, *lambioso!*" he exclaimed. "We've got to get this over. We can't have everyone in the show up all night dealing with your *pelotudo* corpse."

"Mr. Lurrieta, with all due respect, may I ask if Alfredo Nunez is the person who has been spreading these lies about me?"

"Alfredo is my *amigo*," he replied, wiping a hairy, muscular hand down over his face and shaking his head. "He knows you to be *el hijo de la gran puta* and has told me so. You dishonor him by calling him a liar. For that also you must die."

"Show me the evidence," I persisted. "Show me the evidence that I have defiled your daughters."

"The evidence is in your face, *coño*. You have . . . You have . . ."

He didn't finish his explanation. He got an odd grin on his face, then his eyes trampolined up and down, the gun slipped from his hand, and he crumpled to the floor. My strategy had worked. I had proved scientifically that the liquid in the bottle was not shampoo. Now, what to do with my slumbering houseguest? Powered by a fierce jolt of adrenaline, I managed to drag him unseen out the door and across the lot. I left him curled up and clutching the wine bottle by the front entrance to the big tent. He was wearing a heavy jacket, so he shouldn't freeze to death. I don't know what I'll do if he comes after me tomorrow, but this time *I'll* be the guy holding the Luger.

TUESDAY, September 20 — Pretty bleary-eyed. I was too on edge to get much sleep last night. No sign yet of Miren's father. We jumped this morning to Sheridan, Wyoming, and Mrs. Lurrieta drove the truck pulling their trailer. I've never seen her do that before.

Not much difference so far between Montana and Wyoming. Ninety-nine percent of what you see is scenic wilderness and rugged mountains—interrupted only by disfiguring blotches of human habitation. Sheridan appears to be another Old West

town panning for tourists rushing by on the Interstate highway.
11:32 a.m. Things are grim. Mr. Lurrieta is in a hospital in
Sheridan. They thought he was sleeping off a bender, but when
he didn't wake up, they hauled him off to the emergency room.
Very unnerving. I've wiped down both guns and the other incriminating items, crammed them into a plastic bag, and ditched
them behind some bushes on a remote part of the lot. Too bad I
hadn't thought to wipe my fingerprints off that damn wine
bottle!

I must have splashed in too much of Señor Nunez's knockout drops. How was I supposed to know the proper adult dose?
Hell, there were no instructions or warning labels on the bottle.
If he croaks, I'll probably be charged with homicide, even though
the deceased was threatening me with a gun. Plus, I looked in
the doniker mirror this morning and was alarmed to see my loose
tooth is turning brown. I look like a real criminal. I'm sure it
will be one more thing prejudicing the jury against me. I wonder if they gas 15-year-olds in this state?

7:18 p.m. Mr. Lurrieta is still in intensive care. Haven't spoken to Miren or Nerea yet as they've been at the hospital all
day. Meanwhile, the afternoon performance went on without
them. Joe College, volunteering to help fill the gap, ran out and
did some semi-pathetic juggling. It seems he went to circus summer camps as a kid and fancies himself a performer. The audience applauded politely, but I expect they're starved for enter-
tainment in this burg.

Two sheriff's deputies came poking around during the dinner
break. They talked to all the Patsatzises, then worked their way
around to the rest of us. I told them I knew Mr. Lurrieta only by
sight, but had spoken several times to his daughters. They seemed
suspicious and wanted to know why my face was so torn up. I
told them I had been in an altercation recently with a former
employee, but no, the dispute had not involved any of the Lurrieta
family. Don't ask me if they believed me. I'm sure I looked suspicious with my shaky voice, nervous tremor, shifty eyes, ugly

lip scab, and lowlife tooth. They wrote down my name and were disappointed I couldn't produce an I.D. I explained I was too young to have a driver's license.

10:38 p.m. I'm wracked by guilt. I've been trying to read the tattered remnants of my poetry book (it didn't fare well in that clothes dryer), but have been too distracted to concentrate. I keep wondering how I'll cope if I have to spend the rest of my life in prison. I feel I'm especially unsuited to such confinement since I have real problems with authority figures and excessive regimentation. I figure prison may be like being stuck in high school 24 hours a day, only without girls and with a very suspect student body. I'd face a lifetime of conforming to rules, being unpopular, being bossed around, dodging bullies, and disappointing my family. Perhaps it would be best just to get it over with and be dragged whimpering into that gas chamber.

I took a walk earlier to try to clear my head, and was accosted by Señor Nunez near the generator truck. He said he knew it was me who had poisoned Mr. Lurrieta and I would never get away with it. I warned him that if he said a word to the cops, I would tell them where I got the stuff and what he did to me. I reminded him that the incriminating bottle had his fingerprints on it too. Then I demanded he tell me what he knew about Sheeni's missing twin daughter.

"I told you," he insisted. "Her baby died."

"OK, where did she die? It sure as hell wasn't in Albi because we've checked."

"I never said she died in Albi. We had moved to Argentina."

"Where in Argentina?"

"Buenos Aires."

"OK, is your story now that she died in Buenos Aires? Because we can check that."

"It's not a story, Jake. It's the truth."

No call from Veeva. I tried calling her, but got no answer. I don't know how far Albi is from Lyon, but I assume she's spoken to Sheeni by now. I hope their chat went well, and Sheeni isn't trying to weasel out of her responsibilities. I expect, though, there are lots of parents out there with children they'd rather forget—my own, for example.

Not that I can blame them for that.

WEDNESDAY, September 21 — The end of summer. For lots of reasons this is one summer I don't think I'll ever forget.

Two pieces of good news this morning: 1. Mr. Lurrieta is conscious and out of intensive care. 2. I may never have to clean another circus doniker.

The bad news is I'm back slaving as Mr. Povey's 13-hour-a-day kitchen helper. Joe College dropped by my roomette early this morning and made me an offer I couldn't refuse. If I agreed to switch jobs, he wouldn't tell the cops what he'd overheard through the walls two nights ago. I got a little heated and demanded to know why, if he heard Mr. Lurrieta threatening me, he hadn't tried to intervene or gone for help. Joe looked at me like that was a very silly question.

"Why should I get involved in your private argument, Jake? If you guys want to tangle, what business is that of mine?"

"But he intended to kill me!"

"Yeah, that had me a little worried. These trailer walls are way too flimsy to stop a bullet. I had to duck down onto my floor."

So it appears I'm not the only sociopath employed by this circus.

Joe College also made me promise that I would cease all communications with Vrsula Herczegh. The irony is that yesterday she told me she didn't much care for the new guy. She indicated through signs and gestures that she found him pushy, arrogant, and conceited. She feels she could never respect someone who got up in front of an audience with an act that inept. Like most professional showmen, she regards the circus as no place for amateurs.

Mr. Povey was delighted to have me back. After I donned my apron and ceremonial hairnet, he pointed to a 100-pound sack of potatoes and said, "Now maybe we can get some work done around here."

8:14 p.m. I haven't been arrested yet, although I'm not sure jail could be much worse than life in the commissary trailer. I didn't catch this afternoon's show (being ensnared in dinner preparations), but I heard the Lurrietas did a modified act without their dad. Later I was able to steal away for a five-minute chat with Miren. She looked tired but relieved that the worst was over. She reported that the hospital found traces of a common date-rape drug in her father's system.

"Why would anyone do that to my father, Jake?"

I shuffled my feet and looked mortifyingly guilty. "I don't know, Miren. What did your father say?"

"He hasn't been much help. The last thing he remembers is drinking too many cognacs with Alfredo Nunez in his trailer."

"Nothing after that—at all?"

"Unfortunately not. The doctor said that memory lapses are a common side effect of that drug—especially in large doses."

"Oh, that's, uh, interesting. Do the cops suspect the dwarf?"

"They've interrogated him twice. But he's one of my father's oldest friends. The families have known each other for generations."

"What did Alfredo say?"

"He said that after my father left he saw him talking to Randy. I don't know why Randy would come back to harm my father, but after seeing what he did to you, I suppose he's capable of anything."

"Are the cops looking for Randy?"

"They put a bulletin out for his arrest. But I'm not sure they're that interested."

"Why's that?"

"We're transients, Jake. The police don't much care what happens in circuses—as long as no locals are involved or get harmed. I think they just want us to leave town. And how have you been, Jake?"

"Tremendous, Miren," I said, sneaking a kiss. "Never better."

10:26 p.m. Still no call from Veeva. I'm beginning to worry she's been nailed as a runaway by the French cops. Or angry Sheeni has locked her up in that dingy storage room down in her cellar and intends to starve her slowly to death to safeguard her darkest secret. All I know is, it's very unlike Veeva not to call with gossip as potentially explosive as she's been tracking.

Something in France is clearly amiss!

THURSDAY, September 22 — We jumped this morning to Gillette, Wyoming. I don't think I've ever been so happy to leave a town. You might say it was a bit of a close shave. All the Lurrietas came with us, although Mrs. Lurrieta still had to drive their truck. Her husband, riding shotgun in the front seat, seemed pretty perky. He looked right at me as their rig pulled out, and didn't appear at all eager to murder me.

We've left the scenic forests and mountains behind. Gillette is a stark high-plains town that's booming from all the coal mines in the area. I'm feeling right at home here—nearly everyone in this burg lives in a mobile home. Grandma, to her credit, tries to grow a few roses around hers. These folks just park their trailers on the barren prairie and consider themselves moved in.

I took a shower this morning, and I must say, our doniker was not looking its best. Joe College seems most perfunctory in his toilet swabbing. Only the mirrors are kept polished so he can style his wavy locks. Mrs. Patsatzis seems to like him though. The rumor is she's already weighing him as a potential suitor for some of her less-attractive nieces.

Even though I receive a fair amount of kidding in my job, I've been trying to remember not to smile. A guy wearing a hairnet, sporting a fading black eye and an ugly lip scab, and sheathed in a grungy apron can't afford to be flashing a diseased-looking front tooth. If I had the money, I could get it encrusted with diamonds ala Carlyle Bogy. For now, I try not

to smile or I cover my mouth with my hand when I do. I noticed
Miren tried to avoid staring at it this morning when I served her
the A-grade bacon. She's probably having second thoughts. I
imagine she's wondering why a pretty girl like herself is hanging out with a beast like me.

Only three days until our next session "in church." I hope
she doesn't duck out on our date, but it wouldn't surprise me if
she does.

Still no call from Veeva and she's not answering her phone. I
feel such a sense of dread. I fear something terrible has happened. Or is about to.

7:48 p.m. I was serving salisbury steak and mashed potatoes
to the dinner line, when I looked up and there standing in front
of me was my brother.

"Hi, Noel," he said.

"Hi, Nick. You talked to Veeva, huh?"

"Yes, she told me where to find you."

"Where is she now?"

"In Paris with her father. Things are going to be OK, Noel.
Don't worry."

"Uh, right."

"I'll talk to you later, Noel. Don't go anywhere, OK?"

"OK, Nick. You better move along though. You're holding
up the line."

That's the last I've seen of my brother. Ever since then he's
been holed up with the Lurrietas in their trailer. They didn't
even show up for the evening performance, obliging Joe College to fill in with more excruciating juggling.

What I can't figure out is how Nick knew it was me who
poisoned Mr. Lurrieta. I mean, I haven't spoken to Veeva since
before the whole thing happened. And why is my brother butt-
ing in now? I thought I had that rap beat. Jesus, I can't believe
he traveled all the way from Paris to Wyoming just to track me
down and wreck my life.

But I suppose that's what Twisps are for.

FRIDAY, September 23 — The clatter of a diesel engine woke me up in the middle of the night. This morning we discovered that Señor Nunez had pulled out, trailer and all. Some may miss him, but I won't.

More bad news on the incest front. It turns out I've been a naughty uncle again. No, Veeva is not the long-lost daughter of Sheeni Saunders. That honor belongs to Miren and Nerea Lurrieta. Yes, the illustrious Twisp family now embraces a couple of skilled acrobats. I got the whole story and met my new relatives last night in their trailer. I even got a jovial hug from Mr. Lurrieta, whom I may now be related to in some convoluted way. That may explain why we recently tried to murder each other.

I feel it's promising for my genetic makeup that my brother has such good-looking children. He claims they look remarkably like Sheeni, although you can't prove it by me since I've never met the chick. They certainly don't look much like him—not that there's much doubt now of their paternity. Nor do they much resemble Veeva, who is also said to take after Sheeni.

Mr. and Mrs. Lurrieta are being pretty gracious about my brother's sudden *deus ex machina* arrival. They had informed their daughters they were adopted, but were led to believe by Señor Nunez (who had engineered the adoption) that the girls' natural parents had no interest in them. They seem rather proud that their daughters' biological father turned out to be the celebrated juggler Nick Twisp.

Last night Miren and Nerea appeared mostly bewildered by the whole thing, but this morning when we all went out to breakfast in Gillette (Nick paid), they were yucking it up and getting to know their second father. He juggled some steak knives and sliced a donut into small pieces in mid-air. This feat drew a loud round of applause from everyone in the restaurant. Rather embarrassing, I thought, but then I'm not a show-off like he is.

2:27 p.m. I just had a long conversation with Veeva in Paris. It's nighttime there and they're already back from dinner. Young

Nipsie's going to have quite a daunting cell phone bill this month. I finally got through to her by screaming into the phone that I knew the whole story and to stop being a twit and pick up. She took my call and apologized for betraying me to my brother. I said it couldn't be helped, and I'd decided not to despise her.

I filled her in on all the developments here, and she told me about the fascinating places that her aunt Sheeni has been showing her in Paris. Yes, they're still buddies despite Veeva's poking around into her aunt's long-buried affairs. Sheeni says she feels like a weight has been lifted from her shoulders. Her husband has been taking it like a man and wants to meet his new stepkids someday. Sheeni also has been complimenting Veeva's French— saying it is much improved, even though Veeva still feels "totally spastic" in that language.

I said I was surprised that Sheeni was in Paris, and asked if she happened to run into Nick before he left.

"She did more than run into him, Noel. We all went out to dinner one night."

"You did?"

"Yes, and was it amazing. My father, Reina, Uncle Nick, Sheeni, and me. How's that for a guest list?"

"Pretty incredible. So how was it?"

"I believe the operative word was tense. Very tense. Like every utterance carried this incredible baggage of drama. Of course, Uncle Nick was major annoyed at Sheeni for concealing the fact of his children all these years. Plus, things were crashing with him and Reina. And there was my father moving into the picture. Still, everyone was polite and no one threw any food. The fight for the check at the end got pretty vicious. Daddy won out, of course."

"Did Nick and Sheeni talk?"

"Oh sure. They even looked at each other occasionally. One thing I heard her say is that if he had bothered to reply to that letter she sent him a few years ago, she might have told him about the twins. He didn't, so she figured he didn't care. She told me later she thought all those years of incarceration had hardened Nick. But she says if you're going to break the law, you have to be prepared to suffer the consequences."

"I wonder why Nick didn't reply to her letter?"

"I expect it was to retaliate for all the pain she caused him. The thing is you could tell that Nick still loved her. I mean, it was blatantly obvious. I'm sure that was hard for Reina, who is totally great by the way. My father should have grabbed her back when he first met her."

"But then you wouldn't be here, Veeva."

"Sure I would, Noel. I'd just have a nice mother instead of a raging bitch, who is probably going to kill me when I get back to L.A. Plus, I'd be totally fluent in Czech."

"Does Sheeni still love Nick?"

"Of course not, Noel. The woman always moves on. Usually to something better too. It's you guys who hang tough and won't let go. My father has been carrying his torch for nearly as long as Nick. I'm just glad things are working out finally with him and Reina. I think my letter may have helped grease the wheels. I want Reina to adopt me and teach me Czech. Her kids are so cute and I guess we'll all get used to her noisy birds—assuming my mother ever lets me back into France."

"So you're not my niece after all."

"No, but I found you two new ones right there under your nose. Do you like them?"

"Uh, sure. They're nice."

"Are you sure? You don't sound very enthusiastic."

"Well, I'm still getting used to the idea."

"My father told me some things I never knew about Sheeni."

"Like what?"

"Like twins run in the Saunders family. Sheeni had a little twin brother who died 13 days after they were born. Daddy thinks that's why she couldn't quite bring herself to have an abortion. That dwarf clown gave her a way to have her babies and hide out from her parents—so she grabbed it. Then he helped arrange the adoption with this childless couple that he thought would make good parents."

"If Alfredo was so fucking helpful, why was he being such a prick with us?"

"I asked Sheeni about that. She thinks he'd developed very paternal feelings toward those twins and resented the Twisp side coming back into the picture. She used to write to him and once in a while would include a family photo."

"So that's how he got your baby picture?"

"Right. My aunt didn't say so, but I think she was curious about her babies and wanted to know if they looked like me. Anyway, Sheeni told me something else interesting too."

"What's that?"

"Her little brother's name was Frank. It always made her uncomfortable when Nick was raving about how much he loved Frank Sinatra. Of course, then she goes and marries a man named François."

"I don't see the connection."

"I forgot. I always have to connect the dots for you, Noel. The French version of Frank is François."

"Oh. That's kind of sick."

"No, just poetically significant. Well I better go. We don't want to bankrupt my mother."

"I miss you, Veeva."

"I miss you too, Noel. Look on the bright side, honey. Now I can marry Tyler and wind up your niece-in-law."

"I suppose, Veeva, if you can land him. The competition is tough."

"I'm not worried, Noel. I'm my mother's daughter. We always get our man."

"But can you keep him?"

"I think I'll do better than she did. I hope so at any rate. See you soon, Noel. I love you."

"I love you too, Veeva."

4:36 p.m. Nick and I watched this afternoon's performance

together. I was able to do this because I have officially resigned from the Hercules Circus. Joe College is not back in hairnet though. Another unemployed townie wandered on the lot, stated he would rather peel potatoes than mine coal, and got hired on the spot. Mr. Patsatzis paid me off in cash and graciously gave me 24 hours to vacate my roomette. He said he liked the way I handled a toilet brush and would hire me again next summer if I was interested. I told him I'd think about it.

Mr. Lurrieta was back in tights on the trampoline and didn't drop any loved ones. My brother applauded their every trick and whistled enthusiastically when they concluded. I think he may have the best approach to fatherhood: Get someone else to raise your kids, then sit back and applaud the results.

Nick enjoyed the rest of the circus too. He thought Mr. Barker has a great act, but needs flashier showmanship. He was amazed to see tall Marcel pedal into the ring on his tiny tricycle. He said the monkey was a new addition, but it was the same old Marcel, who had started him on the path to juggling stardom. Nick talked to him for a few minutes after the show, but I noticed Marcel only reluctantly shook my brother's hand and never cracked a smile. Those clowns are an odd bunch. Nick had a longer and friendlier conversation with Mr. Barker. While they discussed the intricacies of dog balancing, Kardos made one last effort to get me to stay and devote myself to all things Hungarian. I told him his sister had moved way up on my list, but I wasn't quite ready to propose.

I finally checked in with Grandma, who seemed delighted to hear from me. Yeah, she wants me back, and she claims it's OK with her son too. She told Lance that if I wasn't there to look after her, she'd have to think seriously about moving in with him. I guess a 57-year-old ex-cop figures it'd look bad if he's living with his mom. I should start charging that guy hefty fees for elder care.

8:14 p.m. I had dinner in the cookhouse tent with Miren. We found an unoccupied table and sat by ourselves. I guess her par-

ents don't mind me now since we're related, and they got clued
in that Randy was the actual drug-dealer, not me.

Miren is still pretty amazed by the turn of events. She said it
would be like in *Pride and Prejudice* if Elizabeth Bennet had
gone through the whole rigmarole with Mr. Darcy, only to discover on the last page that he was her uncle.

I hadn't read the book, but I told her I could see her point. I
said I hoped she wouldn't wind up resenting me for molesting
her.

She said that we both cared for each other, and she could see
no reason to feel ashamed about what happened. She said that
we probably would have broken up soon and never seen each
other again. Now that can't happen because "an uncle is for
life." She admitted that Nerea is disappointed that our marriage
is off.

"Why was your sister so hot for us to get married?" I asked.

"Nerea is terrified we'll grow apart. She doesn't want me to
go to college and find a life apart from the circus. She figures if
I'm married and have kids, I'll always stay right here—with the
family and with her."

"I know how she feels," I said. "I don't much like change
either. I'm having a hard time thinking of you as my brother's
daughter."

"I know, Jake. It's a shock. Or should I call you Noel now?"

"No, I prefer Jake."

Miren said she and her sister liked their "Uncle Alfredo"
when they were little kids, but lately he'd been sort of creeping
them out. He was always watching them—as if anyone needs
yet another parent. Plus, it had mystified her why such an inter-
nationally known clown would want to travel with an obscure
one-ring mud show like this one. She wishes her parents had
informed them why he was so obsessed about them, but under-
stands why they hadn't.

Curious about her background, Miren asked me many questions about the Twisps and the Saunders. I told her what I knew,

remembering to sugarcoat some of the nastier Twisp parts. For example, I said her paternal grandfather was "retired and living in Los Angeles." We agreed that it was a shame things hadn't worked out better with Nick and Reina. She suspects that Sheeni and Reina were the two great loves of his life, yet now he has wound up with neither of them.

I'm amazed how chicks always seem to know such things. I mean, she only met the guy yesterday.

11:48 p.m. After the evening show, Nick and I hung out with the Lurrietas in their trailer. We drank Basque wine (I got a watered-down splash), and Nick and Mr. Lurrieta swapped circus stories and discussed mutual show-biz acquaintances. I sat beside Miren and kept reminding myself not to put my arm around her or grab her hand. Incest or no, I really wanted to hold her in inappropriate ways. Despite the wine, everyone was a bit down because the circus jumps to Nebraska tomorrow, while we're heading back to Winnemucca in Nick's rental car.

Then it was time to say good night, and things got even sadder.

Will write more tomorrow. Feel too low now.

SATURDAY, September 24 — The circus pulled out right on the dot at 7:00 a.m. Nick showed up a little after 6:00 with coffee and donuts. I tossed my stuff in his car, and we stood around in the golden light of the rising sun and talked about nothing much. Nerea and Miren looped their arms around mine, and we took Mr. Barker's pugs for a stroll around the lot. Then it was time to go, and we did the final hugs, and I got kissed by all the Lurrietas except their old man. Lots of tears, and I was not entirely exempt either. My brother was such a wreck, it took him 20 minutes to get it together enough to start the car and head down the road.

6:45 p.m. We made it to Salt Lake City. Nick sprung for separate motel rooms because he said he has "problems sleeping with other people in the room." That may explain why he's

30 and still single.

My brother has quite the lead foot. He slams over into the left lane, accelerates like he just broke jail, and holds it steady at a brisk 90 mph. He says he always thrashes his rental cars because, "Hey, it's not my car." On a lightly traveled stretch of interstate between Buffalo and Casper he let me take the wheel. He told me to stay under the speed limit and "try not to hit anything." Driving a car is way better than any video game. Hard to believe adults get tired of it. Nick practically had to pry my hands off the wheel to take over when we hit heavier traffic this afternoon.

Nick said when he was 14 he drove a large Lincoln towing a trailer through heavy rush-hour traffic from Oakland to Berkeley with disastrous consequences. Hard to believe my sedate brother was once so wild. I hope I haven't inherited that same sobering gene.

Can't write any more. Going out to dinner with my bro'. I think I'll order a big steak and let him pick up the check.

10:18 p.m. Not much on the motel TV. I was hoping for a porno channel, but dream on. Both Nick and I agree this town is the cleanest city we've ever seen—and Nick has been all over the world. Our waitress was so scrubbed and fresh-faced, she looked like she'd just been unwrapped from the factory packaging. Incredibly perky too, like she was totally thrilled to be there taking our orders. She almost had an orgasm on the spot when I told her I wanted my filet cooked medium rare. All that enthusiasm, yet the food was mediocre at best.

Over dinner I got Nick to talk about why things went sour for him in Paris. He said too many years had gone by, and both he and Reina had changed. They were too much in their own separate worlds now. Plus, her kids felt totally threatened and wanted their real dad back, not "some American turkey who couldn't speak the language." Nick said Reina had inherited an apartment building in Paris. Since her young kids made it difficult for her to tour with her bird act, she wanted Nick to quit the stage and help her run the building.

"Somehow she imagined that I would want to do that. She thought it was perfect because we could be together all the time. True, but when I get out of bed in the morning, I want to look forward to more than fixing toilets and collecting rent from a bunch of disgruntled tenants. Besides, I had already worked as a janitor in that building—years ago when I lived there with Sheeni. The thought of carrying out the same garbage cans left me cold. I don't think Reina quite realized that I wasn't this marginal person any more. That I had a profession now and had done very well in it."

Nick was skeptical Paul Saunders would fare any better, but said Sheeni's brother had at least one thing going for him: "Reina's parrots love that guy. They just go wild when they see him. Naturally, she takes that as an encouraging sign."

Feeling reckless, I raised the touchiest subject of them all: Sheeni Saunders.

My brother sipped his wine and shifted uneasily on the banquette.

"Yeah, it was interesting seeing Sheeni after all these years. I used to think the sun rose and set on that gal. I thought she was the smartest, most beautiful girl in the world."

"And now?" I asked.

"I think she spends too much time out in the sun. I don't know, I was struck by how coarse her skin had become. Her eyes seemed tired. They'd lost their sparkle."

"And?"

"And what? That's about it. We're strangers now—except I suppose we have our children in common."

"Do you wish you were still married to her?"

"Hard to say. Could be—at least theoretically sometimes. But I didn't feel that way when I was sitting beside her in that Paris restaurant. I was thinking, hey, I don't know this person at all."

Weird. According to Veeva, Nick's been totally hung up on

that chick for half his life, yet he tells me she feels like a complete stranger to him.

Nick pushed aside his plate and asked me if there was anything going on between Miren and me.

Being a full-blooded Twisp, I denied everything. I said we were just pals and Miren wasn't that interested in boys because she intended to go to college and study literature.

"She takes after her mother," he commented. "I think Nerea may have a bit more of the Twisp in her."

A fairly astute observation. My brother may not be as oblivious as I'd always assumed.

SUNDAY, September 25 — Once we were out of Salt Lake City traffic, Nick let me take over and drive the rest of the way. It didn't seem to phase him that I had no license and yesterday was my first time behind the wheel. Perhaps a spark of that youthful rebel still flickers inside my brother. I did have a near-miss in the restaurant parking lot when we stopped for lunch in Elko. How was I supposed to know that ancient idiot would pull right out in front of me? Doddering 90-year-olds are allowed to drive in this state, but me—a teen with all my finely honed faculties in prime condition—is denied my rightful license. Is that fucked up, or what?

At lunch I mentioned to Nick that I was thinking of changing my name to Jake Twisp.

"Jake, huh?" he said. "Is that short for Jacob?"

"No, it's just Jake."

"How about a middle name? Most people have one."

"I don't know, Nick. I never thought about that."

"How about Jake Sinatra Twisp? That has a nice ring to it."

Yeah, maybe. If you're 103 years old. I told him I would pass on the middle name. Nick said if I was serious, he would get his lawyer to file the paperwork. I told him to go ahead.

Jake Twisp. I think that sounds like me. At least for now.

Grandma was thrilled to see us. She gave us both hugs and carried on in a rather embarrassing way about my face bruises and bum tooth. She looked OK, but she'd put on a few pounds. Wescotts tend to do that when they're stressed. I wish I didn't cause her so much worry.

Grandma invited Nick to stay the night, but he was eager to get going. He said he planned to dump the rental car in Reno and catch the next flight to Vegas. I gave him a farewell hug, and he slipped me another $100 bill. That makes two hugs and $200 from that guy. He pays off better than any slot machine in the state.

So here I am back in my cramped and squalid bedroom. Still, it's palace-sized compared to my circus roomette. I lay down on my narrow bed and felt the crinkle of the plastic layer under my sheets. All the trauma I went through on the road, yet I didn't wet the bed once. Not much thumb-sucking to report either. A positive trend that I hope continues.

My computer's back from the cops, minus its violated hard drive. May take me a while to get it back up to speed. So I guess I won't be checking my e-mail tonight.

Grandma phoned out for pizza and we're going to watch a video. I may sew on some sequins too as her costume orders are backing up. She's OK about my new name. She says she was never that nuts about the name Noel—or Wescott for that matter.

MONDAY, September 26 — I spent 45 minutes this morning waiting outside the office of Mr. Tweedy, Winnemucca High School's crankiest guidance counselor. As usual, no one who passed by said hi or acknowledged my existence.

Finally, I was called in, and Mr. Tweedy looked me over with his patented frown.

"You're back, huh, Wescott? I thought you were in jail in Southern California."

"No, that's Carlyle Bogy."

"Aren't you guys gang brothers?"

"Well, it wasn't much of a gang. And I've changed my name to Jake Twisp."

"Oh," he sneered, "since when?"

"Since my brother's lawyer petitioned the court for a name change."

"Well, I'm not altering anything in this computer until I see a legal document."

That didn't surprise me. As everyone knows, Mr. Tweedy hates high school students and goes out of his way to be as unhelpful as possible. A few years ago he achieved notoriety throughout Northern Nevada by suspending 47 girls in one day for showing up for class with their midriffs exposed. The sight of a bare navel drives him wild. He also despises baggy trousers on boys, except he can't really ban them since all objectionable areas are more than covered. He's been known to stop the baggiest boys in the halls to inquire sarcastically if they just lost 200 pounds.

Mr. Tweedy turned to his computer and called up my records. "Any requests?" he asked.

I told him I thought it would be nice if they piped hip-hop music into the classrooms over the P.A. system to help the students concentrate on their studies.

"How would you like a three-day suspension for that smartass remark?" he asked.

"Sorry, Mr. Tweedy. I misunderstood your question."

"I repeat, do you have any *class* requests?"

"Well, I was thinking it might be interesting to take Spanish or Hungarian."

I was in luck. Mr. Tweedy said there was an opening in Spanish I. He also plugged me into some other classes in his usual capricious and arbitrary way, then handed me a printout of my schedule.

I thanked him and told him I would need to be excused for the balance of the day as I had a hearing scheduled at 10:30 in Juvenile Court.

Mr. Tweedy smiled and said in that case I'd probably need to be excused for the next two or three years.

The judge gave me a long lecture on the dire consequences I would face if I didn't give up my trouble-making and gang-ridden ways. She said it was only luck that I hadn't gotten into more serious trouble and wasn't facing "prolonged incarceration" like my peer Carlyle Bogy. She also regarded it as a very bad sign that my face bore evidence of recent hooliganism. I stated I was truly sorry for all the grief and worry I had caused my family and guardian. I got choked up and started bawling into my shirttail. Next time I'll try to remember to take along a handkerchief. She said I appeared remorseful, and she hoped very much that I would reform and never again have to face her in court. She gave me six months' probation and 50 hours of community service. In Winnemucca that usually means being trucked out to the interstate highway to pick up litter. Fortunately, I've had a lot of recent experience at that.

So now Noel Wescott has a police record, a parole officer, and a rap sheet.

All in all, it's a good thing I'm changing my name.

TUESDAY, September 27 — My first day back at school. The biggest problem with missing an entire month is that there are now kids who have gone out, flourished as couples, and subsequently split up whose fleeting connection I may never have any knowledge of. It's like if you go on a long camping trip in the wilderness and never find out that the Pope died or Brad Pitt got divorced.

There was a big pep rally for the football team during the first period; attendance was compulsory. OK, as I view it here's the basic Winnemucca High School dilemma: Are you demonstrating poor school spirit if you're unenthusiastic about supporting sporting competitions in a town that has no reason to exist? Why exactly are we all stuck out here in the middle of nowhere, and why should we care if our football team beats Elko (another totally pointless town)? Like me, Stoney Holt used to sit on her hands at these functions, but today I noticed she was screaming and chanting with the rest of the automatons. Is that the price one must pay for being popular and dating Sloan Chandler?

I didn't run into Uma until fifth-period study hall. To my surprise she came in and took the desk right next to mine. Even without her midriff exposed, she immediately got my heart beating wildly.

"Hi, Noel," she said.

"Hi, Uma. I've changed my name."

"Not to Toby, I hope."

"No. To Jake—Jake Twisp."

"Jake Twisp, huh? Well, that will take some getting used to. How was your summer vacation?"

"I wasn't on vacation, Uma. I was a teen runaway and fugitive from the law."

"Whatever, Jake. Did you have a good time?"

"Well, uh, it was OK. I'm surprised you're talking to me, Uma."

"Your friend Stoney Holt has been e-mailing me unsolicited updates on your hectic love life, Jake."

"She has?"

"Yes. It appears you've been a very busy guy."

"I can explain everything, Uma."

"There's nothing to explain, Jake. I'm relieved, in fact. It appears your ego is not as fragile and your devotion to me not so all-consuming as I had first feared. Therefore, I don't feel I have to worry about wrecking your life by associating with you."

"Can you translate that into English, Uma?"

"In short, Jake, I still like you. Do you know what tomorrow is?"

"Uh, not offhand."

"It's Bingo Night. Shall I drop by at my usual hour?"

A powerful jolt went through my body, paralyzing my tongue.

"You look a little sick, Jake. And what the hell happened to your face?"

WEDNESDAY, September 28 — Uma Spurletti lost her virginity tonight to her desired partner: an experienced male. We performed the act—twice—on my narrow bed to the musical accompaniment of the Pickled Punks. Entry was gained without too much struggle, and Uma reported that the experiment probably bears repeating. My expensive Dockweiler condoms performed flawlessly—transmitting far more tingles per stroke than Grandma's discount brand. Yet more proof that it pays to be rich.

Of all the girls I have slept with, Uma is the reigning world's champion. Everything about her is extremely exciting and pleasing to my nervous system. I really can't get enough of her, although I intend to give it my best shot from now on. Clutching her naked body to mine afterwards was nearly as nice as the actual act. I filled her in on my eventful summer and new nieces, and she brought me up to date on her exciting life. The best news: her aunt Rosa is now in Washington training to be a Peace Corps volunteer. After sampling the Nevada male dating pool, she decided she wasn't quite ready for marriage, and now intends to go to Latin America to help little Catholic babies. Mr. Spurletti has hired a live-in housekeeper to take her place. This woman is a native Nevadan who believes that her job is to cook and clean, not to worry about whether Uma is leaving the house without a bra.

For any concerned parent who wants to know, I can report that Uma was wearing quite an attractive one tonight, although not for long.

FRIDAY, October 14 — On the bus to Las Vegas. Sorry, blog readers, for skipping all these weeks. Sometimes life is just too hectic for rigorous introspection. Now, facing many hours of enforced idleness on a bouncing bus, I've brought along my $5 laptop. Amazingly, I also brought along darling Uma, who is sitting next to me and reading a book by some long-dead Russian. There's a butterfly on the cover, but she says it isn't about insects.

Frankly, I was flabbergasted when her father agreed to let her come along on this trip. Unaccountably, the guy really likes me. He always takes the time to chat when I'm visiting their house or manning the breath-mints kiosk at the Silver Sluice. Yeah, Uma got me a part-time job there—much to fat Marvin Tuelco's annoyance.

The reason we're going to Vegas is that I've been roped into being the best man at my brother Nick's wedding. He probably wants me for the job since I've had so much professional experience at the Dixie Belle. You don't want amateurs bungling the ring handoff when you're paying top dollar to get shackled for life.

As you might expect our bus conversation has touched on many intimate topics, including suicide. Uma doesn't think much of my scheme. She says all that exertion of tunneling into the sand bank would raise your endorphin levels to the point that you would no longer be depressed enough to off yourself. Damn, she may have a point there. Guess I'm back to square one on that project, though lately the prospect of personal nonexistence has lost most of its appeal.

10:38 p.m. I quit the party early to come up to my bedroom to work on my speech. My brother informed me that I'll be expected to propose a toast at the reception tomorrow. I have to do this despite the fact that I am legally too young to drink. That's called getting the short end of both sticks.

Nick hosted a catered wedding-eve buffet dinner at his house tonight for the families and close friends. Great eats, although it was a bit nervous-making sitting on the sofa with Uma, Veeva, and Miren lined up beside me. The famous actor Trent Preston snapped a photo of us that could be captioned "Jake Twisp and His Many Conquests." The girls are getting along fine so far. They've found a common ground in teasing me mercilessly.

This is the first time Veeva has met her new cousins. Seeing them side by side, I can now discern a family resemblance. I'd say the actor they most resemble is Meg Ryan. All three are quite taken with my nephew Tyler, although Veeva has the advantage of being parked all weekend on the same floor at the Normandie as my sister Joanie and her family. Miren and Nerea are staying here at Nick's house with us. Uma has her own bedroom opposite mine. Fortunately, there are no land mines or barbed wire in the hallway and I've always had fairly acute night vision.

My brother said he thought about inviting our mother, but decided there was no reason to spoil everyone's good time. She missed his first wedding too, so I expect she's used to being snubbed. Needless to say, our dad will be missing the fun as well. Both will have to shape up drastically to be invited to any of my weddings.

Well, this isn't getting my speech written. Damn, what do you say in a wedding toast? I suppose everyone expects some snickering allusions to the forthcoming wedding night. But can a nervous 15-year-old really carry that off?

SATURDAY, October 15 — My brother didn't chicken out. He got married at 1:30 this afternoon to Ada Olson in the Art Deco chapel of the Normandie casino. Performing the service was the sharply uniformed "Captain" of the Normandie. He's this very distinguished silver-haired gent, ramrod straight and dripping with gold braid, who normally functions as the maitre d' in the Main Salon. Like my former employer Mr. Dugan, he has a mail-order minister's ordination, so everything was totally legit.

Then we all trooped up two decks to the private "Captain's Salon" for the lavish reception and banquet. The Normandie management provided piles of shiny silver dollars on every table so the guests could feed the slot machines that lined one wall of the room. I put in a dollar, didn't win, and pocketed the rest. Uma won $437—proving once again that it pays to hang out with us Twisps.

It's a good thing Grandma made me take those wretched dancing lessons back in the seventh grade. Nick had sprung for a live (but not lively) band. I had to slow dance with countless females, including the bride, her mother from Connecticut, my own sister, and Violet Preston (Trent's wife), who was grossly pregnant. As you'd expect, my competitive nephew Tyler danced circles around me all afternoon. He also had the most partners lining up for taxi service. If the sports thing doesn't work out, he could have a great career as a gigolo.

Fortunately, the waiters at the open bar weren't checking IDs. The champagne flowed like wine and quite a bit of it flowed into me. At last I've discovered something alcoholic that's an improvement on the original grape juice.

While dancing with Veeva, she told me her mother got monumentally pissed when her husband filed for divorce and completely blames her daughter. To get back at Veeva, she suddenly got honest and informed her that Paul Saunders wasn't her actual father. Nope, Mrs. Saunders claimed she was forced to resort to a sperm donor—some USC student at the time named Bruno Preston. We agreed that her "confession" was a vile maternal mind-fuck and completely bogus to boot. Young Bruno may have been whacking off for beer money, but anyone with eyes can see it was Veeva's daddy who did the deed. The family resemblance is too strong for any doubt on that point.

Veeva also confided that she found out the lawyer Nick shot was her own Bible-banging grandfather in Ukiah. Jesus, my brother nearly killed his own ex-father-in-law. Well, at least he kept it in the family. Now Veeva's worried her grandpa will keel over from shock on that gala future day when she announces her engagement to Tyler Twisp.

I also danced with Miren, who commented that Uma was extremely pretty and seemed very nice. Could be, but I'm still keeping Vrsula Herczegh as backup. Miren reported that Joe College only lasted another week after I left. While he was dusting the office trailer, Mrs. Patsatzis came in and caught him treasure hunting in one of her cash bags.

The Lurrietas will be on the road one more month, then head

back to Bilbao for the winter. They've been invited to spend Christmas in Lyon. Miren's looking forward to it, but I predict there will be some tense moments around the tree since as we all know mothers can be weird. Anyway, Miren's promised to e-mail me regularly.

The main course was poached wild Alaskan salmon with lobster sauce. While we ate, Nick talked a lot with Nerea and Miren about life in the circus. He said he's thinking seriously about buying a trailer and going on the road with them next year. Ada smiled graciously at this news, but even I could sense she was thinking "over my very dead body."

Glamorous Trent Preston gave by far the best speech. He said he was thrilled to be here at Nick's wedding, since Nick had single-handedly engineered his first marriage and also had played a major role in his subsequent divorce. This drew a much bigger laugh than my lame toast, but then I'm not a suave movie star who makes $18 million per picture. The less said about my effort the better.

Then there was more music, more dancing, and more champagne. I remember a big wedding cake being rolled in and Nick juggling some more cutlery. No, Uma didn't catch the bridal bouquet. It went to a surprised waitress in a low-cut sailor's suit. Then things got a little hazy; I remember spending a good deal of time in the lavish nautical-theme restroom throwing up. It was either a nervous stomach from my traumatic toast, a gut-wrenching LSD flashback, or too much champagne.

SUNDAY, October 16 — On the bus to Winnemucca. Since my brother isn't leaving on his honeymoon until tomorrow, Ada roped me into her dental chair this morning to deal with my dead tooth. I think it embarrassed her professionally to have such a trailer-trash smile in the family. She yanked it out, stuck in a fake one that's a perfect match to my other choppers, and— while my jaw was numb—filled two cavities and cleaned out the excess gunk.

While she worked, she told me more about how she met my brother. She noticed him in the skydiving class because he was the only student who proved too chicken to jump out of the plane. She thought that was rather endearing and also indicated that he was a guy with both feet on the ground. She also was attracted by his excellent oral hygiene. The irony is that Nick was attending that class because his philosophy is "When life gets dull, try something new."

Although Ada is a high-priced oral surgeon, she didn't charge me one cent. Nor would she accept a tip. She did make me promise on my sacred honor as her brother-in-law that I will floss faithfully from now on. I had to agree because by then the Novocain was wearing off, and she was still poking around with sharp instruments.

All in all, I'm glad Nick took my advice and married the dentist.

We had to clear out of Nick's house by noon today because his real estate agent was preparing for an open house. My brother claims he's selling his pad so he and Ada can get their own place, but Veeva speculates the sale was motivated by his bride's refusal to live in the same domicile where Nick did the ugly with Reina. Could be, but I will always regard it as Ground Zero of my burgeoning sex life.

Nick took us all out to lunch, then came another round of hugs and sad farewells (plus the obligatory $100 hug payout from Nick). Damn, it's tough suddenly having a family that you keep saying good-bye to. I'd like to hang around those guys some more, although I suppose that impulse wears off.

Uma says she had a good time and enjoyed meeting all those Twisps. She also thinks we should use some of our profits to buy a nice gift for the newlyweds. I suppose, but what could they possibly use that I don't need more?

Traveling with Uma was great. I love her so much I can barely stand it. I suppose the odds aren't very good that we'll wind up together in the future. Uma thinks teen romances are just practice for the real thing when we get to be adults. Could be, except you do hear about people who marry their high-school sweethearts and live happily ever after.

Well, we'll just have to see what happens.

Can't write any more. I see the bus restroom is free now. Time to duck back there again to check out my great new smile.

See you all down the road!

C.D. Payne was born in 1949 in Akron, Ohio, the former "Rubber Capital of the World" famed for its tire factories. He shares a birthday with P.T. Barnum, a fact which has influenced his life profoundly. After graduating from Harvard College in 1971, he moved to California, where he's worked as a newspaper editor, graphic artist, cartoonist, typesetter, photographer, proofreader, carpenter, trailer park handyman, and advertising copywriter. He is married and lives in Sonoma County.